WILDFIRE—a Dream of a Horse

His coat was shaggy and red. It was not glossy.
The color was what made him shine. His
mane was like a crest, mounting, then
falling low. Slone had never seen so much
muscle on a horse. Yet his outline was
graceful, beautiful. The head was indeed that
of the wildest of all wild creatures—a stallion
born wild—and it was beautiful, savage, splendi[d]
everything but noble. Whatever Wildfire was,
he was a devil, a murderer—he had no noble
attributes. Slone thought that if a horse could
express hate, surely Wildfire did.

Slone shook a gauntleted fist at the stallion, as
if the horse were human. Wildfire turned
away, showed bright against the dark
background, and then disappeared. . . .

Now began a desperate pursuit through the
desert. Slone was determined to get a rope
around the wild creature's head—or kill him!

Books by Zane Grey

Arizona Ames
The Arizona Clan
Black Mesa
The Border Legion
Boulder Dam
The Call of the Canyon
Captives of the Desert
Code of the West
The Deer Stalker
Desert Gold
Drift Fence
The Dude Ranger
Fighting Caravans
Forlorn River
The Fugitive Trail
The Hash Knife Outfit
The Heritage of the Desert
Horse Heaven Hill
Knights of the Range
The Light of the Western Stars
Lone Star Ranger
Last Pueblo
The Lost Wagon Train
Majesty's Rancho

The Man of the Forest
The Mysterious Rider
Raiders of Spanish Peaks
The Rainbow Trail
The Reward
Rawhide Justice
Riders of the Purple Sage
Robbers' Roost
Rogue River Feud
Shadow on the Trail
Stranger from the Tonto
Sunset Pass
Thunder Mountain
To the Last Man
The Trail Driver
Twin Sombreros
Under the Tonto Rim
The U.P. Trail
Valley of Wild Horses
Wanderer of the Wasteland
Western Union
West of the Pecos
Wilderness Trek
Wyoming

Published by POCKET BOOKS

ZANE GREY

WILDFIRE

PUBLISHED BY POCKET BOOKS NEW YORK

POCKET BOOKS, a Simon & Schuster division of
GULF & WESTERN CORPORATION
1230 Avenue of the Americas, New York, N.Y. 10020

ISBN: 0-671-43194-3

First Pocket Books printing March, 1976

10 9 8 7 6 5 4 3

POCKET and colophon are trademarks of Simon & Schuster.

Printed in the U.S.A.

Chapter I

FOR some reason the desert scene before Lucy Bostil awoke varying emotions—a sweet gratitude for the fullness of her life there at the Ford, yet a haunting remorse that she could not be wholly content—a vague loneliness of soul—a thrill and a fear for the strangely calling future, glorious, unknown.

She longed for something to happen. It might be terrible, so long as it was wonderful. This day, when Lucy had stolen away on a forbidden horse, she was eighteen years old. The thought of her mother, who had died long ago on their way into this wilderness, was the one drop of sadness in her joy. Lucy loved everybody at Bostil's Ford and everybody loved her. She loved all the horses except her father's favorite racer, that perverse devil of a horse, the great Sage King.

Lucy was glowing and rapt with love for all she beheld from her lofty perch: the green-and-pink blossoming hamlet beneath her, set between the beauty of the gray sage expanse and the ghastliness of the barren heights; the swift Colorado sullenly thundering below in the abyss; the Indians in their bright colors, riding up the river trail; the eagle poised like a feather on the air, and a mile beneath him the grazing cattle making black dots on the sage; the deep velvet azure of the sky; the golden lights on the bare peaks and the lilac veils in the far ravines; the silky rustle of a cañon swallow as he shot downward in the sweep of the wind; the fragrance of cedar, the flowers of the spear-pointed mescal; the brooding silence, the beckoning range, the purple distance.

Whatever it was Lucy longed for, whatever was whispered by the wind and written in the mystery of the waste of sage and stone, she wanted it to happen there at Bostil's Ford. She had no desire for civilization, she flouted the idea of marrying the rich rancher of Durango. Bostil's sister, that stern but lovable woman who had brought her up and taught her, would never persuade her to marry against her will. Lucy imagined herself like a wild horse—free, proud, untamed, meant for the desert; and here she would live her life. The desert and her life seemed as one, yet in what did they resemble each other—in what part of this scene could she read the nature of her future?

Shudderingly she rejected the red, sullen, thundering river, with its swift, changeful, endless, contending strife—for that was tragic. And she rejected the frowning mass of red rock, upreared, riven and split and cañoned, so grim and aloof—for that was barren. But she accepted the vast sloping valley of sage, rolling gray and soft and beautiful, down to the dim mountains and purple ramparts of the horizon. Lucy did not know what she yearned for, she did not know why the desert called to her, she did not know in what it resembled her spirit, but she did know that these three feelings were as one, deep in her heart. For ten years, every day of her life, she had watched this desert scene, and never had there been an hour that it was not different, yet the same. Ten years—and she grew up watching, feeling—till from the desert's thousand moods she assimilated its nature, loved her bonds, and could never have been happy away from the open, the color, the freedom, the wildness. On this birthday, when those who loved her said she had become her own mistress, she acknowledged the claim of the desert forever. And she experienced a deep, rich, strange happiness.

Hers always then the mutable and immutable desert, the leagues and leagues of slope and sage and rolling ridge, the great cañons and the giant cliffs, the dark river with its mystic thunder of waters, the pine-fringed plateaus, the endless stretch of horizon, with its lofty, isolated, noble monuments, and the bold ramparts with their beckoning beyond! Hers always the desert seasons: the shrill, icy blast, the intense cold, the steely skies, the fading snows; the gray old sage and the bleached grass under the pall of the spring sand-storms; the hot furnace breath of summer, with its magnificent cloud pageants in the sky, with the black tempests hanging here and there over the peaks, dark veils floating down and rainbows everywhere, and the lacy waterfalls upon the glistening cliffs and the thunder of the red floods; and the glorious golden autumn when it was always afternoon and time stood still! Hers always the rides in the open, with the sun at her back and the wind in her face! And hers surely, sooner or later, the nameless adventure which had its inception in the strange yearning of her heart and presaged its fulfilment somewhere down that trailless sage-slope she loved so well!

Bostil's house was a crude but picturesque structure of red stone and white clay and bleached cottonwoods, and it stood at the outskirts of the cluster of green-inclosed cabins which composed the hamlet. Bostil was wont to say that in all the world there could hardly be a grander view than the outlook down that gray sea of rolling sage, down to the black-fringed plateaus and the wild, blue-rimmed and gold-spired horizon.

One morning in early spring, as was Bostil's custom, he ordered the racers to be brought from the corrals and turned loose on the slope. He loved to sit there and watch his horses graze, but ever he saw that the riders were close at hand, and that the horses did not get out on the slope of sage. He sat back and gloried in the sight. He owned bands of mustangs; near by was a field of them, fine and mettlesome and racy; yet Bostil had eyes only for the blooded favorites. Strange it was that not one of these was a mustang or a broken wild horse, for many of the riders' best mounts had been captured by them or the Indians. And it was Bostil's supreme ambition to own a great wild stallion. There was Plume, a superb mare that got her name from the way her mane swept in the wind when she was on the run; and there was Two Face, like a coquette, sleek and glossy and cunning; and the huge, rangy bay, Dusty Ben; and the black stallion Sarchedon; and lastly Sage King, the color of the upland sage, a racer in build, a horse splendid and proud and beautiful.

"Where's Lucy?" presently asked Bostil.

As he divided his love, so he divided his anxiety.

Some rider had seen Lucy riding off, with her golden hair flying in the wind. This was an old story.

"She's up on Buckles?" Bostil queried, turning sharply to the speaker.

"Reckon so," was the calm reply.

Bostil swore. He did not have a rider who could equal him in profanity.

"Farlane, you'd orders. Lucy's not to ride them hosses, least of all Buckles. He ain't safe even for a man."

"Wal, he's safe for Lucy."

"But didn't I say no?"

"Boss, it's likely you did, fer you talk a lot," replied Farlane. "Lucy pulled my hat down over my eyes—told me to go to thunder—an' then, zip! she an' Buckles were dustin' it fer the sage."

"She's got to keep out of the sage," growled Bostil. "It ain't safe for her out there. . . . Where's my glass? I want to take a look at the slope. Where's my glass?"

The glass could not be found.

"What's makin' them dust-clouds on the sage? Antelope? . . . Holley, you used to have eyes better 'n me. Use them, will you?"

A gray-haired, hawk-eyed rider, lean and worn, approached with clinking spurs.

"Down in there," said Bostil, pointing.

"That's a bunch of hosses," replied Holley.

"Wild hosses?"

"I take 'em so, seein' how they throw thet dust."

"Huh! I don't like it. Lucy oughtn't be ridin' round alone."

"Wal, boss, who could catch her up on Buckles? Lucy can ride. An' there's the King an' Sarch right under your nose—the only hosses on the sage thet could outrun Buckles."

Farlane knew how to mollify his master and long habit had made him proficient. Bostil's eyes flashed. He was proud of Lucy's power over a horse. The story Bostil first told to any stranger happening by the Ford was how Lucy had been born during a wild ride—almost, as it were, on the back of a horse. That, at least, was her fame, and the riders swore she was a worthy daughter of such a mother. Then, as Farlane well knew, a quick road to Bostil's good will was to praise one of his favorites.

"Reckon you spoke sense for once, Farlane," replied Bostil, with relief. "I wasn't thinkin' so much of danger for Lucy. . . . But she lets thet half-witted Creech go with her."

"No, boss, you're wrong," put in Holley, earnestly. "I know the girl. She has no use fer Joel. But he jest runs after her."

"An' he's harmless," added Farlane.

"We ain't agreed," rejoined Bostil, quickly. "What do you say, Holley?"

The old rider looked thoughtful and did not speak for long.

"Wal, yes an' no," he answered, finally. "I reckon Lucy could make a man out of Joel. But she doesn't care fer him, an' thet settles thet. . . . An' maybe Joel's leanin' toward the bad."

"If she meets him again I'll rope her in the house," declared Bostil.

Another clear-eyed rider drew Bostil's attention from the gray waste of rolling sage.

"Bostil, look! Look at the King! He's watchin' fer somethin'. . . . An' so's Sarch."

The two horses named were facing a ridge some few hundred yards distant, and their heads were aloft and ears straight forward. Sage King whistled shrilly and Sarchedon began to prance.

"Boys, you'd better drive them in," said Bostil. "They'd like nothin' so well as gettin' out on the sage. . . . Hullo! what's thet shootin' up behind the ridge?"

"No more'n Buckles with Lucy makin' him run some," replied Holley, with a dry laugh.

"If it ain't! . . . Lord! look at him come!"

Bostil's anger and anxiety might never have been. The light of the upland rider's joy shone in his keen gaze. The slope before him was open, and almost level, down to the ridge that had hidden the missing girl and horse. Buckles was running for the love of running, as the girl low down over his neck was riding for the love of riding. The Sage King whistled again, and shot off with graceful sweep to meet them; Sarchedon plunged after him; Two Face and Plume jealously trooped down, too, but Dusty Ben, after a toss of his head, went on grazing. The gray and the black met Buckles and could not turn in time to stay with him. A girl's gay scream pealed up the slope, and Buckles went lower and faster. Sarchedon was left behind. Then the gray King began to run as if before he had been loping. He was beautiful in action. This was play—a game—a race—plainly dominated by the spirit of the girl. Lucy's hair was a bright stream of gold in the wind. She rode bareback. It seemed that she was hunched low over Buckles with her knees high on his back—scarcely astride him at all. Yet her motion was one with the horse. Again that wild, gay scream pealed out—call or laugh or challenge. Sage King, with a fleetness that made the eyes of Bostil and his riders glisten, took the lead, and then sheered off to slow down, while Buckles thundered past. Lucy was pulling him hard, and had him plunging to a halt, when the rider Holley ran out to grasp his bridle. Buckles was snorting and his ears were laid back. He pounded the ground and scattered the pebbles.

"No use, Lucy," said Bostil. "You can't beat the King at your own game, even with a runnin' start."

Lucy Bostil's eyes were blue, as keen as her father's, and now they flashed like his. She had a hand twisted in the horse's long mane, and as, lithe and supple, she slipped a knee across his broad back she shook a little gantleted fist at Bostil's gray racer.

"Sage King, I hate you!" she called, as if the horse were human. "And I'll beat you some day!"

Bostil swore by the gods his Sage King was the swiftest horse in all that wild upland country of wonderful horses. He swore the great gray could look back over his shoulder and run away from any broken horse known to the riders.

Bostil himself was half horse, and the half of him that was human he divided between love of his fleet racers and his daughter Lucy. He had seen years of hard riding on that wild Utah border where, in those days, a horse meant all the world to a man. A lucky strike of grassy upland and good water south of the Rio Colorado made him rich in all that he cared to own. The Indians, yet unspoiled by white men, were friendly. Bostil built a boat at the Indian crossing of the Colorado and the place became known as Bostil's Ford. From time to time his personality and his reputation and his need brought horse-hunters, riders, sheep-herders, and men of pioneer spirit, as well as wandering desert travelers, to the Ford, and the lonely, isolated hamlet slowly grew. North of the river it was more than two hundred miles to the nearest little settlement, with only a few lonely ranches on the road; to the west were several villages, equally distant, but cut off for two months at a time by the raging Colorado, flooded by melting snow up in the mountains. Eastward from the Ford stretched a ghastly, broken, unknown desert of cañons. Southward rolled the beautiful uplands, with valleys of sage and grass, and plateaus of pine and cedar, until this rich rolling gray and green range broke sharply on a purple horizon line of upflung rocky ramparts and walls and monuments, wild, dim, and mysterious.

Bostil's cattle and horses were numberless, and many as were his riders, he always could use more.

But most riders did not abide long with Bostil, first
because some of them were of a wandering breed,
wild-horse hunters themselves; and secondly, Bostil
had two great faults: he seldom paid a rider in money, and he never permitted one to own a fleet horse.
He wanted to own all the fast horses himself. And in
those days every rider, especially a wild-horse hunter,
loved his steed as part of himself. If there was a difference between Bostil and any rider of the sage, it
was that, as he had more horses, so he had more love.

Whenever Bostil could not get possession of a
horse he coveted, either by purchase or trade, he in-
variably acquired a grievance toward the owner. This
happened often; for riders were loath to part with their
favorites. And he had made more than one enemy by
his persistent nagging. It could not be said, however,
that he sought to drive hard bargains. Bostil would
pay any price asked for a horse.

Across the Colorado, in a high, red-walled cañon
opening upon the river, lived a poor sheep-herder
and horse-trader named Creech. This man owned a
number of thoroughbreds, two of which he would not
part with for all the gold in the uplands. These racers,
Blue Roan and Peg, had been captured wild on the
ranges by Ute Indians and broken to racing. They
were still young and getting faster every year. Bostil
wanted them because he coveted them and because
he feared them. It would have been a terrible blow to
him if any horse ever beat the gray. But Creech laughed
at all offers and taunted Bostil with a boast that in
another summer he would see a horse out in front
of the King.

To complicate matters and lead rivalry into hatred
young Joel Creech, a great horseman, but worthless
in the eyes of all save his father, had been heard to
say that some day he would force a race between
the King and Blue Roan. And that threat had been
taken in various ways. It alienated Bostil beyond all
hope of reconciliation. It made Lucy Bostil laugh and
look sweetly mysterious. She had no enemies, and she

liked everybody. It was even gossiped by the women
of Bostil's Ford that she had more than liking for the
idle Joel. But the husbands of these gossips said Lucy
was only tender-hearted. Among the riders, when they
sat around their lonely camp-fires, or lounged at the
corrals of the Ford, there was speculation in regard
to this race hinted by Joel Creech. There never had
been a race between the King and Blue Roan, and
there never would be, unless Joel were to ride off
with Lucy. In that case there would be the grandest
race ever run on the uplands, with the odds against
Blue Roan only if he carried double. If Joel put Lucy
up on the Roan and he rode Peg there would be another story. Lucy Bostil was a slip of a girl, born on
a horse, as strong and supple as an Indian, and she
could ride like a burr sticking in a horse's mane. With
Blue Roan carrying her light weight she might run
away from any one up on the King—which for Bostil
would be a double tragedy, equally in the loss of his
daughter and the beating of his best-beloved racer.
But with Joel on Peg, such a race would end in heartbreak for all concerned, for the King would outrun
Peg, and that would bring riders within gunshot.

It had always been a fascinating subject, this long-
looked-for race. It grew more so when Joel's infatuation for Lucy became known. There were fewer riders who believed Lucy might elope with Joel than
there were who believed Joel might steal his father's
horses. But all the riders who loved horses and all
the women who loved gossip were united in at least
one thing, and that was that something like a race or
a romance would soon disrupt the peaceful, sleepy
tenor of Bostil's Ford.

In addition to Bostil's growing hatred for the
Creeches, he had a great fear of Cordts, the horse-
thief. A fear ever restless, ever watchful. Cordts hid
back in the untrodden ways. He had secret friends
among the riders of the ranges, faithful followers back
in the cañon camps, gold for the digging, cattle by
the thousands, and fast horses. He had always gotten

what he wanted—except one thing. That was a certain horse. And the horse was Sage King.

Cordts was a bad man, a product of the early gold-fields of California and Idaho, an outcast from that evil wave of wanderers retreating back over the trails so madly traveled westward. He became a lord over the free ranges. But more than all else he was a rider. He knew a horse. He was as much horse as Bostil. Cordts rode into this wild free-range country, where he had been heard to say that a horse-thief was meaner than a poisoned coyote. Nevertheless, he became a horse-thief. The passion he had conceived for the Sage King was the passion of a man for an unattainable woman. Cordts swore that he would never rest, that he would not die, till he owned the King. So there was reason for Bostil's great fear.

Chapter II

BOSTIL went toward the house with his daughter, turning at the door to call a last word to his riders about the care of his horses.

The house was a low, flat, wide structure, with a corridor running through the middle, from which doors led into the adobe-walled rooms. The windows were small openings high up, evidently intended for defense as well as light, and they had rude wooden shutters. The floor was clay, covered everywhere by Indian blankets. A pioneer's home it was, simple and crude, yet comfortable, and having the rare quality peculiar to desert homes—it was cool in summer and warm in winter.

As Bostil entered with his arm round Lucy a big hound rose from the hearth. This room was immense, running the length of the house, and it contained a huge stone fireplace, where a kettle smoked fragrantly, and rude home-made chairs with blanket coverings, and tables to match, and walls covered with bridles, guns, pistols, Indian weapons and ornaments, and trophies of the chase. In a far corner stood a work-bench, with tools upon it and horse trappings under it. In the opposite corner a door led into the kitchen. This room was Bostil's famous living-room, in which many things had happened, some of which had helped make desert history and were never mentioned by Bostil.

Bostil's sister came in from the kitchen. She was a huge person with a severe yet motherly face. She had her hands on her hips, and she cast a rather disapproving glance at father and daughter.

"So you're back again?" she queried, severely.

"Sure, Auntie," replied the girl, complacently.

"You ran off to get out of seeing Wetherby, didn't you?"

Lucy stared sweetly at her aunt.

"He was waiting for hours," went on the worthy woman. "I never saw a man in such a stew. . . . No wonder, playing fast and loose with him the way you do."

"I told him No!" flashed Lucy.

"But Wetherby's not the kind to take no. And I'm not satisfied to let you mean it. Lucy Bostil, you don't know your mind an hour straight running. You've fooled enough with these riders of your Dad's. If you're not careful you'll marry one of them. . . . One of these wild riders! As bad as a Ute Indian! . . . Wetherby is young and he idolizes you. In all common sense why don't you take him?"

"I don't care for him," replied Lucy.

"You like him as well as anybody. . . . John Bostil, what do you say? You approved of Wetherby. I heard you tell him Lucy was like an unbroken colt and that you'd—"

"Sure, I like Jim," interrupted Bostil; and he avoided Lucy's swift look.

"Well?" demanded his sister.

Evidently Bostil found himself in a corner between two fires. He looked sheepish, then disgusted.

"Dad!" exclaimed Lucy, reproachfully.

"See here, Jane," said Bostil, with an air of finality, "the girl is of age to-day—an' she can do what she damn pleases!"

"That's a fine thing for you to say," retorted Aunt Jane. "Like as not she'll be fetching that hang-dog Joel Creech up here for you to support."

"Auntie!" cried Lucy, her eyes blazing.

"Oh, child, you torment me—worry me so," said the disappointed woman. "It's all for your sake. . . . Look at you, Lucy Bostil! A girl of eighteen who comes of a family! And you riding around and going as you are now—in a man's clothes!"

"But, you dear old goose, I can't ride in a woman's skirt," expostulated Lucy. "Mind you, Auntie, I can *ride!*"

"Lucy, if I live here forever I'd never get reconciled to a Bostil woman in leather pants. We Bostils were somebody once, back in Missouri."

Bostil laughed. "Yes, an' if I hadn't hit the trail west we'd be starvin' yet. Jane, you're a sentimental old fool. Let the girl alone an' reconcile yourself to this wilderness."

Aunt Jane's eyes were wet with tears. Lucy, seeing them, ran to her and hugged and kissed her.

"Auntie, I will promise—from to-day—to have some dignity. I've been free as a boy in these rider clothes. As I am now the men never seem to regard me as a girl. Somehow that's better. I can't explain, but I *like* it. My dresses are what have caused all the trouble. I know that. But if I'm grown up—if it's so tremendous—then I'll wear a dress all the time, except just *when* I ride. Will that do, Auntie?"

"Maybe you will grow up, after all," replied Aunt Jane, evidently surprised and pleased.

Then Lucy with clinking spurs ran away to her room.

"Jane, what's this nonsense about young Joel Creech?" asked Bostil, gruffly.

"I don't know any more than is gossiped. That I told you. Have you ever asked Lucy about him?"

"I sure haven't," said Bostil, bluntly.

"Well, ask her. If she tells you at all she'll tell the truth. Lucy'd never sleep at night if she lied."

Aunt Jane returned to her housewifely tasks, leaving Bostil thoughtfully stroking the hound and watching the fire. Presently Lucy returned—a different Lucy —one that did not rouse his rider's pride, but thrilled his father's heart. She had been a slim, lithe, supple, disheveled boy, breathing the wild spirit of the open and the horse she rode. She was now a girl in the graceful roundness of her slender form, with hair the gold of the sage at sunset, and eyes the blue of the deep haze of distance, and lips the sweet red of the upland rose. And all about her seemed different.

"Lucy—you look—like—like she used to be," said Bostil, unsteadily.

"My mother!" murmured Lucy.

But these two, so keen, so strong, so alive, did not abide long with sad memories.

"Lucy, I want to ask you somethin'," said Bostil, presently. "What about this young Joel Creech?"

Lucy started as if suddenly recalled, then she laughed merrily. "Dad, you old fox, did you see him ride out after me?"

"No. I was just askin' on—on general principles."

"What do you mean?"

"Lucy, is there anythin' between you an' Joel?" he asked, gravely.

"No," she replied, with her clear eyes up to his.

Bostil thought of a bluebell. "I'm beggin' your pardon," he said, hastily.

"Dad, you know how Joel runs after me. I've told you. I let him till lately. I liked him. But that wasn't why. I felt sorry for him—pitied him."

"You did? Seems an awful waste," replied Bostil.

"Dad, I don't believe Joel is—perfectly right in his mind," Lucy said, solemnly.

"Haw! haw! Fine compliments you're payin' yourself."

"Listen. I'm serious. I mean I've grown to see—looking back—that a slow, gradual change has come over Joel since he was kicked in the head by a mustang. I'm sure no one else has noticed it."

"Goin' batty over you. That's no unusual sign round this here camp. Look at—"

"We're talking about Joel Creech. Lately he has done some queer things. To-day, for instance. I thought I gave him the slip. But he must have been watching. Anyway, to my surprise he showed up on Peg. He doesn't often get Peg across the river. He said the feed was getting scarce over there. I was dying to race Buckles against Peg, but I remembered you wouldn't like that."

"I should say not," said Bostil, darkly.

"Well, Joel caught up to me—and he wasn't nice at all. He was worse to-day. We quarreled. I said I'd bet he'd never follow me again and he said he'd bet he would. Then he got sulky and hung back. I rode away, glad to be rid of him, and I climbed to a favorite place of mine. On my way home I saw Peg grazing on the rim of the creek, near that big spring-hole where the water's so deep and clear. And what do you think? There was Joel's head above the water. I remembered in our quarrel I had told him to go wash his dirty face. He was doing it. I had to laugh. When he saw me—he—then—then he—" Lucy faltered, blushing with anger and shame.

"Well, what then?" demanded Bostil, quietly.

"He called, 'Hey, Luce—take off your clothes and come in for a swim!'"

Bostil swore.

"I tell you I was mad," continued Lucy, "and just as surprised. That was one of the queer things. But never before had he dared to—to—"

"Insult you. Then what'd you do?" interrupted Bostil, curiously.

"I yelled, 'I'll fix you, Joel Creech!' . . . His clothes were in a pile on the bank. At first I thought I'd throw them in the water, but when I got to them I thought of something better. I took up all but his shoes, for I remembered the ten miles of rock and cactus between him and home, and I climbed up on Buckles. Joel screamed and swore something fearful. But I didn't look back. And Peg, you know—maybe you don't know—but Peg is fond of me, and he followed me, straddling his bridle all the way in. I dropped Joel's clothes down the ridge a ways, right in the trail, so he can't miss them. And that's all. . . . Dad, was it—was it very bad?"

"Bad! Why, you ought to have thrown your gun on him. At least bounced a rock off his head! But say, Lucy, after all, maybe you've done enough. I guess you never thought of it."

"What?"

"The sun is hot to-day. Hot! An' if Joel's as crazy an' mad as you say he'll not have sense enough to stay in the water or shade till the sun's gone down. An' if he tackles that ten miles before he'll sunburn himself within an inch of his life."

"Sunburn? Oh, Dad! I'm sorry," burst out Lucy, contritely. "I never thought of that. I'll ride back with his clothes."

"You will not," said Bostil.

"Let me send some one, then," she entreated.

"Girl, haven't you the nerve to play your own game? Let Creech get his lesson. He deserves it. . . . An' now, Lucy, I've two more questions to ask."

"Only two?" she queried, archly. "Dad, don't scold me with questions."

"What shall I say to Wetherby for good an' all?"

Lucy's eyes shaded dreamily, and she seemed to look beyond the room, out over the ranges.

"Tell him to go back to Durango and forget the

foolish girl who can care only for the desert and a horse."

"All right. That is straight talk, like an Indian's. An' now the last question—what do you want for a birthday present?"

"Oh, of course," she cried, gleefully clapping her hands. "I'd forgotten that. I'm eighteen!"

"You get that old chest of your mother's. But what from me?"

"Dad, will you give me anything I ask for?"

"Yes, my girl."

"Anything—any *horse?*"

Lucy knew his weakness, for she had inherited it.

"Sure; any horse but the King."

"How about Sarchedon?"

"Why, Lucy, what'd you do with that big black devil? He's too high. Seventeen hands high! You couldn't mount him."

"Pooh! Sarch *kneels* for me."

"Child, listen to reason. Sarch would pull your arms out of their sockets."

"He has got an iron jaw," agreed Lucy. "Well, then—how about Dusty Ben?" She was tormenting her father and she did it with glee.

"No—not Ben. He's the faithfulest hoss I ever owned. It wouldn't be fair to part with him, even to you. Old associations . . . a rider's loyalty . . . now, Lucy, you know—"

"Dad, you're afraid I'd train and love Ben into beating the King. Some day I'll ride some horse out in front of the gray. Remember, Dad! . . . Then give me Two Face."

"Sure not her, Lucy. Thet mare can't be trusted. Look why we named her Two Face."

"Buckles, then, dear generous Daddy who longs to give his grown-up girl *anything!*"

"Lucy, can't you be satisfied an' happy with your mustangs? You've got a dozen. You can have any others on the range. Buckles ain't safe for you to ride."

Bostil was notably the most generous of men, the
kindest of fathers. It was an indication of his strange
obsession, in regard to horses, that he never would see
that Lucy was teasing him. As far as horses were concerned he lacked a sense of humor. Anything connected with his horses was of intense interest.

"I'd dearly love to own Plume," said Lucy, demurely.

Bostil had grown red in the face and now he was
on the rack. The monstrous selfishness of a rider who
had been supreme in his day could not be changed.

"Girl, I—I thought you hadn't no use for Plume,"
he stammered.

"I haven't—the jade! She threw me once. I've never
forgiven her. . . . Dad, I'm only teasing you. Don't
I know you couldn't give one of those racers away?
You couldn't!"

"Lucy, I reckon you're right," Bostil burst out in
immense relief.

"Dad, I'll bet if Cordts gets me and holds me as
ransom for the King—as he's threatened—you'll let
him have me!"

"Lucy, now thet ain't funny!" complained the father.

"Dear Dad, keep your old racers! But, remember,
I'm my father's daughter. I can love a horse, too.
Oh, if I ever get the one I want to love! A wild horse
—a desert stallion—pure Arabian—broken right by
an Indian! If I ever get him, Dad, you look out! For
I'll run away from Sarch and Ben—and I'll beat the
King!"

The hamlet of Bostil's Ford had a singular situation,
though, considering the wonderful nature of that desert country, it was not exceptional. It lay under the
protecting red bluff that only Lucy Bostil cared to
climb. A hard-trodden road wound down through
rough breaks in the cañon wall to the river. Bostil's
house, at the head of the village, looked in the opposite direction, down the sage slope that widened like

a colossal fan. There was one wide street bordered by cottonwoods and cabins, and a number of gardens and orchards, beginning to burst into green and pink and white. A brook ran out of a ravine in the huge bluff, and from this led irrigation ditches. The red earth seemed to blossom at the touch of water.

The place resembled an Indian encampment— quiet, sleepy, colorful, with the tiny streams of water running everywhere, and lazy columns of blue wood-smoke rising, Bostil's Ford was the opposite of a busy village, yet its few inhabitants, as a whole, were prosperous. The wants of pioneers were few. Perhaps once a month the big, clumsy flatboat was rowed across the river with horses or cattle or sheep. And the season was now close at hand when for weeks, sometimes months, the river was unfordable. There were a score of permanent families, a host of merry, sturdy children, a number of idle young men, and only one girl—Lucy Bostil. But the village always had transient inhabitants—friendly Utes and Navajos in to trade, and sheep-herders with a scraggy, woolly flock, and travelers of the strange religious sect identified with Utah going on into the wilderness. Then there were always riders passing to and fro, and sometimes unknown ones regarded with caution. Horse-thieves sometimes boldly rode in, and sometimes were able to sell or trade. In the matter of horse-dealing Bostil's Ford was as bold as the thieves.

Old Brackton, a man of varied Western experience, kept the one store, which was tavern, trading-post, freighter's headquarters, blacksmith's shop, and anything else needful. Brackton employed riders, teamsters, sometimes Indians, to freight supplies in once a month from Durango. And that was over two hundred miles away. Sometimes the supplies did not arrive on time—occasionally not at all. News from the outside world, except that elicited from the taciturn travelers marching into Utah, drifted in at intervals. But it was not missed. These wilderness spirits were the forerunners of a great movement, and as such were big,

strong, stern, sufficient unto themselves. Life there
was made possible by horses. The distant future, that
looked bright to far-seeing men, must be and could
only be fulfilled through the endurance and faithful-
ness of horses. And then, from these men, horses received the meed due them, and the love they were truly
worth. The Navajo was a nomad horseman, an Arab
of the Painted Desert, and the Ute Indian was close
to him. It was they who developed the white riders of
the uplands as well as the wild-horse wrangler or
hunter.

Brackton's ramshackle establishment stood down at
the end of the village street. There was not a sawed
board in all that structure, and some of the pine logs
showed how they had been dropped from the bluff.
Brackton, a little old gray man, with scant beard, and
eyes like those of a bird, came briskly out to meet an
incoming freighter. The wagon was minus a hind
wheel, but the teamster had come in on three wheels
and a pole. The sweaty, dust-caked, weary, thin-ribbed
mustangs, and the gray-and-red-stained wagon, and
the huge jumble of dusty packs, showed something of
what the journey had been.

"Hi thar, Red Wilson, you air some late gettin' in,"
greeted old Brackton.

Red Wilson had red eyes from fighting the flying
sand, and red dust pasted in his scraggy beard, and
as he gave his belt an upward hitch little red clouds
flew from his gun-sheath.

"Yep. An' I left a wheel an' part of the load on the
trail," he said.

With him were Indians who began to unhitch the
teams. Riders lounging in the shade greeted Wilson
and inquired for news. The teamster replied that travel
was dry, the water-holes were dry, and he was dry.
And his reply gave both concern and amusement.

"One more trip out an' back—thet's all, till it
rains," concluded Wilson.

Brackton led him inside, evidently to alleviate part
of that dryness.

Water and grass, next to horses, were the stock subject of all riders.

"It's got oncommon hot early," said one.

"Yes, an' them northeast winds—hard this spring," said another.

"No snow on the uplands."

"Holley seen a dry spell comin'. Wal, we can drift along without freighters. There's grass an' water enough here, even if it doesn't rain."

"Sure, but there ain't none across the river."

"Never was, in early season. An' if there was it'd be sheeped off."

"Creech'll be fetchin' his hosses across soon, I reckon."

"You bet he will. He's trainin' for the races next month."

"An' when air they comin' off?"

"You got me. Mebbe Van knows."

Some one prodded a sleepy rider who lay all his splendid, lithe length, hat over his eyes. Then he sat up and blinked, a lean-faced, gray-eyed fellow, half good-natured and half resentful.

"Did somebody punch me?"

"Naw, you got nightmare! Say, Van, when will the races come off?"

"Huh! An' you woke me for thet? . . . Bostil says in a few weeks, soon as he hears from the Indians. Plans to have eight hundred Indians here, an' the biggest purses an' best races ever had at the Ford."

"You'll ride the King again?"

"Reckon so. But Bostil is kickin' because I'm heavier than I was," replied the rider.

"You're skin an' bones at thet."

"Mebbe you'll need to work a little off, Van. Some one said Creech's Blue Roan was comin' fast this year."

"Bill, your mind ain't operatin'," replied Van, scornfully. "Didn't I beat Creech's hosses last year without the King turnin' a hair?"

"Not if I recollect, you didn't. The Blue Roan wasn't runnin'."

Then they argued, after the manner of friendly riders, but all earnest, all eloquent in their convictions. The prevailing opinion was that Creech's horse had a chance, depending upon condition and luck.

The argument shifted upon the arrival of two newcomers leading mustangs and apparently talking trade. It was manifest that these arrivals were not loath to get the opinions of others.

"Van, there's a hoss!" exclaimed one.

"No, he ain't," replied Van.

And that diverse judgment appeared to be characteristic throughout. The strange thing was that Macomber, the rancher, had already traded his mustang and money to boot for the sorrel. The deal, whether wise or not, had been consummated. Brackton came out with Red Wilson, and they had to have their say.

"Wal, durned if some of you fellers ain't kind an' complimentary," remarked Macomber, scratching his head. "But then every feller can't have hoss sense." Then, looking up to see Lucy Bostil coming along the road, he brightened as if with inspiration.

Lucy was at home among them, and the shy eyes of the younger riders, especially Van, were nothing if not revealing. She greeted them with a bright smile, and when she saw Brackton she burst out:

"Oh, Mr. Brackton, the wagon's in, and did my box come? . . . To-day's my birthday."

" 'Deed it did, Lucy; an' many more happy ones to you!" he replied, delighted in her delight. "But it's too heavy for you. I'll send it up—or mebbe one of the boys—"

Five riders in unison eagerly offered their services and looked as if each had spoken first. Then Macomber addressed her:

"Miss Lucy, you see this here sorrel?"

"Ah! the same lazy crowd and the same old story— a horse trade!" laughed Lucy.

"There's a little difference of opinion," said Macomber, politely indicating the riders. "Now, Miss Lucy, we-all know you're a judge of a hoss. And as good as thet you tell the truth. Thet ain't in some hoss-traders I know. . . . What do you think of this mustang?"

Macomber had eyes of enthusiasm for his latest acquisition, but some of the cock-sureness had been knocked out of him by the blunt riders.

"Macomber, aren't you a great one to talk?" queried Lucy, severely. "Didn't you get around Dad and trade him an old, blind, knock-kneed bag of bones for a perfectly good pony—one I liked to ride?"

The riders shouted with laughter while the rancher struggled with confusion.

" 'Pon my word, Miss Lucy, I'm surprised you could think thet of such an old friend of yours—an' your Dad's, too. I'm hopin' he doesn't side altogether with you."

"Dad and I never agree about a horse. He thinks he got the best of you. But you know, Macomber, what a horse-thief you are. Worse than Cordts!"

"Wal, if I got the best of Bostil I'm willin' to be thought bad. I'm the first feller to take him in. . . . An' now, Miss Lucy, look over my sorrel."

Lucy Bostil did indeed have an eye for a horse. She walked straight up to the wild, shaggy mustang with a confidence born of intuition and experience, and reached a hand for his head, not slowly, nor yet swiftly. The mustang looked as if he was about to jump, but he did not. His eyes showed that he was not used to women.

"He's not well broken," said Lucy. "Some Navajo has beaten his head in breaking him."

Then she carefully studied the mustang point by point.

"He's deceiving at first because he's good to look at," said Lucy. "But I wouldn't own him. A saddle will turn on him. He's not vicious, but he'll never get over his scare. He's narrow between the eyes—a bad

sign. His ears are stiff—and too close. I don't see anything more wrong with him."

"You seen enough?" declared Macomber. "An' so
you wouldn't own him?"

"You couldn't make me a present of him—even on
my birthday."

"Wal, now I'm sorry, for I was thinkin' of thet,"
replied Macomber, ruefully. It was plain that the sorrel had fallen irremediably in his estimation.

"Macomber, I often tell Dad all you horse-traders
get your deserts now and then. It's vanity and desire
to beat the other man that's your downfall."

Lucy went away, with Van shouldering her box,
leaving Macomber trying to return the banter of the
riders. The good-natured raillery was interrupted by a
sharp word from one of them.

"Look! Darn me if thet ain't a naked Indian comin'!"

The riders whirled to see an apparently nude savage
approaching, almost on a run.

"Take a shot at thet, Bill," said another rider. "Miss
Lucy might see— No, she's out of sight. But, mebbe
some other woman is around."

"Hold on, Bill," called Macomber. "You never saw
an Indian run like thet."

Some of the riders swore, others laughed, and all
suddenly became keen with interest.

"Sure his face is white, if his body's red!"

The strange figure neared them. It was indeed red
up to the face, which seemed white in contrast. Yet
only in general shape and action did it resemble a man.

"Damned if it ain't Joel Creech!" sang out Bill
Stark.

The other riders accorded their wondering assent.

"Gone crazy, sure!"

"I always seen it comin'."

"Say, but ain't he wild? Foamin' at the mouth like
a winded hoss!"

Young Creech was headed down the road toward the ford across which he had to go to reach

home. He saw the curious group, slowed his pace, and halted. His face seemed convulsed with rage and pain and fatigue. His body, even to his hands, was incased in a thick, heavy coating of red adobe that had caked hard.

"God's sake—fellers—" he panted, with eyes rolling, "take this—'dobe mud off me! . . . I'm dyin'!'

Then he staggered into Brackton's place. A howl went up from the riders and they surged after him.

That evening after supper Bostil stamped in the big room, roaring with laughter, red in the face; and he astonished Lucy and her aunt to the point of consternation.

"Now—you've—done—it—Lucy Bostil!" he roared

"Oh dear! Oh dear!" exclaimed Aunt Jane.

"Done what?" asked Lucy, blankly.

Bostil conquered his paroxysm, and, wiping his moist red face, he eyed Lucy in mock solemnity.

"Joel!" whispered Lucy, who had a guilty conscience.

"Lucy, I never heard the beat of it. . . . Joel's smarter in some ways than we thought, an' crazier in others. He had the sun figgered, but what'd he want to run through town for? Why, never in my life have I seen such tickled riders."

"Dad!" almost screamed Lucy. "What did Joel do?"

"Wal, I see it this way. He couldn't or wouldn't wait for sundown. An' he wasn't hankerin' to be burned. So he wallows in a 'dobe mud-hole an' covers himself thick with mud. You know that 'dobe mud! Then he starts home. But he hadn't figgered on the 'dobe gettin' hard, which it did—harder 'n rock. An' thet must have hurt more'n sunburn. Late this afternoon he came runnin' down the road, yellin' thet he was dyin'. The boys had conniption fits. Joel ain't over-liked, you know, an' here they had one on him. Mebbe they didn't try hard to clean him off. But the fact is not for hours did they get thet 'dobe off him. They washed an' scrubbed an' curried him, while he yelled an' cussed. Finally they peeled it off, with his skin I guess. He was raw, an', they say, the maddest feller ever seen in Bostil's Ford!"

Lucy was struggling between fear and mirth. She did not look sorry. "Oh! Oh! Oh, Dad!"

"Wasn't it great, Lucy?"

"But what—will he—do?" choked Lucy.

"Lord only knows. Thet worries me some. Because he never said a word about how he come to lose his clothes or why he had the 'dobe on him. An' sure I never told. Nobody knows but us."

"Dad, he'll do something terrible to me!" cried Lucy, aghast at her premonition.

Chapter III

THE days did not pass swiftly at Bostil's Ford. And except in winter, and during the spring sand-storms, the lagging time passed pleasantly. Lucy rode every day, sometimes with Van, and sometimes alone. She was not over-keen about riding with Van—first, because he was in love with her; and secondly, in spite of that, she could not beat him when he rode the King. They were training Bostil's horses for the much-anticipated races.

At last word arrived from the Utes and Navajos that they accepted Bostil's invitation and would come in force, which meant, according to Holley and other old riders, that the Indians would attend about eight hundred strong.

"Thet old chief, Hawk, is comin'," Holley informed Bostil. "He hasn't been here fer several years. Recollect thet bunch of colts he had? They're hosses, not mustangs. . . . So you look out, Bostil!"

No rider or rancher or sheepman, in fact, no one, ever lost a chance to warn Bostil. Some of it was in fun, but most of it was earnest. The nature of events was that sooner or later a horse would beat the King. Bostil knew that as well as anybody, though he would not admit it. Holley's hint made Bostil look worried. Most of Bostil's gray hairs might have been traced to his years of worry about horses.

The day he received word from the Indians he sent for Brackton, Williams, Muncie, and Creech to come to his house that night. These men, with Bostil, had for years formed in a way a club, which gave the Ford distinction. Creech was no longer a friend of Bostil's, but Bostil had always been fair-minded, and now he did not allow his animosities to influence him. Holley, the veteran rider, made the sixth member of the club.

Bostil had a cedar log blazing cheerily in the wide fireplace, for these early spring nights in the desert were cold.

Brackton was the last guest to arrive. He shuffled in without answering the laconic greetings accorded him, and his usually mild eyes seemed keen and hard.

"John, I reckon you won't love me fer this here I've got to tell you, to-night specially," he said, seriously.

"You old robber, I couldn't love you anyhow," retorted Bostil. But his humor did not harmonize with the sudden gravity of his look. "What's up?"

"Who do you suppose I jest sold whisky to?"

"I've no idea," replied Bostil. Yet he looked as if he was perfectly sure.

"Cordts! . . . Cordts, an' four of his outfit. Two of them I didn't know. Bad men, judgin' from appearances, let alone company. The others was Hutchinson an'—Dick Sears."

"Dick Sears!" exclaimed Bostil.

Muncie and Williams echoed Bostil. Holley appeared suddenly interested. Creech alone showed no surprise.

"But Sears is dead," added Bostil.

"He was dead—we thought," replied Brackton, with

a grim laugh. "But he's alive again. He told me he'd been in Idaho for two years, in the gold-fields. Said the work was too hard, so he'd come back here. Laughed when he said it, the little devil! I'll bet he was thinking of thet wagon-train of mine he stole."

Bostil gazed at his chief rider.

"Wal, I reckon we didn't kill Sears, after all," replied Holley. "I wasn't never sure."

"Lord! Cordts an' Sears in camp!" ejaculated Bostil, and he began to pace the room.

"No, they're gone now," said Brackton

"Take it easy, boss. Sit down," drawled Holley. "The King is safe, an' all the racers. I swear to thet. Why, Cordts couldn't chop into thet log-an'-wire corral if he an' his gang chopped all night! They hate work. Besides, Farlane is there, an' the boys."

This reassured Bostil, and he resumed his chair. But his hand shook a little.

"Did Cordts have anythin' to say?" he asked.

"Sure. He was friendly an' talkative," replied Brackton. "He came in just after dark. Left a man I didn't see out with the hosses. He bought two big packs of supplies, an' some leather stuff, an', of course, ammunition. Then some whisky. Had plenty of gold an' wouldn't take no change. Then while his men, except Sears, was carryin' out the stuff, he talked."

"Go on. Tell me," said Bostil.

"Wal, he'd been out north of Durango an' fetched news. There's wild talk back there of a railroad goin' to be built some day, joinin' east an' west. It's interestin', but no sense to it. How could they build a railroad through thet country?"

"North it ain't so cut up an' lumpy as here," put in Holley.

"Grandest idea ever thought of for the West," avowed Bostil. "If thet railroad ever starts we'll all get rich. . . . Go on, Brack."

"Then Cordts said water an' grass was peterin' out back on the trail, same as Red Wilson said last week. Finally he asked, 'How's my friend Bostil?' I told him

you was well. He looked kind of thoughtful then, an'
I knew what was comin'. . . . 'How's the King?' 'Grand'
I told him—'grand.' 'When is them races comin' off?'
I said we hadn't planned the time yet, but it would be
soon—inside of a month or two. 'Brackton,' he said,
sharp-like, 'is Bostil goin' to pull a gun on me at
sight?' 'Reckon he is,' I told him. 'Wal, I'm not powerful glad to know thet. . . . I hear Creech's blue
hoss will race the King this time. How about it?' 'Sure
an' certain this year. I've Creech's an' Bostil's word
for thet.' Cordts put his hand on my shoulder. You
ought to've seen his eyes! . . . 'I want to see thet
race. . . . I'm goin' to.' 'Wal,' I said, 'you'll have to
stop bein'— You'll need to change your bizness.'
Then, Bostil, what do you think? Cordts was sort of
eager an' wild. He said thet was a race he jest couldn't
miss. He swore he wouldn't turn a trick or let a man
of his gang stir a hand till after thet race, if you'd let
him come."

A light flitted across Bostil's face.

"I know how Cordts feels," he said.

"Wal, it's a queer deal," went on Brackton. "Fer
a long time you've meant to draw on Cordts when
you meet. We all know thet."

"Yes, I'll kill him!" The light left Bostil's face. His
voice sounded differently. His mouth opened, drooped
strangely at the corners, then shut in a grim, tense
line. Bostil had killed more than one man. The memory, no doubt, was haunting and ghastly.

"Cordts seemed to think his word was guarantee
of his good faith. He said he'd send an Indian in here
to find out if he can come to the races. I reckon,
Bostil, thet it wouldn't hurt none to let him come. An'
hold your gun hand fer the time he swears he'll be
honest. Queer deal, ain't it, men? A hoss-thief turnin'
honest jest to see a race! Beats me! Bostil, it's a
cheap way to get at least a little honesty from Cordts.
An' refusin' might rile him bad. When all's said
Cordts ain't as bad as he could be."

"I'll let him come," replied Bostil, breathing deep.

"But it'll be hard to see him, rememberin' how he's robbed me, an' what he's threatened. An' I ain't lettin' him come to bribe a few weeks' decency from him. I'm doin' it for only one reason. . . . Because I know how he loves the King—how he wants to see the King run away from the field thet day! Thet's why!"

There was a moment of silence, during which all turned to Creech. He was a stalwart man, no longer young, with a lined face, deep-set, troubled eyes, and white, thin beard.

"Bostil, if Cordts loves the King thet well, he's in fer heartbreak," said Creech, with a ring in his voice.

Down crashed Bostil's heavy boots and fire flamed in his gaze. The other men laughed, and Brackton interposed:

"Hold on, you boy riders!" he yelled. "We ain't a-goin' to have any arguments like thet. . . . Now, Bostil, it's settled, then? You'll let Cordts come?"

"Glad to have him," replied Bostil.

"Good. An' now mebbe we'd better get down to the bizness of this here meetin'."

They seated themselves around the table, upon which Bostil laid an old and much-soiled ledger and a stub of a lead-pencil.

"First we'll set the time," he said, with animation, "an' then pitch into details. . . . What's the date?"

No one answered, and presently they all looked blankly from one to the other.

"It's April, ain't it?" queried Holley.

That assurance was as close as they could get to the time of year.

"Lucy!" called Bostil, in a loud voice.

She came running in, anxious, almost alarmed.

"Goodness! you made us jump! What on earth is the matter?"

"Lucy, we want to know the date," replied Bostil.

"Date! Did you have to scare Auntie and me out of our wits just for that?"

"Who scared you? This is important, Lucy. What's the date?"

"It's a week to-day since last Tuesday," answered Lucy, sweetly.

"Huh! Then it's Tuesday again," said Bostil, laboriously writing it down. "Now, what's the date?"

"Don't you remember?"

"Remember? I never knew."

"Dad! . . . Last Tuesday was my birthday—the day you *did not* give me a horse!"

"Aw, so it was," rejoined Bostil, confused at her reproach. "An' thet date was—let's see—April sixth. . . . Then this is April thirteenth. Much obliged, Lucy. Run back to your aunt now. This hoss talk won't interest you."

Lucy tossed her head. "I'll bet I'll have to straighten out the whole thing." Then with a laugh she disappeared.

"Three days beginnin'—say June first. June first—second, an' third. How about thet for the races?"

Everybody agreed, and Bostil laboriously wrote that down. Then they planned the details. Purses and prizes, largely donated by Bostil and Muncie, the rich members of the community, were recorded. The old rules were adhered to. Any rider or any Indian could enter any horse in any race, or as many horses as he liked in as many races. But by winning one race he excluded himself from the others. Bostil argued for a certain weight in riders, but the others ruled out this suggestion. Special races were arranged for the Indians, with saddles, bridles, blankets, guns as prizes.

All this appeared of absorbing interest to Bostil. He perspired freely. There was a gleam in his eye, betraying excitement. When it came to arranging the details of the big race between the high-class racers, then he grew intense and harder to deal with. Many points had to go by vote. Muncie and Williams both had fleet horses to enter in this race; Holley had one; Creech had two; there were sure to be several Indians enter fast mustangs; and Bostil had the King and four others to choose from. Bostil held out stubbornly for a long race. It was well known that Sage King was

unbeatable in a long race. If there were any chance to
beat him it must be at short distance. The vote went
against Bostil, much to his chagrin, and the great race
was set down for two miles.

"But two miles! . . . Two miles!" he kept repeating.
"Thet's Blue Roan's distance. Thet's his distance. An'
it ain't fair to the King!"

His guests, excepting Creech, argued with him, explained, reasoned, showed him that it was fair to all
concerned. Bostil finally acquiesced, but he was not
happy. The plain fact was that he was frightened.

When the men were departing Bostil called Creech
back into the sitting-room. Creech appeared surprised,
yet it was evident that he would have been glad to
make friends with Bostil.

"What'll you take for the roan?" Bostil asked, terse-
ly, as if he had never asked that before.

"Bostil, didn't we thresh thet out before—an' *fell*
out over it?" queried Creech, with a deprecating
spread of his hands.

"Wal, we can fall in again, if you'll sell or trade
the hoss."

"I'm sorry, but I can't."

"You need money an' hosses, don't you?" demanded
Bostil, brutally. He had no conscience in a matter of
horse-dealing.

"Lord knows, I do," replied Creech.

"Wal, then, here's your chance. I'll give you five
hundred in gold an' Sarchedon to boot."

Creech looked as if he had not heard aright. Bostil
repeated the offer.

"No," replied Creech.

"I'll make it a thousand an' throw Plume in with
Sarch," flashed Bostil.

"No!" Creech turned pale and swallowed hard.

"Two thousand an' Dusty Ben along with the
others?"

This was an unheard-of price to pay for any horse.
Creech saw that Bostil was desperate. It was an almost overpowering temptation. Evidently Creech re-

sisted it only by applying all his mind to the thought of his clean-limbed, soft-eyed, noble horse.

Bostil did not give Creech time to speak. "Twenty-five hundred an' Two Face along with the rest!"

"My God, Bostil—stop it! I can't *part* with Blue Roan. You're rich an' you've no heart. Thet I always knew. At least to me you never had, since I owned them two racers. Didn't I beg you, a little time back, to lend me a few hundred? To meet thet debt? An' you wouldn't, unless I'd sell the hosses. An' I had to lose my sheep. Now I'm a poor man—gettin' poorer all the time. But I won't sell or trade Blue Roan, not for all you've got!"

Creech seemed to gain strength with his speech and passion with the strength. His eyes glinted at the hard, paling face of his rival. He raised a clenching fist.

"An' by G—d, I'm goin' to win thet race!"

During that week Lucy had heard many things about Joel Creech, and some of them were disquieting.

Some rider had not only found Joel's clothes on the trail, but he had recognized the track of the horse Lucy rode, and at once connected her with the singular discovery. Coupling that with Joel's appearance in the village incased in a heaving armor of adobe, the riders guessed pretty close to the truth. For them the joke was tremendous. And Joel Creech was exceedingly sensitive to ridicule. The riders made life unbearable for him. They had fun out of it as long as Joel showed signs of taking the joke manfully, which was not long, and then his resentment won their contempt. That led to sarcasm on their part and bitter anger on his. It came to Lucy's ears that Joel began to act and talk strangely. She found out that the rider Van had knocked Joel down in Brackton's store and had kicked a gun out of his hand. Van laughed off the rumor and Brackton gave her no satisfaction. Moreover, she heard no other rumors. The channels of gossip had suddenly closed to her. Bostil, when questioned by Lucy, swore in a way that amazed her, and all he told her was to leave Creech alone. Finally, when Muncie discharged Joel, who worked now and then, Lucy realized that something was wrong with Joel and that she was to blame for it.

She grew worried and anxious and sorry, but she held her peace, and determined to find out for herself what was wrong. Every day when she rode out into the sage she expected to meet him, or at least see him somewhere; nevertheless days went by and there was no sign of him.

One afternoon she saw some Indians driving sheep down the river road toward the ford, and, acting upon impulse, she turned her horse after them.

Lucy seldom went down the river road. Riding down and up was merely work, and a horse has as little liking for it as she had. Usually it was a hot, dusty trip, and the great, dark, overhanging walls had a depressing effect upon her. She always felt awe at the gloomy cañon and fear at the strange, murmuring red river. But she started down this afternoon in the hope of meeting Joel. She had a hazy idea of telling him she was sorry for what she had done, and of asking him to forget it and pay no more heed to the riders.

The sheep raised a dust-cloud in the sandy wash where the road wound down, and Lucy hung back to let them get farther ahead. Gradually the tiny roar of pattering hoofs and the blended bleating and baaing died away. The dust-cloud, however, hung over the head of the ravine, and Lucy had to force Sarchedon through it. Sarchedon did not mind sand and dust, but he surely hated the smell of sheep. Lucy seldom put a spur to Sarchedon; still, she gave him a lash with her quirt, and then he went on obediently, if disgustedly. He carried his head like a horse that wondered why his mistress preferred to drive him down into an unpleasant hole when she might have been cutting the sweet, cool sage wind up on the slope.

The wash, with its sand and clay walls, dropped

into a gulch, and there was an end of green growths. The road led down over solid rock. Gradually the rims of the gorge rose, shutting out the light and the cliffs. It was a winding road and one not safe to tarry on in a stormy season. Lucy had seen boulders weighing a ton go booming down that gorge during one of the sudden fierce desert storms, when a torrent of water and mud and stone went plunging on to the river. The ride through here was short, though slow. Lucy always had time to adjust her faculties for the overpowering contrast these lower regions presented. Long before she reached the end of the gorge she heard the sullen thunder of the river. The river was low, too, for otherwise there would have been a deafening roar.

Presently she came out upon a lower branch of the cañon, into a great red-walled space, with the river still a thousand feet below, and the cliffs towering as high above her. The road led down along this rim where to the left all was open, across to the split and peaked wall opposite. The river appeared to sweep round a bold, bulging corner a mile above. It was a wide, swift, muddy, turbulent stream. A great bar of sand stretched out from the shore. Beyond it, through the mouth of an intersecting cañon, could be seen a clump of cottonwoods and willows that marked the home of the Creeches. Lucy could not see the shore nearest her, as it was almost directly under her. Besides, in this narrow road, on a spirited horse, she was not inclined to watch the scenery. She hurried Sarchedon down and down, under the overhanging brows of rock, to where the rim sloped out and failed. Here was a half-acre of sand, with a few scant willows, set down seemingly in a dent at the base of the giant, beetling cliffs. The place was light, though the light seemed a kind of veiled red, and to Lucy always ghastly. She could not have been joyous with that river moaning before her, even if it had been up on a level, in the clear and open day. As a little girl eight years old she had conceived a terror and hatred of this huge, jagged rent so full of red haze and purple smoke and the thunder of rushing waters. And she had never wholly outgrown it. The joy of the sun and wind, the rapture in the boundless open, the sweetness in the sage—these were not possible here. Something mighty and ponderous, heavy as those colossal cliffs, weighted down her spirit. The voice of the river drove out any dream. Here was the incessant frowning presence of destructive forces of nature. And the ford was associated with catastrophe—to sheep, to horses and to men.

Lucy rode across the bar to the shore where the Indians were loading the sheep into an immense rude flatboat. As the sheep were frightened, the loading was no easy task. Their bleating could be heard above the roar of the river. Bostil's boatmen, Shugrue and Somers, stood knee-deep in the quicksand of the bar, and their efforts to keep free-footed were as strenuous as their handling of the sheep. Presently the flock was all crowded on board, the Indians followed, and then the boatmen slid the unwieldy craft off the sand-bar. Then, each manning a clumsy oar, they pulled upstream. Along shore were whirling, slow eddies, and there rowing was possible. Out in that swift current it would have been folly to try to contend with it, let alone make progress. The method of crossing was to row up along the shore as far as a great cape of rock jutting out, and there make into the current, and while drifting down pull hard to reach the landing opposite. Heavily laden as the boat was, the chances were not wholly in favor of a successful crossing.

Lucy watched the slow, laborious struggle of the boatmen with the heavy oars until she suddenly remembered the object of her visit down to the ford. She appeared to be alone on her side of the river. At the landing opposite, however, were two men; and presently Lucy recognized Joel Creech and his father. A second glance showed Indians with burros, evidently waiting for the boat. Joel Creech jumped into a skiff and shoved off. The elder man, judging by his

motions, seemed to be trying to prevent his son from
leaving the shore. But Joel began to row up-stream,
keeping close to the shore. Lucy watched him. No
doubt he had seen her and was coming across. Either
the prospect of meeting him or the idea of meeting
him there in the place where she was never herself
made her want to turn at once and ride back home.
But her stubborn sense of fairness overruled that. She
would hold her ground solely in the hope of persuad-
ing Joel to be reasonable. She saw the big flatboat
sweep into line of sight at the same time Joel turned
into the current. But while the larger craft drifted
slowly the other way, the smaller one came swiftly
down and across. Joel swept out of the current into
the eddy, rowed across that, and slid the skiff up on
the sand-bar. Then he stepped out. He was bareheaded
and barefooted, but it was not that which made him
seem a stranger to Lucy.

"Are you lookin' fer me?" he shouted.

Lucy waved a hand for him to come up.

Then he approached. He was a tall, lean young
man, stoop-shouldered and bow-legged from much riding, with sallow, freckled face, a thin fuzz of beard,
weak mouth and chin, and eyes remarkable for their
small size and piercing quality and different color.
For one was gray and the other was hazel. There was
no scar on his face, but the irregularity of his features reminded one who knew that he had once been
kicked in the face by a horse.

Creech came up hurriedly, in an eager, wild way
that made Lucy suddenly pity him. He did not seem
to remember that the stallion had an antipathy for
him. But Lucy, if she had forgotten, would have been
reminded by Sarchedon's action.

"Look out, Joel!" she called, and she gave the
black's head a jerk. Sarchedon went up with a snort
and came down pounding the sand. Quick as an Indian Lucy was out of the saddle.

"Lemme your quirt," said Joel, showing his teeth
like a wolf.

"No. I wouldn't let you hit Sarch. You beat him once, and he's never forgotten," replied Lucy.

The eye of the horse and the man met and clashed, and there was a hostile tension in their attitudes. Then Lucy dropped the bridle and drew Joel over to a huge drift-log, half buried in the sand. Here she sat down, but Joel remained standing. His gaze was now all the stranger for its wistfulness. Lucy was quick to catch a subtle difference in him, but she could not tell wherein it lay.

"What'd you want?" asked Joel.

"I've heard a lot of things, Joel," replied Lucy, trying to think of just what she wanted to say.

"Reckon you have," said Joel, dejectedly, and then he sat down on the log and dug holes in the sand with his bare feet.

Lucy had never before seen him look tired, and it seemed that some of the healthy brown of his cheeks had thinned out. Then Lucy told him, guardedly, a few of the rumors she had heard.

"All thet you say is nothin' to what's happened," he replied, bitterly. "Them riders mocked the life an' soul out of me."

"But, Joel, you shouldn't be so—so touchy," said Lucy, earnestly. "After all, the joke *was* on you. Why didn't you take it like a man?"

"But they knew you stole my clothes," he protested.

"Suppose they did. That wasn't much to care about. If you hadn't taken it so hard they'd have let up on you."

"Mebbe I might have stood that. But they taunted me with bein'—loony about you."

Joel spoke huskily. There was no doubt that he had been deeply hurt. Lucy saw tears in his eyes, and her first impulse was to put a hand on his and tell him how sorry she was. But she desisted. She did not feel at her ease with Joel.

"What'd you and Van fight about?" she asked, presently.

Joel hung his head. "I reckon I ain't a-goin' to tell you."

"You're ashamed of it?"

Joel's silence answered that.

"You said something about me?" Lucy could not resist her curiosity, back of which was a little heat. "It must have been—bad—else Van wouldn't have struck you."

"He hit me—he knocked me flat," passionately said Joel.

"And you drew a gun on him?"

"I did, an' like a fool I didn't wait till I got up. Then he kicked me! . . . Bostil's Ford will never be big enough fer me an' Van now."

"Don't talk foolish. You won't fight with Van. . . . Joel, maybe you deserved what you got. You say some —some rude things."

"I only said I'd pay you back," burst out Joel.

"How?"

"I swore I'd lay fer you—an' steal your clothes— so you'd have to run home naked."

There was indeed something lacking in Joel, but it was not sincerity. His hurt had rankled deep and his voice trembled with indignation.

"But, Joel, I don't go swimming in spring-holes," protested Lucy, divided between amusement and annoyance.

"I meant it, anyhow," said Joel, doggedly.

"Are you absolutely honest? Is that all you said to provoke Van?"

"It's all, Lucy, I swear."

She believed him, and saw the unfortunate circumstance more than ever her fault. "I'm sorry, Joel. I'm much to blame. I shouldn't have lost my temper and played that trick with your clothes. . . . If you'd only had sense enough to stay out till after dark! But no use crying over spilt milk. Now, if you'll do your share I'll do mine. I'll tell the boys I was to blame. I'll persuade them to let you alone. I'll go to Muncie—"

"No you won't go cryin' small fer me!" blurted out Joel.

Lucy was surprised to see pride in him. "Joel, I'll not make it appear—"

"You'll not say one word about me to any one," he went on, with the blood beginning to darken his face. And now he faced her. How strange the blaze in his differently colored eyes! "Lucy Bostil, there's been thet done an' said to me which I'll never forgive. I'm no good in Bostil's Ford. Mebbe I never was much. But I could get a job when I wanted it an' credit when I needed it. Now I can't get nothin'. I'm no good! . . . I'm no good! An' it's your fault!"

"Oh, Joel, what can I do?" cried Lucy.

"I reckon there's only one way you can square me," he replied, suddenly growing pale. But his eyes were like flint. He certainly looked to be in possession of all his wits.

"How?" queried Lucy, sharply.

"You can marry me. Thet'll show thet gang! An' it'll square me. Then I'll go back to work an' I'll stick. Thet's all, Lucy Bostil."

Manifestly he was laboring under strong suppressed agitation. That moment was the last of real strength and dignity ever shown by Joel Creech.

"But, Joel, I can't marry you—even if I am to blame for your ruin," said Lucy, simply.

"Why?"

"Because I don't love you."

"I reckon thet won't make any difference, if you don't love some one else."

Lucy gazed blankly at him. He began to shake, and his eyes grew wild. She rose from the log.

"Do you love anybody else?" he asked, passionately.

"None of your business!" retorted Lucy. Then, at a strange darkening of his face, an aspect unfamiliar to her, she grew suddenly frightened.

"It's Van!" he said, thickly.

"Joel, you're a fool!"

That only infuriated him.

"So they all say. An' they got my old man believin' it, too. Mebbe I am. . . . But I'm a-goin' to kill Van!"

"No! No! Joel, what are you sayin? I don't love Van. I don't care any more for him than for any other rider—or—or you."

"Thet's a lie, Lucy Bostil!"

"How dare you say I lie?" demanded Lucy. "I've a mind to turn my back on you. I'm trying to make up for my blunder and you—you insult me!"

"You talk sweet . . . but talk isn't enough. You made me no-good. . . . Will you marry me?"

"I will not!" And Lucy, with her blood up, could not keep contempt out of voice and look, and she did not care. That was the first time she had ever shown anything approaching ridicule for Joel. The effect was remarkable. Like a lash upon a raw wound it made him writhe; but more significant to Lucy was the sudden convulsive working of his features and the wildness of his eyes. Then she turned her back, not from contempt, but to hurry away from him.

He leaped after her and grasped her with rude hands.

"Let me go!" cried Lucy, standing perfectly motionless. The hard clutch of his fingers roused a fierce, hot anger.

Joel did not heed her command. He was forcing her back. He talked incoherently. One glimpse of his face added terror to Lucy's fury.

"Joel, you're out of your head!" she cried, and she began to wrench and writhe out of his grasp. Then ensued a short, sharp struggle. Joel could not hold Lucy, but he tore her blouse into shreds. It seemed to Lucy that he did that savagely. She broke free from him, and he lunged at her again. With all her strength she lashed his face with the heavy leather quirt. That staggered him. He almost fell.

Lucy bounded to Sarchedon. In a flash she was up in the saddle. Joel was running toward her. Blood on his face! Blood on his hands! He was not the Joel Creech she knew.

"Stop!" cried Lucy, fiercely. "I'll run you down!"

The big black plunged at a touch of spur and came down quivering, ready to bolt.

Creech swerved to one side. His face was lividly white except where the bloody welts crossed it. His jaw seemed to hang loosely, making speech difficult.

"Jest fer—thet—" he panted, hoarsely, "I'll lay fer you—an' I'll strip you—an' I'll tie you on a hoss—an'. I'll drive you naked through Bostil's Ford!"

Lucy saw the utter futility of all her good intentions. Something had snapped in Joel Creech's mind. And in hers kindness had given precedence to a fury she did not know was in her. For the second time she touched a spur to Sarchedon. He leaped out, flashed past Creech, and thundered up the road. It was all Lucy could do to break his gait at the first steep rise.

Chapter IV

THREE wild-horse hunters made camp one night beside a little stream in the Sevier Valley, five hundred miles, as a crow flies, from Bostil's Ford.

These hunters had a poor outfit, excepting, of course, their horses. They were young men, rangy in build, lean and hard from life in the saddle, bronzed like Indians, still-faced, and keen-eyed. Two of them appeared to be tired out, and lagged at the camp-fire duties. When the meager meal was prepared they sat, cross-legged, before a ragged tarpaulin, eating and drinking in silence.

The sky in the west was rosy, slowly darkening. The valley floor billowed away, ridged and cut, growing gray and purple and dark. Walls of stone, pink with the last rays of the setting sun, inclosed the valley, stretching away toward a long, low, black mountain range.

The place was wild, beautiful, open, with something nameless that made the desert different from any other country. It was, perhaps, a loneliness of vast stretches of valley and stone, clear to the eye, even after sunset. That black mountain range, which looked close enough to ride to before dark, was a hundred miles distant.

The shades of night fell swiftly, and it was dark by the time the hunters finished the meal. Then the camp-fire had burned low. One of the three dragged branches of dead cedars and replenished the fire. Quickly it flared up, with the white flame and crackle characteristic of dry cedar. The night wind had risen, moaning through the gnarled, stunted cedars near by, and it blew the fragrant wood-smoke into the faces of the two hunters, who seemed too tired to move.

"I reckon a pipe would help me make up my mind," said one.

"Wal, Bill," replied the other, dryly, "your mind's made up, else you'd not say smoke."

"Why?"

"Because there ain't three pipefuls of thet precious tobacco left."

"Thet's one apiece, then. . . . Lin, come an' smoke the last pipe with us."

The tallest of the three, he who had brought the firewood, stood in the bright light of the blaze. He looked the born rider, light, lithe, powerful.

"Sure, I'll smoke," he replied.

Then, presently, he accepted the pipe tendered him, and, sitting down beside the fire, he composed himself to the enjoyment which his companions evidently considered worthy of a decision they had reached.

"So this smokin' means you both want to turn back?" queried Lin, his sharp gaze glancing darkly bright in the glow of the fire.

"Yep, we'll turn back. An', Lordy! the relief I feel!" replied one.

"We've been long comin' to it, Lin, an' thet was for your sake," replied the other.

Lin slowly pulled at his pipe and blew out the smoke as if reluctant to part with it. "Let's go on," he said, quietly.

"No. I've had all I want of chasin' thet damn wild stallion," returned Bill, shortly.

The other spread wide his hands and bent an expostulating look upon the one called Lin. "We're two hundred miles out," he said. "There's only a little flour left in the bag. No coffee! Only a little salt! All the hosses except your big Nagger are played out. We're already in strange country. An' you know what we've heerd of this an' all to the south. It's all cañons, an' somewheres down there is thet awful canon none of our people ever seen. But we've heerd of it. An awful cut-up country."

He finished with a conviction that no one could say a word against the common sense of his argument. Lin was silent, as if impressed.

Bill raised a strong, lean, brown hand in a forcible gesture. "We can't ketch Wildfire!"

That seemed to him, evidently, a more convincing argument than his comrade's.

"Bill is sure right, if I'm wrong, which I ain't," went on the other. "Lin, we've trailed thet wild stallion for six weeks. Thet's the longest chase he ever had. He's left his old range. He's cut out his band, an' left them, one by one. We've tried every trick we know on him. An' he's too smart for us. There's a hoss! Why, Lin, we're all but gone to the dogs chasin' Wildfire. An' now I'm done, an' I'm glad of it."

There was another short silence, which presently Bill opened his lips to break.

"Lin, it makes me sick to quit. I ain't denyin' thet for a long time I've had hopes of ketchin' Wildfire. He's the grandest hoss I ever laid eyes on. I reckon no man, onless he was an Arab, ever seen as good a one. But now, that's neither here nor there. . . . We've got to hit the back trail."

"Boys, I reckon I'll stick to Wildfire's tracks," said Lin, in the same quiet tone.

Bill swore at him, and the other hunter grew excited and concerned.

"Lin Slone, are you gone plumb crazy over thet red hoss?"

"I—reckon," replied Slone. The working of his throat as he swallowed could be plainly seen by his companions.

Bill looked at his ally as if to confirm some sudden understanding between them. They took Slone's attitude gravely and they wagged their heads doubtfully, as they might have done had Slone just acquainted them with a hopeless and deathless passion for a woman. It was significant of the nature of riders that they accepted his attitude and had consideration for his feelings. For them the situation subtly changed. For weeks they had been three wild-horse wranglers on a hard chase after a valuable stallion. They had failed to get even close to him. They had gone to the limit of their endurance and of the outfit, and it was time to turn back. But Slone had conceived that strange and rare longing for a horse—a passion understood, if not shared, by all riders. And they knew that he would catch Wildfire or die in the attempt. From that moment their attitude toward Slone changed as subtly as had come the knowledge of his feeling. The gravity and gloom left their faces. It seem they might have regretted what they had said about the futility of catching Wildfire. They did not want Slone to see or feel the hopelessness of his task.

"I tell you, Lin," said Bill, "your hoss Nagger's as good as when we started."

"Aw, he's better," vouchsafed the other rider. "Nagger needed to lose some weight. Lin, have you got an extra set of shoes for him?"

"No full set. Only three left," replied Lin, soberly.

"Wal, thet's enough. You can keep Nagger shod. An' *mebbe* thet red stallion will get sore feet an' go lame. Then you'd stand a chance."

"But Wildfire keeps travelin' the valleys—the soft ground," said Slone.

"No matter. He's leavin' the country, an' he's bound to strike sandstone sooner or later. Then, by gosh! mebbe he'll wear off them hoofs!"

"Say, can't he ring bells offen the rocks?" exclaimed Bill. "Oh, Lordy! what a hoss!"

"Boys, do you think he's leavin' the country?" inquired Slone, anxiously.

"Sure he is," replied Bill. "He ain't the first stallion I've chased off the Sevier range. An' I know. It's a stallion thet makes for new country, when you push him hard."

"Yep, Lin, he's sure leavin'," added the other comrade. "Why, he's traveled a bee-line for days! I'll bet he's seen us many a time. Wildfire's about as smart as any man. He was born wild, an' his dam was born wild, an' there you have it. The wildest of all wild creatures—a wild stallion, with the intelligence of a man! A grand hoss, Lin, but one thet'll be hell, if you ever ketch him. He has killed stallions all over the Sevier range. A wild stallion thet's a killer! I never liked him for thet. Could he be broke?"

"I'll break him," said Lin Slone, grimly. "It's gettin' him thet's the job. I've got patience to break a hoss. But patience can't catch a streak of lightnin'."

"Nope; you're right," replied Bill. "If you have some luck you'll get him—mebbe. If he wears out his feet, or if you crowd him into a narrow cañon, or run him into a bad place where he can't get by you. Thet might happen. An' then, with Nagger, you stand a chance. Did you ever tire thet hoss?"

"Not yet."

"An' how fur did you ever run him without a break? Why, when we ketched thet sorrel last year I rode Nagger myself—thirty miles, most at a hard gallop. An' he never turned a hair!"

"I've beat thet," replied Lin. "He could run hard fifty miles—mebbe more. Honestly, I never seen him tired yet. If only he was fast!"

"Wal, Nagger ain't so durned slow, come to think

of thet," replied Bill, with a grunt. "He's good enough for you not to want another hoss."

"Lin, you're goin' to wear out Wildfire, an' then trap him somehow—is thet the plan?" asked the other comrade.

"I haven't any plan. I'll just trail him, like a cougar trails a deer."

"Lin, if Wildfire gives you the slip he'll have to fly. You've got the best eyes for tracks of any wrangler in Utah."

Slone accepted the compliment with a fleeting, doubtful smile on his dark face. He did not reply, and no more was said by his comrades. They rolled with backs to the fire. Slone put on more wood, for the keen wind was cold and cutting; and then he lay down, his head in his saddle, with a goatskin under him and a saddle-blanket over him.

All three were soon asleep. The wind whipped the sand and ashes and smoke over the sleepers. Coyotes barked from near in darkness, and from the valley ridge came the faint mourn of a hunting wolf. The desert night grew darker and colder.

The Stewart brothers were wild-horse hunters for the sake of trades and occasional sales. But Lin Slone never traded nor sold a horse he had captured. The excitement of the game, and the lure of the desert, and the love of a horse were what kept him at the profitless work. His type was rare in the uplands.

These were the early days of the settlement of Utah, and only a few of the hardiest and most adventurous pioneers had penetrated the desert in the southern part of that vast upland. And with them came some of that wild breed of riders to which Slone and the Stewarts belonged. Horses were really more important and necessary than men; and this singular fact gave these lonely riders a calling.

Before the Spaniards came there were no horses in the West. Those explorers left or lost horses all over the southwest. Many of them were Arabian horses of purest blood. American explorers and travelers, at the outset of the nineteenth century, encountered countless droves of wild horses all over the plains. Across the Grand Cañon, however, wild horses were comparatively few in number in the early days; and these had probably come in by way of California.

The Stewarts and Slone had no established mode of catching wild horses. The game had not developed fast enough for that. Every chase of horse or drove was different; and once in many attempts they met with success.

A favorite method originated by the Stewarts was to find a water-hole frequented by the band of horses or the stallion wanted, and to build round this hole a corral with an opening for the horses to get in. Then the hunters would watch the trap at night, and if the horses went in to drink, a gate was closed across the opening. Another method of the Stewarts was to trail a coveted horse up on a mesa or highland, places which seldom had more than one trail of ascent and descent, and there block the escape, and cut lines of cedars, into which the quarry was run till captured. Still another method, discovered by accident, was to shoot a horse lightly in the neck and sting him. This last, called creasing, was seldom successful, and for that matter in any method ten times as many horses were killed as captured.

Lin Slone helped the Stewarts in their own way, but he had no especial liking for their tricks. Perhaps a few remarkable captures of remarkable horses had spoiled Slone. He was always trying what the brothers claimed to be impossible. He was a fearless rider, but he had the fault of saving his mount, and to kill a wild horse was a tragedy for him. He would much rather have hunted alone, and he had been alone on the trail of the stallion Wildfire when the Stewarts had joined him.

Lin Slone awoke next morning and rolled out of his blanket at his usual early hour. But he was not early enough to say good-by to the Stewarts. They were gone.

The fact surprised him and somehow relieved him. They had left him more than his share of the outfit, and perhaps that was why they had slipped off before dawn. They knew him well enough to know that he would not have accepted it. Besides, perhaps they felt a little humiliation at abandoning a chase which he chose to keep up. Anyway, they were gone, apparently without breakfast.

The morning was clear, cool, with the air dark like that before a storm, and in the east, over the steely wall of stone, shone a redness growing brighter.

Slone looked away to the west, down the trail taken by his comrades, but he saw nothing moving against that cedar-dotted waste.

"Good-by," he said, and he spoke as if he was saying good-by to more than comrades.

"I reckon I won't see Sevier Village soon again—an' maybe never," he soliloquized.

There was no one to regret him, unless it was old Mother Hall, who had been kind to him on those rare occasions when he got out of the wilderness. Still, it was with regret that he gazed away across the red valley to the west. Slone had no home. His father and mother had been lost in the massacre of a wagon-train by Indians, and he had been one of the few saved and brought to Salt Lake. That had happened when he was ten years old. His life thereafter had been hard, and but for his sturdy Texas training he might not have survived. The last five years he had been a horse-hunter in the wild uplands of Nevada and Utah.

Slone turned his attention to the pack of supplies. The Stewarts had divided the flour and the parched corn equally, and unless he was greatly mistaken they had left him most of the coffee and all of the salt.

"Now I hold that decent of Bill an' Abe," said Slone, regretfully. "But I could have got along without it better 'n they could."

Then he swiftly set about kindling a fire and getting

a meal. In the midst of his task a sudden ruddy brightness fell around him. Lin Slone paused in his work to
look up.

The sun had risen over the eastern wall.

"Ah!" he said, and drew a deep breath.

The cold, steely, darkling sweep of desert had been
transformed. It was now a world of red earth and gold
rocks and purple sage, with everywhere the endless
straggling green cedars. A breeze whipped in, making
the fire roar softly. The sun felt warm on his cheek.
And at the moment he heard the whistle of his horse.

"Good old Nagger!" he said. "I shore won't have
to track you this mornin'."

Presently he went off into the cedars to find Nagger
and the mustang that he used to carry a pack. Nagger
was grazing in a little open patch among the trees, but
the pack-horse was missing. Slone seemed to know
in what direction to go to find the trail, for he came
upon it very soon. The pack-horse wore hobbles, but
he belonged to the class that could cover a great deal
of ground when hobbled. Slone did not expect the
horse to go far, considering that the grass thereabouts
was good. But in a wild-horse country it was not safe
to give any horse a chance. The call of his wild breth-
ren was irresistible. Slone, however, found the mustang standing quietly in a clump of cedars, and, removing the hobbles, he mounted and rode back to camp.
Nagger caught sight of him and came at his call.

This horse Nagger appeared as unique in his class
as Slone was rare among riders. Nagger seemed of
several colors, though black predominated. His coat
was shaggy, almost woolly, like that of a sheep. He
was huge, rawboned, knotty, long of body and long
of leg, with the head of a war charger. His build did
not suggest speed. There appeared to be something
slow and ponderous about him, similar to an elephant,
with the same suggestion of power and endurance.

Slone discarded the pack-saddle and bags. The latter
were almost empty. He roped the tarpaulin on the back
of the mustang, and, making a small bundle of his few

supplies, he tied that to the tarpaulin. His blanket he
used for a saddle-blanket on Nagger. Of the utensils
left by the Stewarts he chose a couple of small iron
pans, with long handles. The rest he left. In his saddle-
bags he had a few extra horseshoes, some nails, bullets
for his rifle, and a knife with a heavy blade.

"Not a rich outfit for a far country," he mused.
Slone did not talk very much, and when he did he
addressed Nagger and himself simultaneously. Evidently he expected a long chase, one from which he
would not return, and light as his outfit was it would
grow too heavy.

Then he mounted and rode down the gradual slope,
facing the valley and the black, bold, flat mountain to
the southeast. Some few hundred yards from camp he
halted Nagger and bent over in the saddle to scrutinize
the ground.

The clean-cut track of a horse showed in the bare,
hard sand. The hoof-marks were large, almost oval,
perfect in shape, and manifestly they were beautiful to
Lin Slone. He gazed at them for a long time, and
then he looked across the dotted red valley up the vast
ridgy steps, toward the black plateau and beyond. It
was the look that an Indian gives to a strange country.
Then Slone slipped off the saddle and knelt to scrutinize the horse tracks. A little sand had blown into the
depressions, and some of it was wet and some of it
was dry. He took his time about examining it, and he
even tried gently blowing other sand into the tracks,
to compare that with what was already there. Finally
he stood up and addressed Nagger.

"Reckon we won't have to argue with Abe an' Bill
this mornin'," he said, with satisfaction. "Wildfire made
that track yesterday, before sun-up."

Thereupon Slone remounted and put Nagger to a
trot. The pack-horse followed with an alacrity that
showed he had no desire for loneliness.

As straight as a bee-line Wildfire had left a trail
down into the floor of the valley. He had not stopped
to graze, and he had not looked for water. Slone had

hoped to find a water-hole in one of the deep washes in the red earth, but if there had been any water there Wildfire would have scented it. He had not had a drink for three days that Slone knew of. And Nagger had not drunk for forty hours. Slone had a canvas water-bag hanging over the pommel, but it was a habit of his to deny himself, as far as possible, till his horse could drink also. Like an Indian, Slone ate and drank but little.

It took four hours of steady trotting to reach the middle and bottom of that wide, flat valley. A network of washes cut up the whole center of it, and they were all as dry as bleached bone. To cross these Slone had only to keep Wildfire's trail. And it was proof of Nagger's quality that he did not have to veer from the stallion's course.

It was hot down in the lowland. The heat struck up, reflected from the sand. But it was a March sun, and no more than pleasant to Slone. The wind rose, however, and blew dust and sand in the faces of horse and rider. Except lizards Slone did not see any living things.

Miles of low greasewood and sparce yellow sage led to the first almost imperceptible rise of the valley floor on that side. The distant cedars beckoned to Slone. He was not patient, because he was on the trail of Wildfire; but, nevertheless, the hours seemed short.

Slone had no past to think about, and the future held nothing except a horse, and so his thoughts revolved the possibilities connected with this chase of Wildfire. The chase was hopeless in such country as he was traversing, and if Wildfire chose to roam around valleys like this one Slone would fail utterly. But the stallion had long ago left his band of horses, and then, one by one his favorite consorts, and now he was alone, headed with unerring instinct for wild, untrammeled ranges. He had been used to the pure, cold water and the succulent grass of the cold desert uplands. Assuredly he would not tarry in such barren lands as these.

For Slone an ever-present and growing fascination

lay in Wildfire's clear, sharply defined tracks. It was as if every hoof-mark told him something. Once, far up the interminable ascent, he found on a ridge-top tracks showing where Wildfire had halted and turned.

"Ha, Nagger!" cried Sloan, exultingly. "Look there! He's begun facin' about. He's wonderin' if we're still after him. He's worried. . . . But we'll keep out of sight—a day behind."

When Slone reached the cedars the sun was low down in the west. He looked back across the fifty miles of valley to the colored cliffs and walls. He seemed to be above them now, and the cool air, with tang of cedar and juniper, strengthened the impression that he had climbed high.

A mile or more ahead of him rose a gray cliff with breaks in it and a line of dark cedars or piñons on the level rims. He believed these breaks to be the mouths of cañons, and so it turned out. Wildfire's trail led into the mouth of a narrow cañon with very steep and high walls. Nagger snorted his perception of water, and the mustang whistled. Wildfire's tracks led to a point under the wall where a spring gushed forth. There were mountain-lion and deer tracks also, as well as those of smaller game.

Slone made camp here. The mustang was tired. But Nagger, upon taking a long drink, rolled in the grass as if he had just begun the trip. After eating, Slone took his rifle and went out to look for deer. But there appeared to be none at hand. He came across many lion tracks and saw, with apprehension, where one had taken Wildfire's trail. Wildfire had grazed up the cañon, keeping on and on, and he was likely to go miles in a night. Slone reflected that as small as were his own chances of getting Wildfire, they were still better than those of a mountain-lion. Wildfire was the most cunning of all animals—a wild stallion; his speed and endurance were incomparable; his scent as keen as those animals that relied wholly upon scent to warn them of danger, and as for sight, it was Slone's belief that no hoofed creature, except the mountain-sheep used to high altitudes, could see as far as a wild horse.

It bothered Slone a little that he was getting into a lion country. Nagger showed nervousness, something unusual for him. Slone tied both horses with long halters and stationed them on patches of thick grass. Then he put a cedar stump on the fire and went to sleep. Upon awakening and going to the spring he was somewhat chagrined to see that deer had come down to drink early. Evidently they were numerous. A lion country was always a deer country, for the lions followed the deer.

Slone was packed and saddled and on his way before the sun reddened the cañon wall. He walked the horses. From time to time he saw signs of Wildfire's consistent progress. The cañon narrowed and the walls grew lower and the grass increased. There was a decided ascent all the time. Slone could find no evidence that the cañon had ever been traveled by hunters or Indians. The day was pleasant and warm and still. Every once in a while a little breath of wind would bring a fragrance of cedar and piñon, and a sweet hint of pine and sage. At every turn he looked ahead, expecting to see the green of pine and the gray of sage. Toward the middle of the afternoon, coming to a place where Wildfire had taken to a trot, he put Nagger to that gait, and by sundown had worked up to where the cañon was only a shallow ravine. And finally it turned once more, to lose itself in a level where straggling pines stood high above the cedars, and great, dark-green silver spruces stood above the pines. And here were patches of sage, fresh and pungent, and long reaches of bleached grass. It was the edge of a forest. Wildfire's trail went on. Slone came at length to a group of pines, and here he found the remains of a camp-fire, and some flint arrow-heads. Indians had been in there, probably having come from the opposite direction to Slone's. This encouraged him, for where Indians could hunt so could he. Soon he was entering a forest where cedars and piñons and pines began to grow thickly. Presently he came upon a faintly defined trail, just a dim, dark line even to an experienced eye. But it was a trail, and Wildfire had taken it.

Slone halted for the night. The air was cold. And the dampness of it gave him an idea there were snowbanks somewhere not far distant. The dew was already heavy on the grass. He hobbled the horses and put a bell on Nagger. A bell might frighten lions that had never heard one. Then he built a fire and cooked his meal.

It had been long since he had camped high up among the pines. The sough of the wind pleased him, like music. There had begun to be prospects of pleasant experience along with the toil of chasing Wildfire. He was entering new and strange and beautiful country. How far might the chase take him? He did not care. He was not sleepy, but even if he had been it developed that he must wait till the coyotes ceased their barking round his campfire. They came so close that he saw their gray shadows in the gloom. But presently they wearied of yelping at him and went away. After that the silence, broken only by the wind as it roared and lulled, seemed beautiful to Slone. He lost completely that sense of vague regret which had remained with him, and he forgot the Stewarts. And suddenly he felt absolutely free, alone, with nothing behind to remember, with wild, thrilling, nameless life before him. Just then the long mourn of a timber wolf wailed in with the wind. Seldom had he heard the cry of one of those night wanderers. There was nothing like it—no sound like it to fix in the lone camper's heart the great solitude and the wild.

Chapter V

In the early morning when all was gray and the big, dark pines were shadowy specters, Slone was awakened by the cold. His hands were so numb that he had difficulty starting a fire. He stood over the blaze, warming them. The air was nipping, clear and thin, and sweet with frosty fragrance.

Daylight came while he was in the midst of his morning meal. A white frost covered the ground and crackled under his feet as he went out to bring in the horses. He saw fresh deer tracks. Then he went back to camp for his rifle. Keeping a sharp lookout for game, he continued his search for the horses.

The forest was open and park-like. There were no fallen trees or evidences of fire. Presently he came to a wide glade in the midst of which Nagger and the pack-mustang were grazing with a herd of deer. The size of the latter amazed Slone. The deer he had hunted back on the Sevier range were much smaller than these. Evidently these were mule deer, closely allied to the elk. They were so tame they stood facing him curiously, with long ears erect. It was sheer murder to kill a deer standing and watching like that, but Slone was out of meat and hungry and facing a long, hard trip. He shot a buck, which leaped spasmodically away, trying to follow the herd, and fell at the edge of the glade. Slone cut out a haunch, and then, catching the horses, he returned to camp, where he packed and saddled, and at once rode out on the dim trail.

The wildness of the country he was entering was evident in the fact that as he passed the glade where he had shot the deer a few minutes before, there were coyotes quarreling over the carcass.

Slone could see ahead and on each side several hundred yards, and presently he ascertained that the forest

floor was not so level as he had supposed. He had
entered a valley or was traversing a wide, gently sloping pass. He went through thickets of juniper, and had
to go around clumps of quaking asp. The pines grew
larger and farther apart. Cedars and piñons had been
left behind, and he had met with no silver spruces after
leaving camp. Probably that point was the height of a
divide. There were banks of snow in some of the hol-
lows on the north side. Evidently the snow had very
recently melted, and it was evident also that the depth
of snow through here had been fully ten feet, judging
from the mutilation of the juniper-trees where the deer,
standing on the hard, frozen crust, had browsed upon
the branches.

The quiet of the forest thrilled Slone. And the only
movement was the occasional gray flash of a deer or
coyote across the glade. No birds of any species crossed
Slone's sight. He came, presently, upon a lion track
in the trail, made probably a day before. Slone grew
curious about it, seeing how it held, as he was holding,
to Wildfire's tracks. After a mile or so he made sure
the lion had been trailing the stallion, and for a second
he felt a cold contraction of his heart. Already he
loved Wildfire, and by virtue of all this toil of travel
considered the wild horse his property.

"No lion could ever get close to Wildfire," he soliloquized, with a short laugh. Of that he was absolutely
certain.

The sun rose, melting the frost, and a breath of
warm air, laden with the scent of pine, moved heavily
under the huge, yellow trees. Slone passed a point
where the remains of an old camp-fire and a pile of
deer antlers were further proof that Indians visited this
plateau to hunt. From this camp broader, more deeply
defined trails led away to the south and east. Slone
kept to the east trail, in which Wildfire's tracks and
those of the lion showed clearly. It was about the middle of the forenoon when the tracks of the stallion and
lion left the trail to lead up a little draw where grass
grew thick. Slone followed, reading the signs of Wild-

fire's progress, and the action of his pursuer, as well as if he had seen them. Here the stallion had plowed into a snow-bank, eating a hole two feet deep; then he had grazed around a little; then on and on; there his splendid tracks were deep in the soft earth. Slone knew what to expect when the track of the lion veered from those of the horse, and he followed the lion tracks. The ground was soft from the late melting of snow, and Nagger sunk deep. The lion left a plain track. Here he stole steadily along; there he left many tracks at a point where he might have halted to make sure of his scent. He was circling on the trail of the stallion, with cunning intent of ambush. The end of this slow, careful stalk of the lion, as told in his tracks, came upon the edge of a knoll where he had crouched to watch and wait. From this perch he had made a magnificent spring—Slone estimating it to be forty feet —but he had missed the stallion. There were Wildfire's tracks again, slow and short, and then deep and sharp where in the impetus of fright he had sprung out of reach. A second leap of the lion, and then lessening bounds, and finally an abrupt turn from Wildfire's trail told the futility of that stalk. Slone made certain that Wildfire was so keen that as he grazed along he had kept to open ground.

Wildfire had run for a mile, then slowed down to a trot, and he had circled to get back to the trail he had left. Slone believed the horse was just so intelligent. At any rate, Wildfire struck the trail again, and turned at right angles to follow it.

Here the forest floor appeared perfectly level. Patches of snow became frequent, and larger as Slone went on. At length the patches closed up, and soon extended as far as he could see. It was soft, affording difficult travel. Slone crossed hundreds of deer tracks, and the trail he was on eventually became a deer runway.

Presently, far down one of the aisles between the great pines Slone saw what appeared to be a yellow cliff, far away. It puzzled him. And as he went on he received the impression that the forest dropped out of sight ahead. Then the trees grew thicker, obstructing his view. Presently the trail became soggy and he had to help his horse. The mustang floundered in the soft snow and earth. Cedars and piñons appeared again, making travel still more laborious.

All at once there came to Slone a strange consciousness of light and wind and space and void. On the instant his horse halted with a snort. Slone quickly looked up. Had he come to the end of the world? An abyss, a cañon, yawned beneath him, beyond all comparison in its greatness. His keen eye, educated to desert distance and dimension, swept down and across, taking in the tremendous truth, before it staggered his comprehension. But a second sweeping glance, slower, becoming intoxicated with what it beheld, saw gigantic cliff-steps and yellow slopes dotted with cedars, leading down to clefts filled with purple smoke, and these led on and on to a ragged red world of rock, bare, shining, bold, uplifted in mesa, dome, peak, and crag, clear and strange in the morning light, still and sleeping like death.

This, then, was the great cañon, which had seemed like a hunter's fable rather than truth. Slone's sight dimmed, blurring the spectacle, and he found that his eyes had filled with tears. He wiped them away and looked again and again, until he was confounded by the vastness and the grandeur and the vague sadness of the scene. Nothing he had ever looked at had affected him like this cañon, although the Stewarts had tried to prepare him for it.

It was the horse-hunter's passion that reminded him of his pursuit. The deer trail led down through a break in the wall. Only a few rods of it could be seen. This trail was passable, even though choked with snow. But the depth beyond this wall seemed to fascinate Slone and hold him back, used as he was to desert trails. Then the clean mark of Wildfire's hoof brought back the old thrill.

"This place fits you, Wildfire," muttered Slone, dismounting.

He started down, leading Nagger. The mustang followed. Slone kept to the wall side of the trail, fearing the horses might slip. The snow held firmly at first and Slone had no trouble. The gap in the rim-rock widened to a slope thickly grown over with cedars and piñons and manzanita. This growth made the descent more laborious, yet afforded means at least for Slone to go down with less danger. There was no stopping. Once started, the horses had to keep on. Slone saw the impossibility of ever climbing out while that snow was there. The trail zigzagged down and down. Very soon the yellow wall hung tremendously over him, straight up. The snow became thinner and softer. The horses began to slip. They slid on their haunches. Fortunately the slope grew less steep, and Slone could see below where it reached out to comparatively level ground. Still, a mishap might yet occur. Slone kept as close to Nagger as possible, helping him whenever he could do it. The mustang slipped, rolled over, and then slipped past Slone, went down the slope to bring up in a cedar. Slone worked down to him and extricated him. Then the huge Nagger began to slide. Snow and loose rock slid with him, and so did Slone. The little avalanche stopped of its own accord, and then Slone dragged Nagger on down and down, presently to come to the end of the steep descent. Slone looked up to see that he had made short work of a thousand-foot slope. Here cedars and piñons grew thickly enough to make a forest. The snow thinned out to patches, and then failed. But the going remained bad for a while as the horses sank deep in a soft red earth. This eventually grew more solid and finally dry. Slone worked out of the cedars to what appeared a grassy plateau inclosed by the great green-and-white slope with its yellow wall over-hanging, and distant mesas and cliffs. Here his view was restricted. He was down on the first bench of the great cañon. And there was the deer trail, a well-worn path keeping to the edge of the slope.

Slone came to a deep cut in the earth, and the trail headed it, where it began at the last descent of the slope. It was the source of a cañon. He could look down to see the bare, worn rock, and a hundred yards from where he stood the earth was washed from its rims and it began to show depth and something of that ragged outline which told of violence of flood. The trail headed many cañons like this, all running down across this bench, disappearing, dropping invisibly. The trial swung to the left under the great slope, and then presently it climbed to a higher bench. Here were brush and grass and huge patches of sage, so pungent that it stung Slone's nostrils. Then he went down again, this time to come to a clear brook lined by willows. Here the horses drank long and Slone refreshed himself. The sun had grown hot. There was fragrance of flowers he could not see and a low murmur of a waterfall that was likewise invisible. For most of the time his view was shut off, but occasionally he reached a point where through some break he saw towers gleaming red in the sun. A strange place, a place of silence, and smoky veils in the distance. Time passed swiftly. Toward the waning of the afternoon he began to climb to what appeared to be a saddle of land, connecting the cañon wall on the left with a great plateau, gold-rimmed and pine-fringed, rising more and more in his way as he advanced. At sunset Slone was more shut in than for several hours. He could tell the time was sunset by the golden light on the cliff wall again overhanging him. The slope was gradual up to this pass to the saddle, and upon coming to a spring, and the first pine-trees, he decided to halt for camp. The mustang was almost exhausted.

Thereupon he hobbled the horses in the luxuriant grass round the spring, and then unrolled his pack. Once as dusk came stealing down, while he was eating his meal, Nagger whistled in fright. Slone saw a gray, pantherish form gliding away into the shadows. He took a quick shot at it, but missed.

"It's a lion country, all right," he said. And then he

set about building a big fire on the other side of the
grassy plot, so to have the horses between fires. He cut
all the venison into thin strips, and spent an hour
roasting them. Then he lay down to rest, and he said:
"Wonder where Wildfire is to-night? Am I closer to
him? Where's he headin' for?"

The night was warm and still. It was black near the
huge cliff, and overhead velvety blue, with stars of
white fire. It seemed to him that he had become more
thoughtful and observing of the aspects of his wild
environment, and he felt a welcome consciousness of
loneliness. Then sleep came to him and the night
seemed short. In the gray dawn he arose refreshed.

The horses were restive. Nagger snorted a welcome.
Evidently they had passed an uneasy night. Slone
found lion tracks at the spring and in sandy places.
Presently he was on his way up to the notch between
the great wall and the plateau. A growth of thick
scrub-oak made travel difficult. It had not appeared
far up to that saddle, but it was far. There were
straggling pine trees and huge rocks that obstructed
his gaze. But once up he saw that the saddle was only
a narrow ridge, curved to slope up on both sides.

Straight before Slone and under him opened the
cañon, blazing and glorious along the peaks and ramparts, where the rising sun struck, misty and smoky
and shadowy down in those mysterious depths.

It took an effort not to keep on gazing. But Slone
turned to the grim business of his pursuit. The trail he
saw leading down had been made by Indians. It was
used probably once a year by them; and also by wild
animals, and it was exceedingly steep and rough.
Wildfire had paced to and fro along the narrow ridge
of that saddle, making many tracks, before he had
headed down again. Slone imagined that the great
stallion had been daunted by the tremendous chasm,
but had finally faced it, meaning to put this obstacle
between him and his pursuers. It never occurred to
Slone to attribute less intelligence to Wildfire than that.
So, dismounting, Slone took Nagger's bridle and started

down. The mustang with the pack was reluctant. He snorted and whistled and pawed the earth. But he would not be left alone, so he followed.

The trail led down under cedars that fringed a precipice. Slone was aware of this without looking. He attended only to the trail and to his horse. Only an Indian could have picked out that course, and it was cruel to put a horse to it. But Nagger was powerful, sure-footed, and he would go anywhere that Slone led him. Gradually Slone worked down and away from the bulging rim-wall. It was hard, rough work, and risky because it could not be accomplished slowly. Brush and rocks, loose shale and weathered slope, long, dusty inclines of yellow earth, and jumbles of stone—these made bad going for miles of slow, zigzag trail down out of the cedars. Then the trail entered what appeared to be a ravine.

That ravine became a cañon. At its head it was a dry wash, full of gravel and rocks. It began to cut deep into the bowels of the earth. It shut out sight of the surrounding walls and peaks. Water appeared from under a cliff and, augmented by other springs, became a brook. Hot, dry, and barren at its beginning, this cleft became cool and shady and luxuriant with grass and flowers and amber moss with silver blossoms. The rocks had changed color from yellow to deep red. Four hours of turning and twisting, endlessly down and down, over boulders and banks and every conceivable roughness of earth and rock, finished the pack-mustang; and Slone mercifully left him in a long reach of cañon where grass and water never failed. In this place Slone halted for the noon hour, letting Nagger have his fill of the rich grazing. Nagger's three days in grassy upland, despite the continuous travel by day, had improved him. He looked fat, and Slone had not yet caught the horse resting. Nagger was iron to endure. Here Slone left all the outfit except what was on his saddle, and the sack containing the few pounds of meat and supplies, and the two utensils. This sack he tied on the back of his saddle, and resumed his journey.

Presently he came to a place where Wildfire had doubled on his trail and had turned up a side cañon. The climb out was hard on Slone, if not on Nagger. Once up, Slone found himself upon a wide, barren plateau of glaring red rock and clumps of greasewood and cactus. The plateau was miles wide, shut in by great walls and mesas of colored rock. The afternoon sun beat down fiercely. A blast of wind, as if from a furnace, swept across the plateau, and it was laden with red dust. Slone walked here, where he could have ridden. And he made several miles of up-and-down progress over this rough plateau. The great walls of the opposite side of the cañon loomed appreciably closer. What, Slone wondered, was at the bottom of this rent in the earth? The great desert river was down there, of course, but he knew nothing of it. Would that turn back Wildfire? Slone thought grimly how he had always claimed Nagger to be part fish and part bird. Wildfire was not going to escape.

By and by only isolated mescal plants with long, yellow-plumed spears broke the bare monotony of the plateau. And Slone passed from red sand and gravel to a red, soft shale, and from that to hard, red rock. Here Wildfire's tracks were lost, the first time in seven weeks. But Slone had his direction down that plateau with the cleavage lines of cañons to right and left. At times Slone found a vestige of the old Indian trail, and this made him doubly sure of being right. He did not need to have Wildfire's tracks. He let Nagger pick the way, and the horse made no mistake in finding the line of least resistance. But that grew harder and harder. This bare rock, like a file, would soon wear Wildfire's hoofs thin. And Slone rejoiced. Perhaps somewhere down in this awful chasm he and Nagger would have it out with the stallion. Slone began to look far ahead, beginning to believe that he might see Wildfire. Twice he had seen Wildfire, but only at a distance. Then he had resembled a running streak of fire, whence his name, which Slone had given him.

This bare region of rock began to be cut up into gullies. It was necessary to head them or to climb in and out. Miles of travel really meant little progress straight ahead. But Slone kept on. He was hot and Nagger was hot, and that made hard work easier. Sometimes on the wind came a low thunder. Was it a storm or an avalanche slipping or falling water? He could not tell. The sound was significant and haunting.

Of one thing he was sure—that he could not have found his back-trail. But he divined he was never to retrace his steps on this journey. The stretch of broken plateau before him grew wilder and bolder of outline, darker in color, weirder in aspect, and progress across it grew slower, more dangerous. There were many places Nagger should not have been put to—where a slip meant a broken leg. But Slone could not turn back. And something besides an indomitable spirit kept him going. Again the sound resembling thunder assailed his ears, louder this time. The plateau appeared to be ending in a series of great capes or promontories. Slone feared he would soon come out upon a promontory from which he might see the impossibility of further travel. He felt relieved down in the gullies, where he could not see far. He climbed out of one, presently, from which there extended a narrow ledge with a slant too perilous for any horse. He stepped out upon that with far less confidence than Nagger. To the right was a bulge of low wall, and a few feet to the left a dark precipice. The trail here was faintly outlined, and it was six inches wide and slanting as well. It seemed endless to Slone, that ledge. He looked only down at his feet and listened to Nagger's steps. The big horse trod carefully, but naturally, and he did not slip. That ledge extended in a long curve, turning slowly away from the precipice, and ascending a little at the further end. Slone drew a deep breath of relief when he led Nagger up on level rock.

Suddenly a strange yet familiar sound halted Slone,

as if he had been struck. The wild, shrill, high-pitched, piercing whistle of a stallion! Nagger neighed a blast in reply and pounded the rock with his iron-shod hoofs. With a thrill Slone looked ahead.

There, some few hundred yards distant, on a promontory, stood a red horse.

"My Lord! . . . It's Wildfire!" breathed Slone, tensely.

He could not believe his sight. He imagined he was dreaming. But as Nagger stamped and snorted defiance Slone looked with fixed and keen gaze, and knew that beautiful picture was no lie.

Wildfire was as red as fire. His long mane, wild in the wind, was like a whipping, black-streaked flame. Silhouetted there against that cañon background he seemed gigantic, a demon horse, ready to plunge into fiery depths. He was looking back over his shoulder, his head very high, and every line of him was instinct with wildness. Again he sent out that shrill, air-splitting whistle. Slone understood it to be a clarion call to Nagger. If Nagger had been alone Wildfire would have killed him. The red stallion was a killer of horses. All over the Utah ranges he had left the trail of a murderer. Nagger understood this, too, for he whistled back in rage and terror. It took an iron arm to hold him. Then Wildfire plunged, apparently down, and vanished from Slone's sight.

Slone hurried onward, to be blocked by a huge crack in the rocky plateau. This he had to head. And then another and like obstacle checked his haste to reach that promontory. He was forced to go more slowly. Wildfire had been close only as to sight. And this was the great cañon that dwarfed distance and magnified proximity. Climbing down and up, toiling on, he at last learned patience. He had seen Wildfire at close range. That was enough. So he plodded on, once more returning to careful regard of Nagger. It took an hour of work to reach the point where Wildfire had disappeared.

A promontory indeed it was, overhanging a valley a

thousand feet below. A white torrent of a stream
wound through it. There were lines of green cottonwoods following the winding course. Then Slone saw
Wildfire slowly crossing the flat toward the stream.
He had gone down that cliff, which to Slone looked
perpendicular.

Wildfire appeared to be walking lame. Slone, making sure of this, suffered a pang. Then, when the
significance of such lameness dawned upon him he
whooped his wild joy and waved his hat. The red
stallion must have heard, for he looked up. Then he
went on again and waded into the stream, where he
drank long. When he started to cross, the swift current
drove him back in several places. The water wreathed
white around him. But evidently it was not deep; and
finally he crossed. From the other side he looked up
again at Nagger and Slone, and, going on, he soon was
out of sight in the cottonwoods.

"How to get down!" muttered Slone.

There was a break in the cliff wall, a bare stone
slant where horses had gone down and come up. That
was enough for Slone to know. He would have attempted the descent if he were sure no other horse but
Wildfire had ever gone down there. But Slone's hair
began to rise stiff on his head. A horse like Wildfire,
and mountain-sheep and Indian ponies, were all very
different from Nagger. The chances were against Nagger.

"Come on, old boy. If I can do it, you can," he
said.

Slone had never seen a trail as perilous as this. He
was afraid for his horse. A slip there meant death.
The way Nagger trembled in every muscle showed his
feelings. But he never flinched. He would follow Slone
anywhere, providing Slone rode him or led him. And
here, as riding was impossible, Slone went before. If
the horse slipped there would be a double tragedy, for
Nagger would knock his master off the cliff. Slone set
his teeth and stepped down. He did not let Nagger see

his fear. He was taking the greatest risk he had ever run.

The break in the wall led to a ledge, and the ledge dropped from step to step, and these had bare, slippery slants between. Nagger was splendid on a bad trail. He had methods peculiar to his huge build and great weight. He crashed down over the stone steps, both front hoofs at once. The slants he slid down on his haunches with his forelegs stiff and the iron shoes scraping. He snorted and heaved and grew wet with sweat. He tossed his head at some of the places. But he never hesitated and it was impossible for him to go slowly. Whenever Slone came to corrugated stretches in the trail he felt grateful. But these were few. The rock was like smooth red iron. Slone had never seen such hard rock. It took him long to realize that it was marble. His heart seemed a tense, painful knot in his breast, as if it could not beat, holding back in the strained suspense. But Nagger never jerked on the bridle. He never faltered. Many times he slipped, often with both front feet, but never with all four feet. So he did not fall. And the red wall began to loom above Slone. Then suddenly he seemed brought to a point where it was impossible to descend. It was a round bulge, slanting fearfully, with only a few little rough surfaces to hold a foot. Wildfire had left a broad, clear-swept mark at that place, and red hairs on some of the sharp points. He had slid down. Below was an offset that fortunately prevented further sliding. Slone started to walk down this place, but when Nagger began to slide Slone had to let go the bridle and jump. Both he and the horse landed safely. Luck was with them. And they went on, down and down, to reach the base of the great wall, scraped and exhausted, wet with sweat, but unhurt. As Slone gazed upward he felt the impossibility of believing what he knew to be true. He hugged and petted the horse. Then he led on to the roaring stream.

It was green water white with foam. Slone waded in and found the water cool and shallow and very swift.

He had to hold to Nagger to keep from being swept down-stream. They crossed in safety. There in the sand showed Wildfire's tracks. And here were signs of another Indian camp, half a year old.

The shade of the cottonwoods was pleasant. Slone found this valley oppressively hot. There was no wind and the sand blistered his feet through his boots. Wildfire held to the Indian trail that had guided him down into this wilderness of worn rock. And that trail crossed the stream at every turn of the twisting, narrow valley. Slone enjoyed getting into the water. He hung his gun over the pommel and let the water roll him. A dozen times he and Nagger forded the rushing torrent. Then they came to a box-like closing of the valley to cañon walls, and here the trail evidently followed the stream bed. There was no other way. Slone waded in, and stumbled, rolled, and floated ahead of the sturdy horse. Nagger was wet to his breast, but he did not fall. This gulch seemed full of a hollow rushing roar. It opened out into a wide valley. And Wildfire's tracks took to the left side and began to climb the slope.

Here the traveling was good, considering what had been passed. Once up out of the valley floor Slone saw Wildfire far ahead, high on the slope. He did not appear to be limping, but he was not going fast. Slone watched as he climbed. What and where would be the end of this chase?

Sometimes Wildfire was plain in his sight for a moment, but usually he was hidden by rocks. The slope was one great talus, a jumble of weathered rock, fallen from what appeared a mountain of red and yellow wall. Here the heat of the sun fell upon him like fire. The rocks were so hot Slone could not touch them with bare hand. The close of the afternoon was approaching, and this slope was interminably long. Still, it was not steep, and the trail was good.

At last from the height of slope Wildfire appeared, looking back and down. Then he was gone. Slone plodded upward. Long before he reached that summit he heard the dull rumble of the river. It grew to be a roar, yet it seemed distant. Would the great desert river stop Wildfire in his flight? Slone doubted it. He surmounted the ridge, to find the cañon opening in a tremendous gap, and to see down, far down, a glittering, sun-blasted slope merging into a deep, black gulch where a red river swept and chafed and roared.

Somehow the river was what he had expected to see. A force that had cut and ground this cañon could have been nothing but a river like that. The trail led down, and Slone had no doubt that it crossed the river and led up out of the cañon. He wanted to stay there and gaze endlessly and listen. At length he began the descent. As he proceeded it seemed that the roar of the river lessened. He could not understand why this was so. It took half an hour to reach the last level, a ghastly, black, and iron-ribbed cañon bed, with the river splitting it. He had not had a glimpse of Wildfire on this side of the divide, but he found his tracks, and they led down off the last level, through a notch in the black bank of marble to a sand-bar and the river.

Wildfire had walked straight off the sand into the water. Slone studied the river and shore. The water ran slow, heavily, in sluggish eddies. From far up the cañon came the roar of a rapid, and from below the roar of another, heavier and closer. The river appeared tremendous, in ways Slone felt rather than realized, yet it was not swift. Studying the black, rough wall of rock above him, he saw marks where the river had been sixty feet higher than where he stood on the sand. It was low, then. How lucky for him that he had gotten there before flood season! He believed Wildfire had crossed easily, and he knew Nagger could make it. Then he piled and tied his supplies and weapons high on the saddle, to keep them dry, and looked for a place to take to the water.

Wildfire had sunk deep before reaching the edge. Manifestly he had lunged the last few feet. Slone found a better place, and waded in, urging Nagger. The big horse plunged, almost going under, and began to swim. Slone kept up-stream beside him. He found, presently, that the water was thick and made him tired, so it was necessary to grasp a stirrup and be towed. The river appeared only a few hundred feet wide, but probably it was wider than it looked. Nagger labored heavily near the opposite shore; still, he landed safely upon a rocky bank. There were patches of sand in which Wildfire's tracks showed so fresh that the water had not yet dried out of them.

Slone rested his horse before attempting to climb out of that split in the rock. However, Wildfire had found an easy ascent. On this side of the cañon the bare rock did not predominate. A clear trail led up a dusty, gravelly slope, upon which scant greasewood and cactus appeared. Half an hour's climbing brought Slone to where he could see that he was entering a vast valley, sloping up and narrowing to a notch in the dark cliffs, above which towered the great red wall and about that the slopes of cedar and the yellow rim-rock.

And scarcely a mile distant, bright in the westering sunlight, shone the red stallion, moving slowly.

Slone pressed on steadily. Just before dark he came to an ideal spot to camp. The valley had closed up, so that the lofty walls cast shadows that met. A clump of cottonwoods surrounding a spring, abundance of rich grass, willows and flowers lining the banks, formed an oasis in the bare valley. Slone was tired out from the day of ceaseless toil down and up, and he could scarcely keep his eyes open. But he tried to stay awake. The dead silence of the valley, the dry fragrance, the dreaming walls, the advent of night low down, when up on the ramparts the last red rays of the sun lingered, the strange loneliness—these were sweet and comforting to him.

And that night's sleep was as a moment. He opened his eyes to see the crags and towers and peaks and domes, and the lofty walls of that vast, broken chaos of cañons across the river. They were now emerging from the misty gray of dawn, growing pink and lilac and purple under the rising sun.

He arose and set about his few tasks, which, being soon finished, allowed him an early start.

Wildfire had grazed along no more than a mile in the lead. Slone looked eagerly up the narrowing cañon, but he was not rewarded by a sight of the stallion. As he progressed up a gradually ascending trail he became aware of the fact that the notch he had long looked up to was where the great red walls closed in and almost met. And the trail zigzagged up this narrow vent, so steep that only a few steps could be taken without rest. Slone toiled up for an hour—an age—till he was wet, burning, choked, with a great weight on his chest. Yet still he was only half-way up that awful break between the walls. Sometimes he could have tossed a stone down upon a part of the trail, only a few rods below, yet many, many weary steps of actual toil. As he got farther up the notch widened. What had been scarcely visible from the valley below was now colossal in actual dimensions. The trail was like a twisted mile of thread between two bulging mountain walls leaning their ledges and fronts over this tilted pass.

Slone rested often. Nagger appreciated this and heaved gratefully at every halt. In this monotonous toil Slone forgot the zest of his pursuit. And when Nagger suddenly snorted in fright Slone was not prepared for what he saw.

Above him ran a low, red wall, around which evidently the trail led. At the curve, which was a promontory, scarcely a hundred feet in an airline above him, he saw something red moving, bobbing, coming out into view. It was a horse.

Wildfire—no farther away than the length of three lassoes!

There he stood looking down. He fulfilled all of Slone's dreams. Only he was bigger. But he was so magnificently proportioned that he did not seem heavy. His coat was shaggy and red. It was not glossy. The color was what made him shine. His mane was like a crest, mounting, then falling low. Slone had never seen

so much muscle on a horse. Yet his outline was graceful, beautiful. The head was indeed that of the wildest
of all wild creatures—a stallion born wild—and it was
beautiful, savage, splendid, everything but noble. Whatever Wildfire was, he was a devil, a murderer—he had
no noble attributes. Slone thought that if a horse could
express hate, surely Wildfire did then. It was certain
that he did express curiosity and fury.

Slone shook a gauntleted fist at the stallion, as if the
horse were human. That was a natural action for a
rider of his kind. Wildfire turned away, showed bright
against the dark background, and then disappeared.

Chapter VI

THAT was the last Slone saw of Wildfire for three days.

It took all of this day to climb out of the cañon.
The second was a slow march of thirty miles into a
scrub cedar and piñon forest, through which the great
red and yellow walls of the cañon could be seen. That
night Slone found a water-hole in a rocky pocket and
a little grass for Nagger. The third day's travel consisted of forty miles or more through level pine forest,
dry and odorous, but lacking the freshness and beauty
of the forest on the north side of the cañon. On this
south side a strange feature was that all the water, when
there was any, ran away from the rim. Slone camped
this night at a muddy pond in the woods, where Wildfire's tracks showed plainly.

On the following day Slone rode out of the forest
into a country of scanty cedars, bleached and stunted,
and out of this to the edge of a plateau from which
the shimmering desert flung its vast and desolate dis-
tances, forbidding and menacing. This was not the
desert upland country of Utah, but a naked and bony
world of colored rock and sand—a painted desert of

heat and wind and flying sand and waterless wastes
and barren ranges. But it did not daunt Slone. For far
down on the bare, billowing ridges moved a red speck,
at a snail's pace, a slowly moving dot of color which
was Wildfire.

On open ground like this, Nagger, carrying two hundred and fifty pounds, showed his wonderful quality.
He did not mind the heat nor the sand nor the glare
nor the distance nor his burden. He did not tire. He
was an engine of tremendous power.

Slone gained upon Wildfire, and toward evening of
that day he reached to within half a mile of the stallion. And he chose to keep that far behind. That night
he camped where there was dry grass, but no water.

Next day he followed Wildfire down and down, over
the endless swell of rolling red ridges, bare of all but
bleached white grass and meager greasewood, always
descending in the face of that painted desert of bold
and ragged steps. Slone made fifty miles that day, and
gained the valley bed, where a slender stream ran thin
and spread over a wide sandy bottom. It was salty
water, but it was welcome to both man and beast.

The following day he crossed, and the tracks of
Wildfire were still wet on the sand-bars. The stallion
was slowing down. Slone saw him, limping along, not
far in advance. There was a ten-mile stretch of level
ground, blown hard as rock, from which the sustenance
had been bleached, for not a spear of grass grew there.
And following that was a tortuous passage through a
weird region of clay dunes, blue and violet and helio-
trope and lavender, all worn smooth by rain and wind.
Wildfire favored the soft ground now. He had deviated
from his straight course. And he was partial to washes
and dips in the earth where water might have lodged.
And he was not now scornful of a green-scummed
water-hole with its white margin of alkali. That night
Slone made camp with Wildfire in plain sight. The
stallion stopped when his pursuers stopped. And he

began to graze on the same stretch with Nagger. How strange this seemed to Slone!

Here at this camp was evidence of Indians. Wildfire had swung round to the north in his course. Like any pursued wild animal, he had begun to circle. And he had pointed his nose toward the Utah he had left.

Next morning Wildfire was not in sight, but he had left his tracks in the sand. Slone trailed him with Nagger at a trot. Toward the head of this sandy flat Slone came upon old corn-fields, and a broken dam where the water had been stored, and well-defined trails leading away to the right. Somewhere over there in the desert lived Indians. At this point Wildfire abandoned the trail he had followed for many days and cut out more to the north. It took all the morning hours to climb three great steps and benches that led up to the summit of a mesa, vast in extent. It turned out to be a sandy waste. The wind rose and everywhere were moving sheets of sand, and in the distance circular yellow dust-devils, rising high like waterspouts, and back down in the sun-scorched valley a sand-storm moved along majestically, burying the desert in its yellow pall.

Then two more days of sand and another day of a slowly rising ground growing from bare to gray and gray to green, and then to the purple of sage and cedar —these three grinding days were toiled out with only one water-hole.

And Wildfire was lame and in distress and Nagger was growing gaunt and showing strain; and Slone, haggard and black and worn, plodded miles and miles on foot to save his horse.

Slone felt that it would be futile to put the chase to a test of speed. Nagger could never head that stallion. Slone meant to go on and on, always pushing Wildfire, keeping him tired, wearied, and worrying him, till a section of the country was reached where he could drive Wildfire into some kind of a natural trap. The pursuit seemed endless. Wildfire kept to open country where he could not be surprised.

There came a morning when Slone climbed to a
cedared plateau that rose for a whole day's travel, and
then split into a labyrinthine maze of cañons. There
were trees, grass, water. It was a high country, cool
and wild, like the uplands he had left. For days he
camped on Wildfire's trail, always relentlessly driving
him, always watching for the trap he hoped to find.
And the red stallion spent much of this time of flight
in looking backward. Whenever Slone came in sight
of him he had his head over his shoulder, watching.
And on the soft ground of these cañons he had begun
to recover from his lameness. But this did not worry
Slone. Sooner or later Wildfire would go down into a
high-walled wash, from which there would be no outlet; or he would wander into a box-cañon; or he would
climb out on a mesa with no place to descend, unless
he passed Slone; or he would get cornered on a soft,
steep slope where his hoofs would sink deep and make
him slow. The nature of the desert had changed. Slone
had entered a wonderful region, the like of which he
had not seen—a high plateau criss-crossed in every
direction by narrow cañons with red walls a thousand
feet high.

And one of the strange turning cañons opened into
a vast valley of monuments.

The plateau had weathered and washed away, leaving huge sections of stone walls, all standing isolated,
different in size and shape, but all clean-cut, bold, with
straight lines. They stood up everywhere, monumental,
towering, many-colored, lending a singular and beautiful aspect to the great green-and-gray valley, billowing
away to the north, where dim, broken battlements
mounted to the clouds.

The only living thing in Slone's sight was Wildfire.
He shone red down on the green slope.

Slone's heart swelled. This was the setting for that
grand horse—a perfect wild range. But also it seemed
the last place where there might be any chance to trap
the stallion. Still that did not alter Slone's purpose,
though it lost to him the joy of former hopes. He rode

down the slope, out upon the billowing floor of the valley. Wildfire looked back to see his pursuers, and then the solemn stillness broke to a wild, piercing whistle.

Day after day, camping where night found him, Slone followed the stallion, never losing sight of him till darkness had fallen. The valley was immense and the monuments miles apart. But they always seemed close together and near him. The air magnified everything. Slone lost track of time. The strange, solemn, lonely days and the silent, lonely nights, and the endless pursuit, and the wild, weird valley—these completed the work of years on Slone and he became satisfied, unthinking, almost savage.

The toil and privation had worn him down and he was like iron. His garments hung in tatters; his boots were ripped and soleless. Long since his flour had been used up, and all his supplies except the salt. He lived on the meat of rabbits, but they were scarce, and the time came when there were none. Some days he did not eat. Hunger did not make him suffer. He killed a desert bird now and then, and once a wildcat crossing the valley. Eventually he felt his strength diminishing, and then he took to digging out the pack-rats and cooking them. But these, too, were scarce. At length starvation faced Slone. But he knew he would not starve. Many times he had been within rifle-shot of Wildfire. And the grim, forbidding thought grew upon him that he must kill the stallion. The thought seemed involuntary, but his mind rejected it. Nevertheless, he knew that if he could not catch the stallion he would kill him. That had been the end of many a desperate rider's pursuit of a coveted horse.

While Slone kept on his merciless pursuit, never letting Wildfire rest by day, time went on just as relentlessly. Spring gave way to early summer. The hot sun bleached the grass; water-holes failed out in the valley and water could be found only in the cañons; and the dry winds began to blow the sand. It was a sandy valley, green and gray only at a distance, and out toward the north there were no monuments, and the slow heave of sand lifted toward the dim walls.

Wildfire worked away from this open valley, back to the south end, where the great monuments loomed, and still farther back, where they grew closer, till at length some of them were joined by weathered ridges to the walls of the surrounding plateau. For all that Slone could see, Wildfire was in perfect condition. But Nagger was not the horse he had been. Slone realized that in one way or another the pursuit was narrowing down to the end.

He found a water-hole at the head of a wash in a split in the walls, and here he let Nagger rest and graze one whole day—the first day for a long time that he had not kept the red stallion in sight. That day was marked by the good fortune of killing a rabbit, and while eating it his gloomy, fixed mind admitted that he was starving. He dreaded the next sunrise. But he could not hold it back. There, behind the dark monuments, standing sentinel-like, the sky lightened and reddened and burst into gold and pink, till out of the golden glare the sun rose glorious. And Slone, facing the league-long shadows of the monuments, rode out again into the silent, solemn day, on his hopeless quest.

For a change Wildfire had climbed high up a slope of talus, through a narrow pass, rounded over with drifting sand. And Slone gazed down into a huge amphitheater full of monuments, like all that strange country. A basin three miles across lay beneath him. Walls and weathered slants of rock and steep slopes of reddish-yellow sand inclosed this oval depression. The floor was white, and it seemed to move gently or radiate with heatwaves. Studying it, Slone made out that the motion was caused by wind in long bleached grass. He had crossed small areas of this grass in different parts of the region.

Wildfire's tracks led down into this basin, and presently Slone, by straining his eyes, made out the red spot that was the stallion.

"He's lookin' to quit the country," soliloquized Slone, as he surveyed the scene.

With keen, slow gaze Slone studied the lay of wall and slope, and when he had circled the huge depression he made sure that Wildfire could not get out except by the narrow pass through which he had gone in. Slone sat astride Nagger in the mouth of this pass —a wash a few yards wide, walled by broken, rough rock on one side and an insurmountable slope on the other.

"If this hole was only little, now," sighed Slone, as he gazed at the sweeping, shimmering oval floor, "I might have a chance. But down there—we couldn't get near him."

There was no water in that dry bowl. Slone reflected on the uselessness of keeping Wildfire down there, because Nagger could not go without water as long as Wildfire. For the first time Slone hesitated. It seemed merciless to Nagger to drive him down into this hot, windy hole. The wind blew from the west, and it swooped up the slope, hot, with the odor of dry, dead grass.

But that hot wind stirred Slone with an idea, and suddenly he was tense, excited, glowing, yet grim and hard.

"Wildfire, I'll make you run with your namesake in that high grass," called Slone. The speech was full of bitter failure, of regret, of the hardness of a rider who could not give up the horse to freedom.

Slone meant to ride down there and fire the long grass. In that wind there would indeed be wildfire to race with the red stallion. It would perhaps mean his death; at least it would chase him out of that hole, where to follow him would be useless.

"I'd make you hump now to get away if I could get behind you," muttered Slone. He saw that if he could fire the grass on the other side the wind of flame would drive Wildfire straight toward him. The slopes and walls narrowed up to the pass, but high grass grew to within a few rods of where Slone stood. But it seemed impossible to get behind Wildfire.

"At night—then—I could get round him," said Slone, thinking hard and narrowing his gaze to scan the circle of wall and slope. "Why not? . . . No wind at night. That grass would burn slow till mornin'—till the wind came up—an' it's been west for days."

Suddenly Slone began to pound the patient Nagger and to cry out to him in wild exultance.

"Old horse, we've got him! . . . We've got him! . . . We'll put a rope on him before this time to-morrow!"

Slone yielded to his strange, wild joy, but it did not last long, soon succeeding to sober, keen thought. He rode down into the bowl a mile, making absolutely certain that Wildfire could not climb out on that side. The far end, beyond the monuments, was a sheer wall of rock. Then he crossed to the left side. Here the sandy slope was almost too steep for even him to go up. And there was grass that would burn. He returned to the pass assured that Wildfire had at last fallen into a trap the like Slone had never dreamed of. The great horse was doomed to run into living flame or the whirling noose of a lasso.

Then Slone reflected. Nagger had that very morning had his fill of good water—the first really satisfying drink for days. If he was rested that day, on the morrow he would be fit for the grueling work possibly in store for him. Slone unsaddled the horse and turned him loose, and with a snort he made down the gentle slope for the grass. Then Slone carried his saddle to a shady spot afforded by a slab of rock and a dwarf cedar, and here he composed himself to rest and watch and think and wait.

Wildfire was plainly in sight no more than two miles away. Gradually he was grazing along toward the monuments and the far end of the great basin. Slone believed, because the place was so large, that Wildfire thought there was a way out on the other side or over the slopes or through the walls. Never before had the far-sighted stallion made a mistake. Slone suddenly felt the keen, stabbing fear of an outlet somewhere. But it left him quickly. He had studied those slopes and walls. Wildfire could not get out, except by the pass he had entered, unless he could fly.

Slone lay in the shade, his head propped on his saddle, and while gazing down into the shimmering hollow he began to plan. He calculated that he must be able to carry fire swiftly across the far end of the basin, so that he would not be absent long from the mouth of the pass. Fire was always a difficult matter, since he must depend only on flint and steel. He decided to wait till dark, build a fire with dead cedar sticks, and carry a bundle of them with burning ends. He felt assured that the wind caused by riding would keep them burning. After he had lighted the grass all he had to do was to hurry back to his station and there await developments.

The day passed slowly, and it was hot. The heat-waves rose in dark, wavering lines and veils from the valley. The wind blew almost a gale. Thin, curling sheets of sand blew up over the crests of the slopes, and the sound it made was a soft, silken rustling, very low. The sky was a steely blue above and copper close over the distant walls.

That afternoon, toward the close, Slone ate the last of the meat. At sunset the wind died away and the air cooled. There was a strip of red along the wall of rock and on the tips of the monuments, and it lingered there for long, a strange, bright crown. Nagger was not far away, but Wildfire had disappeared, probably behind one of the monuments.

When twilight fell Slone went down after Nagger and, returning with him, put on bridle and saddle. Then he began to search for suitable sticks of wood. Farther back in the pass he found stunted dead cedars, and from these secured enough for his purpose. He kindled a fire and burnt the ends of the sticks into red embers. Making a bundle of these, he put them under his arm, the dull glowing ends backward, and then mounted his horse.

It was just about dark when he faced down into the valley. When he reached level ground he kept to the edge of the left slope and put Nagger to a good trot. The grass and brush were scant here, and the color of the sand was light, so he had no difficulty in traveling. From time to time his horse went through grass, and its dry, crackling rustle, showing how it would burn, was music to Slone. Gradually the monuments began to loom up, bold and black against the blue sky, with stars seemingly hanging close over them. Slone had calculated that the basin was smaller than it really was, in both length and breadth. This worried him. Wildfire might see or hear or scent him, and make a break back to the pass and thus escape. Slone was glad when the huge, dark monuments were indistinguishable from the black, frowning wall. He had to go slower here, because of the darkness. But at last he reached the slow rise of jumbled rock that evidently marked the extent of weathering on that side. Here he turned to the right and rode out into the valley. The floor was level and thickly overgrown with long, dead grass and dead greasewood, as dry as tinder. It was easy to account for the dryness; neither snow nor rain had visited that valley for many months. Slone whipped one of the sticks in the wind and soon had the smoldering end red and showering sparks. Then he dropped the stick in the grass, with curious intent and a strange feeling of regret.

Instantly the grass blazed with a little sputtering roar. Nagger snorted. "Wildfire!" exclaimed Slone. That word was a favorite one with riders, and now Slone used it both to call out his menace to the stallion and to express his feeling for that blaze, already running wild.

Without looking back Slone rode across the valley, dropping a glowing stick every quarter of a mile. When he reached the other side there were a dozen fires behind him, burning slowly, with white smoke rising lazily. Then he loped Nagger along the side back to the sandy ascent, and on up to the mouth of the pass.

There he searched for tracks. Wildfire had not gone
out, and Slone experienced relief and exultation. He
took up a position in the middle of the narrowest part
of the pass, and there, with Nagger ready for anything,
he once more composed himself to watch and wait.

Far across the darkness of the valley, low down,
twelve lines of fire, widely separated, crept toward one
another. They appeared thin and slow, with only an
occasional leaping flame. And some of the black spaces
must have been monuments, blotting out the creeping
snail-lines of red. Slone watched, strangely fascinated.

"What do you think of that?" he said, aloud, and
he meant his query for Wildfire.

As he watched the lines perceptibly lengthened and
brightened and pale shadows of smoke began to appear. Over at the left of the valley the two brightest
fires, the first he had started, crept closer and closer
together. They seemed long in covering distance. But
not a breath of wind stirred, and besides they really
might move swiftly, without looking so to Slone. When
the two lines met a sudden and larger blaze rose.

"Ah!" said the rider, and then he watched the other
lines creeping together. How slowly fire moved, he
thought. The red stallion would have every chance to
run between those lines, if he dared. But a wild horse
feared nothing like fire. This one would not run the
gantlet of flames. Nevertheless, Slone felt more and
more relieved as the lines closed. The hours of the
night dragged past until at length one long, continuous
line of fire spread level across the valley, its bright,
red line broken only where the monuments of stone
were silhouetted against it.

The darkness of the valley changed. The light of the
moon changed. The radiance of the stars changed.
Either the line of fire was finding denser fuel to con-
sume or it was growing appreciably closer, for the
flames began to grow, to leap, and to flare.

Slone strained his ears for the thud of hoofs on sand.

The time seemed endless in its futility of results, but
fleeting after it had passed; and he could tell how the

hours fled by the ever-recurring need to replenish the little fire he kept burning in the pass.

A broad belt of valley grew bright in the light, and behind it loomed the monuments, weird and dark, with columns of yellow and white smoke wreathing them.

Suddenly Slone's sensitive ear vibrated to a thrilling sound. He leaned down to place his ear to the sand. Rapid, rhythmic beat of hoofs made him leap to his feet, reaching for his lasso with right hand and a gun with his left.

Nagger lifted his head, sniffed the air, and snorted. Slone peered into the black belt of gloom that lay below him. It would be hard to see a horse there, unless he got high enough to be silhouetted against that line of fire now flaring to the sky. But he heard the beat of hoofs, swift, sharp, louder—louder. The night shadows were deceptive. That wonderful light confused him, made the place unreal. Was he dreaming? Or had the long chase and his privations unhinged his mind? He reached for Nagger. No! The big black was real, alive, quivering, pounding the sand. He scented an enemy.

Once more Slone peered down into the void or what seemed a void. But it, too, had changed, lightened. The whole valley was brightening. Great palls of curling smoke rose white and yellow, to turn back as the monuments met their crests, and then to roll upward, blotting out the stars. It was such a light as he had never seen, except in dreams. Pale moonlight and dimmed starlight and wan dawn all vague and strange and shadowy under the wild and vivid light of burning grass.

In the pale path before Slone, that fanlike slope of sand which opened down into the valley, appeared a swiftly moving black object, like a fleeting phantom. It was a phantom horse. Slone felt that his eyes, deceived by his mind, saw racing images. Many a wild chase he had lived in dreams on some far desert. But what was that beating in his ears—sharp, swift, even, rhythmic? Never had his ears played him false. Never had he heard things in his dreams. That running object was a horse and he was coming like the wind. Slone felt something grip his heart. All the time and endurance and pain and thirst and suspense and longing and hopelessness—the agony of the whole endless chase—closed tight on his heart in that instant.

The running horse halted just in the belt of light cast by the burning grass. There he stood sharply defined, clear as a cameo, not a hundred paces from Slone. It was Wildfire.

Slone uttered an involuntary cry. Thrill on thrill shot through him. Delight and hope and fear and despair claimed him in swift, successive flashes. And then again the ruling passion of a rider held him—the sheer glory of a grand and unattainable horse. For Slone gave up Wildfire in that splendid moment. How had he ever dared to believe he could capture that wild stallion? Slone looked and looked, filling his mind, regretting nothing, sure that the moment was reward for all he had endured.

The weird lights magnified Wildfire and showed him clearly. He seemed gigantic. He shone black against the fire. His head was high, his mane flying. Behind him the fire flared and the valley-wide column of smoke rolled majestically upward, and the great monuments seemed to retreat darkly and mysteriously as the flames advanced beyond them. It was a beautiful, unearthly spectacle, with its silence the strangest feature.

But suddenly Wildfire broke that silence with a whistle which to Slone's overstrained faculties seemed a blast as piercing as the splitting sound of lightning. And with the whistle Wildfire plunged up toward the pass.

Slone yelled at the top of his lungs and fired his gun before he could terrorize the stallion and drive him back down the slope. Soon Wildfire became again a running black object, and then he disappeared.

The great line of fire had gotten beyond the monuments and now stretched unbroken across the valley from wall to slope. Wildfire could never pierce that line of flames. And now Slone saw, in the paling sky to the east, that dawn was at hand.

Chapter VII

SLONE looked grimly glad when simultaneously with the first red flash of sunrise a breeze fanned his cheek. All that was needed now was a west wind. And here came the assurance of it.

The valley appeared hazy and smoky, with slow, rolling clouds low down where the line of fire moved. The coming of daylight paled the blaze of the grass, though here and there Slone caught flickering glimpses of dull red flame. The wild stallion kept to the center of the valley, restlessly facing this way and that, but never toward the smoke. Slone made sure that Wildfire gradually gave ground as the line of smoke slowly worked toward him.

Every moment the breeze freshened, grew steadier and stronger, until Slone saw that it began to clear the valley of the low-hanging smoke. There came a time when once more the blazing line extended across from slope to slope.

Wildfire was cornered, trapped. Many times Slone nervously uncoiled and recoiled his lasso. Presently the great chance of his life would come—the hardest and most important throw he would ever have with a rope. He did not miss often, but then he missed sometimes, and here he must be swift and sure. It annoyed him that his hands perspired and trembled and that something weighty seemed to obstruct his breathing. He muttered that he was pretty much worn out, not in the best of condition for a hard fight with a wild horse. Still he would capture Wildfire; his mind was unalterably set there. He anticipated that the stallion would make a final and desperate rush past him; and he had his plan of action all outlined. What worried him was the possibility of Wildfire doing some unforeseen feat at the very last. Slone was prepared for hours of strained watching, and then a desperate effort, and then a shock that might kill Wildfire and cripple Nagger, or a long race and fight.

But he soon discovered that he was wrong about the long watch and wait. The wind had grown strong and was driving the fire swiftly. The flames, fanned by the breeze, leaped to a formidable barrier. In less than an hour, though the time seemed only a few moments to the excited Slone, Wildfire had been driven down toward the narrowing neck of the valley, and he had begun to run, to and fro, back and forth. Any moment, then, Slone expected him to grow terrorized and to come tearing up toward the pass.

Wildfire showed evidence of terror, but he did not attempt to make the pass. Instead he went at the right-hand slope of the valley and began to climb. The slope was steep and soft, yet the stallion climbed up and up. The dust flew in clouds; the gravel rolled down, and the sand followed in long streams. Wildfire showed his keenness by zigzagging up the slope.

"Go ahead, you red devil!" yelled Slone. He was much elated. In that soft bank Wildfire would tire out while not hurting himself.

Slone watched the stallion in admiration and pity and exultation. Wildfire did not make much headway, for he slipped back almost as much as he gained. He attempted one place after another where he failed. There was a bank of clay, some few feet high, and he could not round it at either end or surmount it in the middle. Finally he literally pawed and cut a path, much as if he were digging in the sand for water. When he got over that he was not much better off. The slope above was endless and grew steeper, more difficult toward the top. Slone knew absolutely that no horse could climb over it. He grew apprehensive, however, for Wildfire might stick up there on the slope until the line of fire passed. The horse apparently shunned any near proximity to the fire and performed prodigious efforts to escape.

"He'll be ridin' an avalanche pretty soon," muttered Slone.

Long sheets of sand and gravel slid down to spill thinly over the low bank. Wildfire, now sinking to his knees, worked steadily upward till he had reached a point halfway up the slope, at the head of a long, yellow bank on treacherous-looking sand. Here he was halted by a low bulge, which he might have surmounted had his feet been free. But he stood deep in the sand. For the first time he looked down at the sweeping fire, and then at Slone.

Suddenly the bank of sand began to slide with him. He snorted in fright. The avalanche started slowly and was evidently no mere surface slide. It was deep. It stopped—then started again—and again stopped. Wildfire appeared to be sinking deeper and deeper. His struggles only embedded him more firmly. Then the bank of sand, with an ominous, low roar, began to move once more. This time it slipped swiftly. The dust rose in a cloud, almost obscuring the horse. Long streams of gravel rattled down, and waterfalls of sand waved over the steps of the slope.

Just as suddenly the avalanche stopped again. Slone saw, from the great oval hole it had left above, that it was indeed deep. That was the reason it did not slide readily. When the dust cleared away Slone saw the stallion, sunk to his flanks in the sand, utterly helpless.

With a wild whoop Slone leaped off Nagger, and, a lasso in each hand, he ran down the long bank. The fire was perhaps a quarter of a mile distant, and, since the grass was thinning out, it was not coming so fast as it had been. The position of the stallion was halfway between the fire and Slone, and a hundred yards up the slope.

Like a madman Slone climbed up through the drag-

ging, loose sand. He was beside himself with a fury
of excitement. He fancied his eyes were failing him,
that it was not possible the great horse really was up
there, helpless in the sand. Yet every huge stride Slone
took brought him closer to a fact he could not deny.
In his eagerness he slipped, and fell, and crawled, and
leaped, until he reached the slide which held Wildfire
prisoner.

The stallion might have been fast in quicksand, up
to his body, for all the movement he could make. He
could move only his head. He held that up, his eyes
wild, showing the whites, his foaming mouth wide
open, his teeth gleaming. A sound like a scream rent
the air. Terrible fear and hate were expressed in that
piercing neigh. And shaggy, wet, dusty red, with all
of brute savageness in the look and action of his head,
he appeared hideous.

As Slone leaped within roping distance the avalanche
slipped a foot or two, halted, slipped once more, and
slowly started again with that low roar. He did not
care whether it slipped or stopped. Like a wolf he
leaped closer, whirling his rope. The loop hissed round
his head and whistled as he flung it. And when fiercely
he jerked back on the rope, the noose closed tight
round Wildfire's neck.

"By G—d—I—got—a rope—on him!" cried Slone,
in hoarse pants.

He stared, unbelieving. It was unreal, that sight—
unreal like the slow, grinding movement of the avalanche under him. Wildfire's head seemed a demon
head of hate. It reached out, mouth agape, to bite, to
rend. That horrible scream could not be the scream
of a horse.

Slone was a wild-horse hunter, a rider, and when
that second of incredulity flashed by, then came the
moment of triumph. No moment could ever equal that
one, when he realized he stood there with a rope
around that grand stallion's neck. All the days and the
miles and the toil and the endurance and the hopeless-

ness and the hunger were paid for in that moment. His heart seemed too large for his breast.

"I tracked—you!" he cried, savagely. "I stayed—with you! . . . An' I got a rope—on you! An'—I'll ride you—you red devil!"

The passion of the man was intense. That endless, racking pursuit had brought out all the hardness the desert had engendered in him. Almost hate, instead of love, spoke in Slone's words. He hauled on the lasso, pulling the stallion's head down and down. The action was the lust of capture as well as the rider's instinctive motive to make the horse fear him. Life was unquenchably wild and strong in that stallion; it showed in the terror which made him hideous. And man and beast somehow resembled each other in that moment which was inimical to noble life.

The avalanche slipped with little jerks, as if treacherously loosing its hold for a long plunge. The line of fire below ate at the bleached grass and the long column of smoke curled away on the wind.

Slone held the taut lasso with his left hand, and with the right he swung the other rope, catching the noose round Wildfire's nose. Then letting go of the first rope he hauled on the other, pulling the head of the stallion far 'down. Hand over hand Slone closed in on the horse. He leaped on Wildfire's head, pressed it down, and, holding it down on the sand with his knees, with swift fingers he tied the noose in a hackamore—an improvised halter. Then, just as swiftly, he bound his scarf tight round Wildfire's head, blindfolding him.

"All so easy!" exclaimed Slone, under his breath. "Lord! who would believe it! . . . Is it a dream?"

He rose and let the stallion have a free head.

"Wildfire, I got a rope on you—an' a hackamore—an' a blinder," said Slone. "An' if I had a bridle I'd put that on you. . . . Who'd ever believe you'd catch yourself, draggin' in the sand?"

Slone, finding himself falling on the sand, grew alive to the augmented movement of the avalanche. It had begun to slide, to heave and bulge and crack. Dust rose in clouds from all around. The sand appeared to open and let him sink to his knees. The rattle of gravel was drowned in a soft roar. Then he shot down swiftly, holding the lassoes, keeping himself erect, and riding as if in a boat. He felt the successive steps of the slope, and then the long incline below, and then the checking and rising and spreading of the avalanche as it slowed down on the level. All movement then was checked violently. He appeared to be half buried in sand. While he struggled to extricate himself the thick dust blew away and settled so that he could see. Wildfire lay before him, at the edge of the slide, and now he was not so deeply embedded as he had been up on the slope. He was struggling and probably soon would have been able to get out. The line of fire was close now, but Slone did not fear that.

At his shrill whistle Nagger bounded toward him, obedient, but snorting, with ears laid back. He halted. A second whistle started him again. Slone finally dug himself out of the sand, pulled the lassoes out, and ran the length of them toward Nagger. The black showed both fear and fight. His eyes rolled and he half shied away.

"Come on!" called Slone, harshly.

He got a hand on the horse, pulled him round, and, mounting in a flash, wound both lassoes round the pommel of the saddle.

"Haul him out, Nagger, old boy!" cried Slone, and he dug spurs into the black.

One plunge of Nagger's slid the stallion out of the sand. Snorting, wild, blinded, Wildfire got up, shaking in every limb. He could not see his enemies. The blowing smoke, right in his nose, made scent impossible. But in the taut lassoes he sensed the direction of his captors. He plunged, rearing at the end of the plunge, and struck out viciously with his hoofs. Slone, quick with spur and bridle, swerved Nagger aside and Wildfire, off his balance, went down with a crash. Slone dragged him, stretched him out, pulled him over twice before he got forefeet planted. Once up, he reared again, screeching his rage, striking wildly with his hoofs. Slone wheeled aside and toppled him over again.

"Wildfire, it's no fair fight," he called, grimly. "But you led me a chase. . . . An' you learn right now I'm boss!"

Again he dragged the stallion. He was ruthless. He would have to be so, stopping just short of maiming or killing the horse, else he would never break him. But Wildfire was nimble. He got to his feet and this time he lunged out. Nagger, powerful as he was, could not sustain the tremendous shock, and went down. Slone saved himself with a rider's supple skill, falling clear of the horse, and he leaped again into the saddle as Nagger pounded up. Nagger braced his huge frame and held the plunging stallion. But the saddle slipped a little, the cinches cracked. Slone eased the strain by wheeling after Wildfire.

The horses had worked away from the fire, and Wildfire, free of the stifling smoke, began to break and lunge and pitch, plunging round Nagger in a circle, running blindly, but with unerring scent. Slone, by masterly horsemanship, easily avoided the rushes, and made a pivot of Nagger, round which the wild horse dashed in his frenzy. It seemed that he no longer tried to free himself. He lunged to kill.

"Steady, Nagger, old boy!" Slone kept calling. "He'll never get at you. . . . If he slips that blinder I'll kill him!"

The stallion was a fiend in his fury, quicker than a panther, wonderful on his feet, and powerful as an ox. But he was at a disadvantage. He could not see. And Slone, in his spoken intention to kill Wildfire should the scarf slip, acknowledged that he never would have a chance to master the stallion. Wildfire was bigger, faster, stronger than Slone had believed, and as for spirit, that was a grand and fearful thing to see.

The soft sand in the pass was plowed deep before Wildfire paused in his mad plunges. He was wet and heaving. His red coat seemed to blaze. His mane stood up and his ears lay flat.

Slone uncoiled the lassoes from the pommel and slacked them a little. Wildfire stood up, striking at the air, snorting fiercely. Slone tried to wheel Nagger in close behind the stallion. Both horse and man narrowly escaped the vicious hoofs. But Slone had closed in. He took a desperate chance and spurred Nagger in a single leap as Wildfire reared again. The horses collided. Slone hauled the lassoes tight. The impact threw Wildfire off his balance, just as Slone had calculated, and as the stallion plunged down on four feet Slone spurred Nagger close against him. Wildfire was a little in the lead. He could only half rear now, for the heaving, moving Nagger, always against him, jostled him down, and Slone's iron arm hauled on the short ropes. When Wildfire turned to bite, Slone knocked the vicious nose back with a long swing of his fist.

Up the pass the horses plunged. With a rider's wild joy Slone saw the long green-and-gray valley, and the isolated monuments in the distance. There, on that wide stretch, he would break Wildfire. How marvelously luck had favored him at the last!

"Run, you red devil!" Slone called. "Drag us around now till you're done!"

They left the pass and swept out upon the waste of sage. Slone realized, from the stinging of the sweet wind in his face, that Nagger was being pulled along at a tremendous pace. The faithful black could never have made the wind cut so. Lower the wild stallion stretched and swifter he ran, till it seemed to Slone that death must end that thunderbolt race.

Chapter VIII

LUCY BOSTIL had called twice to her father and he had not answered. He was out at the hitching-rail, with Holley, the rider, and two other men. If he heard Lucy he gave no sign of it. She had on her chaps and did not care to go any farther than the door where she stood.

"Somers has gone to Durango an' Shugrue is out huntin' hosses," Lucy heard Bostil say, gruffly.

"Wal now, I reckon I could handle the boat an' fetch Creech's hosses over," said Holley.

Bostil raised an impatient hand, as if to wave aside Holley's assumption.

Then one of the other two men spoke up. Lucy had seen him before, but did not know his name.

"Sure there ain't any need to rustle the job. The river hain't showed any signs of risin' yet. But Creech is worryin'. He allus is worryin' over them hosses. No wonder! Thet Blue Roan is sure a hoss. Yesterday at two miles he showed Creech he was a sight faster than last year. The grass is gone over there. Creech is grainin' his stock these last few days. An' thet's expensive."

"How about the flat up the cañon?" queried Bostil. "Ain't there any grass there?"

"Reckon not. It's the dryest spell Creech ever had," replied the other. "An' if there was grass it wouldn't do him no good. A landslide blocked the only trail up."

"Bostil, them hosses, the racers special, ought to be brought acrost the river," said Holley, earnestly. He loved horses and was thinking of them.

"The boat's got to be patched up," replied Bostil shortly.

It occurred to Lucy that her father was also think-

93

ing of Creech's thoroughbreds, but not like Holley. She grew grave and listened intently.

There was an awkward pause. Creech's rider, whoever he was, evidently tried to conceal his anxiety. He flicked his boots with a quirt. The boots were covered with wet mud. Probably he had crossed the river very recently.

"Wal, when will you have the hosses fetched over?" he asked, deliberately. "Creech 'll want to know."

"Just as soon as the boat's mended," replied Bostil. "I'll put Shugrue on the job to-morrow."

"Thanks, Bostil. Sure, thet 'll be all right. Crech 'll be satisfied," said the rider, as if relieved. Then he mounted, and with his companion trotted down the lane.

The lean, gray Holley bent a keen gaze upon Bostil. But Bostil did not notice that; he appeared preoccupied in thought.

"Bostil, the dry winter an' spring here ain't any guarantee thet there wasn't a lot of snow up in the mountains."

Holley's remark startled Bostil.

"No—it ain't—sure," he replied.

"An' any mornin' along now we might wake up to hear the Colorado boomin'," went on Holley, significantly.

Bostil did not reply to that.

"Creech hain't lived over there so many years. What's he know about the river? An' fer that matter, who knows anythin' sure about thet hell-bent river?"

"It ain't my business thet Creech lives over there riskin' his stock every spring," replied Bostil, darkly.

Holley opened his lips to speak, hesitated, looked away from Bostil, and finally said, "No, it sure ain't." Then he turned and walked away, head bent in sober thought. Bostil came toward the open door where Lucy stood. He looked somber. At her greeting he seemed startled.

"What?" he said.

"I just said, 'Hello, Dad,'" she replied, demurely. Yet she thoughtfully studied her father's dark face.

"Hello yourself. . . . Did you know Van got throwed an' hurt?"

"Yes."

Bostil swore under his breath. "There ain't any riders on the range thet can be trusted," he said, disgustedly. "They're all the same. They like to get in a bunch an' jeer each other an' bet. They want *mean* hosses. They make good hosses buck. They haven't any use for a hoss thet won't buck. They all want to give a hoss a rakin' over. . . . Think of thet fool Van gettin' throwed by a two-dollar Ute mustang. An' hurt so he can't ride for days! With them races comin' soon! It makes me sick."

"Dad, weren't you a rider once?" asked Lucy.

"I never was thet kind."

"Van will be all right in a few days."

"No matter. It's bad business. If I had any other rider who could handle the King I'd let Van go."

"I can get just as much out of the King as Van can," said Lucy, spiritedly.

"You!" exclaimed Bostil. But there was pride in his glance.

"I know I can."

"You never had any use for Sage King," said Bostil, as if he had been wronged.

"I love the King a little, and hate him a lot," laughed Lucy.

"Wal, I might let you ride at thet, if Van ain't in shape," rejoined her father.

"I wouldn't ride him in the race. But I'll keep him in fine fettle."

"I'll bet you'd like to see Sarch beat him," said Bostil jealously.

"Sure I would," replied Lucy, teasingly. "But, Dad, I'm afraid Sarch never will beat him."

Bostil grunted. "See here. I don't want any weight upon the King. You take him out for a few days. An' ride him! Savvy thet?"

"Yes, Dad."

"Give him miles an' miles—an' then comin' home, on good trails, ride him for all your worth. . . . Now, Lucy, keep your eye open. Don't let any one get near you on the sage."

"I won't. . . . Dad, do you still worry about poor Joel Creech?"

"Not Joel. But I'd rather lose all my stock then have Cordts or Dick Sears get within a mile of you."

"A mile!" exclaimed Lucy, lightly, though a fleeting shade crossed her face. "Why, I'd run away from him, if I was on the King, even if he got within ten yards of me."

"A mile is close enough, my daughter," replied Bostil. "Don't ever forget to keep your eye open. Cordts has sworn thet if he can't steal the King he'll get you."

"Oh! he prefers the horse to me."

"Wal, Lucy, I've a sneakin' idea thet Cordts will never leave the uplands unless he gets you an' the King both."

"And, Dad—you consented to let that horse-thief come to our races?" exclaimed Lucy, with heat.

"Why not? He can't do any harm. If he or his men get uppish, the worse for them. Cordts gave his word not to turn a trick till after the races."

"Do you trust him?"

"Yes. But his men might break loose, away from his sight. Especially thet Dick Sears. He's a bad man. So be watchful whenever you ride out."

As Lucy went down toward the corrals she was thinking deeply. She could always tell, woman-like, when her father was excited or agitated. She remembered the conversation between him and Creech's rider. She remembered the keen glance old Holley had bent upon him. And mostly she remembered the somber look upon his face. She did not like that. Once, when a little girl, she had seen it and never forgotten it, nor the thing that it was associated with—something tragical which had happened in the big

room. There had been loud, angry voices of men—
and shots—and then the men carried out a long form
covered with a blanket. She loved her father, but there
was a side to him she feared. And somehow related
to that side was his hardness toward Creech and his
intolerance of any rider owning a fast horse and his
obsession in regard to his own racers. Lucy had often
tantalized her father with the joke that if it ever came
to a choice between her and his favorites they would
come first. But was it any longer a joke? Lucy felt
that she had left childhood behind with its fun and
fancies, and she had begun to look at life thoughtfully.

Sight of the corrals, however, and the King prancing around, drove serious thoughts away. There were
riders there, among them Farlane, and they all had
pleasant greetings for her.

"Farlane, Dad says I'm to take out Sage King," an-
nounced Lucy.

"No!" ejaculated Farlane, as he pocketed his pipe.

"Sure. And I'm to *ride* him. You know how Dad
means that."

"Wal, now, I'm doggoned!" added Farlane, looking
worried and pleased at once. "I reckon, Miss Lucy,
you—you wouldn't fool me?"

"Why, Farlane!" returned Lucy, reproachfully. "Did
I ever do a single thing around horses that you didn't
want me to?"

Farlane rubbed his chin beard somewhat dubiously.
"Wal, Miss Lucy, not exactly while you was around
the hosses. But I reckon when you onct got *up,* you've
sorta forgot a few times."

All the riders laughed, and Lucy joined them.

"I'm safe when I'm up, you know that," she replied.

They brought out the gray, and after the manner of
riders who had the care of a great horse and loved
him, they curried and combed and rubbed him before
saddling him.

"Reckon you'd better ride Van's saddle," suggested

Farlane. "Them races is close now, an' a strange saddle—"

"Of course. Don't change anything he's used to, except the stirrups," replied Lucy.

Despite her antipathy toward Sage King, Lucy could not gaze at him without all a rider's glory in a horse. He was sleek, so graceful, so racy, so near the soft gray of the sage, so beautiful in build and action. Then he was the kind of a horse that did not have to be eternally watched. He was spirited and full of life, eager to run, but when Farlane called for him to stand still he obeyed. He was the kind of a horse that a child could have played around in safety. He never kicked. He never bit. He never bolted. It was splendid to see him with Farlane or with Bostil. He did not like Lucy very well, a fact that perhaps accounted for Lucy's antipathy. For that matter, he did not like any woman. If he had a bad trait, it came out when Van rode him, but all the riders, and Bostil, too, claimed that Van was to blame for that.

"Thar, I reckon them stirrups is right," declared Farlane. "Now, Miss Lucy, hold him tight till he wears off thet edge. He needs work."

Sage King would not kneel for Lucy as Sarchedon did, and he was too high for her to mount from the ground, so she mounted from a rock. She took to the road, and then the first trail into the sage, intending to trot him ten or fifteen miles down into the valley, and give him some fast, warm work on the return.

The day was early in May and promised to grow hot. There was not a cloud in the blue sky. The wind, laden with the breath of sage, blew briskly from the west. All before Lucy lay the vast valley, gray and dusky gray, then blue, then purple where the monuments stood, and, farther still, dark ramparts of rock. Lucy had a habit of dreaming while on horseback, a habit all the riders had tried to break, but she did not give it rein while she rode Sarchedon, and assuredly now, up on the King, she never forgot him for an instant. He shied at mockingbirds and pack-rats and blowing blossoms and even at butterflies; and he did it, Lucy thought, just because he was full of mischief. Sage King had been known to go steady when there had been reason to shy. He did not like Lucy and he chose to torment her. Finally he earned a good dig from a spur, and then, with swift pounding of hoofs, he plunged and veered and danced in the sage. Lucy kept her temper, which was what most riders did not do, and by patience and firmness pulled Sage King out of his prancing back into the trail. He was not the least cross-grained, and, having had his little spurt, he settled down into easy going.

In an hour Lucy was ten miles or more from home, and farther down in the valley than she had ever been. In fact, she had never before been down the long slope to the valley floor. How changed the horizon became! The monuments loomed up now, dark, sentinel-like, and strange. The first one, a great red rock, seemed to her some five miles away. It was lofty, straight-sided, with a green slope at its base. And beyond that the other monuments stretched out down the valley. Lucy decided to ride as far as the first one before turning back. Always these monuments had fascinated her, and this was her opportunity to ride near one. How lofty they were, how wonderfully colored. and how comely!

Presently, over the left, where the monuments were thicker, and gradually merged their slopes and lines and bulk into the yellow walls, she saw low, drifting clouds of smoke.

"Well, what's that, I wonder?" she mused. To see smoke on the horizon in that direction was unusual, though out toward Durango the grassy benches would often burn over. And these low clouds of smoke resembled those she had seen before.

"It's a long way off," she added.

So she kept on, now and then gazing at the smoke. As she grew nearer to the first monument she was surprised, then amazed, at its height and surpassing size. It was mountain-high—a grand tower—smooth, worn, glistening, yellow and red. The trail she had followed petered out in a deep wash, and beyond that she crossed no more trails. The sage had grown meager and the greasewoods stunted and dead; and cacti appeared on barren places. The grass had not failed, but it was not rich grass such as the horses and cattle grazed upon miles back on the slope. The air was hot down here. The breeze was heavy and smelled of fire, and the sand was blowing here and there. She had a sense of the bigness, the openness of this valley, and then she realized its wildness and strangeness. These lonely, isolated monuments made the place different from any she had visited. They did not seem mere standing rocks. They seemed to retreat all the time as she approached, and they watched her. They interested her, made her curious. What had formed all these strange monuments? Here the ground was level for miles and miles, to slope gently up to the bases of these huge rocks. In an old book she had seen pictures of the Egyptian pyramids, but these appeared vaster, higher, and stranger, and they were sheerly perpendicular.

Suddenly Sage King halted sharply, shot up his ears, and whistled. Lucy was startled. That from the King meant something. Hastily, with keen glance she swept the foreground. A mile on, near the monument, was a small black spot. It seemed motionless. But the King's whistle had proved it to be a horse. When Lucy had covered a quarter of the intervening distance she could distinguish the horse and that there appeared something strange about his position. Lucy urged Sage King into a lope and soon drew nearer. The black horse had his head down, yet he did not appear to be grazing. He was as still as a statue. He stood just outside a clump of greasewood and cactus.

Suddenly a sound pierced the stillness. The King jumped and snorted in fright. For an instant Lucy's blood ran cold, for it was a horrible cry. Then she recognized it as the neigh of a horse in agony. She had heard crippled and dying horses utter that long-drawn

and blood-curdling neigh. The black horse had not
moved, so the sound could not have come from him.
Lucy thought Sage King acted more excited than the
occasion called for. Then remembering her father's
warning, she reined in on top of a little knoll, perhaps
a hundred yards from where the black horse stood,
and she bent her keen gaze forward.

It was a huge, gaunt, shaggy black horse she saw,
with the saddle farther up on his shoulders than it
should have been. He stood motionless, as if utterly
exhausted. His forelegs were braced, so that he leaned
slightly back. Then Lucy saw a rope. It was fast to
the saddle and stretched down into the cactus. There
was no other horse in sight, nor any living thing. The
immense monument dominated the scene. It seemed
stupendous to Lucy, sublime, almost frightful.

She hesitated. She knew there was another horse,
very likely at the other end of that lasso. Probably a
rider had been thrown, perhaps killed. Certainly a horse
had been hurt. Then on the moment rang out the
same neigh of agony, only weaker and shorter. Lucy
no longer feared an ambush. That was a cry which
could not be imitated by a man or forced from a
horse. There was probably death, certainly suffering,
near at hand. She spurred the King on.

There was a little slope to descend, a wash to cross,
a bench to climb—and then she rode up to the black
horse. Sage King needed harder treatment than Lucy
had ever given him.

"What's wrong with you?" she demanded, pulling
him down. Suddenly, as she felt him tremble, she
realized that he was frightened. "That's funny!" Then
when she got him quiet she looked around.

The black horse was indeed huge. His mane, his
shaggy flanks, were lathered as if he had been smeared
with heavy soap-suds. He raised his head to look at
her. Lucy, accustomed to horses all her life, saw that
this one welcomed her arrival. But he was almost
ready to drop.

Two taut lassoes stretched from the pommel of his

saddle down a little into a depression full of brush and cactus and rocks. Then Lucy saw a red horse. He was down in a bad position. She heard his low, choking heaves. Probably he had broken legs or back. She could not bear to see a horse in pain. She would do what was possible, even to the extent of putting him out of his misery, if nothing else could be done. Yet she scanned the surroundings closely, and peered into the bushes and behind the rocks before she tried to urge Sage King closer. He refused to go nearer, and Lucy dismounted.

The red horse was partly hidden by overbending brush. He had plunged into a hole full of cactus. There was a hackamore round his nose and a tight noose round his neck. The one round his neck was also round his forelegs. And both lassoes were held taut by the black horse. A torn and soiled rider's scarf hung limp round the red horse's nose, kept from falling off by the hackamore.

"A wild horse, a stallion, being broken!" exclaimed Lucy, instantly grasping the situation. "Oh! where's the rider?"

She gazed around, ran to and fro, glanced down the little slope, and beyond, but she did not see anything resembling the form of a man. Then she ran back.

Lucy took another quick look at the red stallion. She did not believe either his legs or back were hurt. He was just played out and tangled and tied in the ropes, and could not get up. The shaggy black horse stood there braced and indomitable. But he, likewise, was almost ready to drop. Looking at the condition of both horses and the saddle and ropes, Lucy saw what a fight there had been, and a race! Where was the rider? Thrown, surely, and back on the trail, perhaps dead or maimed.

Lucy went closer to the stallion so that she could almost touch him. He saw her. He was nearly choked. Foam and blood wheezed out with his heaves. She must do something quickly. And in her haste she pricked her arms and shoulders on the cactus.

She led the black horse closer in, letting the ropes go slack. The black seemed as glad of that release as she was. What a faithful brute he looked! Lucy liked his eyes.

Then she edged down in among the cactus and brush. The red horse no longer lay in a strained position. He could lift his head. Lucy saw that the noose still held tight round his neck. Fearlessly she jerked it loose. Then she backed away, but not quite out of his reach. He coughed and breathed slowly, with great heaves. Then he snorted.

"You're all right now," said Lucy, soothingly. Slowly she reached a hand toward his head. He drew it back as far as he could. She stepped around, closer, and more back of him, and put a hand on him, gently, for an instant. Then she slipped out of the brush and, untying one lasso from the pommel, she returned to the horse and pulled it from round his legs. He was free now, except the hackamore, and that rope was slack. Lucy stood near him, watching him, talking to him, waiting for him to get up. She could not be sure he was not badly hurt till he stood up. At first he made no efforts to rise. He watched Lucy, less fearfully, she imagined. And she never made a move. She wanted him to see, to understand that she had not hurt him and would not hurt him. It began to dawn upon her that he was magnificent.

Finally, with a long, slow heave he got to his feet. Lucy led him out of the hole to open ground. She seemed somehow confident. There occurred to her only one way to act.

"A little horse sense, as Dad would say," she soliloquized, and then, when she got him out of the brush, she stood thrilled and amazed.

"Oh, what a wild, beautiful horse! What a giant! He's bigger than the King. Oh, if Dad could see him!"

The red stallion did not appear to be hurt. The twitching of his muscles must have been caused by the cactus spikes embedded in him. There were drops of blood all over one side. Lucy thought she dared to try to pull these thorns out. She had never in her life been afraid of any horse. Farlane, Holley, all the riders, and her father, too, had tried to make her realize the danger in a horse, sooner or later. But Lucy could not help it; she was not afraid; she believed that the meanest horse was actuated by natural fear of a man; she was not a man and she had never handled a horse like a man. This red stallion showed hate of the black horse and the rope that connected them; he showed some spirit at the repeated blasts of Sage King. But he showed less fear of her.

"He has been a proud, wild stallion," mused Lucy. "And he's now broken—terribly broken—all but ruined."

Then she walked up to him naturally and spoke softly, and reached a hand for his shoulder.

"Whoa, Reddy. Whoa now. . . . There. That's a good fellow. Why, I wouldn't rope you or hit you. I'm only a girl."

He drew up, made a single effort to jump, which she prevented, and then he stood quivering, eying her, while she talked soothingly, and patted him and looked at him in the way she had found infallible with most horses. Lucy believed horses were like people, or easier to get along with. Presently she gently pulled out one of the cactus spikes. The horse flinched, but he stood. Lucy was slow, careful, patient, and dexterous. The cactus needles were loose and easily removed or brushed off. At length she got him free of them, and was almost as proud as she was glad. The horse had gradually dropped his head; he was tired and his spirit was broken.

"Now, what shall I do?" she queried. "I'll take the back trail of these horses. They certainly hadn't been here long before I saw them. And the rider may be close. If not I'll take the horses home."

She slipped the noose from the stallion's head, leaving the hackamore, and, coiling the loose lasso, she hung it over the pommel of the black's saddle. Then she took up his bridle.

"Come on," she called.

The black followed her, and the stallion, still fast to him by the lasso Lucy had left tied, trooped behind with bowed head. Lucy was elated. But Sage King did not like the matter at all. Lucy had to drop the black's bridle and catch the King, and then ride back to lead the other again.

A broad trail marked the way the two horses had come, and it led off to the left, toward where the monuments were thickest, and where the great sections of wall stood, broken and battlemented. Lucy was hard put to it to hold Sage King, but the horses behind plodded along. The black horse struck Lucy as being an ugly, but a faithful and wonderful animal. He understood everything. Presently she tied the bridle she was leading him by to the end of her own lasso, and thus let him drop back a few yards, which lessened the King's fretting.

Intent on the trail, Lucy failed to note time or distance till the looming and frowning monuments stood aloft before her. What weird effect they had! Each might have been a colossal statue left there to mark the work of the ages. Lucy realized that the whole vast valley had once been solid rock, just like the monuments, and through the millions of years the softer parts had eroded and weathered and blown away—gone with the great sea that had once been there. But the beauty, the solemnity, the majesty of these monuments fascinated her most. She passed the first one, a huge square butte, and then the second, a ragged, thin, double shaft, and then went between two much alike, reaching skyward in the shape of monstrous mittens. She watched and watched them, sparing a moment now and then to attend to the trail. She noticed that she was coming into a region of grass, and faint signs of water in the draws. She was getting high again, not many miles now from the wall of rock.

All at once Sage King shied, and Lucy looked down to see a man lying on the ground. He lay inert. But his eyes were open—dark, staring eyes. They moved. And he called. But Lucy could not understand him.

In a flash she leaped off the King. She ran to the prostrate man—dropped to her knees.

"Oh!" she cried. His face was ghastly. "Oh! are you—you badly hurt?"

"Lift me—my head," he said, faintly.

She raised his head. What a strained, passionate, terrible gaze he bent upon the horses.

"Boy, they're mine—the black an' the red!" he cried.

"They surely must be," replied Lucy. "Oh! tell me. Are you hurt?"

"Boy! did you catch them—fetch them back—lookin' for me?"

"I sure did."

"You caught—that red devil—an' fetched him—back to me?" went on the wondering, faint voice. "Boy—oh—boy!"

He lifted a long, ragged arm and pulled Lucy down. The action amazed her equally as his passion of gratitude. He might have been injured, but he had an arm of iron. Lucy was powerless. She felt her face against his—and her breast against his. The pounding of his heart was like blows. The first instant she wanted to laugh, despite her pity. Then the powerful arm—the contact affected her as nothing ever before. Suppose this crippled rider had taken her for a boy— She was not a boy! She could not help being herself. And no man had ever put a hand on her. Consciousness of this brought shame and anger. She struggled so violently that she freed herself. And he lay back.

"See here—that's no way to act—to hug—a person," she cried, with flaming cheeks.

"Boy, I—"

"I'm *not* a boy. I'm a girl."

"What!"

Lucy tore off her sombrero, which had been pulled far forward, and this revealed her face fully, and her

hair came tumbling down. The rider gazed, stupefied.
Then a faint tingle of red colored his ghastly cheeks.

"A girl! . . . Why—why 'scuse me, miss. I—I took
you—for a boy."

He seemed so astounded, he looked so ashamed,
so scared, and withal, so haggard and weak, that Lucy
immediately recovered her equanimity.

"Sure I'm a girl. But that's no matter. . . . You've
been thrown. Are you hurt?"

He smiled a weak assent.

"Badly?" she queried. She did not like the way he
lay—so limp, so motionless.

"I'm afraid so. I can't move."

"Oh! . . . What shall I do?"

"Can you—get me water?" he whispered, with dry
lips.

Lucy flew to her horse to get the small canteen
she always carried. But that had been left on her saddle, and she had ridden Van's. Then she gazed around.
The wash she had crossed several times ran near
where the rider lay. Green grass and willows bordered
it. She ran down and, hurrying along, searched for
water. There was water in places, yet she had to go
a long way before she found water that was drinkable.
Filling her sombrero, she hurried back to the side
of the rider. It was difficult to give him a drink.

"Thanks, miss," he said, gratefully. His voice was
stronger and less hoarse.

"Have you any broken bones?" asked Lucy.

"I don't know. I can't feel much."

"Are you in pain?"

"Hardly. I feel sort of thick."

Lucy, being an intelligent girl, born in the desert
and used to its needs, had not often encountered a
situation with which she was unable to cope.

"Let me feel if you have any broken bones. . . .
That arm isn't broken, I'm positive."

The rider smiled faintly again. How he stared with
his strained, dark eyes! His face showed ghastly
through the thin, soft beard and the tan. Lucy found

his right arm badly bruised, but not broken. She made sure his collar-bones and shoulder-blades were intact. Broken ribs were harder to locate; still, as he did not feel pain from pressure, she concluded there were no fractures there. With her assistance he moved his legs, proving no broken bones there.

"I'm afraid it's my—spine," he said.

"But you raised your head once," she replied. "If your back was—was broken or injured you couldn't raise your head."

"So I couldn't. I guess I'm just knocked out. I was —pretty weak before Wildfire knocked me—off Nagger."

"Wildfire?"

"That's the red stallion's name."

"Oh, he's named already?"

"I named him—long ago. He's known on many a range."

"Where?"

"I think far north of here. I—trailed him—days— weeks—months. We crossed the great cañon—"

"The Grand Cañon?"

"It must be that."

"The Grand Cañon is down there," said Lucy, pointing. "I live on it. . . . You've come a long way."

"Hundreds of miles! . . . Oh, the ground I covered— that awful cañon country! . . . But I stayed with Wildfire. An' I put a rope on him. An' he got away. . . . An' it was a boy—no—a *girl* who—saved him for me —an' maybe saved my life, too!"

Lucy looked away from the dark, staring eyes. A light in them confused her.

"Never mind me. You say you were weak? Have you been ill?"

"No, miss. Just starved. . . . I starved on Wildfire's trail."

Lucy ran to her saddle and got the biscuits out of the pockets of her coat, and she ran back to the rider.

"Here. I never thought. Oh, you've had a hard time of it! I understand. That wonderful flame of a horse! I'd have stayed, too. My father was a rider once. Bostil. Did you ever hear of him?"

"Bostil. The name—I've heard." Then the rider lay thinking, as he munched a biscuit. "Yes, I remember, but it was long ago. I spent a night with a wagon-train, a camp of many men and women, religious people, working into Utah. Bostil had a boat at the crossing of the Fathers."

"Yes, they called the Ferry that."

"I remember well now. They said Bostil couldn't count his horses—that he was a rich man, hard on riders—an' he'd used a gun more than once."

Lucy bowed her head. "Yes, that's my dad."

The rider did not seem to see how he had hurt her.

"Here we are talking—wasting time," she said. "I must start home. You can't be moved. What shall I do?"

"That's for you to say, Bostil's daughter."

"My name's Lucy," replied the girl, blushing painfully. "I mean I'll be glad to do anything you think best."

"You're very good."

Then he turned his face away. Lucy looked closely at him. He was indeed a beggared rider. His clothes and his boots hung in tatters. He had no hat, no coat, no vest. His gaunt face bore traces of what might have been a fine, strong comeliness, but now it was only thin, worn, wan, pitiful, with that look which always went to a woman's heart. He had the look of a homeless rider. Lucy had seen a few of his wandering type, and his story was so plain. But he seemed to have a touch of pride, and this quickened her interest.

"Then I'll do what I think best for you," said Lucy.

First she unsaddled the black Nagger. With the saddle she made a pillow for the rider's head, and she covered him with the saddle blanket. Before she had finished this task he turned his eyes upon her. And Lucy felt she would be haunted. Was he badly hurt, after all? It seemed probable. How strange he was!

"I'll water the horses—then tie Wildfire here on a double rope. There's grass."

"But you can't lead him," replied the rider.

"He'll follow me."

"That red devil!" The rider shuddered as he spoke.

Lucy had some faint inkling of what a terrible fight that had been between man and horse. "Yes; when I found him he was broken. Look at him now."

But the rider did not appear to want to see the stallion. He gazed up at Lucy, and she saw something in his eyes that made her think of a child. She left him, had no trouble in watering the horses, and haltered Wildfire among the willows on a patch of grass. Then she returned.

"I'll go now," she said to the rider.

"Where?"

"Home. I'll come back to-morrow, early, and bring some one to help you—"

"Girl, if *you* want to help me more—bring me some bread an' meat. Don't tell any one. Look what a ragamuffin I am. . . . An' there's Wildfire. I don't want him seen till I'm—on my feet again. I know riders. . . . That's all. If you want to be so good— come."

"I'll come," replied Lucy, simply.

"Thank you. I owe you—a lot. . . . What did you say your name was?"

"Lucy—Lucy Bostil."

"Oh, I forgot. . . . Are you sure you tied Wildfire good an' tight?"

"Yes, I'm sure. I'll go now. I hope you'll be better to-morrow."

Lucy hesitated, with her hand on the King's bridle. She did not like to leave this young man lying there helpless on the desert. But what else could she do? What a strange adventure had befallen her! At the following thought that it was not yet concluded she felt a little stir of excitement at her pulses. She was so

strangely preoccupied that she forgot it was necessary
for her to have a step to mount Sage King. She realized
it quickly enough when she attempted it. Then she
led him off in the sage till she found a rock. Mounting,
she turned him straight across country, meaning to cut
out miles of travel that would have been necessary
along her back-trail. Once she looked back. The rider
was not visible; the black horse, Nagger, was out of
sight, but Wildfire, blazing in the sun, watched her
depart.

Chapter IX

LUCY BOSTIL could not control the glow of strange
excitement under which she labored, but she could
put her mind on the riding of Sage King. She did not
realize, however, that she was riding him under the
stress and spell of that excitement.

She had headed out to make a short cut, fairly sure
of her direction, yet she was not unaware of the fact
that she would be lost till she ran across her trail.
That might be easy to miss and time was flying. She
put the King to a brisk trot, winding through the aisles
of the sage.

Soon she had left the monument region and was
down on the valley floor again. From time to time she
conquered a desire to look back. Presently she was
surprised and very glad to ride into a trail where she
saw the tracks she had made coming out. With much
relief she turned Sage King into this trail, and then
any anxiety she had felt left her entirely. But that
did not mitigate her excitement. She eased the King
into a long, swinging lope. And as he warmed to the
work she was aroused also. It was hard to hold him
in, once he got out of a trot, and after miles and miles
of this, when she thought best to slow down he nearly

pulled her arms off. Still she finally got him in hand. Then followed miles of soft and rough going, which seemed long and tedious. Beyond that was the home stretch up the valley, whose gradual slope could be seen only at a distance. Here was a straight, broad trail, not too soft nor too hard, and for all the years she could remember riders had tried out and trained their favorites on that course.

Lucy reached down to assure herself that the cinch was tight, then she pulled her sombrero down hard, slackened the bridle, and let the King go. He simply broke his gait, he was so surprised. Lucy saw him trying to look back at her, as if he could not realize that this young woman rider had given him a free rein. Perhaps one reason he disliked her had been always and everlastingly that tight rein. Like the wary horse he was he took to a canter, to try out what his new freedom mean.

"Say, what's the matter with you?" called Lucy, disdainfully. "Are you lazy? Or don't you believe I can ride you?"

Whereupon she dug him with her spurs. Sage King snorted. His action shifted marvelously. Thunder rolled from under his hoofs. And he broke out of that clattering roar into his fleet stride, where his hoof-beats were swift, regular, rhythmic.

Lucy rode him with teeth and fists clenched, bending low. After all, she thought, it was no trick to ride him. In that gait he was dangerous, for a fall meant death; but he ran so smoothly that riding him was easy and certainly glorious. He went so fast that the wind blinded her. The trail was only a white streak in blurred gray. She could not get her breath; the wind seemed to whip the air away from her. And then she felt the lessening of the tremendous pace. Sage King had run himself out and the miles were behind her. Gradually her sight became clear, and as the hot and wet horse slowed down, satisfied with his wild run, Lucy realized that she was up on the slope only a few miles from home. Suddenly she thought she saw

something dark stir behind a sage-bush just ahead.
Before she could move a hand at the bridle Sage King
leaped with a frantic snort. It was a swerving, nimble,
tremendous bound. He went high. Lucy was un-
seated. but somehow clung on, and came down with
him, finding the saddle. And it seemed, while in the
air, she saw a long, snaky, whipping loop of rope
shoot out and close just where Sage King's legs had
been.

She screamed. The horse broke and ran. Lucy,
righting herself, looked back to see Joel Creech holding
a limp lasso. He had tried to rope the King.

The blood of her father was aroused in Lucy. She
thought of the horse—not herself. If the King had not
been so keen-sighted, so swift, he would have gone
down with a broken leg. Lucy never in her life had
been so furious.

Joel shook his fist at her and yelled, "I'd 'a' got you
—on any other hoss!"

She did not reply, though she had to fight herself
to keep from pulling her gun and shooting at him.
She guided the running horse back into the trail,
rapidly leaving Creech out of sight.

"He's gone crazy, that's sure," said Lucy. "And he
means me harm!"

She ran the King clear up to the corrals, and he
was still going hard when she turned down the lane
to the barns. Then she pulled him in.

Farlane was there to meet her. She saw no other
riders and was glad.

"Wal, Miss Lucy, the King sure looks good," said
Farlane, as she jumped off and flung him the bridle.
"He's just had about right, judgin'. . . . Say, girl,
you're all pale! Oh, say, you wasn't scared of the
King, now?"

"No," replied Lucy, panting.

"Wal, what's up, then?" The rider spoke in an entirely different voice, and into his clear, hazel eyes a
little dark gleam shot.

"Joel Creech waylaid me out in the sage—and—and

tried to catch me." Lucy checked herself. It might
not do to tell how Joel had tried to catch her.

"He did? An' you on the King!" Farlane laughed,
as if relieved. "Wal, he's tried thet before, Miss Lucy.
But when you was up on the gray—thet shows Joel's
crazy, sure."

"He sure is. Farlane, I—I am mad!"

"Wal, cool off, Miss Lucy. It ain't nothin' to git
set up about. An' don't tell the old man."

"Why not?" demanded Lucy.

"Wal, because he's in a queer sort of bad mood
lately. It wouldn't be safe. He hates them Creeches.
So don't tell him."

"All right, Farlane, I won't. Don't you tell, either,"
replied Lucy, soberly.

"Sure I'll keep mum. But if Joel doesn't watch out
I'll put a crimp in him myself."

Lucy hurried away down the lane and entered the
house without meeting any one. In her room she
changed her clothes and lay down to rest and think.

Strangely enough, Lucy might never have encountered Joel Creech out in the sage, for all the thought
she gave him. Her mind was busy with the crippled
rider. Who was he? Where was he from? What strange
passion he had shown over the recovery of that wonderful red horse! Lucy could not forget the feeling
of his iron arm when he held her in a kind of frenzied
gratitude. A wild upland rider, living only for a wild
horse! How like Indians some of these riders! Yet
this fellow had seemed different from most of the
uncouth riders she had known. He spoke better. He
appeared to have had some little schooling. Lucy
did not realize that she was interested in him. She
thought she was sorry for him and interested in the
stallion. She began to compare Wildfire with Sage
King, and if she remembered rightly Wildfire, even
in his disheveled state, had appeared a worthy rival
of the King. What would Bostil say at sight of that
flame-colored stallion? Lucy thrilled.

Later she left her room to see if the hour was opportune for her plan to make up a pack of supplies for the rider. Her aunt was busy in the kitchen, and Bostil had not come in. Lucy took advantage of the moment to tie up a pack and carry it to her room. Somehow the task pleased her. She recalled the lean face of the rider. And that recalled his ragged appearance. Why not pack up an outfit of clothes? Bostil had a stock-room full of such accessories for his men. Then Lucy, glowing with the thought, hurried to Bostil's stock-room, and with deft hands and swift judgment selected an outfit for the rider, even down to a comb and razor. All this she carried quickly to her room, where in her thoughtfulness she added a bit of glass from a broken mirror, and soap and a towel. Then she tied up a second pack.

Bostil did not come home to supper, a circumstance that made Lucy's aunt cross. They ate alone, and, waiting awhile, were rather late in clearing away the table. After this Lucy had her chance in the dusk of early evening, and she carried both packs way out into the sage and left them near the trail.

"Hope a coyote doesn't come along," she said. That possibility, however, did not worry her as much as getting those packs up on the King. How in the world would she ever do it?

She hurried back to the house, stealthily keeping to the shadow of the cottonwoods, for she would have faced an embarrassing situation if she had met her father, even had he been in a good humor. And she reached the sitting-room unobserved. The lamps had been lighted and a log blazed on the hearth. She was reading when Bostil entered.

"Hello, Lucy!" he said.

He looked tired, and Lucy knew he had been drinking, because when he had been he never offered to kiss her. The strange, somber shade was still on his face, but it brightened somewhat at sight of her. Lucy greeted him as always.

"Farlane tells me you handled the King great—better 'n Van has worked him lately," said Bostil. "But don't tell him I told you."

That was sweet praise from Farlane. "Oh, Dad, it could hardly be true," expostulated Lucy. "Both you and Farlane are a little sore at Van now."

"I'm a lot sore," replied Bostil, gruffly.

"Anyway, how did Farlane know how I handled Sage King?" queried Lucy.

"Wal, every hair on a hoss talks to Farlane, so Holley says. . . . Lucy, you take the King out every day for a while. Ride him now an' watch out! Joel Creech was in the village to-day. He sure sneaked when he seen me. He's up to some mischief."

Lucy did not want to lie and she did not know what to say. Presently Bostil bade her good night. Lucy endeavored to read, but her mind continually wandered back to the adventure of the day.

Next morning she had difficulty in concealing her impatience, but luck favored her. Bostil was not in evidence, and Farlane, for once, could spare no more time than it took to saddle Sage King. Lucy rode out into the sage, pretty sure that no one watched her.

She had hidden the packs near the tallest bunch of greasewood along the trail; and when she halted behind it she had no fear of being seen from the corrals. She got the packs. The light one was not hard to tie back of the saddle, but the large one was a very different matter. She decided to carry it in front. There was a good-sized rock near, upon which she stepped, leading Sage King alongside; and after an exceedingly trying moment she got up, holding the pack. For a wonder Sage King behaved well.

Then she started off, holding the pack across her lap, and she tried the King's several gaits to see which one would lend itself more comfortably to the task before her. The trouble was that Sage King had no slow gait, even his walk was fast. And Lucy was compelled to hold him into that. She wanted to hurry, but that seemed out of the question. She tried to keep from gazing out toward the monuments, because they were so far away.

How would she find the crippled rider? It flashed into her mind that she might find him dead, and this seemed horrible. But her common sense persuaded her that she would find him alive and better. The pack was hard to hold, and Sage King fretted at the monotonous walk. The hours dragged. The sun grew hot. And it was noon, almost, when she reached the point where she cut off the trail to the left. Thereafter, with the monuments standing ever higher, and the distance perceptibly lessening, the minutes passed less tediously.

At length she reached the zone of lofty rocks, and found them different, how, she could not tell. She rode down among them, and was glad when she saw the huge mittens—her landmarks. At last she espied the green-bordered wash and the few cedar-trees. Then a horse blazed red against the sage and another shone black. That sight made Lucy thrill. She rode on, eager now, but moved by the stangeness of the experience.

Before she got quite close to the cedars she saw a man. He took a few slow steps out of the shade. His back was bent. Lucy recognized the rider, and in her gladness to see him on his feet she cried out. Then, when Sage King reached the spot, Lucy rolled the pack off to the ground.

"Oh, that was a job!" she cried.

The rider looked up with eyes that seemed keener, less staring than she remembered. "You came? . . . I was afraid you wouldn't," he said.

"Sure I came. . . . You're better—not badly hurt?" she said, gravely. "I—I'm so glad."

"I've got a crimp in my back, that's all."

Lucy was quick to see that after the first glance at her he was all eyes for Sage King. She laughed. How like a rider! She watched him, knowing that presently he would realize what a horse she was riding. She slipped off and threw the bridle, and then, swiftly untying the second pack, she laid it down.

The rider, with slow, painful steps and bent back,

approached Sage King and put a lean, strong, brown hand on him, and touched him as if he wished to feel if he were real. Then he whistled softly. When he turned to Lucy his eyes shone with a beautiful light.

"It's Sage King, Bostil's favorite," said Lucy.

"Sage King! . . . He looks it. . . . But never a wild horse?"

"No."

"A fine horse," replied the rider. "Of course he can run?" This last held a note of a rider's jealousy.

Lucy laughed. "Run! . . . The King is Bostil's favorite. He can run away from any horse in the uplands."

"I'll bet you Wildfire can beat him," replied the rider, with a dark glance.

"Come on!" cried Lucy, daringly.

Then the rider and girl looked more earnestly at each other. He smiled in a way that changed his face —brightened out the set hardness.

"I reckon I'll have to crawl," he said, ruefully. "But maybe I can ride in a few days—if you'll come back again."

His remark brought to Lucy the idea that of course she would hardly see this rider again after to-day. Even if he went to the Ford, which event was unlikely, he would not remain there long. The sensation of blankness puzzled her, and she felt an unfamiliar confusion.

"I—I've brought you—some things," she said, pointing to the larger pack.

"Grub, you mean?"

"No."

"That was all I asked you for, miss," he said, somewhat stiffly.

"Yes, but—I—I thought—" Lucy became unaccountably embarrassed. Suppose this strange rider would be offended. "Your clothes were—so torn. . . . And no wonder you were thrown—in those boots! . . . So I thought I'd—"

"You thought I needed clothes as bad as grub," he said, bitterly. "I reckon that's so."

His look, more than his tone, cut Lucy; and involuntarily she touched his arm. "Oh, you won't refuse to take them! Please don't!"

At her touch a warmth came into his face. "Take them? I should smile I will."

He tried to reach down to lift the pack, but as it was obviously painful for him to bend, Lucy intercepted him.

"But you've had no breakfast," she protested. "Why not eat before you open that pack?"

"Nope. I'm not hungry. . . . Maybe I'll eat a little, after I dress up." He started to walk away, then turned. "Miss Bostil, have you been so good to every wanderin' rider you happened to run across?"

"Good!" she exclaimed, flushing. She dropped her eyes before his. "Nonsense. . . . Anyway, you're the first wandering rider I ever met—like this."

"Well, you're good," he replied, with emotion. Then he walked away with slow, stiff steps and disappeared behind the willows in the little hollow.

Lucy uncoiled the rope on her saddle and haltered Sage King on the best grass near at hand. Then she opened the pack of supplies, thinking the while that she must not tarry here long.

"But on the King I can run back like the wind," she mused.

The pack contained dried fruits and meat and staples, also an assortment of good things to eat that were of a perishable nature, already much the worse for the long ride. She spread all this out in the shade of a cedar. The utensils were few—two cups, two pans, and a tiny pot. She gathered wood, and arranged it for a fire, so that the rider could start it as soon as he came back. He seemed long in coming. Lucy waited, yet still he did not return. Finally she thought of the red stallion, and started off down the wash to take a look at him. He was grazing. He had lost some of the dirt and dust and the bedraggled appearance. When he caught sight of her he lifted his head high and whistled. How wild he looked! And his whistle was shrill, clear, strong. Both the other horses answered it.

Lucy went on closer to Wildfire. She was fascinated now.

"If he doesn't know me!" she cried. Never had she been so pleased. She had expected evry sign of savageness on his part, and certainly had not intended to go near him. But Wildfire did not show fear or hate in his recognition. Lucy went directly to him and got a hand on him. Wildfire reared a little and shook a little, but this disappeared presently under her touch. He held his head very high and watched her with wonderful eyes. Gradually she drew his head down. Standing before him, she carefully and slowly changed the set of the hackamore, which had made a welt on his nose. It seemed to have been her good fortune that every significant move she had made around this stallion had been to mitigate his pain. Lucy believed he knew this as well as she knew it. Her theory, an often disputed one, was that horses were as intelligent as human beings and had just the same fears, likes, and dislikes. Lucy knew she was safe when she untied the lasso from the strong root where she had fastened it, and led the stallion down the wash to a pool of water. And she stood beside him with a hand on his shoulder while he bent his head to sniff at the water. He tasted it, plainly with disgust. It was stagnant water, full of vermin. But finally he drank. Lucy led him up the wash to another likely place, and tied him securely.

When she got back to the camp in the cedars the rider was there, on his knees, kindling the fire. His clean-shaved face and new apparel made him vastly different. He was young, and, had he not been so gaunt, he would have been fine-looking, Lucy thought.

"Wildfire remembered me," Lucy burst out. "He wasn't a bit scary. Let me handle him. Followed me to water."

"He's taken to you," replied the rider, seriously. "I've heard of the like, but not so quick. Was he in a bad fix when you got to him yesterday?"

Lucy explained briefly.

"Aha! . . . If that red devil has any love in him I'll

never get it. I wish I could have done so much for him. But always when he sees me he'll remember."

Lucy saw that the rider was in difficulties. He could not bend his back, and evidently it pained him to try. His brow was moist.

"Let me do that," she said.

"Thanks. It took about all my strength to get into this new outfit," he said, relinquishing his place to Lucy.

When she looked up from her task, presently, he was sitting in the shade of the cedar, watching her. He had the expression of a man who hardly believed what he saw.

"Did you have any trouble gettin' away, without tellin'—about me?" he asked.

"No. But I sure had a job with those packs," she replied.

"You must be a wonder with a horse."

As far as vanity was concerned Lucy had only one weakness—and he had touched upon it.

"Well, Dad and Holley and Farlane argue much about me. Still, I guess they all agree I can ride."

"Holley an' Farlane are riders?" he questioned.

"Yes, Dad's right-hand men."

"Your dad hires many riders, I suppose?"

"Sure I never heard of him turning any rider down, at least not without a try."

"I wonder if he would give me a job?"

Lucy glanced up quickly. The idea surprised her—pleased her. "In a minute," she replied. "And he'd be grand to you. You see, he'd have an eye for Wildfire."

The rider nodded his head as if he understood how that would be.

"And of course you'd never sell nor trade Wildfire?" went on Lucy.

The rider's smile was sad, but it was conclusive.

"Then you'd better stay away from Bostil," returned Lucy, shortly.

He remained silent, and Lucy, busy about the camp-fire, did not speak again till the simple fare was ready. Then she spread a tarpaulin in the shade.

"I'm pretty hungry myself," she said. "But I don't suppose I know what hunger is."

"After a while a fellow loses the feelin' of hunger," he replied. "I reckon it 'll come back quick. . . . This all looks good."

So they began to eat. Lucy's excitement, her sense of the unreality of this adventure, in no wise impaired her appetite. She seemed acutely sensitive to the perceptions of the moment. The shade of the cedars was cool. And out on the desert she could see the dark smoky veils of heat lifting. The breeze carried a dry odor of sand and grass. She heard bees humming by. And all around the great isolated monuments stood up, red tops against the blue sky. It was a silent, dreaming, impressive place, where she felt unlike herself.

"I mustn't stay long," she said, suddenly remembering.

"Will you come back—again?" he asked.

The question startled Lucy. "Why—I—I don't know. . . . Won't you ride in to the Ford just as soon as you're able?"

"I reckon not."

"But it's the only place where there's people in hundreds of miles. Surely you won't try to go back— the way you came?"

"When Wildfire left that country I left it. We can't go back."

"Then you've no people—no one you care for?" she asked, in sweet seriousness.

"There's no one. I'm an orphan. My people were lost in an Indian massacre—with a wagon-train crossin' Wyomin'. A few escaped, an' I was one of the youngsters. I had a tough time, like a stray dog, till I grew up. An' then I took to the desert."

"Oh, I see. I—I'm sorry," replied Lucy. "But that's not very different from my dad's story, of his early years. . . . What will you do now?"

"I'll stay here till my back straightens out. . . . Will you ride out again?"

"Yes," replied Lucy, without looking at him; and she wondered if it were really she who was speaking.

Then he asked her about the Ford, and Bostil, and the ranches and villages north, and the riders and horses. Lucy told him everything she knew and could think of, and, lastly, after waxing eloquent on the horses of the uplands, particularly Bostil's, she gave him a graphic account of Cordts and Dick Sears.

"Horse-thieves!" exclaimed the rider, darkly. There was a grimness as well as fear in his tone. "I've heard of Sears, but not Cordts. Where does this band hang out?"

"No one knows. Holley says they hide up in the cañon country. None of the riders have ever tried to track them far. It would be useless. Holley says there are plateaus of rich grass and great forests. The Ute Indians say that much, too. But we know little about the wild country."

"Aren't there any hunters at Bostil's Ford?"

"Wild-horse hunters, you mean?"

"No. Bear an' deer hunters."

"There's none. And I suppose that's why we're not familiar with the wild cañon country. I'd like to ride in there sometime and camp. But our people don't go in for that. They love the open ranges. No one I know, except a half-witted boy, ever rode down among these monuments. And how wonderful a place! It can't be more than twenty miles from home. . . . I must be going soon. I'm forgetting Sage King. Did I tell you I was training him for the races?"

"No, you didn't. What races? Tell me," he replied, with keen interest.

Then Lucy told him about the great passion of her father—about the long, time-honored custom of free-for-all races, and the great races that had been run in the past; about the Creeches and their swift horses; about the rivalry and speculation and betting; and lastly about the races to be run in a few weeks—races so wonderful in prospect that even the horse-thief, Cordts, had begged to be allowed to attend.

"I'm going to see the King beat Creech's roan," shouted the rider, with red in his cheeks and a flash in his eye.

His enthusiasm warmed Lucy's interest, yet it made her thoughtful. Ideas flashed into her mind. If the rider attended the races he would have that fleet stallion with him. He could not be separated from the horse that had cost him so dearly. What would Bostil and Holley and Farlane say at sight of Wildfire? Suppose Wildfire was to enter the races! It was probable that he could run away from the whole field —even beat the King. Lucy thrilled and thrilled. What a surprise it would be! She had the rider's true love of seeing the unheralded horse win over the favorite. She had for years wanted to see a horse—and ride a horse—out in front of Sage King. Then suddenly all these flashing ideas coruscated seemingly into a gleam—a leaping, radiant, wonderful thought. Irresistibly it burst from her.

"Let *me* ride your Wildfire in the great race?" she cried, breathlessly.

His response was instantaneous—a smile that was keen and sweet and strong, and a proffered hand. Impulsively Lucy clasped that hand with both hers.

"You don't mean it," she said. "Oh, it's what Auntie would call one of my wild dreams! . . . And I'm growing up—they say. . . . But— Oh, if I could ride Wildfire against the field in that race. . . . *If I only could!*"

She was on fire with the hope, flushing, tingling. She was unconscious of her effect upon the rider, who gazed at her with a new-born light in his eyes.

"You can ride him. I reckon I'd like to see that race just as much as Bostil or Cordts or any man. . . . An' see here, girl, Wildfire can beat this gray racer of your father's."

"Oh!" cried Lucy.

"Wildfire can beat the King," repeated the rider,

intensely. "The tame horse doesn't step on this earth that can run with Wildfire. He's a stallion. He has been a killer of horses. It's in him to *kill*. If he ran a race it would be that instinct in him."

"How can we plan it?" went on Lucy, impulsively. She had forgotten to withdraw her hands from his. "It must be a surprise—a complete surprise. If you came to the Ford we couldn't keep it secret. And Dad or Farlane would prevent me, somehow."

"It's easy. Ride out here as often as you can. Bring a light saddle an' let me put you up on Wildfire. You'll run him, train him, get him in shape. Then the day of the races or the night before I'll go in an' hide out in the sage till you come or send for Wildfire."

"Oh, it 'll be glorious," she cried, with eyes like stars. "I know just where to have you hide. A pile of rocks near the racecourse. There's a spring and good grass. I could ride out to you just before the big race, and we'd come back, with me on Wildfire. The crowd always stays down at the end of the racecourse. Only the starters stay out there. . . . Oh, I can see Bostil when that red stallion runs into sight!"

"Well, is it settled?" queried the rider, strangely.

Lucy was startled into self-consciousness by his tone. How strangely he must have felt. And his eyes were piercing.

"You mean—that I ride Wildfire?" she replied, shyly. "Yes, if you'll let me."

"I'll be proud."

"You're very good. . . . And do you think Wildfire can beat the King?"

"I know it."

"How do you?"

"I've seen both horses."

"But it will be a grand race."

"I reckon so. It's likely to be the grandest ever seen. But Wildfire will win, because he's run wild all his life —an' run to kill other horses. . . . The only question is—*can* you ride him?"

"Yes. I never saw the horse I couldn't ride. Bostil says there are some I can't ride. Farlane says not. Only two horses have thrown me, the King and Sarchedon. But that was before they knew me. And I was sort of wild. I can make your Wildfire love me."

"*That's* the last part of it I'd ever doubt," replied the rider. "It's settled, then. I'll camp here. I'll be well in a few days. Then I'll take Wildfire in hand. You will ride out whenever you have a chance, without bein' seen. An' the two of us will train the stallion to upset that race."

"Yes—then—it's settled."

Lucy's gaze was impelled and held by the rider's. Why was he so pale? But then he had been injured—weakened. This compact between them had somehow changed their relation. She seemed to have known him long.

"What's your name?" she asked.

"Lin Slone," replied the rider.

Then she released her hands. "I must ride in now. If this isn't a dream I'll come back soon." She led Sage King to a rock and mounted him.

"It's good to see you up there," said Slone. "An' that splendid horse! . . . He knows what he is. It'll break Bostil's heart to see that horse beat."

"Dad 'll feel bad, but it 'll do him good," replied Lucy.

That was the old rider's ruthless spirit speaking out of his daughter's lips.

Slone went close to the King and, putting a hand on the pommel, he looked up at Lucy. "Maybe—it is—a dream—an' you won't come back," he said, with unsteady voice.

"Then I'll come in dreams," she flashed. "Be careful of yourself. . . . Good-by."

And at a touch the impatient King was off. From far up the slope near a monument Lucy looked back. Slone was watching her. She waved a gauntleted hand—and then looked back no more.

Chapter X

Two weeks slipped by on the wings of time and opportunity and achievement, all colored so wonderfully for Lucy, all spelling that adventure for which she had yearned.

Lucy was riding down into the sage toward the monuments with a whole day before her. Bostil kept more and more to himself, a circumstance that worried her, though she thought little about it. Van had taken up the training of the King; and Lucy had deliberately quarreled with him so that she would be free to ride where she listed. Farlane nagged her occasionally about her rides into the sage, insisting that she must not go so far and stay so long. And after Van's return to work he made her ride Sarchedon.

Things had happened at the Ford which would have concerned Lucy greatly had she not been over-excited about her own affairs. Some one had ambushed Bostil in the cottonwoods near his house and had shot at him, narrowly missing him. Bostil had sworn he recognized the shot as having come from a rifle, and that he knew to whom it belonged. The riders did not believe this, and said some boy, shooting at a rabbit or coyote, had been afraid to confess he had nearly hit Bostil. The riders all said Bostil was not wholly himself of late. The river was still low. The boat had not been repaired. And Creech's horses were still on the other side.

These things concerned Lucy, yet they only came and went swiftly through her mind. She was obsessed by things intimately concerning herself.

"Oh, I oughtn't to go," she said, aloud. But she did not even check Sarchedon's long swing, his rocking-chair lope. She had said a hundred times that she

ought not go again out to the monuments. For Lin
Slone had fallen despairingly, terribly in love with her.

It was not this, she averred, but the monuments
and the beautiful Wildfire that had woven a spell
round her she could not break. She had ridden Wildfire all through that strange region of monuments and
now they claimed something of her. Just as wonderful
was Wildfire's love for her. The great stallion hated
Slone and loved Lucy. Of all the remarkable circumstances she had seen or heard about a horse, this fact
was the most striking. She could do anything with him.
All that savageness and wildness disappeared when
she approached him. He came at her call. He whistled
at sight of her. He sent out a ringing blast of disapproval when she rode away. Every day he tried to bite
or kick Slone, but he was meek under Lucy's touch.

But this morning there came to Lucy the first vague
doubt of herself. Once entering her mind, that doubt
became clear. And then she vowed she liked Slone as
she might a brother. And something within her accused her own conviction. The conviction was her
real self, and the accusation was some other girl lately
born in her. Lucy did not like this new person. She
was afraid of her. She would not think of her unless
she had to.

"I never cared for him—that way," she said, aloud.
"I don't—I couldn't—ever—I—I—love Lin Slone!"

The spoken thought—the sound of the words played
havoc with Lucy's self-conscious calmness. She burned.
She trembled. She was in a rage with herself. She
spurred Sarchedon into a run and tore through the
sage, down into the valley, running him harder than
she should have run him. Then she checked him, and,
penitent, petted him out of all proportion to her
thoughtlessness. The violent exercise only heated her
blood and, if anything, increased this sudden and new
torment. Why had she discarded her boy's rider outfit
and chaps for a riding-habit made by her aunt, and
one she had scorned to wear? Some awful, accusing
voice thundered in Lucy's burning ears that she had

done this because she was ashamed to face Lin Slone any more in that costume—she wanted to appear different in his eyes, to look like a girl. If that shameful suspicion was a fact why was it—what did it mean? She could not tell, yet she was afraid of the truth.

All of a sudden Lin Slone stood out clearer in her mental vision—the finest type of a rider she had ever known—a strong, lithe, magnificent horseman, whose gentleness showed his love for horses, whose roughness showed his power—a strange, intense, lonely man in whom she had brought out pride, gratitude, kindness, passion, and despair. She felt her heart swell at the realization that she had changed him, made him kinder, made him divide his love as did her father, made him human, hopeful, longing for a future unfettered by the toils of desert allurement. She could not control her pride. She must like him very much. She confessed that, honestly, without a qualm. It was only bewildering moments of strange agitation and uncertainty that bothered her. She had refused to be concerned by them until they had finally impinged upon her peace of mind. Then they accused her; now she accused herself. She ought not go to meet Lin Slone any more.

"But then—the race!" she murmured. "I couldn't give that up. . . . And oh! I'm afraid the harm is done! What can I do?"

After the race—what then? To be sure, all of Bostil's Ford would know she had been meeting Slone out in the sage, training his horse. What would people say?

"Dad will simply be radiant, *if* he can buy Wildfire —and a fiend if he can't," she muttered.

Lucy saw that her own impulsiveness had amounted to daring. She had gone too far. She excused that—for she had a rider's blood—she was Bostil's girl. But she had, in her wildness and joy and spirit, spent many hours alone with a rider, to his undoing. She could not excuse that. She was ashamed. What would he say when she told him she could see him no more?

The thought made her weak. He would accept and go his way—back to that lonely desert, with only a horse.

"Wildfire doesn't love him!" she said.

And the scarlet fired her neck and cheek and temple. That leap of blood seemed to release a riot of emotions. What had been a torment became a torture. She turned Sarchedon homeward, but scarcely had faced that way when she wheeled him again. She rode slowly and she rode swiftly. The former was hateful because it held her back—from what she no longer dared think; the latter was fearful because it hurried her on swiftly, irresistibly to her fate.

Lin Slone had changed his camp and had chosen a pass high up where the great walls had begun to break into sections. Here there was intimacy with the sheer cliffs of red and yellow. Wide avenues between the walls opened on all points of the compass, and that one to the north appeared to be a gateway down into the valley of monuments. The monuments trooped down into the valley to spread out and grow isolated in the distance. Slone's camp was in a clump of cedars surrounding a spring. There was grass and white sage where rabbits darted in and out.

Lucy did not approach this camp from that roundabout trail which she had made upon the first occasion of her visiting Slone. He had found an opening in the wall, and by riding this way into the pass Lucy cut off miles. In fact, the camp was not over fifteen miles from Bostil's Ford. It was so close that Lucy was worried lest some horse-tracker should stumble on the trail and follow her up into the pass.

This morning she espied Slone at his outlook on a high rock that had fallen from the great walls. She always looked to see if he was there, and she always saw him. The days she had not come, which were few, he had spent watching for her there. His tasks were not many, and he said he had nothing to do but wait for her. Lucy had a persistent and remorseful, yet sweet memory of Slone at his lonely lookout. Here was a fine, strong, splendid young man who had nothing to do but watch for her—a waste of precious hours!

She waved her hand from afar, and he waved in reply. Then as she reached the cedared part of the pass Slone was no longer visible. She put Sarchedon to a run up the hard, wind-swept sand, and reached the camp before Slone had climbed down from his perch.

Lucy dismounted reluctantly. What would he say about the riding-habit that she wore? She felt very curious to learn, and shyer than ever before, and altogether different. The skirt made her more of a girl, it seemed.

"Hello, Lin!" she called. There was nothing in her usual greeting to betray the state of her mind.

"Good mornin'—Lucy," he replied, very slowly. He was looking at her, she thought, with different eyes. And he seemed changed, too, though he had long been well, and his tall, lithe rider's form, his lean, strong face, and his dark eyes were admirable in her sight. Only this morning, all because she had worn a girl's riding-skirt instead of boy's chaps, everything seemed different. Perhaps her aunt had been right, after all, and now things were natural.

Slone gazed so long at her that Lucy could not keep silent. She laughed.

"How do you like—me—in this?"

"I like you much better," Slone said, bluntly.

"Auntie made this—and she's been trying to get me to ride in it."

"It changes you, Lucy. . . . But can you ride as well?"

"I'm afraid not. . . . What's Wildfire going to think of me?"

"He'll like you better, too. . . . Lucy, how's the King comin' on?"

"Lin, I'll tell you, if I wasn't as crazy about Wildfire as you are, I'd say he'll have to kill himself to beat the King," replied Lucy, with gravity.

"Sometimes I doubt, too," said Slone. "But I only have to look at Wildfire to get back my nerve. . . . Lucy, that will be the grandest race ever run!"

"Yes," sighed Lucy.

"What's wrong? Don't you want Wildfire to win?"

"Yes and no. But I'm going to beat the King, anyway. . . . Bring on your Wildfire!"

Lucy unsaddled Sarchedon and turned him loose to graze while Slone went out after Wildfire. And presently it appeared that Lucy might have some little time to wait. Wildfire had lately been trusted to hobbles, which fact made it likely that he had strayed.

Lucy gazed about her at the great looming red walls and out through the avenues to the gray desert beyond. This adventure of hers would soon have an end, for the day of the races was not far distant, and after that it was obvious she would not have occasion to meet Slone. To think of never coming to the pass again gave Lucy a pang. Unconsciously she meant that she would never ride up here again, because Slone would not be here. A wind always blew through the pass, and that was why the sand was so clean and hard. To-day it was a pleasant wind, not hot, nor laden with dust, and somehow musical in the cedars. The blue smoke from Slone's fire curled away and floated out of sight. It was lonely, with the haunting presence of the broken walls ever manifest. But the loneliness seemed full of content. She no longer wondered at Slone's desert life. That might be well for a young man, during those years when adventure and daring called him, but she doubted that it would be well for all of a man's life. And only a little of it ought to be known by a woman. She saw how the wildness and loneliness and brooding of such a life would prevent a woman's development. Yet she loved it all and wanted to live near it, so that when the need pressed her she could ride out into the great open stretches and see the dark monuments grow nearer and nearer, till she was under them, in the silent and colored shadows.

Slone returned presently with Wildfire. The stallion shone like a flame in the sunlight. His fear and hatred of Slone showed in the way he obeyed. Slone had mastered him, and must always keep the upper hand of him. It had from the first been a fight between man and beast, and Lucy believed it would always be so.

But Wildfire was a different horse when he saw Lucy. Day by day evidently Slone loved him more and tried harder to win a little of what Wildfire showed at sight of Lucy. Still Slone was proud of Lucy's control over the stallion. He was just as much heart and soul bent on winning the great race as Lucy was. She had ridden Wildfire bareback at first, and then they had broken him to the saddle.

It was serious business, that training of Wildfire, and Slone had peculiar ideas regarding it. Lucy rode him up and down the pass until he was warm. Then Slone got on Sarchedon. Wildfire always snorted and showed fight at sight of Sage King or Nagger, and the stallion Sarchedon infuriated him because Sarchedon showed fight, too. Slone started out ahead of Lucy, and then they raced down the long pass. The course was hard-packed sand. Fast as Sarchedon was, and matchless as a horseman as was Slone, the race was over almost as soon as it began. Wildfire ran indeed like fire before the wind. He wanted to run, and the other horse made him fierce. Like a burr Lucy stuck low over his neck, a part of the horse, and so light he would not have known he was carrying her but for the repeated calls in his ears. Lucy never spurred him. She absolutely refused to use spurs on him. This day she ran away from Slone, and, turning at the end of the two-mile course they had marked out, she loped Wildfire back. Slone turned with her, and they were soon in camp.

Lucy did not jump off. She was in a transport. Every race kindled a mounting fire in her. She was scarlet of face, out of breath, her hair flying. And she lay on Wildfire's neck and hugged him and caressed him and talked to him in low tones of love.

Slone dismounted and got Sarchedon out of the way, then crossed to where Lucy still fondled Wildfire. He paused a moment to look at her, but when she saw him he started again, and came close up to her as she sat the saddle.

"You went past me like a bullet," he said.

"Oh, can't he run!" murmured Lucy.

"Could he beat the King to-day?"

Slone had asked that question every day, more than once.

"Yes, he could—to-day. I know it," replied Lucy. "Oh—I get so—so excited. I—I make a fool of myself—over him. But to ride him—going like that—Lin! It's just glorious!"

"You sure can ride him," replied Slone. "I can't see a fault anywhere—in him—or in your handling him. He never breaks. He goes hard, but he saves something. He gets mad—fierce—all the time, yet he *wants* to go your way. Lucy, I never saw the like of it. Somehow you an' Wildfire make a combination. You can't be beat."

"Do I ride him—well?" she asked, softly.

"*I* could never ride him so well."

"Oh, Lin—you just want to please me. Why, Van couldn't ride with you."

"I don't care, Lucy," replied Slone, stoutly. "You rode this horse perfect. I've found fault with you on the King, on your mustangs, an' on this black horse Sarch. But on Wildfire! You grow there."

"What will Dad say, and Farlane, and Holley, and Van? Oh, I'll crow over Van," said Lucy. "I'm crazy to ride Wildfire out before all the Indians and ranchers and riders, before the races, just to show him off, to make them stare."

"No, Lucy. The best plan is to surprise them all. Enter your horse for the race, but don't show up till all the riders are at the start."

"Yes, that'll be best. . . . And, Lin, only five days more—five days!"

Her words made Slone thoughtful, and Lucy, seeing that, straightway grew thoughtful, too.

"Sure—only five days more," repeated Slone, slowly.

His tone convinced Lucy that he meant to speak again as he had spoken once before, precipitating the only quarrel they had ever had.

"Does *any one* at Bostil's Ford know you meet me out here?" he asked, suddenly.

"Only Auntie. I told her the other day. She had been watching me. She thought things. So I told her."

"What did she say?" went on Slone, curiously.

"She was mad," replied Lucy. "She scolded me. She said. . . . But, anyway, I coaxed her not to tell on me."

"I want to know what she said," spoke up the rider, deliberately.

Lucy blushed, and it was a consciousness of confusion as well as Slone's tone that made her half-angry.

"She said when I was found out there'd be a—a great fuss at the Ford. There would be talk. Auntie said I'm now a grown-up girl. . . . Oh, she carried on! . . . Bostil would likely shoot you. And if he didn't some of the riders would. . . . Oh, Lin, it was perfectly ridiculous the way Auntie talked."

"I reckon not," replied Slone. "I'm afraid I've done wrong to let you come out here. . . . But I never thought. I'm not used to girls. I'll—I'll deserve what I get for lettin' you come."

"It's my own business," declared Lucy, spiritedly. "And I guess they'd better let you alone."

Slone shook his head mournfully. He was getting one of those gloomy spells that Lucy hated. Nevertheless, she felt a stir of her pulses.

"Lucy, there won't be any doubt about my stand—when I meet Bostil," said Slone. Some thought had animated him.

"What do you mean?" Lucy trembled a little.

There was a sternness about Slone, a dignity that seemed new. "I'll ask him to—to let you marry me."

Lucy stared aghast. Slone appeared in dead earnest.

"Nonsense!" she exclaimed, shortly.

"I reckon the possibility is—that," replied Slone, bitterly, "but my motive isn't."

"It *is*. Why, you've known me only a few days. . . . Dad would be mad. Like as not he'd knock you down. . . . I tell you, Lin, my dad is—is pretty rough. And just at this time of the races. . . . And if Wildfire beats the King! . . . Whew!"

"*When* Wildfire beats the King, not *if*," corrected Slone.

"Dad will be dangerous," warned Lucy. "Please don't—don't ask him that. Then everybody would know I—I—you—you—"

"That's it. I want everybody at your home to know."

"But it's a little place," flashed Lucy. "Every one knows me. I'm the only girl. There have been—other fellows who. . . . And oh! I don't want you made fun of!"

"Why?" he asked.

Lucy turned away her head without answering. Something deep within her was softening her anger. She must fight to keep angry; and that was easy enough, she thought, if she could only keep in mind Slone's opposition to her. Strangely, she discovered that it had been sweet to find him always governed by her desire or will.

"Maybe you misunderstand," he began, presently. And his voice was not steady. "I don't forget I'm only —a beggarly rider. I couldn't have gone into the Ford at all—I was such a ragamuffin—"

"Don't talk like that!" interrupted Lucy, impatiently.

"Listen," he replied. "My askin' Bostil for you doesn't mean I've any hope. . . . It's just I want him an' everybody to know that I asked."

"But Dad—everybody will think that *you* think there's reason—why—I—why, you *ought* to ask," burst out Lucy, with scarlet face.

"Sure, that's it," he replied.

"But there's no reason. None! Not a reason under the sun," retorted Lucy, hotly. "I found you out here.

I did you a—a little service. We planned to race Wild-fire. And I came out to ride him. . . . That's all."

Slone's dark, steady gaze disconcerted Lucy. "But, no one knows me, and we've been alone in secret."

"It's not altogether—that. I—I told Auntie," faltered Lucy.

"Yes, just lately."

"Lin Slone, I'll never forgive you if you ask Dad that," declared Lucy, with startling force.

"I reckon that's not so important."

"Oh!—so you don't care." Lucy felt herself indeed in a mood not comprehensible to her. Her blood raced. She wanted to be furious with Slone, but somehow she could not wholly be so. There was something about him that made her feel small and thoughtless and selfish. Slone had hurt her pride. But the thing that she feared and resented and could not understand was the strange gladness Slone's declaration roused in her. She tried to control her temper so she could think. Two emotions contended within her—one of intense annoyance at the thought of embarrassment surely to follow Slone's action, and the other a vague, disturbing element, all sweet and furious and inexplicable. She must try to dissuade him from approaching her father.

"Please don't go to Dad." She put a hand on Slone's arm as he stood close up to Wildfire.

"I reckon I will," he said.

"Lin!" In that word there was the subtle, nameless charm of an intimacy she had never granted him until that moment. He seemed drawn as if by invisible wires. He put a shaking hand on hers and crushed her gauntleted fingers. And Lucy, in the current now of her woman's need to be placated, if not obeyed, pressed her small hand to his. How strange to what lengths a little submission to her feeling had carried her! Every spoken word, every movement, seemed to exact more from her. She did not know herself.

"Lin! . . . Promise not to—speak to Dad!"

"No." His voice rang.

"Don't give me away—don't tell my Dad!"

"What?" he queried, incredulously.

Lucy did not understand what. But his amazed voice, his wide-open eyes of bewilderment, seemed to aid her into piercing the maze of her own mind. A hundred thoughts whirled together, and all around them was wrapped the warm, strong feeling of his hand on hers. What did she mean that he would tell her father? There seemed to be a deep, hidden self in her. Up out of these depths came a whisper, like a ray of light, and it said to her that there was more hope for Lin Slone than he had ever had in one of his wildest dreams.

"Lin, if you tell Dad—then he'll know—and there *won't* be any hope for you!" cried Lucy, honestly.

If Slone caught the significance of her words he did not believe it.

"I'm goin' to Bostil after the race an' ask him. That's settled," declared Slone, stubbornly.

At this Lucy utterly lost her temper. "Oh! you—you fool!" she cried.

Slone drew back suddenly as if struck, and a spot of dark blood leaped to his lean face. "No! It seems to me the right way."

"Right or wrong there's no sense in it—because—because. Oh! can't you see?"

"I see more than I used to," he replied. "I was a fool over a horse. An' now I'm a fool over a girl. . . . I wish you'd never found me that day!"

Lucy whirled in the saddle and made Wildfire jump. She quieted him, and, leaping off, threw the bridle to Slone. "I won't ride your horse in the race!" she declared, with sudden passion. She felt herself shaking all over.

"Lucy Bostil, I wish I was as sure of Heaven as I am you'll be up on Wildfire in that race," he said.

"I won't ride your horse."

"*My* horse. Oh, I see. . . . But you'll ride Wildfire."

"I won't."

Slone suddenly turned white, and his eyes flashed

dark fire. "You won't be able to help ridin' him any more than I could help it."

"A lot you know about me, Lin Slone!" returned Lucy, with scorn. "I can be as—as bull-headed as you, any day."

Slone evidently controlled his temper, though his face remained white. He even smiled at her.

"You are Bostil's daughter," he said.

"Yes."

"You are blood an' bone, heart an' soul a rider, if any girl ever was. You're a wonder with a horse—as good as any man I ever saw. You love Wildfire. An' look—how strange! That wild stallion—that killer of horses, why he follows you, he whistles for you, he runs like lightnin' for you; he *loves* you."

Slone had attacked Lucy in her one weak point. She felt a force rending her. She dared not look at Wildfire. Yes—all that was true Slone had said. How desperately hard to think of forfeiting the great race she knew she could win!

"Never! I'll never ride your Wildfire *again!*" she said, very low.

"*Mine!* . . . So that's the trouble. Well, Wildfire won't be mine when you ride the race."

"What do you mean?" demanded Lucy. "You'll sell him to Bostil. . . . Bah! you couldn't!"

"Sell Wildfire!—after what it cost me to catch an' break him? . . . Not for all your father's lands an' horses an' money!"

Slone's voice rolled out with deep, ringing scorn. And Lucy, her temper quelled, began to feel the rider's strength, his mastery of the situation, and something vague, yet splendid about him that hurt her.

Slone strode toward her. Lucy backed against the cedar-tree and could go no farther. How white he was now! Lucy's heart gave a great, fearful leap, for she imagined Slone intended to take her in his arms. But he did not.

"When you ride—Wildfire in that—race he'll be—*yours!*" said Slone, huskily.

"How can that be?" questioned Lucy, in astonishment.

"I give him to you."

"You—give—Wildfire—to me?" gasped Lucy.

"Yes. Right now."

The rider's white face and dark eyes showed the strain of great and passionate sacrifice.

"Lin Slone! . . . I can't—understand you."

"You've got to ride Wildfire in that race. You've got to beat the King. . . . So I give Wildfire to you. An' now you can't help but ride him."

"Why—why do you give him—to me?" faltered Lucy. All her pride and temper had vanished, and she seemed lost in blankness.

"Because you love Wildfire. An' Wildfire loves you. . . . If that isn't reason enough—then . . . because I love him—as no rider ever loved a horse. . . . An' I love you as no man ever loved a girl!"

Slone had never before spoken words of love to Lucy. She dropped her head. She knew of his infatuation. But he had always been shy except once when he had been bold, and that had caused a quarrel. With a strange pain at her breast Lucy wondered why Slone had not spoken that way before? It made as great a change in her as if she had been born again. It released something. A bolt shot back in her heart. She knew she was quivering like a leaf, with no power to control her muscles. She knew if she looked up then Slone might see the depths of her soul. Even with her hands shutting out the light she thought the desert around had changed and become all mellow gold and blue and white, radiant as the moonlight of dreams— and that the monuments soared above them grandly, and were beautiful and noble, like the revelations of love and joy to her. And suddenly she found herself sitting at the foot of the cedar, weeping, with tear-wet hands over her face.

"There's nothin' to—to cry about," Slone was saying. "But I'm sorry if I hurt you."

"Will—you—please—fetch Sarch?" asked Lucy, tremulously.

While Slone went for the horse and saddled him Lucy composed herself outwardly. And she had two very strong desires—one to tell Slone something, and the other to run. She decided she would do both together.

Slone brought Sarchedon. Lucy put on her gauntlets, and, mounting the horse, she took a moment to arrange her skirts before she looked down at Slone. He was now pale, rather than white, and instead of fire in his eyes there was sadness. Lucy felt the swelling and pounding of her heart—and a long, delicious shuddering thrill that ran over her.

"Lin, I won't take Wildfire," she said.

"Yes, you will. You can't refuse. Remember he's grown to look to you. It wouldn't be right by the horse."

"But he's all you have in the world," she protested. Yet she knew any protestations would be in vain.

"No. I have good old faithful Nagger."

"Would you go try to hunt another wild stallion—like Wildfire?" asked Lucy, curiously. She was playing with the wonderful sweet consciousness of her power to render happiness when she chose.

"No more horse-huntin' for me," declared Slone. "An' as for findin' one like Wildfire—that 'd never be."

"Suppose I won't accept him?"

"How could you refuse? Not for me, but for Wildfire's sake! . . . But if you could be mean an' refuse, why, Wildfire can go back to the desert."

"No!" exclaimed Lucy.

"I reckon so."

Lucy paused a moment. How dry her tongue seemed! And her breathing was labored. An unreal shimmering gleam shone on all about her. Even the red stallion appeared enveloped in a glow. And the looming monuments looked down upon her, paternal, old, and wise, bright with the color of happiness.

"Wildfire ought to have several more days' training

—then a day of rest—and then the race," said Lucy, turning again to look at Slone.

A smile was beginning to change the hardness of his face. "Yes, Lucy," he said.

"And I'll *have* to ride him?"

"You sure will—if he's ever to beat the King."

Lucy's eyes flashed blue. She saw the crowd—the curious, friendly Indians—the eager riders—the spirited horses—the face of her father—and last the race itself, such a race as had never been run, so swift, so fierce, so wonderful.

"Then Lin," began Lucy, with a slowly heaving breast, "if I accept Wildfire will you keep him for me —until . . . and if I accept him, and tell you why, will you promise to say—"

"Don't ask me again!" interrupted Slone, hastily. "I *will* speak to Bostil."

"Wait, will you . . . promise not to say a word— a single word *to me*—till after the race?"

"A word—to you! What about?" he queried, wonderingly. Something in his eyes made Lucy think of the dawn.

"About—the— Because— Why, I'm— I'll accept your horse."

"Yes," he replied, swiftly.

Lucy settled herself in the saddle and, shortening the bridle, she got ready to spur Sarchedon into a bolt.

"Lin, I'll accept Wildfire because I love you."

Sarchedon leaped forward. Lucy did not see Slone's face nor hear him speak. Then she was tearing through the sage, out past the whistling Wildfire, with the wind sweet in her face. She did not look back.

Chapter XI

ALL through May there was an idea, dark and sinister, growing in Bostil's mind. Fiercely at first he had rejected it as utterly unworthy of the man he was. But it returned. It would not be denied. It was fostered by singular and unforeseen circumstances. The meetings with Creech, the strange, sneaking actions of young Joel Creech, and especially the gossip of riders about the improvement in Creech's swift horse—these things appeared to loom larger and larger and to augment in Bostil's mind the monstrous idea which he could not shake off. So he became brooding and gloomy.

It appeared to be an indication of his intense preoccupation of mind that he seemed unaware of Lucy's long trips down into the sage. But Bostil had observed them long before Holley and other riders had approached him with the information.

"Let her alone," he growled to his men. "I gave her orders to train the King. An' after Van got well mebbe Lucy just had a habit of ridin' down there. She can take care of herself."

To himself, when alone, Bostil muttered: "Wonder what the kid has looked up now? Some mischief, I'll bet!"

Nevertheless, he did not speak to her on the subject. Deep in his heart he knew he feared his keen-eyed daughter, and during these days he was glad she was not in evidence at the hours when he could not very well keep entirely to himself. Bostil was afraid Lucy might divine what he had on his mind. There was no one else he cared for. Holley, that old hawk-eyed rider, might see through him but Bostil knew Holley would be loyal, whatever he saw.

Toward the end of the month, when Somers returned from horse-hunting, Bostil put him and Shugrue to work upon the big flatboat down at the crossing. Bostil himself went down, and he walked—a fact apt to be considered unusual if it had been noticed.

"Put in new planks," was his order to the men. "An' pour hot tar in the cracks. Then when the tar dries shove her in . . . but I'll tell you when."

Every morning young Creech rowed over to see if the boat was ready to take the trip across to bring his father's horses back. The third morning of work on the boat Bostil met Joel down there. Joel seemed eager to speak to Bostil. He certainly was a wild-looking youth.

"Bostil, my ole man is losin' sleep waitin' to git the hosses over," he said, frankly. "Feed's almost gone."

"That'll be all right, Joel," replied Bostil. "You see, the river ain't begun to raise yet. . . . How're the hosses comin' on?"

"Grand, sir—grand!" exclaimed the simple Joel. "Peg is runnin' faster than last year, but Blue Roan is leavin' her a mile. Dad's goin' to bet all he has. The roan can't lose this year."

Bostil felt like a bull bayed at by a hound. Blue Roan was a young horse, and every season he had grown bigger and faster. The King had reached the limit of his speed. That was great, Bostil knew, and enough to win over any horse in the uplands, providing the luck of the race fell even. Luck, however, was a fickle thing.

"I was advisin' Dad to swim the hosses over," declared Joel, deliberately.

"A-huh! You was? . . . An' why?" rejoined Bostil.

Joel's simplicity and frankness vanished, and with them his rationality. He looked queer. His contrasting eyes shot little malignant gleams. He muttered incoherently, and moved back toward the skiff, making violent gestures, and his muttering grew to shouting, though still incoherent. He got in the boat and started to row back over the river.

"Sure he's got a screw loose," observed Somers.

Shugrue tapped his grizzled head significantly.

Bostil made no comment. He strode away from his men down to the river shore, and, finding a seat on a stone, he studied the slow eddying red current of the river and he listened. If any man knew the strange and remorseless Colorado, that man was Bostil. He never made any mistakes in anticipating what the river was going to do.

And now he listened, as if indeed the sullen, low roar, the murmuring hollow gurgle, the sudden strange splash, were spoken words meant for his ears alone. The river was low. It seemed tired out. It was a dirty red in color, and it swirled and flowed along lingeringly. At times the current was almost imperceptible; and then again it moved at varying speed. It seemed a petulant, waiting, yet inevitable stream, with some remorseless end before it. It had a thousand voices, but not the one Bostil listened to hear.

He plodded gloomily up the trail, resting in the quiet, dark places of the cañon, loath to climb out into the clear light of day. And once in the village, Bostil shook himself as if to cast off an evil, ever-present, pressing spell.

The races were now only a few days off. Piutes and Navajos were camped out on the sage, and hourly the number grew as more came in. They were building cedar sunshades. Columns of blue smoke curled up here and there. Mustangs and ponies grazed everywhere, and a line of Indians extended along the racecourse, where trials were being held. The village was full of riders, horse-traders and hunters, and ranchers. Work on the ranges had practically stopped for the time being, and in another day or so every inhabitant of the country would be in Bostil's Ford.

Bostil walked into the village, grimly conscious that the presence of the Indians and riders and horses, the action and color and bustle, the near approach of the great race-day—these things that in former years had brought him keen delight and speculation—had somehow lost their tang. He had changed. Something was wrong in him. But he must go among these visitors and welcome them as of old; he who had always been the life of these racing-days must be outwardly the same. And the task was all the harder because of the pleasure shown by old friends among the Indians and the riders at meeting him. Bostil knew he had been a cunning horse-trader, but he had likewise been a good friend. Many were the riders and Indians who owed much to him. So everywhere he was hailed and beseiged, until finally the old excitement of betting and bantering took hold of him and he forgot his brooding.

Brackton's place, as always, was a headquarters for all visitors. Macomber had just come in full of enthusiasm and pride over the horse he had entered, and he had money to wager. Two Navajo chiefs, called by white men Old Horse and Silver, were there for the first time in years. They were ready to gamble horse against horse. Cal Blinn and his riders of Durango had arrived; likewise Colson, Sticks, and Burthwait, old friends and rivals of Bostil's.

For a while Brackton's was merry. There was some drinking and much betting. It was characteristic of Bostil that he would give any odds asked on the King in a race; and, furthermore, he would take any end of wagers on other horses. As far as his own horses were concerned he bet shrewdly, but in races where his horses did not figure he seemed to find fun in the betting, whether or not he won.

The fact remained, however, that there were only two wagers against the King, and both were put up by Indians. Macomber was betting on second or third place for his horse in the big race. No odds of Bostil's tempted him.

"Say, where's Wetherby?" rolled out Bostil. "He'll back his hoss."

"Wetherby's ridin' over to-morrow," replied Macomber. "But you gotta bet him two to one."

"See hyar, Bostil," spoke up old Cal Blinn, "you jest wait till I git an eye on the King's runnin'. Mebbe I'll go you even money."

"An as fer me, Bostil," said Colson, "I ain't set up yit which hoss I'll race."

Burthwait, an old rider, came forward to Brackton's desk and entered a wager against the field that made all the men gasp.

"By George! pard, you ain't a-limpin' along!" ejaculated Bostil, admiringly, and he put a hand on the other's shoulder.

"Bostil, I've a grand hoss," replied Burthwait. "He's four years old, I guess, fer he was born wild, an' you never seen him."

"Wild hoss? . . . Huh!" growled Bostil. "You must think he can run."

"Why, Bostil, a streak of lightnin' ain't anywheres with him."

"Wal, I'm glad to hear it," said Bostil, gruffly. "Brack, how many hosses entered now for the big race?"

The lean, gray Brackton bent earnestly over his soiled ledger, while the riders and horsemen round him grew silent to listen.

"Thar's the Sage King, by Bostil," replied Brackton. "Blue Roan an' Peg, by Creech; Whitefoot, by Macomber; Rocks, by Holley; Hossshoes, by Blinn; Bay Charley, by Burthwait. Then thar's the two mustangs entered by Old Hoss an' Silver—an' last—Wildfire, by Lucy Bostil."

"What's thet last?" queried Bostil.

"Wildfire, by Lucy Bostil," repeated Brackton.

"Has the girl gone an' entered a hoss?"

"She sure has. She came in to-day, regular an' business-like, writ her name an' her hoss's—here 'tis—an' put up the entrance money."

"Wal, I'll be d—d!" exclaimed Bostil. He was astonished and pleased. "She said she'd do it. But I didn't take no stock in her talk. . . . An' the hoss's name?"

"Wildfire."

"Huh! . . . Wildfire. Mebbe thet girl can't think of names for hosses! What's this hoss she calls Wildfire?"

"She sure didn't say," replied Brackton. "Holley an' Van an' some more of the boys was here. They joked her a little. You oughter seen the look Lucy give them. But fer once she seemed mum. She jest walked away mysterious like."

"Lucy's got a pony off some Indian, I reckon," returned Bostil, and he laughed. "Then thet makes ten hosses entered so far?"

"Right. An' there's sure to be one more. I guess the track's wide enough for twelve."

"Wal, Brack, there'll likely be one hoss out in front an' some stretched out behind," replied Bostil, dryly. "The track's sure wide enough."

"Won't thet be a grand race!" exclaimed an enthusiastic rider. "Wisht I had about a million to bet!"

"Bostil, I 'most forgot," went on Brackton, "Cordts sent word by the Piutes who come to-day thet he'd be here sure."

Bostil's face subtly changed. The light seemed to leave it. He did not reply to Brackton—did not show that he heard the comment on all sides. Public opinion was against Bostil's permission to allow Cordts and his horse-thieves to attend the races. Bostil appeared grave, regretful. Yet it was known by all that in the strangeness and perversity of his rider's nature he wanted Cordts to see the King win that race. It was his rider's vanity and defiance in the teeth of a great horse-thief. But no good would come of Cordts's presence—that much was manifest.

There was a moment of silence. All these men, if they did not fear Bostil, were sometimes uneasy when near him. Some who were more reckless than discreet liked to irritate him. That, too, was a rider's weakness.

"When's Creech's hosses comin' over?" asked Colson, with sudden interest.

"Wal, I reckon—soon," replied Bostil, constrainedly, and he turned away.

By the time he got home all the excitement of the past hour had left him and gloom again abided in his mind. He avoided his daughter and forgot the fact of her entering a horse in the race. He ate supper alone, without speaking to his sister. Then in the dusk he went out to the corrals and called the King to the fence. There was love between master and horse. Bostil talked low, like a woman, to Sage King. And the hard old rider's heart was full and a lump swelled in his throat, for contact with the King reminded him that other men loved other horses.

Bostil returned to the house and went to his room, where he sat thinking in the dark. By and by all was quiet. Then seemingly with a wrench he bestirred himself and did what for him was a strange action. Removing his boots, he put on a pair of moccasins. He slipped out of the house; he kept to the flagstone of the walk; he took to the sage till out of the village, and then he sheered round to the river trail. With the step and sureness and the eyes of an Indian he went down through that pitch-black cañon to the river and the ford.

The river seemed absolutely the same as during the day. He peered through the dark opaqueness of gloom. It moved there, the river he knew, shadowy, mysterious, murmuring. Bostil went down to the edge of the water, and, sitting there, he listened. Yes—the voices of the stream were the same. But after a long time he imagined there was among them an infinitely low voice, as if from a great distance. He imagined this; he doubted; he made sure; and then all seemed fancy again. His mind held only one idea and was riveted round it. He strained his hearing, so long, so intently, that at last he knew he had heard what he was longing for. Then in the gloom he took to the trail, and returned home as he had left, stealthily, like an Indian.

But Bostil did not sleep nor rest.

Next morning early he rode down to the river. Somers and Shugrue had finished the boat and were waiting. Other men were there, curious and eager. Joel Creech, barefooted and ragged, with hollow eyes and strange actions, paced the sands.

The boat was lying bottom up. Bostil examined the

new planking and the seams. Then he straightened his form.

"Turn her over," he ordered. "Shove her in. An' let her soak up to-day."

The men seemed glad and relieved. Joel Creech heard and he came near to Bostil.

"You'll—you'll fetch Dad's hosses over?" he queried.

"Sure. To-morrow," replied Bostil, cheerily.

Joel smiled, and that smile showed what might have been possible for him under kinder conditions of life. "Now, Bostil, I'm sorry fer what I said," blurted Joel.

"Shut up. Go tell your old man."

Joel ran down to his skiff and, leaping in, began to row vigorously across. Bostil watched while the workmen turned the boat over and slid it off the sand-bar and tied it securely to the mooring. Bostil observed that not a man there saw anything unusual about the river. But, for that matter, there was nothing to see. The river was the same.

That night when all was quiet in and around the village Bostil emerged from his house and took to his stealthy stalk down toward the river.

The moment he got out into the night oppression left him. How interminable the hours had been! Suspense, doubt, anxiety, fear no longer burdened him. The night was dark, with only a few stars, and the air was cool. A soft wind blew across his heated face. A neighbor's dog, baying dismally, startled Bostil. He halted to listen, then stole on under the cottonwoods, through the sage, down the trail, into the jet-black cañon. Yet he found his way as if it had been light. In the darkness of his room he had been a slave to his indecision; now in the darkness of the looming cliffs he was free, resolved, immutable.

The distance seemed short. He passed out of the narrow cañon, skirted the gorge over the river, and hurried down into the shadowy amphitheater under the looming walls.

The boat lay at the mooring, one end resting lightly on the sand-bar. With strong, nervous clutch Bostil felt the knots of the cables. Then he peered into the opaque gloom of that strange and huge V-shaped split between the great cañon walls. Bostil's mind had begun to relax from the single idea. Was he alone? Except for the low murmur of the river there was dead silence—a silence like no other—a silence which seemed held under imprisoning walls. Yet Bostil peered long into the shadows. Then he looked up. The ragged ramparts far above frowned bold and black at a few cold stars, and the blue of its sky was without the usual velvety brightness. How far it was up to that corrugated rim! All of a sudden Bostil hated this vast ebony pit.

He strode down to the water and, sitting upon the stone he had occupied so often, he listened. He turned his ear up-stream, then down-stream, and to the side, and again up-stream and listened.

The river seemed the same.

It was slow, heavy, listless, eddying, lingering, moving—the same apparently as for days past. It splashed very softly and murmured low and gurgled faintly. It gave forth fitful little swishes and musical tinkles and lapping sounds. It was flowing water, yet the proof was there of tardiness. Now it was almost still, and then again it moved on. It was a river of mystery telling a lie with its low music. As Bostil listened all those soft, watery sounds merged into what seemed a moaning, and that moaning held a roar so low as to be only distinguishable to the ear trained by years.

No—the river was not the same. For the voice of its soft moaning showed to Bostil its meaning. It called from the far north—the north of great ice-clad peaks beginning to glisten under the nearing sun; of vast snow-filled cañons dripping and melting; of the crystal brooks suddenly colored and roiled and filled bank-full along the mountain meadows; of many brooks plunging down and down, rolling the rocks, to pour their volume into the growing turbid streams on the slopes. It was the voice of all that widely separated water spilled suddenly with magical power into the desert river to make it a mighty, thundering torrent, red and defiled, terrible in its increasing onslaught into the cañon, deep, ponderous, but swift—the Colorado in flood.

And as Bostil heard that voice he trembled. What was the thing he meant to do? A thousand thoughts assailed him in answer and none were clear. A chill passed over him. Suddenly he felt that the cold stole up from his feet. They were both in the water. He pulled them out and, bending down, watched the dim, dark line of water. It moved up and up, inch by inch, swiftly. The river was on the rise!

Bostil leaped up. He seemed possessed of devils. A rippling hot gush of blood fired his every vein and tremor after tremor shook him.

"By G—d! I had it right—she's risin'!" he exclaimed, hoarsely.

He stared in fascinated certainty at the river. All about it and pertaining to it had changed. The murmur and moan changed to a low, sullen roar. The music was gone. The current chafed at its rock-bound confines. Here was an uneasy, tormented, driven river! The light from the stars shone on dark, glancing, restless waters, uneven and strange. And while Bostil watched, whether it was a short time or long, the remorseless, destructive nature of the river showed itself.

Bostil began to pace the sands. He thought of those beautiful race-horses across the river.

"It's not too late!" he muttered. "I can get the boat over an' back—yet!"

He knew that on the morrow the Colorado in flood would bar those horses, imprison them in a barren cañon, shut them in to starve.

"It'd be hellish! . . . Bostil, you can't do it. You ain't thet kind of a man. . . . Bostil poison a water-hole where hosses loved to drink, or burn over grass! . . . What would Lucy think of you? . . . No, Bostil, you've let spite rule bad. Hurry now and save them hosses!"

He strode down to the boat. It swung clear now, and there was water between it and the shore. Bostil laid hold of the cables. As he did so he thought of Creech and a blackness enfolded him. He forgot Creech's horses. Something gripped him, burned him—some hard and bitter feeling which he thought was hate of Creech. Again the wave of fire ran over him, and his huge hands strained on the cables. The fiend of that fiendish river had entered his soul. He meant ruin to a man. He meant more than ruin. He meant to destroy what his enemy, his rival loved. The darkness all about him, the gloom and sinister shadow of the cañon, the sullen increasing roar of the river—these lent their influence to the deed, encouraged him, drove him onward, fought and strangled the resistance in his heart. As he brooded all the motives for the deed grew like that remorseless river. Had not his enemy's son shot at him from ambush? Was not his very life at stake? A terrible blow must be dealt Creech, one that would crush him or else lend him manhood enough to come forth with a gun. Bostil, in his torment, divined that Creech would know who had ruined him. They would meet then, as Bostil had tried more than once to bring about a meeting. Bostil saw into his soul, and it was a gulf like this cañon pit where the dark and sullen river raged. He shrank at what he saw, but the furies of passion held him fast. His hands tore at the cables. Then he fell to pacing to and fro in the gloom. Every moment the river changed its voice. In an hour flood would be down. Too late, then! Bostil again remembered the sleek, slim, racy thoroughbreds—Blue Roan, a wild horse he had longed to own, and Peg, a mare that had no equal in the uplands. Where did Bostil's hate of a man stand in comparison with love of a horse? He began to sweat and the sweat burned him.

"How soon 'll Creech hear the river an' know what's comin'?" muttered Bostil, darkly. And that question showed him how he was lost. All this strife of doubt and fear and horror were of no use. He meant to doom Creech's horses. The thing had been unalterable from the inception of the insidious, hateful idea. It was irresistible. He grew strong, hard, fierce, and implacable. He found himself. He strode back to the cables. The knots, having dragged in the water, were soaking wet and swollen. He could not untie them. Then he cut one strand after another. The boat swung out beyond his reach.

Instinctively Bostil reached to pull it back.

"My God! . . . It's goin'!" he whispered. "What have I done?"

He—Bostil—who had made this Crossing of the Fathers more famous as Bostil's Ford—he—to cut the boat adrift! The thing was inconceivable.

The roar of the river rose weird and mournful and incessant, with few breaks, and these were marked by strange ripping and splashing sounds made as the bulges of water broke on the surface. Twenty feet out the boat floated, turning a little as it drifted. It seemed loath to leave. It held on the shore eddy. Hungrily, spitefully the little, heavy waves lapped it. Bostil watched it with dilating eyes. There! the current caught one end and the water rose in a hollow splash over the corner. An invisible hand, like a mighty giant's, seemed to swing the boat out. It had been dark; now it was opaque, now shadowy, now dim. How swift this cursed river! Was there any way in which Bostil could recover his boat? The river answered him with hollow, deep mockery. Despair seized upon him. And the vague shape of the boat, spectral and instinct with meaning, passed from Bostil's strained gaze.

"So help me God, I've done it!" he groaned, hoarsely. And he staggered back and sat down. Mind and heart and soul were suddenly and exquisitely acute to the shame of his act. Remorse seized upon his vitals. He suffered physical agony, as if a wolf gnawed him internally.

"To hell with Creech an' his hosses, but where do I come in as a man?" he whispered. And he sat there, arms tight around his knees, locked both mentally and physically into inaction.

The rising water broke the spell and drove him back. The river was creeping no longer. It swelled. And the roar likewise swelled. Bostil hurried across the flat to get to the rocky trail before he was cut off, and the last few rods he waded in water up to his knees.

"I'll leave no trail there," he muttered, with a hard laugh. It sounded ghastly to him, like the laugh of the river.

And there at the foot of the rocky trail he halted to watch and listen. The old memorable boom came to his ears. The flood was coming. For twenty-three years he had heard the vanguard boom of the Colorado in flood. But never like this, for in the sound he heard the strife and passion of his blood, and realized himself a human counterpart of that remorseless river. The moments passed and each one saw a swelling of the volume of sound. The sullen roar just below him was gradually lost in a distant roar. A steady wind now blew through the cañon. The great walls seemed to gape wider to prepare for the torrent. Bostil backed slowly up the trail as foot by foot the water rose. The floor of the amphitheater was now a lake of choppy, angry waves. The willows bent and seethed in the edge of the current. Beyond ran an uneven, bulging mass that resembled some gray, heavy moving monster. In the gloom Bostil could see how the river turned a corner of wall and slanted away from it toward the center, where it rose higher. Black objects that must have been driftwood appeared on this crest. They showed an instant, then flashed out of sight. The boom grew steadier, closer, louder, and the reverberations, like low detonations of thunder, were less noticeable because all sounds were being swallowed up.

A harder breeze puffed into Bostil's face. It brought a tremendous thunder, as if all the colossal walls were falling in avalanche. Bostil knew the crest of the flood had turned the corner above and would soon reach him. He watched. He listened, but sound had ceased. His ears seemed ringing and they hurt. All his body felt cold, and he backed up and up, with dead feet.

The shadows of the cañon lightened. A river-wide froth, like a curtain, moved down, spreading mushroom-wise· before it, a rolling, heaving maelstrom. Bostil ran to escape the great wave that surged into the amphitheater, up and up the rocky trail. When he turned again he seemed to look down into hell. Murky depths, streaked by pale gleams, and black, sinister, changing forms yawned beneath them. He watched with fixed eyes until once more the feeling of filled ears left him and an awful thundering boom assured him of actualities. It was only the Colorado in flood.

Chapter XII

BOSTIL slept that night, but his sleep was troubled, and a strange, dreadful roar seemed to run through it, like a mournful wind over a dark desert. He was awakened early by a voice at his window. He listened. There came a rap on the wood.

"Bostil! . . . Bostil!" It was Holley's voice.

Bostil rolled off the bed. He had slept without removing any apparel except his boots.

"Wal, Hawk, what d'ye mean wakin' a man at this unholy hour?" growled Bostil.

Holley's face appeared above the rude sill. It was pale and grave, with the hawk eyes like glass. "It ain't so awful early," he said. "Listen, boss."

Bostil halted in the act of pulling on a boot. He looked at his man while he listened. The still air outside seemed filled with a low boom, like thunder at a distance. Bostil tried to look astounded.

"Hell! . . . It's the Colorado! She's boomin'!"

"Reckon it's hell- all right—for Creech," replied Holley. "Boss, why didn't you fetch them hosses over?"

Bostil's face darkened. He was a bad man to oppose

—to question at times. "Holley, you're sure powerful anxious about Creech. Are you his friend?"

"Naw! I've little use fer Creech," replied Holley. "An, you know thet. But I hold for his hosses as I would any man's."

"A-huh! An' what's your kick?"

"Nothin'—except you could have fetched them over before the flood come down. That's all."

The old horse-trader and his right-hand rider looked at each other for a moment in silence. They understood each other. Then Bostil returned to the task of pulling on wet boots and Holley went away.

Bostil opened his door and stepped outside. The eastern ramparts of the desert were bright red with the rising sun. With the night behind him and the morning cool and bright and beautiful, Bostil did not suffer a pang nor feel a regret. He walked around under the cottonwoods where the mocking-birds were singing. The shrill, screeching bray of a burro split the morning stillness, and with that the sounds of the awakening village drowned that sullen, dreadful boom of the river. Bostil went in to breakfast.

He encountered Lucy in the kitchen, and he did not avoid her. He could tell from her smiling greeting that he seemed to her his old self again. Lucy wore an apron and she had her sleeves rolled up, showing round, strong, brown arms. Somehow to Bostil she seemed different. She had been pretty, but now she was more than that. She was radiant. Her blue eyes danced. She looked excited. She had been telling her aunt something, and that worthy woman appeared at once shocked and delighted. But Bostil's entrance had caused a mysterious break in everything that had been going on, except the preparation of the morning meal.

"Now I rode in on some confab or other, that's sure," said Bostil, good-naturedly.

"You sure did, Dad," replied Lucy, with a bright smile.

"Wal, let me sit in the game," he rejoined.

"Dad, you can't even ante," said Lucy.

"Jane, what's this kid up to?" asked Bostil, turning to his sister.

"The good Lord only knows!" replied Aunt Jane, with a sigh.

"Kid? . . . See here, Dad, I'm eighteen long ago. I'm grown up. I can do as I please, go where I like, and anything. . . . Why, Dad, I could get—married."

"Haw! haw!" laughed Bostil. "Jane, hear the girl."

"I hear her, Bostil," sighed Aunt Jane.

"Wal, Lucy, I'd just like to see you fetch some fool love-sick rider around when I'm feelin' good," said Bostil.

Lucy laughed, but there was a roguish, daring flash in her eyes. "Dad, you do seem to have all the young fellows scared. Some day maybe one will ride along— a rider like you used to be—that nobody could bluff. . . . And he can have me!"

"A-huh! . . . Lucy, are you in fun?"

Lucy tossed her bright head, but did not answer.

"Jane, what's got into her?" asked Bostil, appealing to his sister.

"Bostil, she's in fun, of course," declared Aunt Jane. "Still, at that, there's some sense in what she says. Come to your breakfast, now."

Bostil took his seat at the table, glad that he could once more be amiable with his women-folk. "Lucy, to-morrow 'll be the biggest day Bostil's Ford ever seen," he said.

"It sure will be, Dad. The biggest *surprising* day the Ford ever had," replied Lucy.

"Surprisin'?"

"Yes, Dad."

"Who's goin' to get surprised?"

"Everybody."

Bostil said to himself that he had been used to Lucy's banter, but during his moody spell of days past he had forgotten how to take her or else she was different.

"Brackton tells me you've entered a hoss against the field."

"It's an open race, isn't it?"

"Open as the desert, Lucy," he replied. "What's this hoss Wildfire you've entered?"

"Wouldn't you like to know?" taunted Lucy.

"If he's as good as his name you might be in at the finish. . . . But, Lucy, my dear, talkin' good sense now —you ain't a-goin' to go up on some unbroken mustang in this big race?"

"Dad, I'm going to ride a horse."

"But, Lucy, ain't it a risk you'll be takin'—all for fun?"

"Fun! . . . I'm in dead earnest."

Bostil liked the look of her then. She had paled a little; her eyes blazed; she was intense. His question had brought out her earnestness, and straightway Bostil became thoughtful. If Lucy had been a boy she would have been the greatest rider on the uplands; and even girl as she was, superbly mounted, she would have been dangerous in any race.

"Wal, I ain't afraid of your handlin' of a hoss," he said, soberly. "An' as long as you're in earnest I won't stop you. But, Lucy, no bettin'. I won't let you gamble."

"Not even with you?" she coaxed.

Bostil stared at the girl. What had gotten into her? "What'll you bet?" he queried, with blunt curiosity.

"Dad, I'll go you a hundred dollars in gold that I finish one—two—three."

Bostil threw back his head to laugh heartily. What a chip of the old block she was! "Child, there's some fast hosses that'll be back of the King. You'd be throwin' away money."

Blue fire shone in his daughter's eyes. She meant business, all right, and Bostil thrilled with pride in her.

"Dad, I'll bet you two hundred, even, that I beat the King!" she flashed.

"Wal, of all the nerve!" ejaculated Bostil. "No, I won't take you up. Reckon I never before turned down an even bet. Understand, Lucy, ridin' in the race is enough for you."

"All right, Dad," replied Lucy, obediently.

At that juncture Bostil suddenly shoved back his plate and turned his face to the open door. "Don't I hear a runnin' hoss?"

Aunt Jane stopped the noise she was making, and Lucy darted to the door. Then Bostil heard the sharp, rhythmic hoof-beats he recognized. They shortened to clatter and pound—then ceased somewhere out in front of the house.

"It's the King with Van up," said Lucy, from the door. "Dad, Van's jumped off—he's coming in . . . he's running. Something has happened. . . . There are other horses coming—riders—Indians."

Bostil knew what was coming and prepared himself. Rapid footsteps sounded without.

"Hello, Miss Lucy! Where's Bostil?"

A lean, supple rider appeared before the door. It was Van, greatly excited.

"Come in, boy," said Bostil. "What're you flustered about?"

Van strode in, spurs jangling, cap in hand. "Boss, there's—a sixty-foot raise—in the river!" Van panted.

"Oh!" cried Lucy, wheeling toward her father.

"Wal, Van, I reckon I knowed thet," replied Bostil. "Mebbe I'm gettin' old, but I can still hear. . . . Listen."

Lucy tiptoed to the door and turned her head side-wise and slowly bowed it till she stiffened. Outside were sounds of birds and horses and men, but when a lull came it quickly filled with a sullen, low boom.

"Highest flood we—ever seen," said Van.

"You've been down?" queried Bostil, sharply.

"Not to the river," replied Van. "I went as far as —where the gulch opens—on the bluff. There was a string of Navajos goin' down. An' some comin' up. I stayed there watchin' the flood, an' pretty soon Somers come up the trail with Blakesley an' Brack an' some riders. . . . An' Somers hollered out, 'The boat's gone!' "

"Gone!" exclaimed Bostil, his loud cry showing consternation.

"Oh, Dad! Oh, Van!" cried Lucy, with eyes wide and lips parted.

"Sure she's gone. An' the whole place down there—where the willows was an' the sand-bar—it was deep under water."

"What will become of Creech's horses?" asked Lucy, breathlessly.

"My God! ain't it a shame!" went on Bostil, and he could have laughed aloud at his hypocrisy. He felt Lucy's blue eyes riveted upon his face.

"Thet's what we all was sayin'," went on Van. "While we was watchin' the awful flood an' listenin' to the deep bum—bum—bum of rollin' rocks some one seen Creech an' two Piutes leadin' the hosses up thet trail where the slide was. We counted the hosses—nine. An' we saw the roan shine blue in the sunlight."

"Piutes with Creech!" exclaimed Bostil, the deep gloom in his eyes lighting. "By all thet's lucky! Mebbe them Indians can climb the hosses out of thet hole an' find water an' grass enough."

"Mebbe," replied Van, doubtfully. "Sure them Piutes could if there's a chance. But there ain't any grass."

"It won't take much grass travelin' by night."

"So lots of the boys say. But the Navajos they shook their heads. An' Farlane an' Holley, why, they jest held up their hands."

"With them Indians Creech has a chance to get his hosses out," declared Bostil. He was sure of his sincerity, but he was not certain that his sincerity was not the birth of a strange, sudden hope. And then he was able to meet the eyes of his daughter. That was his supreme test.

"Oh, Dad, why, why didn't you hurry Creech's horses over?" said Lucy, with her tears falling.

Something tight within Bostil's breast seemed to ease and lessen. "Why didn't I? . . . Wal, Lucy, I reckon I wasn't in no hurry to oblige Creech. I'm sorry now."

"It won't be so terrible if he doesn't lose the horses," murmured Lucy.

"Where's young Joel Creech?" asked Bostil.

"He stayed on this side last night," replied Van. "Fact is, Joel's the one who first knew the flood was on. Some one said he said he slept in the cañon last night. Anyway, he's ravin' crazy now. An' if he doesn't do harm to some one or hisself I'll miss my guess."

"A-huh!" grunted Bostil. "Right you are."

"Dad, can't anything be done to help Creech now?" appealed Lucy, going close to her father.

Bostil put his arm around her and felt immeasurably relieved to have the golden head press close to his shoulder. "Child, we can't fly acrost the river. Now don't you cry about Creech's hosses. They ain't starved yet. It's hard luck. But mebbe it'll turn out so Creech 'll lose only the race. An', Lucy, it was a dead sure bet he'd have lost thet anyway."

Bostil fondled his daughter a moment, the first time in many a day, and then he turned to his rider at the door. "Van, how's the King?"

"Wild to run, Bostil, jest plumb wild. There won't be any hoss with the ghost of a show to-morrow."

Lucy raised her drooping head. "Is *that* so, Van Sickle? . . . Listen here. If you and Sage King don't get more wild running to-morrow than you ever had I'll never ride again!" With this retort Lucy left the room.

Van stared at the door and then at Bostil. "What'd I say, Bostil?" he asked, plaintively. "I'm always r'ilin' her."

"Cheer up, Van. You didn't say much. Lucy is fiery these days. She's got a hoss somewhere an' she's goin' to ride him in the race. She offered to bet on him— against the King! It certainly beat me all hollow. But see here, Van. I've a hunch there's a dark hoss goin' to show up in this race. So don't underrate Lucy an' her mount, whatever he is. She calls him Wildfire. Ever see him?"

"I sure haven't. Fact is, I haven't seen Lucy for days an' days. As for the hunch you gave, I'll say I was figurin' Lucy for some real race. Bostil, she doesn't *make* a hoss run. He'll run jest to please her. An'

Lucy's lighter 'n a feather. Why, Bostil, if she happened to ride out there on Blue Roan or some other hoss as fast I'd—I'd jest wilt."

Bostil uttered a laugh full of pride in his daughter. "Wal, she won't show up on Blue Roan," he replied, with grim gruffness. "Thet's sure as death. . . . Come on out now. I want a look at the King."

Bostil went into the village. All day long he was so busy with a thousand and one things referred to him, put on him, undertaken by him, that he had no time to think. Back in his mind, however, there was a burden of which he was vaguely conscious all the time. He worked late into the night and slept late the next morning.

Never in his life had Bostil been gloomy or retrospective on the day of a race. In the press of matters he had only a word for Lucy, but that earned a saucy, dauntless look. He was glad when he was able to join the procession of villagers, visitors, and Indians moving out toward the sage.

The racecourse lay at the foot of the slope, and now the gray and purple sage was dotted with more horses and Indians, more moving things and colors, than Bostil had ever seen there before. It was a spectacle that stirred him. Many fires sent up blue columns of smoke from before the hastily built brush huts where the Indians cooked and ate. Blankets shone bright in the sun; burros grazed and brayed; horses whistled piercingly across the slope; Indians lolled before the huts or talked in groups, sitting and lounging on their ponies; down in the valley, here and there, were Indians racing, and others were chasing the wiry mustangs. Beyond this gay and colorful spectacle stretched the valley, merging into the desert marked so strikingly and beautifully by the monuments.

Bostil was among the last to ride down to the high bench that overlooked the home end of the racecourse. He calculated that there were a thousand Indians and whites congregated at that point, which was the best vantage-ground to see the finish of a race. And the occasion of his arrival, for all the gaiety, was one of dignity and importance. If Bostil reveled in anything it was in an hour like this. His liberality made this event a great race-day. The thoroughbreds were all there, blanketed, in charge of watchful riders. In the center of the brow of this long bench lay a huge, flat rock which had been Bostil's seat in the watching of many a race. Here were assembled his neighbors and visitors actively interested in the races, and also the important Indians of both tribes, all waiting for him.

As Bostil dismounted, throwing the bridle to a rider, he saw a face that suddenly froze the thrilling delight of the moment. A tall, gaunt man with cavernous black eyes and huge, drooping black mustache fronted him and seemed waiting. Cordts! Bostil had forgotten. Instinctively Bostil stood on guard. For years he had prepared himself for the moment when he would come face to face with this noted horse-thief.

"Bostil, how are you?" said Cordts. He appeared pleasant, and certainly grateful for being permitted to come there. From his left hand hung a belt containing two heavy guns.

"Hello, Cordts," replied Bostil, slowly unbending. Then he met the other's proffered hand.

"I've bet heavy on the King," said Cordts.

For the moment there could have been no other way to Bostil's good graces, and this remark made the gruff old rider's hard face relax.

"Wal, I was hopin' you'd back some other hoss, so I could take your money," replied Bostil.

Cordts held out the belt and guns to Bostil. "I want to enjoy this race," he said, with a smile that somehow hinted of the years he had packed those guns day and night.

"Cordts, I don't want to take your guns," replied Bostil, bluntly. "I've taken your word an' that's enough."

"Thanks, Bostil. All the same, as I'm your guest I won't pack them," returned Cordts, and he hung the belt on the horn of Bostil's saddle. "Some of my men are with me. They were all right till they got outside of Brackton's whisky. But now I won't answer for them."

"Wal, you're square to say thet," replied Bostil. "An' I'll run this race an' answer for everybody."

Bostil recognized Hutchinson and Dick Sears, but the others of Cordts's gang he did not know. They were a hard-looking lot. Hutchinson was a spare, stoop-shouldered, red-faced, squinty-eyed rider, branded all over with the marks of a bad man. And Dick Sears looked his notoriety. He was a little knot of muscle, short and bow-legged, rough in appearance as cactus. He wore a ragged slouch-hat pulled low down. His face and stubby beard were dust-colored, and his eyes seemed sullen, watchful. He made Bostil think of a dusty, scaly, hard, desert rattlesnake. Bostil eyed this right-hand man of Cordts's and certainly felt no fear of him, though Sears had the fame of swift and deadly skill with a gun. Bostil felt that he was neither afraid nor loath to face Sears in gun-play, and he gazed at the little horse-thief in a manner that no one could mistake. Sears was not drunk, neither was he wholly free from the unsteadiness caused by the bottle. Assuredly he had no fear of Bostil and eyed him insolently. Bostil turned away to the group of his riders and friends, and he asked for his daughter.

"Lucy's over there," said Farlane, pointing to a merry crowd.

Bostil waved a hand to her, and Lucy, evidently mistaking his action, came forward, leading one of her ponies. She wore a gray blouse with a red scarf, and a skirt over overalls and boots. She looked pale, but she was smiling, and there was a dark gleam of excitement in her blue eyes. She did not have on her sombrero. She wore her hair in a braid, and had a red band tight above her forehead. Bostil took her in all at a glance. She meant business and she looked dangerous. Bostil knew once she slipped out of that skirt she could ride with any rider there. He saw that she had become the center toward which all eyes shifted. It pleased him. She was his, like her mother, and as beautiful and thoroughbred as any rider could wish his daughter.

"Lucy, where's your hoss?" he asked, curiously.

"Never you mind, Dad. I'll be there at the finish," she replied.

"Red's your color for to-day, then?" he questioned, as he put a big hand on the bright-banded head.

She nodded archly.

"Lucy, I never thought you'd flaunt red in your old Dad's face. Red, when the color of the King is like the sage out yonder. You've gone back on the King."

"No, Dad, I never was for Sage King, else I wouldn't wear red to-day."

"Child, you sure mean to run in this race—the big one?"

"Sure and certain."

"Wal, the only bitter drop in my cup to-day will be seein' you get beat. But if you run second I'll give you a present thet 'll make the purse look sick."

Even the Indian chiefs were smiling. Old Horse, the Navajo, beamed benignly upon this daughter of the friend of the Indians. Silver, his brother chieftain, nodded as if he understood Bostil's pride and regret. Some of the young riders showed their hearts in their eyes. Farlane tried to look mysterious, to pretend he was in Lucy's confidence.

"Lucy, if you are really goin' to race I'll withdraw my hoss so you can win," said Wetherby, gallantly.

Bostil's sonorous laugh rolled down the slope.

"Miss Lucy, I sure hate to run a hoss against yours," said old Cal Blinn. Then Colson, Sticks, Burthwait, the other principals, paid laughing compliments to the bright-haired girl.

Bostil enjoyed this hugely until he caught the strange intensity of regard in the cavernous eyes of Cordts. That gave him a shock. Cordts had long wanted this girl as much probably as he wanted Sage King. There were dark and terrible stories that stained the name of

Cordts. Bostil regretted his impulse in granting the horse-thief permission to attend the races. Sight of Lucy's fair, sweet face might inflame this Cordts—this Kentuckian who had boasted of his love of horses and women. Behind Cordts hung the little dust-colored Sears, like a coiled snake, ready to strike. Bostil felt stir in him a long-dormant fire—a stealing along his veins, a passion he hated.

"Lucy, go back to the women till you're ready to come out on your hoss," he said. "An' mind you, be careful to-day!"

He gave her a meaning glance, which she understood perfectly, he saw, and then he turned to start the day's sport.

The Indian races run in twos and threes, and on up to a number that crowded the racecourse; the betting and yelling and running; the wild and plunging mustangs; the heat and dust and pounding of hoofs; the excited betting; the surprises and defeats and victories; the trial tests of the principals, jealously keeping off to themselves in the sage; the endless moving, colorful procession, gaudy and swift and thrilling—all these Bostil loved tremendously.

But they were as nothing to what they gradually worked up to—the climax—the great race.

It was afternoon when all was ready for this race, and the sage was bright gray in the westering sun. Everybody was resting, waiting. The tense quiet of the riders seemed to settle upon the whole assemblage. Only the thoroughbreds were restless. They quivered and stamped and tossed their small, fine heads. They knew what was going to happen. They wanted to run. Blacks, bays, and whites were the predominating colors; and the horses and mustangs were alike in those points of race and speed and spirit that proclaimed them thoroughbreds.

Bostil himself took the covering off his favorite. Sage King was on edge. He stood out strikingly in contrast with the other horses. His sage-gray body was as sleek and shiny as satin. He had been trained to the hour. He tossed his head as he champed the bit, and every moment his muscles rippled under his fine skin. Proud, mettlesome, beautiful!

Sage King was the favorite in the betting, the Indians, who were ardent gamblers, plunging heavily on him.

Bostil saddled the horse and was long at the task. Van stood watching. He was pale and nervous. Bostil saw this.

"Van," he said, "it's your race."

The rider reached a quick hand for bridle and horn, and when his foot touched the stirrup Sage King was in the air. He came down, springy—quick, graceful, and then he pranced into line with the other horses.

Bostil waved his hand. Then the troop of riders and racers headed for the starting-point, two miles up the valley. Macomber and Blinn, with a rider and a Navajo, were up there as the official starters of the day.

Bostil's eyes glistened. He put a friendly hand on Cordts's shoulder, an action which showed the stress of the moment. Most of the men crowded around Bostil. Sears and Hutchinson hung close to Cordts. And Holley, keeping near his employer, had keen eyes for other things than horses.

Suddenly he touched Bostil and pointed down the slope. "There's Lucy," he said. "She's ridin' out to join the bunch."

"Lucy! Where? I'd forgotten my girl! . . . Where?"

"There," repeated Holley, and he pointed. Others of the group spoke up, having seen Lucy riding down.

"She's on a red hoss," said one.

" 'Pears all-fired big to me—her hoss," said another. "Who's got a glass?"

Bostil had the only field-glass there and he was using it. Across the round, magnified field of vision moved a giant red horse, his mane waving like a flame. Lucy rode him. They were moving from a jumble of broken rocks a mile down the slope. She had kept her horse hidden there. Bostil felt an added stir in his pulse-beat.

Certainly he had never seen a horse like this one. But the distance was long, the glass not perfect; he could not trust his sight. Suddenly that sight dimmed.

"Holley, I can't make out nothin'," he complained. "Take the glass. Give me a line on Lucy's mount."

"Boss, I don't need the glass to see that she's up on a *hoss*," replied Holley, as he took the glass. He leveled it, adjusted it to his eyes, and then looked long. Bostil grew impatient. Lucy was rapidly overhauling the troop of racers on her way to the post. Nothing ever hurried or excited Holley.

"Wal, can't you see any better 'n me?" queried Bostil, eagerly.

"Come on, Holl, give us a tip before she gits to the post," spoke up a rider.

Cordts showed intense eagerness, and all the group were excited. Lucy's advent, on an unknown horse that even her father could not disparage, was the last and unexpected addition to the suspense. They all knew that if the horse was fast Lucy would be dangerous.

Holley at last spoke: "She's up on a wild stallion. He's red, like fire. He's mighty big—strong. Looks as if he didn't want to go near the bunch. Lord! what action! . . . Bostil, I'd say—a great hoss!"

There was a moment's intense silence in the group round Bostil. Holley was never known to mistake a horse or to be extravagant in judgment or praise.

"A wild stallion!" echoed Bostil. "A-huh! An' she calls him Wildfire. Where'd she get him? . . . Gimme thet glass."

But all Bostil could make out was a blur. His eyes were wet. He realized now that his first sight of Lucy on the strange horse had been clear and strong, and it was that which had dimmed his eyes.

"Holley, you use the glass—an' tell me what comes off," said Bostil, as he wiped his eyes with his scarf. He was relieved to find that his sight was clearing. "My God! if I couldn't see this finish!"

Then everybody watched the close, dark mass of

horses and riders down the valley. And all waited for Holley to speak. "They're linin' up," began the rider. "Havin' some muss, too, it 'pears. . . . Bostil, thet red hoss is raisin' hell! He wants to fight. There! he's up in the air. . . . Boys, he's a devil—a hoss-killer like all them wild stallions. . . . He's plungin' at the King—strikin'! There! Lucy's got him down. She's handlin' him. . . . Now they've got the King on the other side. Thet's better. But Lucy's hoss won't stand. Anyway, it's a runnin' start. . . . Van's got the best position. Foxy Van! . . . He'll be leadin' before the rest know the race's on. . . . Them Indian mustangs are behavin' scandalous. Guess the red stallion scared 'em. Now they're all lined up back of the post. . . . Ah! gun-smoke! They move. . . . It looks like a go."

Then Holley was silent, strained in watching. So were all the watchers silent. Bostil saw far down the valley a moving, dark line of horses.

"They're off! They're off!" called Holley, thrillingly.

Bostil uttered a deep and booming yell, which rose above the shouts of the men round him and was heard even in the din of Indian cries. Then as quickly as the yells had risen they ceased.

Holley stood up on the rock with leveled glass.

"Mac's dropped the flag. It's a sure go. Now! . . . Van's out there front—inside. The King's got his stride. Boss, the King's stretchin' out! . . . Look! Look! see thet red hoss leap! . . . Bostil, he's runnin' down the King! I knowed it. He's like lightnin'. He's pushin' the King over—off the course! See him plunge! Lord! Lucy can't pull him! She goes up—down—tossed—but she sticks like a burr. Good, Lucy! Hang on! . . . My Gawd, Bostil, the King's thrown! He's down! . . . He comes up, off the course. The others flash by. . . . Van's out of the race! . . . An', Bostil—an', gentlemen, there ain't anythin' more to this race but a red hoss!"

Bostil's heart gave a great leap and then seemed to stand still. He was half cold, half hot.

What a horrible, sickening disappointment. Bostil rolled out a cursing query. Holley's answer was short

and sharp. The King was out! Bostil raved. He could
not see. He could not believe. After all the weeks of
preparation, of excitement, of suspense—only this!
There was no race. The King was out! The thing did
not seem possible. A thousand thoughts flitted through
Bostil's mind. Rage, impotent rage, possessed him. He
cursed Van, he swore he would kill that red stallion.
And some one shook him hard. Some one's incisive
words cut into his thick, throbbing ears: "Luck of the
game! The King ain't beat! He's only out!"

Then the rider's habit of mind asserted itself and
Bostil began to recover. For the King to fall was hard
luck. But he had not lost the race! Anguish and pride
battled for mastery over him. Even if the King were
out it was a Bostil who would win the great race.

"He ain't beat!" muttered Bostil. "It ain't fair! He's
run off the track by a wild stallion!"

His dimmed sight grew clear and sharp. And with
a gasp he saw the moving, dark line take shape as
horses. A bright horse was in the lead. Brighter and
larger he grew. Swiftly and more swiftly he came on.
The bright color changed to red. Bostil heard Holley
calling and Cordts calling—and other voices, but he
did not distinguish what was said. The line of horses
began to bob, to bunch. The race looked close, despite
what Holley had said. The Indians were beginning to
lean forward, here and there uttering a short, sharp
yell. Everything within Bostil grew together in one
great, throbbing, tingling mass. His rider's eye, keen
once more, caught a gleam of gold above the red, and
that gold was Lucy's hair. Bostil forgot the King.

Then Holley bawled into his ear, "They're half-way!"

The race was beautiful. Bostil strained his eyes. He
gloried in what he saw—Lucy low over the neck of
that red stallion. He could see plainer now. They were
coming closer. How swiftly! What a splendid race! But
it was too swift—it would not last. The Indians began
to yell, drowning the hoarse shouts of the riders. Out
of the tail of his eye Bostil saw Cordts and Sears and
Hutchinson. They were acting like crazy men. Strange

that horse-thieves should care! The million thrills within Bostil coalesced into one great shudder of rapture. He grew wet with sweat. His stentorian voice took up the call for Lucy to win.

"Three-quarters!" bawled Holley into Bostil's ear. "An' Lucy's give thet wild hoss free rein! Look, Bostil! You never in your life seen a hoss run like thet!"

Bostil never had. His heart swelled. Something shook him. Was that his girl—that tight little gray burr half hidden in the huge stallion's flaming mane? The distance had been close between Lucy and the bunched riders.

But it lengthened. How it widened! That flame of a horse was running away from the others. And now they were close—coming into the home stretch. A deafening roar from the onlookers engulfed all other sounds. A straining, stamping, arm-flinging horde surrounded Bostil.

Bostil saw Lucy's golden hair whipping out from the flame-streaked mane. And then he could only see that red brute of a horse. Wildfire before the wind! Bostil thought of the leaping prairie flame, storm-driven.

On came the red stallion—on—on! What a tremendous stride! What a marvelous recovery! What ease! What savage action!

He flashed past, low, pointed, long, going faster every magnificent stride—winner by a dozen lengths.

Chapter XIII

WILDFIRE ran on down the valley far beyond the yelling crowd lined along the slope. Bostil was deaf to the throng; he watched the stallion till Lucy forced him to stop and turn.

Then Bostil whirled to see where Van was with the

King. Most of the crowd surged down to surround the racers, and the yells gave way to the buzz of many voices. Some of the ranchers and riders remained near Bostil, all apparently talking at once. Bostil gathered that Holley's Whitefoot had run second, and the Navajo's mustang third. It was Holley himself who verified what Bostil had heard. The old rider's hawk eyes were warm with delight.

"Boss, he run second!" Holley kept repeating.

Bostil had the heart to shake hands with Holley and say he was glad, when it was on his lips to blurt out there had been no race. Then Bostil's nerves tingled at sight of Van trotting the King up the course toward the slope. Bostil watched with searching eyes. Sage King did not appear to be injured. Van rode straight up the slope and leaped off. He was white and shaking.

The King's glossy hide was dirty with dust and bits of cactus and brush. He was not even hot. There did not appear to be a bruise or mark on him. He whinnied and rubbed his face against Bostil, and then, flinching, he swept up his head, ears high. Both fear and fire shone in his eyes.

"Wal, Van, get it out of your system," said Bostil, kindly. He was a harder loser before a race was run than after he had lost it.

"Thet red hoss run in on the King before the start an' scared the race out of him," replied Van, swiftly. "We had a hunch, you know, but at thet Lucy's hoss was a surprise. I'll say, sir, thet Lucy rode her wild hoss an' handled him. Twice she pulled him off the King. He meant to kill the King! . . . Ask any of the boys. . . . We got started. I took the lead, sir. The King was in the lead. I never looked back till I heard Lucy scream. She couldn't pull Wildfire. He was rushin' the King—meant to kill him. An' Sage King wanted to fight. If I could only have kept him runnin'! Thet would have been a race! . . . But Wildfire got in closer an' closer. He crowded us. He bit at the King's flank an' shoulder an' neck. Lucy pulled till I yelled she'd throw the hoss an' kill us both. Then Wildfire jumped for us.

Runnin' an' strikin' with both feet at once! Bostil, thet hoss's hell! Then he hit us an' down we went. I had a bad spill. But the King's not hurt an' thet's a blessed wonder."

"No race, Van! It was hard luck. Take him home," said Bostil.

Van's story of the accident vindicated Bostil's doubts. A new horse had appeared on the scene, wild and swift and grand, but Sage King was still unbeaten in a fair race. There would come a reckoning, Bostil grimly muttered. Who owned this Wildfire?

Holley might as well have read his mind. "Reckon this feller ridin' up will take down the prize money," remarked Holley, and he pointed to a man who rode a huge, shaggy, black horse and was leading Lucy's pony.

"A-huh!" exclaimed Bostil. "A strange rider."

"An' here comes Lucy coaxin' the stallion back," added Holley.

"A wild stallion never clear broke!" ejaculated Cordts.

All the men looked and all had some remark of praise for Lucy and her mount.

Bostil gazed with a strange, irresistible attraction. Never had he expected to live to see a wild stallion like this one, to say nothing of his daughter mounted on him, with the record of having put Sage King out of the race!

A thousand pairs of eyes watched Wildfire. He pranced out there beyond the crowd of men and horses. He did not want to come closer. Yet he did not seem to fight his rider. Lucy hung low over his neck, apparently exhausted, and she was patting him and caressing him. There were horses and Indians on each side of the racetrack, and between these lines Lucy appeared reluctant to come.

Bostil strode down and, waving and yelling for everybody to move back to the slope, he cleared the way and then stood out in front alone.

"Ride up, now," he called to Lucy.

It was then Bostil discovered that Lucy did not wear a spur and she had neither quirt nor whip. She turned Wildfire and he came prancing on, head and mane and tail erect. His action was beautiful, springy, and every few steps, as Lucy touched him, he jumped with marvelous ease and swiftness.

Bostil became all eyes. He did not see his daughter as she paraded the winner before the applauding throng. And Bostil recorded in his mind that which he would never forget—a wild stallion, with unbroken spirit; a giant of a horse, glistening red, with mane like dark-striped, wind-blown flame, all muscle, all grace, all power; a neck long and slender and arching to the small, savagely beautiful head; the jaws open, and the thin-skinned, pink-colored nostrils that proved the Arabian blood; the slanting shoulders and the deep, broad chest, the powerful legs and knees not too high nor too low, the symmetrical dark hoofs that rang on the little stones—all these marks so significant of speed and endurance. A stallion with a wonderful physical perfection that matched the savage, ruthless spirit of the desert killer of horses!

Lucy waved her hand, and the strange rider to whom Holley had called attention strode out of the crowd toward Wildfire.

Bostil's gaze took in the splendid build of this lithe rider, the clean-cut face, the dark eye. This fellow had a shiny, coiled lasso in hand. He advanced toward Wildfire. The stallion snorted and plunged. If ever Bostil saw hate expressed by a horse he saw it then. But he seemed to be tractable to the control of the girl. Bostil swiftly grasped the strange situation. Lucy had won the love of the savage stallion. That always had been the secret of her power. And she had hated Sage King because he alone had somehow taken a dislike to her. Horses were as queer as people, thought Bostil.

The rider walked straight up to the trembling Wildfire. When Wildfire plunged and reared up and up the rider leaped for the bridle and with an iron arm pulled the horse down. Wildfire tried again, almost lifting the rider, but a stinging cut from the lasso made him come to a stand. Plainly the rider held the mastery.

"Dad!" called Lucy, faintly.

Bostil went forward, close, while the rider held Wildfire. Lucy was as wan-faced as a flower by moonlight. Her eyes were dark with emotions, fear predominating. Then for Bostil the half of his heart that was human reasserted itself. Lucy was only a girl now, and weakening. Her fear, her pitiful little smile, as if she dared not hope for her father's approval yet could not help it, touched Bostil to the quick, and he opened his arms. Lucy slid down into them.

"Lucy, girl, you've won the King's race an' doublecrossed your poor old dad!"

"Oh, Dad, I never knew—I never dreamed Wildfire —would jump the King," Lucy faltered. "I couldn't hold him. He was terrible. . . . It made me sick. . . . Daddy, tell me Van wasn't hurt—or the King!"

"The hoss's all right an' so's Van," replied Bostil. "Don't cry, Lucy. It was a fool trick you pulled off, but you did it great. By Gad! you sure was ridin' thet red devil. . . . An' say, it's all right with me!"

Lucy did not faint then, but she came near it. Bostil put her down and led her through the lines of admiring Indians and applauding riders, and left her with the women.

When he turned again he was in time to see the strange rider mount Wildfire. It was a swift and hazardous mount, the stallion being in the air. When he came down he tore the turf and sent it flying, and when he shot up again he was doubled in a red knot, bristling with fiery hair, a furious wild beast, mad to throw the rider. Bostil never heard as wild a scream uttered by a horse. Likewise he had never seen so incomparable a horseman as this stranger. Indians and riders alike thrilled at a sight which was after their own hearts. The rider had hooked his long spurs under the horse and now appeared a part of him. He could not be dislodged. This was not a bucking mustang, but a fierce, powerful, fighting stallion. No doubt, thought Bostil, this fight took place every time the rider mounted his horse. It was the sort of thing riders loved. Most of them would not own a horse that would not pitch. Bostil presently decided, however, that in the case of this red stallion no rider in his right senses would care for such a fight, simply because of the extraordinary strength, activity, and ferocity of the stallion.

The riders were all betting the horse would throw the stranger. And Bostil, seeing the gathering might of Wildfire's momentum, agreed with them. No horseman could stick on that horse. Suddenly Wildfire tripped in the sage, and went sprawling in the dust, throwing his rider ahead. Both man and beast were quick to rise, but the rider had a foot in the stirrup before Wildfire was under way. Then the horse plunged, ran free, came circling back, and slowly gave way to the rider's control. Those few moments of frenzied activity had brought out the foam and the sweat—Wildfire was wet. The rider pulled him in before Bostil and dismounted.

"Sometimes I ride him; then sometimes I don't," he said, with a smile.

Bostil held out his hand. He liked this rider. He would have liked the frank face, less hard than that of most riders, and the fine, dark eyes, straight and steady, even if their possessor had not come with the open sesame to Bostil's regard—a grand, wild horse, and nerve to ride him.

"Wal, you rode him longer 'n any of us figgered," said Bostil, heartily shaking the man's hand. "I'm Bostil. Glad to meet you."

"My name's Slone—Lin Slone," replied the rider, frankly. "I'm a wild-horse hunter an' hail from Utah."

"Utah? How'd you ever get over? Wal, you've got a grand hoss—an' you put a grand rider up on him in the race. . . . My girl Lucy—"

Bostil hesitated. His mind was running swiftly. Back of his thoughts gathered the desire and the determination to get possession of this horse Wildfire. He had forgotten what he might have said to this stranger under different circumstances. He looked keenly into Slone's face and saw no fear, no subterfuge. The young man was honest.

"Bostil, I chased this wild horse days an' weeks an' months, hundreds of miles—across the cañon an' the river—"

"No!" interrupted Bostil, blankly.

"Yes. I'll tell you how later. . . . Out here somewhere I caught Wildfire, broke him as much as he'll ever be broken. He played me out an' got away. Your girl rode along—saved my horse—an' saved my life, too. I was in bad shape for days. But I got well—an'—an' then she wanted me to let her run Wildfire in the big race. I couldn't refuse. . . . An' it would have been a great race but for the unlucky accident to Sage King. I'm sorry, sir."

"Slone, it jarred me some, thet disappointment. But it's over," replied Bostil. "An' so thet's how Lucy found her hoss. She sure was mysterious. . . . Wal, wal." Bostil became aware of others behind him. "Holley, shake hands with Slone, hoss-wrangler out of Utah. . . . You, too, Cal Blinn. . . . An' Macomber—an' Wetherby, meet my friend here—young Slone. . . . An', Cordts, shake hands with a feller thet owns a grand hoss!"

Bostil laughed as he introduced the horse-thief to Slone. The others laughed, too, even Cordts joining in. There was much of the old rider daredevil spirit left in Bostil, and it interested and amused him to see Cordts and Slone meet. Assuredly Slone had heard of the noted stealer of horses. The advantage was certainly on Cordts's side, for he was good-natured and pleasant while Slone stiffened, paling slightly as he faced about to acknowledge the introduction.

"Howdy, Slone," drawled Cordts, with hand outstretched. "I sure am glad to meet yuh. I'd like to trade the Sage King for this red stallion!"

A roar of laughter greeted this sally, all but Bostil and Slone joining in. The joke was on Bostil, and he showed it. Slone did not even smile.

"Howdy, Cordts," he replied. "I'm glad to meet you —so I'll know you when I see you again."

"Wal, we're all good fellers to-day," interposed Bostil. "An' now let's ride home an' eat. Slone, you come with me."

The group slowly mounted the slope where the horses waited. Macomber, Wetherby, Burthwait, Blinn —all Bostil's friends proffered their felicitations to the young rider, and all were evidently prepossessed with him.

The sun was low in the west; purple shades were blotting out the gold lights down the valley; the day of the great races was almost done. Indians were still scattered here and there in groups; others were turning out the mustangs; and the majority were riding and walking with the crowd toward the village.

Bostil observed that Cordts had hurried ahead of the group and now appeared to be saying something emphatic to Dick Sears and Hutchinson. Bostil heard Cordts curse. Probably he was arraigning the sullen Sears. Cordts had acted first rate—had lived up to his word, as Bostil thought he would do. Cordts and Hutchinson mounted their horses and rode off, somewhat to the left of the scattered crowd. But Sears remained behind. Bostil thought this strange and put it down to the surliness of the fellow, who had lost on the races. Bostil, wishing Sears would get out of his sight, resolved never to make another blunder like inviting horse-thieves to a race.

All the horses except Wildfire stood in a bunch back on the bench. Sears appeared to be fussing with the straps on his saddle. And Bostil could not keep his glance from wandering back to gloat over Wildfire's savage grace and striking size.

Suddenly there came a halt in the conversation of the men, a curse in Holley's deep voice, a violent split in the group. Bostil wheeled to see Sears in a menacing position with two guns leveled low.

"Don't holler!" he called. "An' don't move!"

"What'n the h—l now, Sears?" demanded Bostil.

"I'll bore you if you move—thet's what!" replied Sears. His eyes, bold, steely, with a glint that Bostil knew, vibrated as he held in sight all points before him. A vicious little sand-rattlesnake about to strike!

"Holley, turn yer back!" ordered Sears.

The old rider, who stood foremost of the group, instantly obeyed, with hands up. He took no chances here, for he alone packed a gun. With swift steps Sears moved, pulled Holley's gun, flung it aside into the sage.

"Sears, it ain't a hold-up!" expostulated Bostil. The act seemed too bold, too wild even for Dick Sears.

"Ain't it?" scoffed Sears, malignantly. "Bostil, I was after the King. But I reckon I'll git the hoss thet beat him!"

Bostil's face turned dark-blood color and his neck swelled. "By Gawd, Sears! You ain't a-goin' to steal this boy's hoss!"

"Shut up!" hissed the horse-thief. He pushed a gun close to Bostil. "I've always laid fer you! I'm achin' to bore you now. I would but fer scarin' this hoss. If you yap again I'll *kill you,* anyhow, an' take a chance!"

All the terrible hate and evil and cruelty and deadliness of his kind burned in his eyes and stung in his voice.

"Sears, if it's my horse you want you needn't kill Bostil," spoke up Slone. The contrast of his cool, quiet voice eased the terrible strain.

"Lead him round hyar!" snapped Sears.

Wildfire appeared more shy of the horses back of him than of the men. Slone was able to lead him, however, to within several paces of Sears. Then Slone dropped the reins. He still held a lasso which was loosely coiled, and the loop dropped in front of him as he backed away.

Sears sheathed the left-hand gun. Keeping the group covered with the other, he moved backward, reaching for the hanging reins. Wildfire snorted, appeared about to jump. But Sears got the reins. Bostil, standing like a stone, his companions also motionless, could not help but admire the daring of this upland horse-thief. How was he to mount that wild stallion? Sears was noted for two qualities—his nerve before men and his skill with horses. Assuredly he would not risk an ordinary mount. Wildfire began to suspect Sears—to look at him instead of the other horses. Then quick as a cat Sears vaulted into the saddle. Wildfire snorted and lifted his forefeet in a lunge that meant he would bolt.

Sears in vaulting up had swung the gun aloft. He swept it down, but waveringly, for Wildfire had begun to rear.

Bostil saw how fatal that single instant would have been for Sears if he or Holley had a gun.

Something whistled. Bostil saw the leap of Slone's lasso—the curling, snaky dart of the noose which flew up to snap around Sears. The rope sung taut. Sears was swept bodily clean from the saddle, to hit the ground in sodden impact.

Almost swifter than Bostil's sight was the action of Slone—flashing by—in the air—himself on the plunging horse. Sears shot once, twice. Then Wildfire bolted as his rider whipped the lasso around the horn. Sears, half rising, was jerked ten feet. An awful shriek was throttled in his throat.

A streak of dust on the slope—a tearing, parting line in the sage!

Bostil stood amazed. The red stallion made short plunges. Slone reached low for the tripping reins. When he straightened up in the saddle Wildfire broke wildly into a run.

It was characteristic of Holley that at this thrilling, tragic instant he walked over into the sage to pick up his gun.

"Throwed a gun on me, got the drop, an' pitched mine away!" muttered Holley, in disgust. The way he spoke meant that he was disgraced.

"My Gawd! I was scared thet Sears would get the hoss!" rolled out Bostil.

Holley thought of his gun; Bostil thought of the splendid horse. The thoughts were characteristic of these riders. The other men, however, recovering from a horror-broken silence, burst out in acclaim of Slone's feat.

"Dick Sears's finish! Roped by a boy rider!" exclaimed Cal Blinn, fervidly.

"Bostil, that rider is worthy of his horse," said Wetherby. "I think Sears would have bored you. I saw his finger pressing—pressing on the trigger. Men like Sears can't help but pull at that stage."

"Thet was the quickest trick I ever seen," declared Macomber.

They watched Wildfire run down the slope, out into the valley, with a streak of rising dust out behind. They all saw when there ceased to be that peculiar rising of dust. Wildfire appeared to shoot ahead at greater speed. Then he slowed up. The rider turned him and faced back toward the group, coming at a stiff gallop. Soon Wildfire breasted the slope, and halted, snorting, shaking before the men. The lasso was still trailing out behind, limp and sagging. There was no weight upon it now.

Bostil strode slowly ahead. He sympathized with the tension that held Slone; he knew why the rider's face was gray, why his lips only moved mutely, why there was horror in the dark, strained eyes, why the lean, strong hands, slowly taking up the lasso, now shook like leaves in the wind.

There was only dust on the lasso. But Bostil knew —they all knew that none the less it had dealt a terrible death to the horse-thief.

Somehow Bostil could not find words for what he wanted to say. He put a hand on the red stallion—patted his shoulder. Then he gripped Slone close and hard. He was thinking how he would have gloried in a son like this young, wild rider. Then he again faced his comrades.

"Fellers, do you think Cordts was in on thet trick?" he queried.

"Nope. Cordts was on the square," replied Holley.

"But he must have seen it comin' an' left Sears to his fate. It sure was a fittin' last ride for a hoss-thief."

Bostil sent Holley and Farlane on ahead to find Cordts and Hutchinson, with their comrades, to tell them the fate of Sears, and to warn them to leave before the news got to the riders.

The sun was setting golden and red over the broken battlements of the cañons to the west. The heat of the day blew away on a breeze that bent the tips of the sage-brush. A wild song drifted back from the riders to the fore. And the procession of Indians moved along, their gay trappings and bright colors beautiful in the fading sunset light.

When Bostil and his guests arrived at the corrals, Holley, with Farlane and other riders, were waiting.

"Boss," said Holley, "Cordts an' his outfit never rid in. They was last seen by some Navajos headin' for the cañons."

"Thet's good!" ejaculated Bostil, in relief. "Wal, boys, look after the hosses. . . . Slone, just turn Wildfire over to the boys with instructions, an' feel safe."

Farlane scratched his head and looked dubious. "I'm wonderin' how safe it 'll be fer us."

"I'll look after him," said Slone.

Bostil nodded as if he had expected Slone to refuse to let any rider put the stallion away for the night. Wildfire would not go into the barn, and Slone led him into one of the high-barred corrals. Bostil waited, talking with his friends, until Slone returned, and then they went toward the house.

"I reckon we couldn't get inside Brack's place now," remarked Bostil. "But in a case like this I can scare up a drink." Lights from the windows shone bright through the darkness under the cottonwoods. Bostil halted at the door, as if suddenly remembering, and he whispered, huskily: "Let's keep the women from learnin' about Sears—to-night, anyway."

Then he led the way through the big door into the huge living-room. There were hanging-lights on the walls and blazing sticks on the hearth. Lucy came running in to meet them. It did not escape Bostil's keen eyes that she was dressed in her best white dress. He had never seen her look so sweet and pretty, and, for that matter, so strange. The flush, the darkness of her eyes, the added something in her face, tender, thoughtful, strong—these were new. Bostil pondered while she welcomed his guests. Slone, who had hung back, was last in turn. Lucy greeted him as she had the others. Slone met her with awkward constraint. The gray had not left his face. Lucy looked up at him again, and differently.

"What—what has happened?" she asked.

It annoyed Bostil that Slone and all the men suddenly looked blank.

"Why, nothin'," replied Slone, slowly, " 'cept I'm fagged out."

Lucy, or any other girl, could have seen that he was evading the truth. She flashed a look from Slone to her father.

"Until to-day we never had a big race that something dreadful didn't happen," said Lucy. "This was my day—my race. And, oh! I wanted it to pass without—without—"

"Wal, Lucy dear," replied Bostil, as she faltered. "Nothin' came off thet'd make you feel bad. Young Slone had a scare about his hoss. Wildfire's safe out there in the corral, an' he'll be guarded like the King an' Sarch. Slone needs a drink an' somethin' to eat, same as all of us."

Lucy's color returned and her smile, but Bostil noted that, while she was serving them and brightly responsive to compliments, she gave more than one steady glance at Slone. She was deep, thought Bostil, and it angered him a little that she showed interest in what concerned this strange rider.

Then they had dinner, with twelve at table. The wives of Bostil's three friends had been helping Aunt Jane prepare the feast, and they added to the merriment. Bostil was not much given to social intercourse

—he would have preferred to be with his horses and riders—but this night he outdid himself as host, amazed his sister Jane, who evidently thought he drank too much, and delighted Lucy. Bostil's outward appearance and his speech and action never reflected all the workings of his mind. No one would ever know the depth of his bitter disappointment at the outcome of the race. With Creech's Blue Roan out of the way, another horse, swifter and more dangerous, had come along to spoil the King's chance. Bostil felt a subtly increasing covetousness in regard to Wildfire, and this colored all his talk and action. The upland country, vast and rangy, was for Bostil too small to hold Sage King and Wildfire unless they both belonged to him. And when old Cal Blinn gave a ringing toast to Lucy, hoping to live to see her up on Wildfire in the grand race that must be run with the King, Bostil felt stir in him the birth of a subtle, bitter fear. At first he mocked it. He—Bostil—afraid to race! It was a lie of the excited mind. He repudiated it. Insidiously it returned. He drowned it down—smothered it with passion. Then the ghost of it remained, hauntingly.

After dinner Bostil with the men went down to Brackton's, where Slone and the winners of the day received their prizes.

"Why, it's more money than I ever had in my whole life!" exclaimed Slone, gazing incredulously at the gold.

Bostil was amused and pleased, and back of both amusement and pleasure was the old inventive, driving passion to gain his own ends.

Bostil was abnormally generous in many ways; monstrously selfish in one way.

"Slone, I seen you didn't drink none," he said, curiously.

"No; I don't like liquor."

"Do you gamble?"

"I like a little bet—on a race," replied Slone, frankly.

"Wal, thet ain't gamblin'. These fool riders of mine

will bet on the switchin' of a hoss's tail." He drew Slone a little aside from the others, who were interested in Brackton's delivery of the different prizes. "Slone, how'd you like to ride for me?"

Slone appeared surprised. "Why, I never rode for any one," he replied, slowly. "I can't stand to be tied down. I'm a horse-hunter, you know."

Bostil eyed the young man, wondering what he knew about the difficulties of the job offered. It was no news to Bostil that he was at once the best and the worst man to ride for in all the uplands.

"Sure, I know. But thet doesn't make no difference," went on Bostil, persuasively. "If we got along—wal, you'd save some of thet yellow coin you're jinglin'. A roamin' rider never builds no corral!"

"Thank you, Bostil," replied Slone, earnestly. "I'll think it over. It would seem kind of tame now to go back to wild-horse wranglin', after I've caught Wildfire. I'll think it over. Maybe I'll do it, if you're sure I'm good enough with rope an' horse."

"Wal, by Gawd!" blurted out Bostil. "Holley says he'd rather you throwed a gun on him than a rope! So would I. An' as for your handlin' a hoss, I never seen no better."

Slone appeared embarrassed and kept studying the gold coins in his palm. Some one touched Bostil, who, turning, saw Brackton at his elbow. The other men were now bantering with the Indians.

"Come now while I've got a minnit," said Brackton, taking up a lantern. "I've somethin' to show you."

Bostil followed Brackton, and Slone came along. The old man opened a door into a small room, half full of stores and truck. The lantern only dimly lighted the place.

"Look thar!" And Brackton flashed the light upon a man lying prostrate.

Bostil recognized the pale face of Joel Creech. "Brack! . . . What's this? Is he dead?" Bostil sustained a strange, incomprehensible shock. Sight of a dead man had never before shocked him.

"Nope, he ain't dead, which if he was might be good for this community," replied Brackton. "He's only fallen in a fit. Fust off I reckoned he was drunk. But it ain't thet."

"Wal, what do you want to show him to me for?" demanded Bostil, gruffly.

"I reckoned you oughter see him."

"An' why, Brackton?"

Brackton set down the lantern and, pushing Slone outside, said: "Jest a minnit, son," and then he closed the door. "Joel's been on my hands since the flood cut him off from home," said Brackton. "An' he's been some trial. But nobody else would have done nothin' for him, so I had to. I reckon I felt sorry for him. He cried like a baby thet had lost its mother. Then he gets wild-lookin' an' raved around. When I wasn't busy I kept an eye on him. But some of the time I couldn't, an' he stole drinks, which made him wuss. An' when I seen he was tryin' to sneak one of my guns, I up an' gets suspicious. Once he said, 'My dad's hosses are goin' to starve, an' I'm goin' to kill somebody!' He was out of his head an' dangerous. Wal, I was worried some, but all I could do was lock up my guns. Last night I caught him confabin' with some men out in the dark, behind the store. They all skedaddled except Joel, but I recognized Cordts. I didn't like this, nuther. Joel was surly an' ugly. An' when one of the riders called him he said: 'Thet boat *never drifted off*. Fer the night of the flood I went down there myself an' tied the ropes. They never come untied. Somebody cut them—jest before the flood—to make sure my dad's hosses couldn't be crossed. Somebody figgered the river an' the flood. An' if my dad's hosses starve I'm goin' to kill somebody!' "

Brackton took up the lantern and placed a hand on the door ready to go out.

"Then a rider punched Joel—I never seen who—an' Joel had a fit. I dragged him in here. An' as you see, he ain't come to yet."

"Wal, Brackton, the boy's crazy," said Bostil.

"So I reckon. An' I'm afeared he'll burn us out—he's crazy on fires, anyway—or do somethin' like."

"He's sure a problem. Wal, we'll see," replied Bostil, soberly.

And they went out to find Slone waiting. Then Bostil called his guests, and with Slone also accompanying him, went home.

Bostil threw off the recurring gloom, and he was good-natured when Lucy came to his room to say good night. He knew she had come to say more than that.

"Hello, daughter!" he said. "Aren't you ashamed to come facin' your poor old dad?"

Lucy eyed him dubiously. "No, I'm not ashamed. But I'm still a little—afraid."

"I'm harmless, child. I'm a broken man. When you put Sage King out of the race you broke me."

"Dad, that isn't funny. You make me an—angry when you hint I did something underhand."

"Wal, you didn't consult *me.*"

"I thought it would be fun to surprise you all. Why, you're always delighted with a surprise in a race, unless it beats *you.* . . . Then, it was my great and only chance to get out in front of the King. Oh, how grand it 'd have been! Dad, I'd have run away from him the same as the others!"

"No, you wouldn't," declared Bostil.

"Dad, Wildfire can beat the King!"

"Never, girl! Knockin' a good-tempered hoss off his pins ain't beatin' him in a runnin'-race."

Then father and daughter fought over the old score, the one doggedly, imperturbably, the other spiritedly, with flashing eyes. It was different this time, however, for it ended in Lucy saying Bostil would never risk another race. That stung Bostil, and it cost him an effort to control his temper.

"Let thet go now. Tell me—all about how you saved Wildfire, an' Slone, too."

Lucy readily began the narrative, and she had scarcely started before Bostil found himself intensely in-

terested. Soon he became absorbed. That was the most
thrilling and moving kind of romance to him, like his
rider's dreams.

"Lucy, you're sure a game kid," he said, fervidly,
when she had ended. "I reckon I don't blame Slone for
fallin' in love with you."

"Who said *that?*" inquired Lucy.

"Nobody. But it's true—ain't it?"

She looked up with eyes as true as ever they were,
yet a little sad, he thought, a little wistful and wondering, as if a strange and grave thing confronted her.

"Yes, Dad—it's—it's true," she answered, haltingly.

"Wal, you didn't need to tell me, but I'm glad you
did."

Bostil meant to ask her then if she in any sense returned the rider's love, but unaccountably he could not
put the question. The girl was as true as ever—as good
as gold. Bostil feared a secret that might hurt him. Just
as sure as life was there and death but a step away,
some rider, sooner or later, would win this girl's love.
Bostil knew that, hated it, feared it. Yet he would never
give his girl to a beggarly rider. Such a man as Wetherby ought to win Lucy's hand. And Bostil did not want
to know too much at present; he did not want his swift-
mounting animosity roused so soon. Still he was curious,
and, wanting to get the drift of Lucy's mind, he took
to his old habit of teasing.

"Another moonstruck rider!" he said. "Your eyes
are sure full moons, Lucy. I'd be ashamed to trifle with
these poor fellers."

"Dad!"

"You're a heartless flirt—same as your mother was
before she met *me.*"

"I'm not. And I don't believe mother was, either,"
replied Lucy. It was easy to strike fire from her.

"Wal, you did dead wrong to ride out there day after
day meetin' Slone, because—young woman—if he ever
has the nerve to ask me for you I'll beat him up bad."

"Then you'd be a brute!" retorted Lucy.

"Wal, mebbe," returned Bostil, secretly delighted

and surprised at Lucy's failure to see through him. But she was looking inward. He wondered what hid there deep in her. "But I can't stand for the nerve of thet."

"He—he means to—to ask you."

"The h—. . . . A-huh!"

Lucy did not catch the slip of tongue. She was flushing now. "He said he'd never have let me meet him out there alone—unless—he—he loved me—and as our neighbors and the riders would learn of it—and talk—he wanted you and them to know he'd asked to—to marry me."

"Wal, he's a square young man!" ejaculated Bostil, involuntarily. It was hard for Bostil to hide his sincerity and impulsiveness; much harder than to hide unworthy attributes. Then he got back on the other track. "Thet'll make me treat him decent, so when he rides up to ask for you I'll let him off with, 'No!'"

Lucy dropped her head. Bostil would have given all he had, except his horses, to feel sure she did not care for Slone.

"Dad—I said—'No'—for myself," she murmured.

This time Bostil did not withhold the profane word of surprise. ". . . So he's asked you, then? Wal, wal! When?"

"To-day—out there in the rocks where he waited with Wildfire for me. He—he—"

Lucy slipped into her father's arms, and her slender form shook. Bostil instinctively felt what she then needed was her mother. Her mother was dead, and he was only a rough, old, hard rider. He did not know what to do—to say. His heart softened and he clasped her close. It hurt him keenly to realize that he might have been a better, kinder father if it were not for the fear that she would find him out. But that proved he loved her, craved her respect and affection.

"Wal, little girl, tell me," he said.

"He—he broke his word to me."

"A-huh! Thet's too bad. An' how did he?"

"He—he—" Lucy seemed to catch her tongue.

Bostil was positive she had meant to tell him something and suddenly changed her mind. Subtly the child vanished—a woman remained. Lucy sat up self-possessed once more. Some powerfully impelling thought had transformed her. Bostil's keen sense gathered that what she would not tell was not hers to reveal. For herself, she was the soul of simplicity and frankness.

"Days ago I told him I cared for him," she went on. "But I forbade him to speak of it to me. He promised. I wanted to wait till after the race—till after I had found courage to confess to you. He broke his word. . . . To-day when he put me up on Wildfire he—he suddenly lost his head."

The slow scarlet welled into Lucy's face and her eyes grew shamed, but bravely she kept facing her father.

"He—he pulled me off—he hugged me—he k-kissed me. . . . Oh, it was dreadful—shameful! . . . Then I gave him back—some—something he had given me. And I told him I—I hated him—and I told him, 'No!' "

"But you rode his hoss in the race," said Bostil.

Lucy bowed her head at that. "I—I couldn't resist!"

Bostil stroked the bright head. What a quandary for a thick-skulled old horseman! "Wal, it seems to me Slone didn't act so bad, considerin'. You'd told him you cared for him. If it wasn't for thet! . . . I remember I did much the same to your mother. She raised the devil, but I never seen as she cared any less for me."

"I'll never forgive him," Lucy cried, passionately. "I hate him. A man who breaks his word in one thing will do it in another."

Bostil sadly realized that his little girl had reached womanhood and love, and with them the sweet, bitter pangs of life. He realized also that here was a crisis when a word—an unjust or lying word from him would forever ruin any hope that might still exist for Slone. Bostil realized this acutely, but the realization was not even a temptation.

"Wal, listen. I'm bound to confess your new rider is sure swift. An', Lucy, to-day if he hadn't been as swift with a rope as he is in love—wal, your old daddy might be dead!"

She grew as white as her dress. "Oh, Dad! I *knew* something had happened," she cried, reaching for him.

Then Bostil told her how Dick Sears had menaced him—how Slone had foiled the horse-thief. He told the story bluntly, but eloquently, with all a rider's praise.

Lucy rose with hands pressed against her breast. When had Bostil seen eyes like those—dark, shining, wonderful? Ah! he remembered her mother's once—only once, as a girl.

Then Lucy kissed him and without a word fled from the room.

Bostil stared after her. "D—n me!" he swore, as he threw a boot against the wall. "I reckon I'll never let her marry Slone, but I just had to tell her what I think of him!"

Chapter XIV

SLONE lay wide awake under an open window, watching the stars glimmer through the rustling foilage of the cottonwoods. Somewhere a lonesome hound bayed. Very faintly came the silvery tinkle of running water.

For five days Slone had been a guest of Bostil's, and the whole five days had been torment.

On the morning of the day after the races Lucy had confronted him. Would he ever forget her eyes—her voice? "Bless you for saving my dad!" she had said. "It was brave. . . . But don't let dad fool you. Don't believe in his kindness. Above all, don't ride for him! He only wants Wildfire, and if he doesn't get him he'll hate you!"

That speech of Lucy's had made the succeeding days hard for Slone. Bostil loaded him with gifts and kindnesses, and never ceased importuning him to accept his offers. But for Lucy, Slone would have accepted. It was she who cast the first doubt of Bostil into his mind.

Lucy averred that her father was splendid and good in every way except in what pertained to fast horses; there he was impossible.

The great stallion that Slone had nearly sacrificed his life to catch was like a thorn in the rider's flesh. Slone lay there in the darkness, restless, hot, rolling from side to side, or staring out at the star-studded sky—miserably unhappy all on account of that horse. Almost he hated him. What pride he had felt in Wildfire! How he had gloried in the gift of the stallion to Lucy! Then, on the morning of the race had come that unexpected, incomprehensible and wild act of which he had been guilty. Yet not to save his life, his soul, could he regret it! Was it he who had been responsible, or an unknown savage within him? He had kept his word to Lucy, when day after day he had burned with love until that fatal moment when the touch of her, as he lifted her to Wildfire's saddle, had made a madman out of him. He had swept her into his arms and held her breast to his, her face before him, and he had kissed the sweet, parting lips till he was blind.

Then he had learned what a little fury she was. Then he learned how he had fallen, what he had forfeited. In his amaze at himself, in his humility and shame, he had not been able to say a word in his own defense. She did not know yet that his act had been ungovernable and that he had not known what he was doing till too late. And she had finished with: "I'll ride Wildfire in the race—but I won't have him—and I won't have *you! No!*"

She had the steel and hardness of her father.

For Slone, the watching of that race was a blend of rapture and despair. He lived over in mind all the time between the race and this hour when he lay there sleepless and full of remorse. His mind was like a race-course with many races; and predominating in it was that swift, strange, stinging race of his memory of Lucy Bostil's looks and actions.

What an utter fool he was to believe she had meant those tender words when, out there under the looming

monuments, she had accepted Wildfire! She had been
an impulsive child. Her scorn and fury that morning of
the race had left nothing for him except footless
fancies. She had mistaken love of Wildfire for love of
him. No, his case was hopeless with Lucy, and if it had
not been so Bostil would have made it hopeless. Yet
there were things Slone could not fathom—the wilful,
contradictory, proud and cold and unaccountably
sweet looks and actions of the girl. They haunted
Slone. They made him conscious he had a mind and
tortured him with his development. But he had no
experience with girls to compare with what was happening now. It seemed that accepted fact and remembered scorn and cold certainty were somehow at vari-
ance with hitherto unknown intuitions and instincts.
Lucy avoided him, if by chance she encountered him
alone. When Bostil or Aunt Jane or any one else was
present Lucy was kind, pleasant, agreeable. What made
her flush red at sight of him and then pale? Why did
she often at table or in the big living-room softly
brush against him when it seemed she could have
avoided that? Many times he had felt some inconceivable drawing power, and looked up to find her
eyes upon him, strange eyes full of mystery, that were
suddenly averted. Was there any meaning attachable to
the fact that his room was kept so tidy and neat, that
every day something was added to its comfort or color,
that he found fresh flowers whenever he returned, or a
book, or fruit, or a dainty morsel to eat, and once a
bunch of Indian paint-brush, wild flowers of the desert
that Lucy knew he loved? Most of all, it was Lucy's
eyes which haunted Slone—eyes that had changed,
darkened, lost their audacious flash, and yet seemed all
the sweeter. The glances he caught, which he fancied
were stolen—and then derided his fancy—thrilled him
to his heart. Thus Slone had spent waking hours by
day and night, mad with love and remorse, tormented
one hour by imagined grounds for hope and resigned
to despair the next.

Upon the sixth morning of his stay at Bostil's Slone

rose with something of his former will reasserting itself.
He could not remain in Bostil's home any longer unless he accepted Bostil's offer, and this was not to be
thought of. With a wrench Slone threw off the softening indecision and hurried out to find Bostil while the
determination was hot.

Bostil was in the corral with Wildfire. This was the
second time Slone had found him there. Wildfire appeared to regard Bostil with a much better favor than
he did his master. As Slone noted this a little heat stole
along his veins. That was gall to a rider.

"I like your hoss," said Bostil, with gruff frankness.
But a tinge of red showed under his beard.

"Bostil, I'm sorry I can't take you up on the job,"
rejoined Slone, swiftly. "It's been hard for me to decide. You've been good to me. I'm grateful. But it's
time I was tellin' you."

"Why can't you?" demanded Bostil, straightening up
with a glint in his big eyes. It was the first time he had
asked Slone that.

"I can't ride for you," replied Slone, briefly.

"Anythin' to do with Lucy?" queried Bostil.

"How so?" returned Slone, conscious of more heat.

"Wal, you was sweet on her an' she wouldn't have
you," replied Bostil.

Slone felt the blood swell and boil in his veins. This
Bostil could say as harsh and hard things as repute
gave him credit for.

"Yes, I *am* sweet on Lucy, an' she won't have me,"
said Slone, steadily. "I asked her to let me come to you
an' tell you I wanted to marry her. But she wouldn't."

"Wal, it's just as good you didn't come, because I
might. . . ." Bostil broke off his speech and began
again. "You don't lack nerve, Slone. What 'd you have
to offer Lucy?"

"Nothin' except— But that doesn't matter," replied
Slone, cut to the quick by Bostil's scorn. "I'm glad you
know, an' so much for that."

Bostil turned to look at Wildfire once more, and he
looked long. When he faced around again he was an-

other man. Slone felt the powerful driving passion of
this old horse-trader.

"Slone, I'll give you pick of a hundred mustangs an'
a thousand dollars for Wildfire!"

So he unmasked his power in the face of a beggarly
rider! Though it struck Slone like a thunderbolt, he felt
amused. But he did not show that. Bostil had only one
possession, among all his uncounted wealth, that could
win Wildfire from his owner.

"No," said Slone, briefly.

"I'll double it," returned Bostil, just as briefly.

"No!"

"I'll—"

"Save your breath, Bostil," flashed Slone. "You don't
know me. But let me tell you—you *can't buy* my
horse!"

The great veins swelled and churned in Bostil's bull
neck; a thick and ugly contortion worked in his face;
his eyes reflected a sick rage.

Slone saw that two passions shook Bostil—one, a
bitter, terrible disappointment, and the other, the passion of a man who could not brook being crossed. It
appeared to Slone that the best thing he could do was
to get away quickly, and to this end he led Wildfire out
of the corral to the stable courtyard, and there quickly
saddled him. Then he went into another corral for his
other horse, Nagger, and, bringing him out, returned to
find Bostil had followed as far as the court. The old
man's rage apparently had passed or had been smothered.

"See here," he began, in thick voice, "don't be a
d— fool an' ruin your chance in life. I'll—"

"Bostil, my one chance was ruined—an' you know
who did it," replied Slone, as he gathered Nagger's
rope and Wildfire's bridle together. "I've no hard
feelin's. . . . But I can't sell you my horse. An' I can't
ride for you—because—well, because it would breed
trouble."

"An' what kind?" queried Bostil.

Holley and Farlane and Van, with several other

riders, had come up and were standing open-mouthed. Slone gathered from their manner and expression that anything might happen with Bostil in such a mood.

"We'd be racin' the King an' Wildfire, wouldn't we?" replied Slone.

"An' supposin' we would?" returned Bostil, ominously. His huge frame vibrated with a slight start.

"Wildfire would run off with your favorite—an' you wouldn't like that," answered Slone. It was his rider's hot blood that prompted him to launch this taunt. He could not help it.

"You wild-hoss chaser," roared Bostil, "your Wildfire may be a bloody killer, but he can't beat the King in a race!"

"Excuse *me*, Bostil, but Wildfire did beat the King!"

This was only adding fuel to the fire. Slone saw Holley making signs that must have meant silence would be best. But Slone's blood was up. Bostil had rubbed him the wrong way.

"You're a liar!" declared Bostil, with a tremendous stride forward. Slone saw then how dangerous the man really was. "It was no race. Your wild hoss knocked the King off the track."

"Sage King had the lead, didn't he? Why didn't he keep it?"

Bostil was like a furious, intractable child whose favorite precious treasure had been broken; and he burst out into a torrent of incoherent speech, apparently reasons why this and that were so. Slone did not make out what Bostil meant and he did not care. When Bostil got out of breath Slone said:

"We're both wastin' talk. An' I'm not wantin' you to call me a liar twice. . . . Put your rider up on the King an' come on, right now. I'll—"

"Slone, shut up an' chase yourself," interrupted Holley.

"You go to h—l!" returned Slone, coolly.

There was a moment's silence, in which Slone took Holley's measure. The hawk-eyed old rider may have been square, but he was then thinking only of Bostil.

"What am I up against here?" demanded Slone. "Am I goin' to be shot because I'm takin' my own part? Holley, you an' the rest of your pards are all afraid of this old devil. But I'm not—an' you stay out of this."

"Wal, son, you needn't git r'iled," replied Holley, placatingly. "I was only tryin' to stave off talk you might be sorry for."

"Sorry for nothin'! I'm goin' to make this great horse-trader, this rich an' mighty rancher, this judge of grand horses, this *Bostil!* . . . I'm goin' to make him race the King or take water!" Then Slone turned to Bostil. That worthy evidently had been stunned by the rider who dared call him to his face. "Come on! Fetch the King! Let your own riders judge the race!"

Bostil struggled both to control himself and to speak. "Naw! I ain't goin' to see that red hoss-killer jump the King again!"

"Bah! you're afraid. You know there'd be no girl on his back. You know he can outrun the King an' that's why you want to buy him."

Slone caught his breath then. He realized suddenly, at Bostil's paling face, that perhaps he had dared too much. Yet, maybe the truth flung into this hard old rider's teeth was what he needed more than anything else. Slone divined, rather than saw, that he had done an unprecedented thing.

"I'll go now, Bostil."

Slone nodded a good-by to the riders, and, turning away, he led the two horses down the lane toward the house. It scarcely needed sight of Lucy under the cottonwoods to still his anger and rouse his regret. Lucy saw him coming, and, as usual, started to avoid meeting him, when sight of the horses, or something else, caused her to come toward him instead.

Slone halted. Both Wildfire and Nagger whinnied at sight of the girl. Lucy took one flashing glance at them, at Slone, and then she evidently guessed what was amiss.

"Lucy, I've done it now—played hob, sure," said Slone.

"What?" she cried.

"I called your dad—called him good an' hard—an' he—he—"

"Lin! Oh, don't say Dad." Lucy's face whitened and she put a swift hand upon his arm—a touch that thrilled him. "Lin! there's blood—on your face. Don't —don't tell me Dad hit you?"

"I should say not," declared Slone, quickly lifting his hand to his face. "Must be from my cut, that blood. I barked my hand holdin' Wildfire."

"Oh! I—I was sick with—with—" Lucy faltered and broke off, and then drew back quickly, as if suddenly conscious of her actions and words.

Then Slone began to relate everything that had been said, and before he concluded his story his heart gave a wild throb at the telltale face and eyes of the girl.

"You said that to Dad!" she cried, in amaze and fear and admiration. "Oh, Dad richly deserved it! But I wish you hadn't. Oh, I wish you hadn't!"

"Why?" asked Slone.

But she did not answer that. "Where are you going?" she questioned.

"Come to think of that, I don't know," replied Slone, blankly. "I started back to fetch my things out of my room. That's as far as my muddled thoughts got."

"Your things? . . . Oh!" Suddenly she grew intensely white. The little freckles that had been so indistinct stood out markedly, and it was as if she had never had any tan. One brown hand went to her breast, the other fluttered to his arm again. "You mean to—to go away —for good?"

"Sure. What else can I do?"

"Lin! . . . Oh, there comes Dad! He mustn't see me. I must run. . . . Lin, don't leave Bostil's Ford—don't go—*don't!*"

Then she flew round the corner of the house, to disappear. Slone stood there transfixed and thrilling. Even Bostil's heavy tread did not break the trance, and a meeting would have been unavoidable had not Bostil turned down the path that led to the back of the house.

Slone, with a start collecting his thoughts, hurried into the little room that had been his and gathered up his few belongings. He was careful to leave behind the gifts of guns, blankets, gloves, and other rider's belongings which Bostil had presented to him. Thus laden, he went outside and, tingling with emotions utterly sweet and bewildering, he led the horses down into the village.

Slone went down to Brackton's, and put the horses into a large, high-fenced pasture adjoining Brackton's house. Slone felt reasonably sure his horses would be safe there, but he meant to keep a mighty close watch on them. And old Brackton, as if he read Slone's mind, said this: "Keep your eye on thet daffy boy, Joel Creech. He hangs round my place, sleeps out somewheres, an' he's crazy about hosses."

Slone did not need any warning like that, nor any information to make him curious regarding young Creech. Lucy had seen to that, and, in fact, Slone was anxious to meet this half-witted fellow who had so grievously offended and threatened Lucy. That morning, however, Creech did not put in an appearance. The village had nearly returned to its normal state now, and the sleepy tenor of its way. The Indians had been the last to go, but now none remained. The days were hot while the sun stayed high, and only the riders braved its heat.

The morning, however, did not pass without an interesting incident. Brackton approached Slone with an offer that he take charge of the freighting between the Ford and Durango. "What would I do with Wildfire?" was Slone's questioning reply, and Brackton held up his hands. A later incident earned more of Slone's attention. He had observed a man in Brackton's store, and it chanced that this man heard Slone's reply to Brackton's offer, and he said: "You'll sure need to corral thet red stallion. Grandest hoss I ever seen!"

That praise won Slone, and he engaged in conversation with the man, who said his name was Vorhees. It developed soon that Vorhees owned a little house, a

corral, and a patch of ground on a likely site up under
the bluff, and he was anxious to sell cheap because he
had a fine opportunity at Durango, where his people
lived. What interested Slone most was the man's remark that he had a corral which could not be broken
into. The price he asked was ridiculously low if the
property was worth anything. An idea flashed across
Slone's mind. He went up to Vorhees's place and was
much pleased with everything, especially the corral,
which had been built by a man who feared horse-
thieves as much as Bostil. The view from the door of
the little cabin was magnificent beyond compare. Slone
remembered Lucy's last words. They rang like bells in
his ears. "Don't go—don't!" They were enough to
chain him to Bostil's Ford until the crack of doom. He
dared not dream of what they meant. He only listened
to their music as they pealed over and over in his ears.

"Vorhees, are you serious?" he asked. "The money
you ask is little enough."

"It's enough an' to spare," replied the man. "An' I'd
take it as a favor of you."

"Well, I'll go you," said Slone, and he laughed a little
irrationally. "Only you needn't tell right away that I
bought you out."

The deal was consummated, leaving Slone still with
half of the money that had been his prize in the race.
He felt elated. He was rich. He owned two horses—
one the grandest in all the uplands, the other the faithfulest—and he owned a neat little cabin where it was a
joy to sit and look out, and a corral which would let
him sleep at night, and he had money to put into supplies and furnishings, and a garden. After he drank out
of the spring that bubbled from under the bluff he told
himself it alone was worth the money.

"Looks right down on Bostil's place," Slone soliloquized, with glee. "Won't he just be mad! An' Lucy!
. . . Whatever's she goin' to think?"

The more Slone looked around and thought, the
more he became convinced that good fortune had
knocked at his door at last. And when he returned to

Brackton's he was in an exultant mood. The old store-keeper gave him a nudge and pointed underhand to a young man of ragged aspect sitting gloomily on a box. Slone recognized Joel Creech. The fellow surely made a pathetic sight, and Slone pitied him. He looked needy and hungry.

"Say," said Slone, impulsively, "want to help me carry some grub an' stuff?"

"Howdy!" replied Creech, raising his hand. "Sure do."

Slone sustained the queerest shock of his life when he met the gaze of those contrasting eyes. Yet he did not believe that his strange feeling came from sight of different-colored eyes. There was an instinct or portent in that meeting.

He purchased a bill of goods from Brackton, and, with Creech helping, carried it up to the cabin under the bluff. Three trips were needed to pack up all the supplies, and meanwhile Creech had but few words to say, and these of no moment. Slone offered him money, which he refused.

"I'll help you fix up, an' eat a bite," he said. "Nice up hyar."

He seemed rational enough and certainly responded to kindness. Slone found that Vorhees had left the cabin so clean there was little cleaning to do. An open fireplace of stone required some repair and there was wood to cut.

"Joel, you start a fire while I go down after my horses," said Slone.

Young Creech nodded and Slone left him there. It was not easy to catch Wildfire, nor any easier to get him into the new corral; but at last Slone saw him safely there. And the bars and locks on the gate might have defied any effort to open or break them quickly. Creech was standing in the doorway, watching the horses, and somehow Slone saw, or imagined he saw, that Creech wore a different aspect.

"Grand wild hoss! He did what Blue was a-goin' to do—beat thet there d—d Bostil's King!"

Creech wagged his head. He was gloomy and strange. His eyes were unpleasant to look into. His face changed. And he mumbled. Slone pitied him the more, but wished to see the last of him. Creech stayed on, however, and grew stranger and more talkative during the meal. He repeated things often—talked disconnectedly, and gave other indications that he was not wholly right in his mind. Yet Slone suspected that Creech's want of balance consisted only in what concerned horses and the Bostils. And Slone, wanting to learn all he could, encouraged Creech to talk about his father and the racers and the river and boat, and finally Bostil.

Slone became convinced that, whether young Creech was half crazy or not, he knew his father's horses were doomed, and that the boat at the ferry had been cut adrift. Slone could not understand why he was convinced, but he was. Finally Creech told how he had gone down to the river only a day before; how he had found the flood still raging, but much lower; how he had worked round the cliffs and had pulled up the rope cables to find they had been cut.

"You see, Bostil cut them when he didn't need to," continued Creech, shrewdly. "But he didn't know the flood was comin' down so quick. He was afeared we'd come across an' git the boat thet night. An' he meant to take away them cut cables. But he hadn't no time."

"Bostil?" queried Slone, as he gazed hard at Creech. The fellow had told that rationally enough. Slone wondered if Bostil could have been so base. No! and yet— when it came to horses Bostil was scarcely human.

Slone's query served to send Creech off on another tangent which wound up in dark, mysterious threats. Then Slone caught the name of Lucy. It abruptly killed his sympathy for Creech.

"What's the girl got to do with it?" he demanded, angrily. "If you want to talk to me don't use her name."

"I'll use her name when I want," shouted Creech.

"Not to me!"

"Yes, to you, mister. I ain't carin' a d——n fer you!"

"You crazy loon!" exclaimed Slone, with impatience and disgust added to anger. "What's the use of being decent to you?"

Creech crouched low, his hands digging like claws into the table, as if he were making ready to spring. At that instant he was hideous.

"Crazy, am I?" he yelled. "Mebbe not d——n crazy! I kin tell you're gone on Lucy Bostil! I seen you with her out there in the rocks the mornin' of the race. I seen what you did to her. An' I'm a-goin' to tell it! . . . An' I'm a-goin' to ketch Lucy Bostil an' strip her naked, an' when I git through with her I'll tie her on a hoss an' fire the grass! By Gawd! I am!" Livid and wild, he breathed hard as he got up, facing Slone malignantly.

"Crazy or not, here goes!" muttered Slone, grimly; and, leaping up, with one blow he knocked Creech half out of the door, and then kicked him the rest of the way. "Go on and have a fit!" cried Slone. "I'm liable to kill you if you don't have one!"

Creech got up and ran down the path, turning twice on the way. Then he disappeared among the trees.

Slone sat down. "Lost my temper again!" he said. "This has been a day. Guess I'd better cool off right now an' stay here. . . . That poor devil! Maybe he's not so crazy. But he's wilder than an Indian. I must warn Lucy. . . . Lord! I wonder if Bostil could have held back repairin' that boat, an' then cut it loose? I wonder? Yesterday I'd have sworn never. To-day—"

Slone drove the conclusion of that thought out of his consciousness before he wholly admitted it. Then he set to work cutting the long grass from the wet and shady nooks under the bluff where the spring made the ground rich. He carried an armful down to the corral. Nagger was roaming around outside, picking grass for himself. Wildfire snorted as always when he saw Slone, and Slone as always, when time permitted, tried to coax the stallion to him. He had never succeeded, nor did he this time. When he left the bundle

of grass on the ground and went outside Wildfire
readily came for it.

"You're that tame, anyhow, you hungry red devil,"
said Slone, jealously. Wildfire would take a bunch of
grass from Lucy Bostil's hand. Slone's feelings had
undergone some reaction, though he still loved the
horse. But it was love mixed with bitterness. More than
ever he made up his mind that Lucy should have Wildfire. Then he walked around his place, planning the
work he meant to start at once.

Several days slipped by with Slone scarcely realizing
how they flew. Unaccustomed labor tired him so that
he went to bed early and slept like a log. If it had not
been for the ever-present worry and suspense and
longing, in regard to Lucy, he would have been happier
than ever he could remember. Almost at once he had
become attached to his little home, and the more he
labored to make it productive and comfortable the
stronger grew his attachment. Practical toil was not
conducive to day-dreaming, so Slone felt a loss of
something vague and sweet. Many times he caught
himself watching with eager eyes for a glimpse of Lucy
Bostil down there among the cottonwoods. Still, he
never saw her, and, in fact, he saw so few villagers that
the place began to have a loneliness which endeared
it to him the more. Then the view down the gray
valley to the purple monuments was always thrillingly
memorable to Slone. It was out there Lucy had saved
his horse and his life. His keen desert gaze could make
out even at that distance the great, dark monument,
gold-crowned, in the shadow of which he had heard
Lucy speak words that had transformed life for him.
He would ride out there some day. The spell of those
looming grand shafts of colored rock was still strong
upon him.

One morning Slone had a visitor—old Brackton.
Slone's cordiality died on his lips before it was half uttered. Brackton's former friendliness was not in evidence; indeed, he looked at Slone with curiosity and
disfavor.

"Howdy, Slone! I jest wanted to see what you was doin' up hyar," he said.

Slone spread his hands and explained in few words.

"So you took over the place, hey? We all figgered thet. But Vorhees was mum. Fact is, he was sure mysterious." Brackton sat down and eyed Slone with interest. "Folks are talkin' a lot about you," he said, bluntly.

"Is that so?"

"You 'pear to be a pretty mysterious kind of a feller, Slone. I kind of took a shine to you at first, an' thet's why I come up hyar to tell you it'd be wise fer you to vamoose."

"What!" exclaimed Slone.

Brackton repeated substantially what he had said, then, pausing an instant, continued: "I've no call to give you a hunch, but I'll do it jest because I did like you fust off."

The old man seemed fussy and nervous and patronizing and disparaging all at once.

"What'd you beat up thet poor Joel Creech fer?" demanded Brackton.

"He got what he deserved," replied Slone, and the memory, coming on the head of this strange attitude of Brackton's, roused Slone's temper.

"Wal, Joel tells some queer things about you—fer instance, how you took advantage of little Lucy Bostil, grabbin' her an' maulin' her the way Joel seen you."

"D—n the loon!" muttered Slone, rising to pace the path.

"Wal, Joel's a bit off, but he's not loony all the time. He's seen you an' he's tellin' it. When Bostil hears it you'd better be acrost the cañon!"

Slone felt the hot, sick rush of blood to his face, and humiliation and rage overtook him.

"Joel's down at my house. He had fits after you beat him, an' he 'ain't got over them yet. But he could blab to the riders. Van Sickle's lookin' fer you. An' to-day when I was alone with Joel he told me some more queer things about you. I shut him up quick. But I ain't guaranteein' I can keep him shut up."

"I'll bet you I shut him up," declared Slone. "What more did the fool say?"

"Slone, hev you been round these hyar parts—down among the monuments—fer any considerable time?" queried Brackton.

"Yes, I have—several weeks out there, an' about ten days or so around the Ford."

"Where was you the night of the flood?"

The shrewd scrutiny of the old man, the suspicion, angered Slone.

"If it's any of your mix, I was out on the slope among the rocks. I heard that flood comin' down long before it got here," replied Slone, deliberately.

Brackton averted his gaze, and abruptly rose as if the occasion was ended. "Wal, take my hunch an' leave!" he said, turning away.

"Brackton, if you mean well, I'm much obliged," returned Slone, slowly, ponderingly. "But I'll not take the hunch."

"Suit yourself," added Brackton, coldly, and he went away.

Slone watched him go down the path and disappear in the lane of cottonwoods.

"I'll be darned!" muttered Slone. "Funny old man. Maybe Creech's not the only loony one hereabouts."

Slone tried to laugh off the effect of the interview, but it persisted and worried him all day. After supper he decided to walk down into the village, and would have done so but for the fact that he saw a man climbing his path. When he recognized the rider Holley he sensed trouble, and straightway he became gloomy. Bostil's right-hand man could not call on him for any friendly reason. Holley came up slowly, awkwardly, after the manner of a rider unused to walking. Slone had built a little porch on the front of his cabin and a bench, which he had covered with goatskins. It struck him a little strange that he should bend over to rear-range these skins just as Holley approached the porch.

"Howdy, son!" was the rider's drawled remark. "Sure makes—me—puff to climb—up this mountain."

Slone turned instantly, surprised at the friendly tone, doubting his own ears, and wanting to verify them. He was the more surprised to see Holley unmistakably amiable.

"Hello, Holley! How are you?" he replied. "Have a seat."

"Wal, I'm right spry fer an old bird. But I can't climb wuth a d—n. . . . Say, this here beats Bostil's view."

"Yes, it's fine," replied Slone, rather awkwardly, as he sat down on the porch step. What could Holley want with him? This old rider was above curiosity or gossip.

"Slone, you ain't holdin' it ag'in me—thet I tried to shut you up the other day?" he drawled, with dry frankness.

"Why, no, Holley, I'm not. I saw your point. You were right. But Bostil made me mad."

"Sure! He'd make anybody mad. I've seen riders bite themselves, they was so mad at Bostil. You called him, an' you sure tickled all the boys. But you hurt yourself, fer Bostil owns an' runs this here Ford."

"So I've discovered," replied Slone.

"You got yourself in bad right off, fer Bostil has turned the riders ag'in you, an' this here punchin' of Creech has turned the village folks ag'in you. What 'd you pitch into him fer?"

Slone caught the kindly interest and intent of the rider, and it warmed him as Brackton's disapproval had alienated him

"Wal, I reckon I'd better tell you," drawled Holley, as Slone hesitated, "thet Lucy wants to know *if* you beat up Joel an' *why* you did."

"Holley! Did she ask you to find out?"

"She sure did. The girl's worried these days, Slone. . . . You see, you haven't been around, an' you don't know what's comin' off."

"Brackton was here today an' he told me a good deal. I'm worried, too," said Slone, dejectedly.

"Thet hoss of yours, Wildfire, he's enough to make you hated in Bostil's camp, even if you hadn't made a fool of yourself, which you sure have."

Slone dropped his head as admission.

"What Creech swears he seen you do to Miss Lucy, out there among the rocks, where you was hid with Wildfire—is there any truth in thet?" asked Holley, earnestly. "Tell me, Slone. Folks believe it. An' it's hurt you at the Ford. Bostil hasn't heard it yet, an' Lucy she doesn't know. But I'm figgerin' thet you punched Joel because he throwed it in your face."

"He did, an' I lambasted him," replied Slone, with force.

"You did right. But what I want to know, is it true what Joel seen?"

"It's true, Holley. But what I did isn't so bad—so bad as he'd make it look."

"Wal, I knowed thet. I knowed for a long time how Lucy cares for you," returned the old rider, kindly.

Slone raised his head swiftly, incredulously. "Holley! You can't be serious."

"Wal, I am. I've been sort of a big brother to Lucy Bostil for eighteen years. I carried her in these here hands when she weighed no more'n my spurs. I taught her how to ride—what she knows about hosses. An' she knows more'n her dad. I taught her to shoot. I know her better'n anybody. An' lately she's been different. She's worried an' unhappy."

"But, Holley, all that—it doesn't seem—"

"I reckon not," went on Holley, as Slone halted. "I think she cares fer you. An' I'm your friend, Slone. You're goin' to buck up ag'in some hell round here sooner or later. An' you'll need a friend."

"Thanks—Holley," replied Slone, unsteadily. He thrilled under the iron grasp of the rider's hard hand.

"You've got another friend you can gamble on," said Holley, significantly.

"Another! Who?"

"Lucy Bostil. An' don't you forget thet. I'll bet she'll raise more trouble than Bostil when she hears what Joel Creech is tellin'. Fer she's bound to hear it. Van Sickle swears he's a-goin' to tell her an' then beat you up with a quirt."

"He is, is he?" snapped Slone, darkly.

"I've a hunch Lucy's guessed why you punched Joel. But she wants to know fer sure. Now, Slone, I'll tell her why."

"Oh, don't!" said Slone, involuntarily.

"Wall, it 'll be better comin' from you an' me. Take my word fer thet. I'll prepare Lucy. An' she's as good a scrapper as Bostil, any day."

"It all scares me," replied Slone. He did feel panicky, and that was from thoughts of what shame might befall Lucy. The cold sweat oozed out of every pore. What might not Bostil do? "Holley, I love the girl. So I—I didn't insult her. Bostil will never understand. An' what's he goin' to do when he finds out?"

"Wal, let's hope you won't git any wuss'n you give Joel."

"Let Bostil beat me!" ejaculated Slone. "I think I'm willin'—now—the way I feel. But I've a temper, and Bostil rubs me the wrong way."

"Wal, leave your gun home, an' fight Bostil. You're pretty husky. Sure he'll lick you, but mebbe you could give the old cuss a black eye." Holley laughed as if the idea gave him infinite pleasure.

"Fight Bostil? . . . Lucy would hate me!" cried Slone.

"Nix! You don't know thet kid. If the old man goes after you Lucy 'll care more fer you. She's just like him in some ways." Holley pulled out a stubby black pipe and, filling and lighting it, he appeared to grow more thoughtful. "It wasn't only Lucy thet sent me up here to see you. Bostil had been pesterin' me fer days. But I kept fightin' shy of it till Lucy got hold of me."

"Bostil sent you? Why?"

"Reckon you can guess. He can't sleep, thinkin' about your red hoss. None of us ever seen Bostil have

sich a bad case. He raised Sage King. But he's always
been crazy fer a great wild stallion. An' here you come
along—an' your hoss jumps the King—an' there's trouble generally."

"Holley, do you think Wildfire can beat Sage King?"
asked Slone, eagerly.

"Reckon I do. Lucy says so, an' I'll back her any
day. But, son, I ain't paradin' what I think. I'd git
in bad myself. Farlane an' the other boys, they're
with Bostil. Van he's to blame fer thet. He's takin' a
dislike to you, right off. An' what he tells Bostil an' the
boys about thet race don't agree with what Lucy tells
me. Lucy says Wildfire ran fiery an' cranky at the
start. He wanted to run round an' kill the King instead
of racin'. So he was three lengths behind when Macomber dropped the flag. Lucy says the King got into his
stride. She knows. An' there Wildfire comes from behind an' climbs all over the King! . . . Van tells a
different story."

"It came off just as Lucy told you," declared Slone.
"I saw every move."

"Wal, thet's neither here nor there. What you're up
ag'in is this. Bostil is sore since you called him. But he
holds himself in because he hasn't given up hope of
gittin' Wildfire. An', Slone, you're sure wise, ain't you,
thet if Bostil doesn't buy him you can't stay on here?"

"I'm wise. But I won't sell Wildfire," replied Slone,
doggedly.

"Wal, I'd never wasted my breath tellin' you all this
if I hadn't figgered about Lucy. You've got her to
think of."

Slone turned on Holley passionately. "You keep
hintin' there's a hope for me, when I know there's
none!"

"You're only a boy," replied Holley. "Son, where
there's life there's hope. I ain't a-goin' to tell you agin
thet I know Lucy Bostil."

Slone could not stand nor walk nor keep still. He
was shaking from head to foot.

"Wildfire's not mine to sell. He's Lucy's!" confessed Slone.

"The devil you say!" ejaculated Holley, and he nearly dropped his pipe.

"I gave Wildfire to her. She accepted him. It was *done*. Then—then I lost my head an' made her mad. . . . An'—she said she'd ride him in the race, but wouldn't keep him. But he *is* hers."

"Oho! I see. Slone, I was goin' to advise you to sell Wildfire—all on account of Lucy. You're young an' you'd have a big start in life if you would. But Lucy's your girl an' you give her the hoss. . . . Thet settles thet!"

"If I go away from here an' leave Wildfire for Lucy —do you think she could keep him? Wouldn't Bostil take him from her?"

"Wal, son, if he tried thet on Lucy she'd jump Wildfire an' hit your trail an' hang on to it till she found you."

"What 'll you tell Bostil?" asked Slone, half beside himself.

"I'm consarned if I know," replied Holley. "Mebbe I'll think of some idee. I'll go back now. An' say, son, I reckon you'd better hang close to home. If you meet Bostil down in the village you two'd clash sure. I'll come up soon, but it 'll be after dark."

"Holley, all this is—is good of you," said Slone. "I —I'll—"

"Shut up, son," interrupted the rider, dryly. "Thet's your only weakness, so far as I can see. You say too much."

Holley started down then, his long, clinking spurs digging into the deep path. He left Slone a prey to deep thoughts at once anxious and dreamy.

Next day Slone worked hard all day, looking forward to nightfall, expecting that Holley would come up. He tried to resist the sweet and tantalizing anticipation of a message from Lucy, but in vain. The rider had immeasurably lifted Slone's hope that Lucy, at least, cared for him. Not for a moment all day could Slone

drive away the hope. At twilight he was too eager to
eat—too obsessed to see the magnificent sunset. But
Holley did not come, and Slone went to bed late, half
sick with disappointment.

The next day was worse. Slone found work irksome,
yet he held to it. On the third day he rested and
dreamed, and grew doubtful again, and then moody.
On the fourth day Slone found he needed supplies that
he must obtain from the store. He did not forget Holley's warning, but he disregarded it, thinking there
would scarcely be a chance of meeting Bostil at midday.

There were horses standing, bridles down, before
Brackton's place, and riders lounging at the rail and
step. Some of these men had been pleasant to Slone on
earlier occasions. This day they seemed not to see him.
Slone was tingling all over when he went into the
store. Some deviltry was afoot! He had an angry
thought that these riders could not have minds of their
own. Just inside the door Slone encountered Wetherby,
the young rancher from Durango. Slone spoke, but
Wetherby only replied with an insolent stare. Slone did
not glance at the man to whom Wetherby was talking.
Only a few people were inside the store, and Brackton
was waiting upon them. Slone stood back a little in the
shadow. Brackton had observed his entrance, but did
not greet him. Then Slone absolutely knew that for
him the good will of Bostil's Ford was a thing of the
past.

Presently Brackton was at leisure, but he showed no
disposition to attend to Slone's wants. Then Slone
walked up to the counter and asked for supplies.

"Have you got the money?" asked Brackton, as if
addressing one he would not trust.

"Yes," replied Slone, growing red under an insult
that he knew Wetherby had heard.

Brackton handed out the supplies and received the
money without a word. He held his head down. It was
a singular action for a man used to dealing fairly with
every one. Slone felt outraged. He hurried out of the

place, with shame burning him, with his own eyes downcast, and in his hurry he bumped square into a burly form. Slone recoiled—looked up. Bostil! The old rider was eying him with cool speculation.

"Wal, are you drunk?" he queried, without any particular expression.

Yet the query was to Slone like a blow. It brought his head up with a jerk, his glance steady and keen on Bostil's.

"Bostil, you know I don't drink," he said.

"A-huh! I know a lot about you, Slone. . . . I heard you bought Vorhees's place, up on the bench."

"Yes."

"Did he tell you it was mortgaged to me for more'n it's worth?"

"No, he didn't."

"Did he make over any papers to you?"

"No."

"Wal, if it interests you I'll show you papers thet proves the property's mine."

Slone suffered a pang. The little home had grown dearer and dearer to him.

"All right, Bostil. If it's yours—it's yours," he said, calmly enough.

"I reckon I'd drove you out before this if I hadn't felt we could make a deal."

"We can't agree on any deal, Bostil," replied Slone, steadily. It was not what Bostil said, but the way he said it, the subtle meaning and power behind it, that gave Slone a sense of menace and peril. These he had been used to for years; he could meet them. But he was handicapped here because it seemed that, though he could meet Bostil face to face, he could not fight him. For he was Lucy's father. Slone's position, the impotence of it, rendered him less able to control his temper.

"Why can't we?" demanded Bostil. "If you wasn't so touchy we could. An' let me say, young feller, thet there's more reason now that you *do* make a deal with me."

"Deal? What about?"

"About your red hoss."

"Wildfire! . . . No deals, Bostil," returned Slone, and made as if to pass him.

The big hand that forced Slone back was far from gentle, and again he felt the quick rush of blood.

"Mebbe I can tell you somethin' thet 'll make you sell Wildfire," said Bostil.

"Not if you talked yourself dumb!" flashed Slone. There was no use to try to keep cool with this Bostil, if he talked horses. "I'll race Wildfire against the King. But no more."

"Race! Wal, we don't run races around here without stakes," replied Bostil, with deep scorn. "An' what can you bet? Thet little dab of prize money is gone, an' it wouldn't be enough to meet me. You're a strange one in these parts. I've pride an' reputation to uphold. You brag of racin' with me—an' you a beggarly rider! . . . You wouldn't have them clothes an' boots if my girl hadn't fetched them to you."

The riders behind Bostil laughed. Wetherby's face was there in the door, not amused, but hard with scorn and something else. Slone felt a sickening, terrible gust of passion. It fairly shook him. And as the wave subsided the quick cooling of skin and body pained him like a burn made with ice.

"Yes, Bostil, I'm what you say," responded Slone, and his voice seemed to fill his ears. "But you're dead wrong when you say I've nothin' to bet on a race."

"An' what 'll you bet?"

"My life an' my horse!"

The riders suddenly grew silent and intense. Bostil vibrated to that. He turned white. He more than any rider on the uplands must have felt the nature of that offer.

"Ag'in what?" he demanded, hoarsely.

"Your daughter Lucy!"

One instant the surprise held Bostil mute and motionless. Then he seemed to expand. His huge bulk jerked into motion and he bellowed like a mad bull.

Slone saw the blow coming, made no move to avoid it. The big fist took him square on the mouth and chin and laid him flat on the ground. Sight failed Slone for a little, and likewise ability to move. But he did not lose consciousness. His head seemed to have been burst into rays and red mist that blurred his eyes. Then these cleared away, leaving intense pain. He started to get up, his brain in a whirl. Where was his gun? He had left it home. But for that he would have killed Bostil He had already killed one man. The thing was a burning flash—then all over! He could do it again. But Bostil was Lucy's father!

Slone gathered up the packages of supplies, and without looking at the men he hurried away. He seemed possessed of a fury to turn and run back. Some force, like an invisible hand, withheld him. When he reached the cabin he shut himself in, and lay on his bunk, forgetting that the place did not belong to him, alive only to the mystery of his trouble, smarting with the shame of the assault upon him. It was dark before he composed himself and went out, and then he had not the desire to eat. He made no move to open the supplies of food, did not even make a light. But he went out to take grass and water to the horses. When he returned to the cabin a man was standing at the porch. Slone recognized Holley's shape and then his voice.

"Son, you raised the devil to-day."

"Holley, don't you go back on me!" cried Slone. "I was driven!"

"Don't talk so loud," whispered the rider in return. "I've only a minnit. . . . Here—a letter from Lucy. . . . An', son, don't git the idee thet I'll go back on you."

Slone took the letter with trembling fingers. All the fury and gloom instantly fled. Lucy had written him! He could not speak.

"Son, I'm double-crossin' the boss, right this minnit!" whispered Holley, hoarsely. "An' the same time I'm playin' Lucy's game. If Bostil finds out he'll kill

me. I mustn't be ketched up here. But I won't lose
track of you—wherever you go."

Holley slipped away steathily in the dusk, leaving
Slone with a throbbing heart.

"Wherever you go!" he echoed. "Ah! I forgot! I
can't stay here."

Lucy's letter made his fingers tingle—made them so
hasty and awkward that he had difficulty in kindling
blaze enough to see to read. The letter was short,
written in lead-pencil on the torn leaf of a ledger. Slone
could not read rapidly—those years on the desert had
seen to that—and his haste to learn what Lucy said
bewildered him. At first all the words blurred:

> Come at once to the bench in the cottonwoods.
> I'll meet you there. My heart is breaking. It's a
> lie—a lie—what they say. I'll swear you were with
> me the night the boat was cut adrift. I *know* you
> didn't do that. I know who. . . . Oh, come! I will
> stick to you. I will run off with you. I love you!

Chapter XV

SLONE'S heart leaped to his throat, and its beating
choked his utterances of rapture and amaze and dread.
But rapture dominated the other emotions. He could
scarcely control the impulse to run to meet Lucy, without a single cautious thought.

He put the precious letter inside his blouse, where it
seemed to warm his breast. He buckled on his gun-
belt, and, extinguishing the light, he hurried out.

A crescent moon had just tipped the bluff. The village lanes and cabins and trees lay silver in the moonlight. A lonesome coyote barked in the distance. All
else was still. The air was cool, sweet, fragrant. There

appeared to be a glamour of light, of silence, of beauty over the desert.

Slone kept under the dark lee of the bluff and worked around so that he could be above the village, where there was little danger of meeting any one. Yet presently he had to go out of the shadow into the moon-blanched lane. Swift and silent as an Indian he went along, keeping in the shade of what trees there were, until he came to the grove of cottonwoods. The grove was a black mystery lanced by silver rays. He slipped in among the trees, halting every few steps to listen. The action, the realization had helped to make him cool, to steel him, though never before in his life had he been so exalted. The pursuit and capture of Wildfire, at one time the desire of his heart, were as nothing to this. Love had called him—and life—and he knew death hung in the balance. If Bostil found him seeking Lucy there would be blood spilled. Slone quaked at the thought, for the cold and ghastly oppression following the death he had meted out to Sears came to him at times. But such thoughts were fleeting; only one thought really held his mind—and the one was that Lucy loved him, had sent strange, wild, passionate words to him.

He found the narrow path, its white crossed by slowly moving black bars of shadow, and stealthily he followed this, keen of eye and ear, stopping at every rustle. He well knew the bench Lucy had mentioned. It was in a remote corner of the grove, under big trees near the spring. Once Slone thought he had a glimpse of white. Perhaps it was only moonlight. He slipped on and on, and when beyond the branching paths that led toward the house he breathed freer. The grove appeared deserted. At last he crossed the runway from the spring, smelled the cool, wet moss and watercress, and saw the big cottonwood, looming dark above the other trees. A patch of moonlight brightened a little glade just at the edge of dense shade cast by the cottonwood. Here the bench stood. It was empty!

Slone's rapture vanished. He was suddenly chilled.

She was not there! She might have been intercepted.
He would not see her. The disappointment, the sudden
relaxation, was horrible. Then a white, slender shape
flashed from beside the black tree-trunk and flew toward him. It was noiseless, like a specter, and swift as
the wind. Was he dreaming? He felt so strange. Then
—the white shape reached him and he knew.

Lucy leaped into his arms.

"Lin! Lin! Oh, I'm so—so glad to see you!" she
whispered. She seemed breathless, keen, new to him,
not in the least afraid nor shy. Slone could only hold
her. He could not have spoken, even if she had given
him a chance. "I know everything—what they accuse
you of—how the riders treated you—how my dad
struck you. Oh! . . . He's a brute! I hate him for that.
Why didn't you keep out of his way? . . . Van saw it
all. Oh, I hate him, too! He said you lay still—where
you fell! . . . Dear Lin, that blow may have hurt you
dreadfully—shamed you because you couldn't strike
back at my dad—but it reached me, too. It hurt me. It
woke my heart. . . . Where—where did he hit you? Oh,
I've seen him hit men! His terrible fists!"

"Lucy, never mind," whispered Slone. "I'd stood to
be shot just for this."

He felt her hands softly on his face, feeling around
tenderly till they found the swollen bruise on mouth
and chin.

"Ah! . . . He struck you. And I—I'll kiss you," she
whispered. "If kisses will make it well—it'll be well!"

She seemed strange, wild, passionate in her tender-
ness. She lifted her face and kissed him softly again and
again and again, till the touch that had been exquisitely painful to his bruised lips became rapture. Then
she leaned back in his arms, her hands on his shoulders, white-faced, dark-eyed, and laughed up in his
face, lovingly, daringly, as if she defied the world to
change what she had done.

"Lucy! Lucy! . . . He can beat me—again!" said
Slone, low and hoarsely.

"If you love me you'll keep out of his way," replied the girl.

"If I love you? . . . My God! . . . I've felt my heart die a thousand times since that mornin'—when—when you—"

"Lin, I didn't know," she interrupted, with sweet, grave earnestness. "I know now!"

And Slone could not but know, too, looking at her; and the sweetness, the eloquence, the noble abandon of her avowal sounded to the depths of him. His dread, his resignation, his shame, all sped forever in the deep, full breath of relief with which he cast off that burden. He tasted the nectar of happiness, the first time in his life. He lifted his head—never, he knew, to lower it again. He would be true to what she had made him.

"Come in the shade," he whispered, and with his arm round her he led her to the great tree-trunk. "Is it safe for you here? An' how long can you stay?"

"I had it out with Dad—left him licked once in his life," she replied. "Then I went to my room, fastened the door, and slipped out of my window. I can stay out as long as I want. No one will know."

Slone's heart throbbed. She was his. The clasp of her hands on his, the gleam of her eyes, the white, daring flash of her face in the shadow of the moon— these told him she was his. How it had come about was beyond him, but he realized the truth. What a girl! This was the same nerve which she showed when she had run Wildfire out in front of the fleetest horses in the uplands.

"Tell me, then," he began, quietly, with keen gaze roving under the trees and eyes strained tight, "tell me what's come off."

"Don't you know?" she queried, in amaze.

"Only that for some reason I'm done in Bostil's Ford. It can't be because I punched Joel Creech. I felt it before I met Bostil at the store. He taunted me. We had bitter words. He told before all of them how the outfit I wore you gave me. An' then I dared him to race the King. My horse an' my life against *you!*"

"Yes, I know," she whispered, softly. "It's all over town. . . . Oh, Lin! it was a grand bet! And Bostil four-flushed, as the riders say. For days a race between Wildfire and the King had been in the air. There'll never be peace in Bostil's Ford again till that race is run."

"But, Lucy, could Bostil's wantin' Wildfire an' hatin' me because I won't sell—could that ruin me here at the Ford?"

"It could. But, Lin, there's more. Oh, I hate to tell you!" she whispered, passionately. "I thought you'd know. . . . Joel Creech swore you cut the ropes on the ferry-boat and sent it adrift."

"The loon!" ejaculated Slone, and he laughed low in both anger and ridicule. "Lucy, that's only a fool's talk."

"He's crazy. Oh, if I ever get him in front of me again when I'm on Sarch—I'll—I'll. . . ." She ended with a little gasp and leaned a moment against Slone. He felt her heart beat—felt the strong clasp of her hands. She was indeed Bostil's flesh and blood, and there was that in her dangerous to arouse.

"Lin, the folks here are queer," she resumed, more calmly. "For long years Dad has ruled them. They see with his eyes and talk with his voice. Joel Creech swore you cut those cables. Swore he trailed you. Brackton believed him. Van believed him. They told my father. And he—my dad—God forgive him! he jumped at that. The village as one person now believes you sent the boat adrift so Creech's horses could not cross and you could win the race."

"Lucy, if it wasn't so—so funny I'd be mad as—as—" burst out Slone.

"It isn't funny. It's terrible. . . . I know who cut those cables. . . . Holley knows. . . . *Dad* knows—an', oh, Lin—I—I hate—I hate my own father!"

"My God!" gasped Slone, as the full signification burst upon him. Then his next thought was for Lucy. "Listen, dear—you mustn't say that," he entreated. "He's your father. He's a good man every way except when he's after horses. Then he's half horse. I understand him. I feel sorry for him. . . . An' if he's throwed the blame on me, all right. I'll stand it. What do I care? I was queered, anyhow, because I wouldn't part with my horse. It can't matter so much if people think I did that just to help win a race. But if they knew your —your father did it, an' if Creech's horses starve, why it 'd be a disgrace for him—an' you."

"Lin Slone—you'll accept the blame!" she whispered, with wide, dark eyes on him, hands at his shoulders.

"Sure I will," replied Slone. "I can't be any worse off."

"You're better than all of them—my rider!" she cried, full-voiced and tremulous. "Lin, you make me love you so—it—it hurts!" And she seemed about to fling herself into his arms again. There was a strangeness about her—a glory. "But you'll not take the shame of that act. For I won't let you. I'll tell my father I was with you when the boat was cut loose. He'll believe me."

"Yes, an' he'll *kill* me!" groaned Slone. "Good Lord! Lucy, don't do that!"

"I will! An' he'll not kill you. Lin, Dad took a great fancy to you. I know that. He thinks he hates you. But in his heart he doesn't. If he got hold of Wildfire—why, he'd never be able to do enough for you. He never could make it up. What do you think? I told him you hugged and kissed me shamefully that day."

"Oh, Lucy! you didn't!" implored Slone.

"I sure did. And what do you think? He said he once did the same to my mother! . . . No, Lin, Dad 'd never kill you for anything except a fury about horses. All the fights he ever had were over horse deals. The two men—he—he—" Lucy faltered and her shudder was illuminating to Slone. "Both of them—fights over horse trades!"

"Lucy, if I'm ever unlucky enough to meet Bostil again I'll be deaf an' dumb. An' now you promise me you won't tell him you were with me that night."

"Lin, if the occasion comes, I will—I couldn't help it," replied Lucy.

"Then fight shy of the occasion," he rejoined, earnestly. "For that would be the end of Lin Slone!"

"Then—what on earth can—we do?" Lucy said, with sudden break of spirit.

"I think we must wait. You wrote in you letter you'd stick to me—you'd—" He could not get the words out, the thought so overcame him.

"If it comes to a finish, I'll go with you," Lucy returned, with passion rising again.

"Oh! to ride off with you, Lucy—to have you all to myself—I daren't think of it. But that's only selfish."

"Maybe it's not so selfish as you believe. If you left the Ford—now—it'd break my heart. I'd never get over it."

"Lucy! You love me—that well?"

Then their lips met again and their hands locked, and they stood silent, straining toward each other. He held the slight form, so pliant, so responsive, so alive, close to him, and her face lay hidden on his breast; and he looked out over her head into the quivering moonlit shadows. The night was as still as one away on the desert far from the abode of men. It was more beautiful than any dream of a night in which he had wandered far into strange lands where wild horses were and forests lay black under moon-silvered peaks.

"We'll run—then—if it comes to a finish," said Slone, huskily. "But I'll wait. I'll stick it out here. I'll take what comes. So—maybe I'll not disgrace you more."

"I told Van I—I gloried in being hugged by you that day," she replied, and her little defiant laugh told what she thought of the alleged disgrace.

"You torment him," remonstrated Slone. "You set him against us. It would be better to keep still."

"But my blood is up!" she said, and she pounded his shoulder with her fist. "I'll fight—I'll fight! . . . I couldn't avoid Van. It was Holley who told me Van was threatening you. And when I met Van he told me

how everybody said you insulted me—had been worse
than a drunken rider—and that he'd beat you half to
death. So I told Van Joel Creech might have seen us
—I didn't doubt that—but he didn't see that I liked
being hugged."

"What did Van say then?" asked Slone, all aglow
with his wonderful joy.

"He wilted. He slunk away. . . . And so I'll tell them
all."

"But, Lucy, you've always been so—so truthful."

"What do you mean?"

"Well, to say you liked being hugged that day was—
was a story, wasn't it?"

"That was what made me so furious," she admitted,
shyly. "I was surprised when you grabbed me off Wildfire. And my heart beat—beat—beat so when you
hugged me. And when you kissed me I—I was petri-
fied. I knew I liked it then—and I was furious with
myself."

Slone drew a long, deep breath of utter enchant-
ment. "You'll take back Wildfire?"

"Oh, Lin—don't—ask—me," she implored.

"Take him back—an' me with him."

"Then I will. But no one must know that yet."

They drew apart then.

"An' now you must go," said Slone, reluctantly.
"Listen. I forgot to warn you about Joel Creech.
Don't ever let him near you. He's crazy an' he means
evil."

"Oh, I know, Lin! I'll watch. But I'm not afraid of
him."

"He's strong, Lucy. I saw him lift bags that were
hefty for me. . . . Lucy, do you ride these days?"

"Every day. If I couldn't ride I couldn't live."

"I'm afraid," said Slone, nervously. "There's Creech
an' Cordts—both have threatened you."

"I'm afraid of Cordts," replied Lucy, with a shiver.
"You should have seen him look at me race-day. It
made me hot with anger, yet weak, too, somehow. But

Dad says I'm never in any danger if I watch out. And I do. Who could catch me on Sarch?"

"Any horse can be tripped in the sage. You told me how Joel tried to rope Sage King. Did you ever tell your dad that?"

"I forgot. But then I'm glad I didn't. Dad would shoot for that, quicker than if Joel tried to rope him. . . . Don't worry, Lin, I always pack a gun."

"But can you use it?"

Lucy laughed. "Do you think I can only ride?"

Slone remembered that Holley had said he had taught Lucy how to shoot as well as ride. "You'll be watchful—careful," he said, earnestly.

"Oh, Lin, you need to be that more than I. . . . What will you do?"

"I'll stay up at the little cabin I thought I owned till to-day."

"Didn't you buy it?" asked Lucy, quickly.

"I thought I did. But . . . never mind. Maybe I won't get put out just yet. An' when will I see you again?"

"Here, every night. Wait till I come," she replied. "Good night, Lin."

"I'll—wait!" he exclaimed, with a catch in his voice. "Oh, my luck! . . . I'll wait, Lucy, every day—hopin' an' prayin' that this trouble will lighten. An' I'll wait at night—for you!"

He kissed her goodby and watched the slight form glide away, flit to and fro, white in the dark patches, grow indistinct and vanish. He was left alone in the silent grove.

Slone stole back to the cabin and lay sleepless and tranced, watching the stars, till late that night.

All the next day he did scarcely anything but watch and look after his horses and watch and drag the hours out and dream despite his dread. But no one visited him. The cabin was left to him that day.

It had been a hot day, with great thunderhead, black and creamy white clouds rolling down from the cañon country. No rain had fallen at the Ford, though storms near by had cooled the air. At sunset Slone saw a rainbow bending down, ruddy and gold, connecting the purple of cloud with the purple of horizon.

Out beyond the valley the clouds were broken, showing rifts of blue, and they rolled low, burying the heads of the monuments, creating a wild and strange spectacle. Twilight followed, and appeared to rise to meet the darkening clouds. And at last the gold on the shafts faded; the monuments faded; and the valley grew dark.

Slone took advantage of the hour before moonrise to steal down into the grove, there to wait for Lucy. She came so quickly he scarcely felt that he had waited at all; and then the time spent with her, sweet, fleeting, precious, left him stronger to wait for her again, to hold himself in, to cease his brooding, to learn faith in something deeper than he could fathom.

The next day he tried to work, but found idle waiting made the time fly swifter because in it he could dream. In the dark of the rustling cottonwoods he met Lucy, as eager to see him as he was to see her, tender, loving, remorseful—a hundred sweet and bewildering things all so new, so unbelievable to Slone.

That night he learned that Bostil had started for Durango with some of his riders. This trip surprised Slone and relieved him likewise, for Durango was over two hundred miles distant, and a journey there even for the hard riders was a matter of days.

"He left no orders for me," Lucy said, "except to behave myself. . . . Is this behaving?" she whispered, and nestled close to Slone, audacious, tormenting as she had been before this dark cloud of trouble. "But he left orders for Holley to ride with me and look after me. Isn't that funny? Poor old Holley! He hates to double-cross Dad, he says."

"I'm glad Holley's to look after you," replied Slone. "Yesterday I saw you tearin' down into the sage on Sarch. I wondered what you'd do, Lucy, if Cordts or that loon Creech should get hold of you?"

"I'd fight!"

"But, child, that's nonsense. You couldn't fight either of them."

"Couldn't I? Well, I just could. I'd—I'd shoot Cordts. And I'd whip Joel Creech with my quirt. And if he kept after me I'd let Sarch run him down. Sarch hates him."

"You're a brave sweetheart," mused Slone. "Suppose you were caught an' couldn't get away. Would you leave a trail somehow?"

"I sure would."

"Lucy, I'm a wild-horse hunter," he went on, thoughtfully, as if speaking to himself. "I never failed on a trail. I could track you over bare rock."

"Lin, I'll leave a trail, so never fear," she replied. "But don't borrow trouble. You're always afraid for me. Look at the bright side. Dad seems to have forgotten you. Maybe it all isn't so bad as we thought. Oh, I hope so! . . . How is my horse, Wildfire? I want to ride him again. I can hardly keep from going after him."

And so they whispered while the moments swiftly passed.

It was early during the afternoon of the next day that Slone, hearing the clip-clop of unshod ponies, went outside to look. One part of the lane he could see plainly, and into it stalked Joel Creech, leading the leanest and gauntest ponies Slone had ever seen. A man as lean and gaunt as the ponies stalked behind.

The sight shocked Slone. Joel Creech and his father! Slone had no proof, because he had never seen the elder Creech, yet strangely he felt convinced of it. And grim ideas began to flash into his mind. Creech would hear who was accused of cutting the boat adrift. What would he say? If he believed, as all the villagers believed, then Bostil's Ford would become an unhealthy place for Lin Slone. Where were the great race-horses —Blue Roan and Peg—and the other thoroughbreds? A pang shot through Slone.

"Oh, not lost—not starved!" he muttered. "That would be hell!"

Yet he believed just this had happened. How strange he had never considered such an event as the return of Creech.

"I'd better look him up before he looks me," said Slone.

It took but an instant to strap on his belt and gun. Then Slone strode down his path, out into the lane toward Brackton's. Whatever before boded ill to Slone had been nothing to what menaced him now. He would have a man to face—a man whom repute called just, but stern.

Before Slone reached the vicinity of the store he saw riders come out to meet the Creech party. It so happened there were more riders than usually frequented Brackton's at that hour. The old storekeeper came stumbling out and raised his hands. The riders could be heard, loud-voiced and excited. Slone drew nearer, and the nearer he got the swifter he strode. Instinct told him that he was making the right move. He would face this man whom he was accused of ruining. The poor mustangs hung their heads dejectedly.

"Bags of bones," some rider loudly said.

And then Slone drew close to the excited group. Brackton held the center; he was gesticulating; his thin voice rose piercingly.

"Creech! Whar's Peg an' the Roan? Gawd Almighty, man! You ain't meanin' them cayuses thar are all you've got left of thet grand bunch of hosses?"

There was scarcely a sound. All the riders were still. Slone fastened his eyes on Creech. He saw a gaunt, haggard face almost black with dust—worn and sad —with big eyes of terrible gloom. He saw an unkempt, ragged form that had been wet and muddy, and was now dust-caked.

Creech stood silent in a dignity of despair that wrung Slone's heart. His silence was an answer. It was Joel Creech who broke the suspense.

"Didn't I tell you-all what'd happen?" he shrilled. *"Parched an' starved!"*

"Aw no!" chorused the riders.

Brackton shook all over. Tears dimmed his eyes— tears that he had no shame for. "So help me Gawd— I'm sorry!" was his broken exclamation.

Slone had forgotten himself and possible revelation concerning him. But when Holley appeared close to him, with a significant warning look, Slone grew keen once more on his own account. He felt a hot flame in- side him—a deep and burning anger at the man who might have saved Creech's horses. And he, like Brack- ton, felt sorrow for Creech, and a rider's sense of loss, of pain. These horses—these dumb brutes—faithful and sometimes devoted, had to suffer an agonizing death because of the selfishness of men.

"I reckon we'd all like to hear what come off, Creech, if you don't feel too bad to tell us," said Brackton.

"Gimme a drink," replied Creech.

"Wal, d—n my old head!" exclaimed Brackton. "I'm gittin' old. Come on in. All of you! We're glad to see Creech home."

The riders filed in after Brackton and the Creeches. Holley stayed close beside Slone, both of them in the background.

"I heerd the flood comin' thet night," said Creech to his silent and tense-faced listeners. "I heard it miles up the cañon. 'Peared a bigger roar than any flood be- fore. As it happened, I was alone, an' it took time to git the hosses up. If there'd been an Indian with me— or even Joel—mebbe—" His voice quavered slightly, broke, and then he resumed. "Even when I got the hosses over to the landin' it wasn't too late—if only some one had heerd me an' come down. I yelled an' shot. Nobody heerd. The river was risin' fast. An' thet roar had begun to make my hair raise. It seemed like years the time I waited there. . . . Then the flood came down—black an' windy an' awful. I had hell gittin' the hosses back.

"Next mornin' two Piutes come down. They had lost mustangs up on the rocks. All the feed on my place was gone. There wasn't nothin' to do but try to git out. The Piutes said there wasn't no chance north—no water—no grass—an' so I decided to go south, if we could climb over thet last slide. Peg broke her leg there, an'—I—I had to shoot her. But we climbed out with the rest of the bunch. I left it then to the Piutes. We traveled five days west to head the cañons. No grass an' only a little water, salt at thet. Blue Roan was game if ever I seen a game hoss. Then the Piutes took to workin' in an' out an' around, not to git out, but to find a little grazin'. I never knowed the earth was so barren. One by one them hosses went down. . . . An' at last, I couldn't—I couldn't see Blue Roan starvin'— dyin' right before my eyes—an' I shot him, too. . . . An' what hurts me most now is thet I didn't have the nerve to kill him fust off."

There was a long pause in Creech's narrative.

"Them Piutes will git paid if ever I can pay them. I'd parched myself but for them. . . . We circled an' crossed them red cliffs an' then the strip of red sand, an' worked down into the cañon. Under the wall was a long stretch of beach—sandy—an' at the head of this we found Bostil's boat."

"Wal, ——!" burst out the profane Brackton. "Bostil's boat! . . . Say, 'ain't Joel told you yet about thet boat?"

"No, Joel 'ain't said a word about the boat," replied Creech. "What about it?"

"It was cut loose jest before the flood."

Manifestly Brackton expected this to be staggering to Creech. But he did not even show surprise.

"There's a rider here named Slone—a wild-hoss wrangler," went on Brackton, "an' Joel swears this Slone cut the boat loose so's he'd have a better chance to win the race. Joel swears he tracked this feller Slone."

For Slone the moment was fraught with many emotions, but not one of them was fear. He did not need the sudden force of Holley's strong hand, pushing him forward. Slone broke into the group and faced Creech.

"It's not true. I never cut that boat loose," he declared, ringingly.

"Who're you?" queried Creech.

"My name's Slone. I rode in here with a wild horse, an' he won a race. Then I was blamed for this trick."

Creech's steady, gloomy eyes seemed to pierce Slone through. They were terrible eyes to look into, yet they held no menace for him. "An' Joel accused you?"

"So they say. I fought with him—struck him for an insult to a girl."

"Come round hyar, Joel," called Creech, sternly. His big, scaly, black hand closed on the boy's shoulder. Joel cringed under it. "Son, you've lied. What for?"

Joel showed abject fear of his father. "He's gone on Lucy—an' I seen him with her," muttered the boy.

"An' you lied to hurt Slone?"

Joel would not reply to this in speech, though that was scarcely needed to show he had lied. He seemed to have no sense of guilt. Creech eyed him pityingly and then pushed him back.

"Men, my son has done this rider dirt," said Creech. "You-all see thet. Slone never cut the boat loose. . . . An' say, you-all seem to think cuttin' thet boat loose was the crime. . . . No! Thet wasn't the crime. The crime was keepin' the boat out of the water fer days when my hosses could have been crossed."

Slone stepped back, forgotten, it seemed to him. Both joy and sorrow swayed him. He had been exonerated. But this hard and gloomy Creech—he knew things. And Slone thought of Lucy.

"Who did cut thet thar boat loose?" demanded Brackton, incredulously.

Creech gave him a strange glance. "As I was sayin', we come on the boat fast at the head of the long stretch. I seen the cables had been cut. An' I seen more'n thet. . . . Wal, the river was high an' swift. But this was a long stretch with good landin' way below on the other side. We got the boat in, an' by rowin' hard

an' driftin' we got acrost, leadin' the hosses. We had
five when we took to the river. Two went down on the
way over. We climbed out then. The Piutes went to
find some Navajos an' get hosses. An' I headed fer the
Ford—made camp twice. An' Joel seen me comin' out
a ways."

"Creech, was there anythin' left in thet boat?" began
Brackton, with intense but pondering curiosity. "Anythin' on the ropes—or so—thet might give an idee who
cut her loose?"

Creech made no reply to that. The gloom burned
darker in his eyes. He seemed a man with a secret. He
trusted no one there. These men were all friends of
his, but friends under strange conditions. His silence
was tragic, and all about the man breathed vengeance.

Chapter XVI

No moon showed that night, and few stars twinkled
between the slow-moving clouds. The air was thick and
oppressive, full of the day's heat that had not blown
away. A dry storm moved in dry majesty across the
horizon, and the sheets and ropes of lightning, blazing
white behind the black monuments, gave weird and
beautiful grandeur to the desert.

Lucy Bostil had to evade her aunt to get out of the
house, and the window, that had not been the means
of exit since Bostil left, once more came into use. Aunt
Jane had grown suspicious of late, and Lucy, much as
she wanted to trust her with her secret, dared not do
it. For some reason unknown to Lucy, Holley had also
been hard to manage, particularly to-day. Lucy certainly did not want Holley to accompany her on her
nightly rendezvous with Slone. She changed her light
gown to the darker and thicker riding-habit.

There was a longed-for, all-satisfying flavor in this

night adventure—something that had not all to do with love. The stealth, the outwitting of guardians, the darkness, the silence, the risk—all these called to some deep, undeveloped instinct in her, and thrilled along her veins, cool, keen, exciting. She had the blood in her of the greatest adventurer of his day.

Lucy feared she was a little late. Allaying the suspicions of Aunt Jane and changing her dress had taken time. Lucy hurried with less cautious steps. Still she had only used caution in the grove because she had promised Slone to do so. This night she forgot or disregarded it. And the shadows were thick—darker than at any other time when she had undertaken this venture. She had always been a little afraid of the dark—a fact that made her contemptuous of herself. Nevertheless, she did not peer into the deeper pits of gloom. She knew her way and could slip swiftly along with only a rustle of leaves she touched.

Suddenly she imagined she heard a step and she halted, still as a tree-trunk. There was no reason to be afraid of a step. It had been a surprise to her that she had never encountered a rider walking and smoking under the trees. Listening, she assured herself she had been mistaken, and then went on. But she looked back. Did she see a shadow—darker than others—moving? It was only her imagination. Yet she sustained a slight chill. The air seemed more oppressive, or else there was some intangible and strange thing hovering in it. She went on—reached the lane that divided the grove. But she did not cross at once. It was lighter in this lane; she could see quite far.

As she stood there, listening, keenly responsive to all the influences of the night, she received an impression that did not have its origin in sight nor sound. And only the leaves touched her—and only their dry fragrance came to her. But she felt a presence—a strange, indefinable presence.

But Lucy was brave, and this feeling, whatever it might be, angered her. She entered the lane and stole swiftly along toward the end of the grove. Paths crossed the lane at right angles, and at these points she went swifter. It would be something to tell Slone—she had been frightened. But thought of him drove away her fear and nervousness, and her anger with herself.

Then she came to a wider path. She scarcely noted it and passed on. Then came a quick rustle—a swift shadow. Between two steps—as her heart leaped—violent arms swept her off the ground. A hard hand was clapped over her mouth. She was being carried swiftly through the gloom.

Lucy tried to struggle. She could scarcely move a muscle. Iron arms wrapped her in coils that crushed her. She tried to scream, but her lips were tight-pressed. Her nostrils were almost closed between two hard fingers that smelled of horse.

Whoever had her, she was helpless. Lucy's fury admitted of reason. Then both succumbed to a paralyzing horror. Cordts had got her! She knew it. She grew limp as a rag and her senses dulled. She almost fainted. The sickening paralysis of her faculties lingered. But she felt her body released—she was placed upon her feet—she was shaken by a rough hand. She swayed, and but for that hand might have fallen. She could see a tall, dark form over her, and horses, and the gloomy gray open of the sage slope. The hand left her face.

"Don't yap, girl!" This command in a hard, low voice pierced her ears. She saw the glint of a gun held before her. Instinctive fear revived her old faculties. The horrible sick weakness, the dimness, the shaking internal collapse all left her.

"I'll—be—quiet!" she faltered. She knew what her father had always feared had come to pass. And though she had been told to put no value on her life, in that event, she could not run. All in an instant—when life had been so sweet—she could not face pain or death.

The man moved back a step. He was tall, gaunt, ragged. But not like Cordts! Never would she forget Cordts. She peered up at him. In the dim light of the few stars she recognized Joel Creech's father.

"Oh, thank God!" she whispered, in the shock of blessed relief. "I thought—you were—Cordts!"

"Keep quiet!" he whispered back, sternly, and with rough hand he shook her.

Lucy awoke to realities. Something evil menaced her, even though this man was not Cordts. Her mind could not grasp it. She was amazed—stunned. She struggled to speak, yet to keep within that warning command.

"What—on earth—does this—mean?" she gasped, very low. She had no sense of fear of Creech. Once, when he and her father had been friends, she had been a favorite of Creech's. When a little girl she had ridden his knee many times. Between Creech and Cordts there was immeasurable distance. Yet she had been violently seized and carried out into the sage and menaced.

Creech leaned down. His gaunt face, lighted by terrible eyes, made her recoil. "Bostil ruined me—an' killed my hosses," he whispered, grimly. "An' I'm takin' you away. An' I'll hold you in ransom for the King —an' Sarchedon—an' all his racers!"

"Oh!" cried Lucy, in startling surprise that yet held a pang. "Oh, Creech! . . . Then you mean me no harm!"

The man straightened up and stood a moment, darkly silent, as if her query had presented a new aspect of the case. "Lucy Bostil, I'm a broken man an' wild an' full of hate. But God knows I never thought of thet— of harm to you. . . . No, child, I won't harm you. But you must obey an' go quietly, for there's a devil in me."

"Where will you take me?" she asked.

"Down in the cañons, where no one can track me," he said. "It'll be hard goin' fer you, child, an' hard fare. . . . But I'm strikin' at Bostil's heart as he has broken mine. I'll send him word. An' I'll tell him if he won't give his hosses thet I'll sell you to Cordts."

"Oh, Creech—but you wouldn't!" she whispered, and her hand went to his brawny arm.

"Lucy, in thet case I'd make as poor a blackguard

as anythin' else I've been," he said, forlornly. "But I'm figgerin' Bostil will give up his hosses fer you."

"Creech, I'm afraid he won't. You'd better give me up. Let me go back. I'll never tell. I don't blame you. I think you're square.. My dad is. . . . But, oh, don't make *me* suffer! You used to—to care for me, when I was little."

"Thet ain't no use," he replied. "Don't talk no more. . . . Git up hyar now an' ride in front of me."

He led her to a lean mustang. Lucy swung into the saddle. She thought how singular a coincidence it was that she had worn a riding-habit. It was dark and thick, and comfortable for riding. Suppose she had worn the flimsy dress, in which she had met Slone every night save this one? Thought of Slone gave her a pang. He would wait and wait and wait. He would go back to his cabin, not knowing what had befallen her.

Suddenly Lucy noticed another man, near at hand, holding two mustangs. He mounted, rode before her, and then she recognized Joel Creech. Assurance of this brought back something of the dread. But the father could control the son!

"Ride on," said Creech, hitting her horse from behind.

And Lucy found herself riding single file, with two men and a pack-horse, out upon the windy, dark sage slope. They faced the direction of the monuments, looming now and then so weirdly black and grand against the broad flare of lightning-blazed sky.

Ever since Lucy had reached her teens there had been predictions that she would be kidnapped, and now the thing had come to pass. She was in danger, she knew, but in infinitely less than had any other wild character of the uplands been her captor. She believed, if she went quietly and obediently with Creech, that she would be, at least, safe from harm. It was hard luck for Bostil, she thought, but no worse than he deserved. Retribution had overtaken him. How terribly hard he would take the loss of his horses! Lucy wondered if he really ever would part with the King, even to save her from privation and peril. Bostil was more likely to trail her with his riders and to kill the Creeches than to concede their demands. Perhaps, though, that threat to sell her to Cordts would frighten the hard old man.

The horses trotted and swung up over the slope, turning gradually, evidently to make a wide détour round the Ford, until Lucy's back was toward the monuments. Before her stretched the bleak, barren, dark desert, and through the opaque gloom she could see nothing. Lucy knew she was headed for the north, toward the wild cañons, unknown to the riders. Cordts and his gang hid in there. What might not happen if the Creeches fell in with Cordts? Lucy's confidence sustained a check. Still, she remembered the Creeches were like Indians. And what would Slone do? He would ride out on her trail. Lucy shivered for the Creeches if Slone ever caught up with them, and remembering his wild-horse-hunter's skill at tracking, and the fleet and tireless Wildfire, she grew convinced that Creech could not long hold her captive. For Slone would be wary. He would give no sign of his pursuit. He would steal upon the Creeches in the dark and— Lucy shivered again. What an awful fate had been that of Dick Sears!

So as she rode on Lucy's mind was full. She was used to riding, and in the motion of a horse there was something in harmony with her blood. Even now, with worry and dread and plotting strong upon her, habit had such power over her that riding made the hours fleet. She was surprised to be halted, to see dimly low, dark mounds of rock ahead.

"Git off," said Creech.

"Where are we?" asked Lucy.

"Reckon hyar's the rocks. An' you sleep some, fer you'll need it." He spread a blanket, laid her saddle at the head of it, and dropped another blanket. "What I want to know is—shall I tie you up or not?" asked Creech. "If I do you'll git sore. An' this'll be the toughest trip you ever made."

"You mean will I try to get away from you—or not?" queried Iucy.

"Jest thet."

Lucy pondered. She divined some fineness of feeling in this coarse man. He wanted to spare her not only pain, but the necessity of watchful eyes on her every moment. Lucy did not like to promise not to try to escape, if opportunity presented. Still, she reasoned, that once deep in the cañons, where she would be in another day, she would be worse off if she did get away. The memory of Cordts's cavernous, hungry eyes upon her was not a small factor in Lucy's decision.

"Creech, if I give my word not to try to get away, would you believe me?" she asked.

Creech was slow in replying. "Reckon I would," he said, finally.

"All right, I'll give it."

"An' thet's sense. Now you lay down."

Lucy did as she was bidden and pulled the blanket over her. The place was gloomy and still. She heard the sound of mustangs' teeth on grass, and the soft footfalls of the men. Presently these sounds ceased. A cold wind blew over her face and rustled in the sage near her. Gradually the chill passed away, and a stealing warmth took its place. Her eyes grew tired. What had happened to her? With eyes closed she thought it was all a dream. Then the feeling of the hard saddle as a pillow under her head told her she was indeed far from her comfortable little room. What would poor Aunt Jane do in the morning when she discovered who was missing? What would Holley do? When would Bostil return? It might be soon and it might be days. And Slone—Lucy felt sorriest for him. For he loved her best. She thrilled at thought of Slone on that grand horse—on her Wildfire. And with her mind running on and on, seemingly making sleep impossible, the thoughts at last became dreams.

Lucy awakened at dawn. One hand ached with cold, for it had been outside the blanket. Her hard bed had cramped her muscles. She heard the crackling of fire and smelled cedar smoke. In the gray of morning she saw the Creeches round a camp-fire.

Lucy got up then. Both men saw her, but made no comment. In that cold, gray dawn she felt her predicament more gravely. Her hair was damp. She had ridden nearly all night without a hat. She had absolutely nothing of her own except what was on her body. But Lucy thanked her lucky stars that she had worn the thick riding-suit and her boots, for otherwise, in a summer dress, her condition would soon have been miserable.

"Come an' eat," said Creech. "You have sense—an' eat if it sticks in your throat."

Bostil had always contended in his arguments with riders that a man should eat heartily on the start of a trip so that the finish might find him strong. And Lucy ate, though the coarse fare sickened her. Once she looked curiously at Joel Creech. She felt his eyes upon her, but instantly he averted them. He had grown more haggard and sullen than ever before.

The Creeches did not loiter over the camp tasks. Lucy was left to herself. The place appeared to be a kind of depression from which the desert rolled away to a bulge against the rosy east, and the rocks behind rose broken and yellow, fringed with cedars.

"Git the hosses in, if you want to," Creech called to her, and then as Lucy started off to where the mustangs grazed she heard him curse his son. "Come back hyar! Leave the girl alone or I'll rap you one!"

Lucy drove three of the mustangs into camp, where Creech began to saddle them. The remaining one, the pack animal, Lucy found among the scrub cedars at the base of the low cliffs. When she drove him in Creech was talking hard to Joel, who had mounted.

"When you come back, work up this cañon till you git up. It heads on the pine plateau. I can't miss seein' you, or any one, long before you git up on top. An' you needn't come without Bostil's hosses. You know what to tell Bostil if he threatens you, or refuses to send his hosses, or turns his riders on my trail. Thet's all. Now git!"

Joel Creech rode away toward the rise in the rolling, barren desert.

"An' now we'll go on," said Creech to Lucy.

When he had gotten all in readiness he ordered Lucy to follow closely in his tracks. He entered a narrow cleft in the low cliffs which wound in and out, and was thick with sage and cedars. Lucy, riding close to the cedars, conceived the idea of plucking the little green berries and dropping them on parts of the trail where their tracks would not show. Warily she filled the pockets of her jacket.

Creech led the way without looking back, and did not seem to care where the horses stepped. The time had not yet come, Lucy concluded, when he was ready to hide his trail. Presently the narrow cleft opened into a low-walled cañon, full of debris from the rotting cliffs, and this in turn opened into a main cañon with mounting yellow crags. It appeared to lead north. Far in the distance above rims and crags rose in a long, black line like a horizon of dark cloud.

Creech crossed this wide cañon and entered one of the many breaks in the wall. This one was full of splintered rock and weathered shale—the hardest kind of travel for both man and beast. Lucy was nothing if not considerate of a horse, and here she began to help her animal in all the ways a good rider knows. Much as this taxed her attention, she remembered to drop some of the cedar berries upon hard ground or rocks. And she knew she was leaving a trail for Slone's keen eyes.

That day was the swiftest and the most strenuous in all Lucy Bostil's experience in the open. At sunset, when Creech halted in a niche in a gorge between lowering cliffs, Lucy fell off her horse and lay still and spent on the grass.

Creech had a glance of sympathy and admiration for her, but he did not say anything about the long day's ride. Lucy never in her life before appreciated rest nor the softness of grass nor the relief at the end of a ride. She lay still with a throbbing, burning ache

in all her body. Creech, after he had turned the horses
loose, brought her a drink of cold water from the brook
she heard somewhere near by.

"How—far—did—we—come?" she whispered.

"By the way round I reckon nigh on to sixty miles,"
he replied. "But we ain't half thet far from where we
camped last night."

Then he set to work at camp tasks. Lucy shook her
head when he brought her food, but he insisted, and
she had to force it down. Creech appeared rough but
kind. After she had become used to the hard, gaunt,
black face she saw sadness and thought in it. One thing
Lucy had noticed was that Creech never failed to spare
a horse, if it was possible. He would climb on foot over
bad places.

Night soon mantled the gorge in blackness thick as
pitch. Lucy could not tell whether her eyes were open
or shut, so far as what she saw was concerned. Her
eyes seemed filled, however, with a thousand pictures
of the wild and tortuous cañons and gorges through
which she had ridden that day. The ache in her limbs
and the fever in her blood would not let her sleep. It
seemed that these were forever to be a part of her.
For twelve hours she had ridden and walked with
scarce a thought of the nature of the wild country, yet
once she lay down to rest her mind was an endless
hurrying procession of pictures—narrow red clefts
choked with green growths—yellow gorges and
weathered slides—dusty, treacherous divides connecting cañons—jumbles of ruined cliffs and piles of shale
—miles and miles and endless winding miles of yellow,
low, beetling walls. And through it all she had left a
trail.

Next day Creech climbed out of that low-walled
cañon, and Lucy saw a wild, rocky country cut by
gorges, green and bare, or yellow and cedared. The
long, black-fringed line she had noticed the day before
loomed closer, overhanging this crisscrossed region of
cañons. Every half-hour Creech would lead them downward and presently climb out again. There were sand

and hard ground and thick turf and acres and acres of
bare rock where even a shod horse would not leave a
track.

But the going was not so hard—there was not so
much travel on foot for Lucy—and she finished that
day in better condition than the first one.

Next day Creech proceeded with care and caution.
Many times he left the direct route, bidding Lucy wait
for him, and he would ride to the rims of cañons or
the tops of ridges of cedar forests, and from these van-
tage-points he would survey the country. Lucy gathered
after a while that he was apprehensive of what might
be encountered, and particularly so of what might be
feared in pursuit. Lucy thought this strange, because
it was out of the question for any one to be so soon
on Creech's trail.

These peculiar actions of Creech were more noticeable on the third day, and Lucy grew apprehensive
herself. She could not divine why. But when Creech
halted on a high crest that gave a sweeping vision of
the broken table-land they had traversed Lucy made
out for herself faint moving specks miles behind.

"I reckon you see thet," said Creech.

"Horses," replied Lucy.

He nodded his head gloomily, and seemed pondering a serious question.

"Is some one trailing us?" asked Lucy, and she could
not keep the tremor out of her voice.

"Wal, I should smile! Fer two days—an' it sure beats
me. They've never had a sight of us. But they keep
comin'."

"They! Who?" she asked, swiftly.

"I hate to tell you, but I reckon I ought. Thet's
Cordts an' two of his gang."

"Oh—don't tell me so!" cried Lucy, suddenly terrified. Mention of Cordts had not always had power to
frighten her, but this time she had a return of that
shaking fear which had overcome her in the grove the
night she was captured.

"Cordts all right," replied Creech. "I knowed thet

before I seen him. Fer two mornin's back I seen his hoss grazin' in thet wide cañon. But I thought I'd slipped by. Some one seen us. Or they seen our trail. Anyway, he's after us. What beats me is how he sticks to thet trail. Cordts never was no tracker. An' since Dick Sears is dead there ain't a tracker in Cordts's outfit. An' I always could hide my tracks. . . . Beats me!"

"Creech, I've been leaving a trail," confessed Lucy.

"What!"

Then she told him how she had been dropping cedar berries and bits of cedar leaves along the bare and stony course they had traversed.

"Wal, I'm—" Creech stifled an oath. Then he laughed, but gruffly. "You air a cute one. But I reckon you didn't promise not to do thet. . . . An' now if Cordts gits you there'll be only yourself to blame."

"Oh!" cried Lucy, frantically looking back. The moving specks were plainly in sight. "How can he know he's trailing me?"

"Thet I can't say. Mebbe he doesn't know. His hosses air fresh, though, an' if I can't shake him he'll find out soon enough who he's trailin'."

"Go on! We must shake him. I'll never do *that* again! . . . For God's sake, Creech, don't let him get me!"

And Creech led down off the high open land into cañons again.

The day ended, and the night seemed a black blank to Lucy. Another sunrise found Creech leading on, sparing neither Lucy nor the horses. He kept on a steady walk or trot, and he picked out ground less likely to leave any tracks. Like an old deer he doubled on his trail. He traveled down stream-beds where the water left no trail. That day the mustangs began to fail. The others were wearing out.

The cañons ran like the ribs of a wash-board. And they grew deep and verdant, with looming, towered walls. That night Lucy felt lost in an abyss. The dreaming silence kept her awake many moments while sleep had already seized upon her eyelids. And then she dreamed of Cordts capturing her, of carrying her miles deeper into these wild and purple cliffs, of Slone in pursuit on the stallion Wildfire, and of a savage fight. And she awoke terrified and cold in the blackness of the night.

On the next day Creech traveled west. This seemed to Lucy to be far to the left of the direction taken before. And Lucy, in spite of her utter weariness, and the necessity of caring for herself and her horse, could not but wonder at the wild and frowning cañon. It was only a tributary of the great cañon, she supposed, but it was different, strange, impressive, yet intimate, because all about it was overpowering, near at hand, even the beetling crags. And at every turn it seemed impossible to go farther over that narrow and rock-bestrewn floor. Yet Creech found a way on.

Then came hours of climbing such slopes and benches and ledges as Lucy had not yet encountered. The grasping spikes of dead cedar tore her dress to shreds, and many a scratch burned her flesh. About the middle of the afternoon Creech led up over the last declivity, a yellow slope of cedar, to a flat upland covered with pine and high bleached grass. They rested.

"We've fooled Cordts, you can be sure of thet," said Creech. "You're a game kid, an', by Gawd! if I had this job to do over I'd never tackle it again!"

"Oh, you're sure we've lost him?" implored Lucy.

"Sure as I am of death. An' we'll make surer in crossin' this bench. It's miles to the other side where I'm to keep watch fer Joel. An' we won't leave a track all the way."

"But this grass?" questioned Lucy. "It'll show our tracks."

"Look at the lanes an' trails between. All pine mats thick an' soft an' springy. Only an Indian could follow us hyar on Wild Hoss Bench."

Lucy gazed before her under the pines. It was a beautiful forest, with trees standing far apart, yet not so far but that their foliage intermingled. A dry fra-

grance, thick as a heavy perfume, blew into her face.
She could not help but think of fire—how it would
race through here, and that recalled Joel Creech's horrible threat. Lucy shuddered and put away the memory.

"I can't go—any further—to-day," she said.

Creech looked at her compassionately. Then Lucy
became conscious that of late he had softened.

"You'll have to come," he said. "There's no water
on this side, short of thet cañon-bed. An' acrost there's
water close under the wall."

So they set out into the forest. And Lucy found
that after all she could go on. The horses walked and
on the soft, springy ground did not jar her. Deer and
wild turkey abounded there and showed little alarm at
sight of the travelers. And before long Lucy felt that
she would become intoxicated by the dry odor. It was
so strong, so thick, so penetrating. Yet, though she
felt she would reel under its influence, it revived her.

The afternoon passed; the sun set off through the
pines, a black-streaked, golden flare; twilight shortly
changed to night. The trees looked spectral in the
gloom, and the forest appeared to grow thicker. Wolves
murmured, and there were wild cries of bat and owl.
Lucy fell asleep on her horse. At last, sometime late
in the night, when Creech lifted her from the saddle
and laid her down, she stretched out on the soft mat
of pine needles and knew no more.

She did not awaken until the afternoon of the next
day.

The site where Creech had made his final camp overlooked the wildest of all that wild upland country. The
pines had scattered and trooped around a beautiful
park of grass that ended abruptly upon bare rock.
Yellow crags towered above the rim, and under them
a yawning narrow gorge, overshadowed from above,
blue in its depths, split the end of the great plateau and
opened out sheer into the head of the cañon, which,
according to Creech, stretched away through that wil-

derness of red stone and green clefts. When Lucy's fascinated gaze looked afar she was stunned at the vast, billowy, bare surfaces. Every green cleft was a short cañon running parallel with this central and longer one. The dips and breaks showed how all these cañons were connected. They led the gaze away, descending gradually to the dim purple of distance—the bare, rolling desert upland.

Lucy did nothing but gaze. She was unable to walk or eat that day. Creech hung around her with a remorse he apparently felt, yet could not put into words.

"Do you expect Joel to come up this big cañon?"

"I reckon I do—some day," replied Creech. "An' I wish he'd hurry."

"Does he know the way?"

"Nope. But he's good at findin' places. An' I told him to stick to the main cañon. Would you believe you could ride off er this rim, straight down thar fer fifty miles, an' never git off your hoss?"

"No, I wouldn't believe it possible."

"Wal, it's so. I've done it. An' I didn't want to come up thet way because I'd had to leave tracks."

"Do you think we're safe—from Cordts now?" she asked.

"I reckon so. He's no tracker."

"But suppose he *does* trail us?"

"Wal, I reckon I've a shade the best of Cordts at gunplay, any day."

Lucy regarded the man in surprise. "Oh, it's so—strange!" she said. "You'd fight for me. Yet you dragged me for days over these awful rocks! . . . Look at me, Creech. Do I look much like Lucy Bostil?"

Creech hung his head. "Wal, I reckon I wasn't a blackguard, but I *am*."

"You used to care for me when I was little. I remember how I used to take rides on your knee."

"Lucy, I never thought of thet when I ketched you. You was only a means to an end. Bostil hated me. He ruined me. I give up to revenge. An' I could only git thet through you."

"Creech, I'm not defending Dad. He's—he's no good where horses are concerned. I know he wronged you. Then why didn't you wait and meet him like a man instead of dragging me to this misery?"

"Wal, I never thought of thet, either. I wished I had." He grew gloomier then and relapsed into silent watching.

Lucy felt better next day, and offered to help Creech at the few camp duties. He would not let her. There was nothing to do but rest and wait, and the idleness appeared to be harder on Creech than on Lucy. He had always been exceedingly active. Lucy divined that every hour his remorse grew keener, and she did all she could think of to make it so. Creech made her a rude brush by gathering small roots and binding them tightly and cutting the ends square. And Lucy, after the manner of an Indian, got the tangles out of her hair. That day Creech seemed to want to hear Lucy's voice, and so they often fell into conversation. Once he said, thoughtfully:

"I'm tryin' to remember somethin' I heerd at the Ford. I meant to ask you—" Suddenly he turned to her with animation. He who had been so gloomy and lusterless and dead showed a bright eagerness. "I heerd you beat the King on a red hoss—a wild hoss! . . . Thet must have been a joke—like one of Joel's."

"No. It's true. An' Dad nearly had a fit!"

"Wal!" Creech simply blazed with excitement. "I ain't wonderin' if he did. His own girl! Lucy, come to remember, you always said you'd beat thet gray racer. . . . Fer the Lord's sake tell me all about it."

Lucy warmed to him because, broken as he was, he could be genuinely glad some horse but his own had won a race. Bostil could never have been like that. So Lucy told him about the race—and then she had to tell about Wildfire, and then about Slone. But at first all of Creech's interest centered round Wildfire and the race that had not really been run. He asked a hundred questions. He was as pleased as a boy listening to a good story. He praised Lucy again and again. He crowed over Bostil's discomfiture. And when Lucy told him that Slone had dared her father to race, had offered to bet Wildfire and his own life against her hand, then Creech was beside himself.

"This hyar Slone—he *called* Bostil's hand!"

"He's a wild-horse hunter. And *he* can trail us!"

"Trail us! Slone? . . . Say, Lucy, are you in love with him?"

Lucy uttered a strange little broken sound, half laugh, half sob. "Love him! Ah!"

"An' your Dad's ag'in him! Sure Bostil'll hate any rider with a fast hoss. Why didn't the darn fool sell his stallion to your father?"

"He gave Wildfire to me."

"I'd have done the same. Wal, now, when you git back home what's comin' of it all?"

Lucy shook her head sorrowfully. "God only knows. Dad will never own Wildfire, and he'll never let me marry Slone. And when you take the King away from him to ransom me—then my life will be hell, for if Dad sacrifices Sage King, afterward he'll hate me as the cause of his loss."

"I can sure see the sense of all that," replied Creech, soberly. And he pondered.

Lucy saw through this man as if he had been an inch of crystal water. He was no villain, and just now in his simplicity in his plodding thought of sympathy for her he was lovable.

"It's one hell of a muss, if you'll excuse my talk," said Creech. "An' I don't like the looks of what I 'pear to be throwin' in your way. . . . But see hyar, Lucy, if Bostil didn't give up—or, say, he gits the King back, thet wouldn't make your chance with Slone any brighter."

"I don't know."

"Thet race will have to be run!"

"What good will that do?" cried Lucy, with tears in her eyes. "I don't want to lose Dad. I—I—love him—mean as he is. And it'll kill me to lose Lin. Because

Wildfire can beat Sage King, and that means Dad will be forever against him."

"Couldn't this wild-horse feller *let* the King win thet race?"

"Oh, he could, but he wouldn't."

"Can't you be sweet round him—fetch him over to thet?"

"Oh, I could, but I won't."

Creech might have been plotting the happiness of his own daughter, he was so deeply in earnest.

"Wal, mebbe you don't love each other so much, after all. . . . Fast hosses mean much to a man in this hyar country. I know, fer I lost mine! . . . But they ain't all. . . . I reckon you young folks don't love so much, after all."

"But—we—do!" cried Lucy, with a passionate sob. All this talk had unnerved her.

"Then the only way is fer Slone to lie to Bostil."

"Lie!" exclaimed Lucy.

"Thet's it. Fetch about a race, somehow—one Bostil can't see—an' then lie an' say the King run Wildfire off his legs."

Suddenly it occurred to Lucy that one significance of this idea of Creech's had not dawned upon him. "You forget that soon my father will no longer own Sage King or Sarchedon or Dusty Ben—or any racer. He loses them or me, I thought. That's what I am here for."

Creech's aspect changed. The eagerness and sympathy fled from his face, leaving it once more hard and stern. He got up and stood a tall, dark, and gloomy man, brooding over his loss, as he watched the cañon. Still, there was in him then a struggle that Lucy felt. Presently he bent over and put his big hand on her head. It seemed gentle and tender compared with former contacts, and it made Lucy thrill. She could not see his face. What did he mean? She divined something startling, and sat there trembling in suspense.

"Bostil won't lose his only girl—or his favorite hoss! . . . Lucy, I never had no girl. But it seems I'm rememberin' them rides you used to have on my knee when you was little!"

Then he strode away toward the forest. Lucy watched him with a full heart, and as she thought of his overcoming the evil in him when her father had yielded to it, she suffered poignant shame. This Creech was not a bad man. He was going to let her go, and he was going to return Bostil's horses when they came. Lucy resolved with a passionate determination that her father must make ample restitution for the loss Creech had endured. She meant to tell Creech so.

Upon his return, however, he seemed so strange and forbidding again that her heart failed her. Had he reconsidered his generous thought? Lucy almost believed so. These old horse-traders were incomprehensible in any relation concerning horses. Recalling Creech's intense interest in Wildfire and in the inevitable race to be run between him and Sage King, Lucy almost believed that Creech would sacrifice his vengeance just to see the red stallion beat the gray. If Creech kept the King in ransom for Lucy he would have to stay deeply hidden in the wild breaks of the cañon country or leave the uplands. For Bostil would never let that deed go unreckoned with. Like Bostil, old Creech was half horse and half human. The human side had warmed to remorse. He had regretted Lucy's plight; he wanted her to be safe at home again and to find happiness; he remembered what she had been to him when she was a little girl. Creech's other side was more complex.

Before the evening meal ended Lucy divined that Creech was dark and troubled because he had resigned himself to a sacrifice harder than it had seemed in the first flush of noble feeling. But she doubted him no more. She was safe. The King would be returned. She would compel her father to pay Creech horse for horse. And perhaps the lesson to Bostil would be worth all the pain of effort and distress of mind that it had cost her.

That night as she lay awake listening to the roar of the wind in the pines a strange premonition—like a mysterious voice—came to her with the assurance that Slone was on her trail.

On the following day Creech appeared to have cast off the brooding mood. Still, he was not talkative. He applied himself to constant watching from the rim.

Lucy began to feel rested. That long trip with Creech had made her thin and hard and strong. She spent the hours under the shade of a cedar on the rim that protected her from sun and wind. The wind, particularly, was hard to stand. It blew a gale out of the west, a dry, odorous, steady rush that roared through the pine-tops and flattened the long, white grass. This day Creech had to build up a barrier of rock round his camp-fire, to keep it from blowing away. And there was a constant danger of firing the grass.

Once Lucy asked Creech what would happen in that case.

"Wal, I reckon the grass would burn back even ag'in thet wind," replied Creech. "I'd hate to see fire in the woods now before the rains come. It's been the longest, dryest spell I ever lived through. But fer thet my hosses— This hyar's a west wind, an' it's blowin' harder every day. It'll fetch the rains."

Next day about noon, when both wind and heat were high, Lucy was awakened from a doze. Creech was standing near her. When he turned his long gaze away from the cañon he was smiling. It was a smile at once triumphant and sad.

"Joel's comin' with the hosses!"

Lucy jumped up, trembling and agitated. "Oh! . . . Where? Where?"

Creech pointed carefully with bent hand, like an Indian, and Lucy either could not get the direction or see far enough.

"Right down along the base of thet red wall. A line of hosses. Jest like a few crawlin' ants! . . . An' now they're creepin' out of sight."

"Oh, I can't see them!" cried Lucy. "Are you *sure?*"

"Positive an' sartin," he replied. "Joel's comin'. He'll be up hyar before long. I reckon we'd jest as well let him come. Fer there's water an' grass hyar. An' down below grass is scarce."

It seemed an age to Lucy, waiting there, until she did see horses zigzagging the ridges below. They disappeared, and then it was another age before they reappeared close under the bulge of wall. She thrilled at sight of Sage King and Sarchedon. She got only a glimpse of them. They must pass round under her to climb a split in the wall, and up a long draw that reached level ground back in the forest. But they were near, and Lucy tried to wait. Creech showed eagerness at first, and then went on with his camp-fire duties. While in camp he always cooked a midday meal.

Lucy saw the horses first. She screamed out. Creech jumped up in alarm.

Joel Creech, mounted on Sage King, and leading Sarchedon, was coming at a gallop. The other horses were following.

"What's his hurry?" demanded Lucy. "After climbing out of that cañon Joel ought not to push the horses."

"He'll git it from me if there's no reason," growled Creech. "Them hosses is wet."

"Look at Sarch! He's wild. He always hated Joel."

"Wal, Lucy, I reckon I ain't likin' this hyar. Look at Joel!" muttered Creech, and he strode out to meet his son.

Lucy ran out, too, and beyond him. She saw only Sage King. He saw her, recognized her, and whistled even while Joel was pulling him in. For once the King showed he was glad to see Lucy. He had been having rough treatment. But he was not winded—only hot and wet. She assured herself of that, then ran to quiet the plunging Sarch. He came down at once, and pushed his big nose almost into her face. She hugged his great, hot neck. He was quivering all over. Lucy heard the other horses pounding up; she recognized Two Face's high whinny, like a squeal; and in her delight she was about to run to them when Creech's harsh voice arrested her. And sight of Joel's face suddenly made her weak.

"What'd you say?" demanded Creech.

"I'd a good reason to run the hosses up-hill—thet's what!" snapped Joel. He was frothing at the mouth.

"Out with it!"

"Cordts an' Hutch!"

"What?" roared Creech, grasping the pale Joel and shaking him.

"Cordts an' Hutch rode in behind me down at thet cross cañon. They seen me. An' they're after me hard!"

Creech gave close and keen scrutiny to the strange face of his son. Then he wheeled away.

"Help me pack. An' you, too, Lucy. We've got to rustle out of hyar."

Lucy fought a sick faintness that threatened to make her useless. But she tried to help, and presently action made her stronger.

The Creeches made short work of that breaking of camp. But when it came to getting the horses there appeared danger of delay. Sarchedon had led Dusty Ben and Two Face off in the grass. When Joel went for them they galloped away toward the woods. Joel ran back.

"Son, you're a smart hossman!" exclaimed Creech, in disgust.

"Shall I git on the King an' ketch them?"

"No. Hold the King." Creech went out after Plume, but the excited and wary horse eluded him. Then Creech gave up, caught his own mustangs, and hurried into camp.

"Lucy, if Cordts gits after Sarch an' the others it'll be as well fer us," he said.

Soon they were riding into the forest, Creech leading, Lucy in the center, and Joel coming behind on the King. Two unsaddled mustangs carrying the packs were driven in front. Creech limited the gait to the best that the pack-horses could do. They made fast time. The level forest floor, hard and springy, afforded the best kind of going.

A cold dread had once more clutched Lucy's heart. What would be the end of this flight? The way Creech looked back increased her dread. How horrible it would be if Cordts accomplished what he had always threatened—to run off with both her and the King! Lucy lost her confidence in Creech. She did not glance again at Joel. Once had been enough. She rode on with heavy heart. Anxiety and dread and conjecture and a gradual sinking of spirit weighed her down. Yet she never had a clearer perception of outside things. The forest loomed thicker and darker. The sky was seen only through a green, crisscross of foliage waving in the roaring gale. This strong wind was like a blast in Lucy's face and its keen dryness cracked her lips.

When they rode out of the forest, down a gentle slope of wind-swept grass, to an opening into a cañon Lucy was surprised to recognize the place. How quickly the ride through the forest had been made!

Creech dismounted. "Git off, Lucy, You, Joel, hurry an' hand me the little pack. . . . Now I'll take Lucy an' the King down in hyar. You go thet way with the hosses an' make as if you was hidin' your trail, but don't. Do you savvy?"

Joel shook his head. He looked sullen, somber, strange. His father repeated what he had said.

"You're wantin' Cordts to split on the trail?" asked Joel.

"Sure. He'll ketch up with you sometime. But you needn't be afeared if he does."

"I ain't a-goin' to do thet."

"Why not?" Creech demanded, slowly, with a rising voice.

"I'm a-goin' with you. What d'ye mean, Dad, by this move? You'll be headin' back fer the Ford. An' we'd git safer if we go the other way."

Creech evidently controlled his temper by an effort. "I'm takin' Lucy an' the King back to Bostil."

Joel echoed those words, slowly divining them. "Takin' them *both!* The girl. . . . An' givin' up the King!"

"Yes, both of them. I've changed my mind, Joel. Now—you—"

But Creech never finished what he meant to say. Joel Creech was suddenly seized by a horrible madness. It was then, perhaps, that the final thread which linked his mind to rationality stretched and snapped. His face turned green. His strange eyes protruded. His jaw worked. He frothed at the mouth. He leaped, apparently to get near his father, but he missed his direction. Then, as if sight had come back, he wheeled and made strange gestures, all the while cursing incoherently. The father's shocked face began to show disgust. Then part of Joel's ranting became intelligible.

"Shut up!" suddenly roared Creech.

"No, I won't!" shrieked Joel, wagging his head in spent passion. "An' you ain't a-goin' to take thet girl home. . . . I'll take her with me. . . . An' you take the hosses home!"

"You're crazy!" hoarsely shouted Creech, his face going black. "They allus said so. But I never believed thet."

"An' if I'm crazy, thet girl made me. . . . You know what I'm a-goin' to do? . . . I'll strip her naked—an' I'll—"

Lucy saw old Creech lunge and strike. She heard the sodden blow. Joel went down. But he scrambled up with his eyes and mouth resembling those of a mad hound Lucy once had seen. The fact that he reached twice for his gun and could not find it proved the breaking connection of nerve and sense.

Creech jumped and grappled with Joel. There was a wrestling, strained struggle. Creech's hair stood up and his face had a kind of sick fury, and he continued to curse and command. They fought for the possession of the gun. But Joel seemed to have superhuman strength. His hold on the gun could not be broken. Moreover, he kept straining to point the gun at his father. Lucy screamed. Creech yelled hoarsely. But the boy was beyond reason or help, and he was beyond overpowering! Lucy saw him bend his arm in spite of the desperate hold upon it and fire the gun. Creech's hoarse entreaties ceased as his hold on Joel broke. He staggered. His arms went up with a tragic, terrible gesture. He fell. Joel stood over him, shaking and livid, but he showed only the vaguest realization of the deed. His actions were instinctive. He was the animal that had clawed himself free. Further proof of his aberration stood out in the action of sheathing his gun; he made the motion to do so, but he only dropped it in the grass.

Sight of that dropped gun broke Lucy's spell of horror, which had kept her silent but for one scream. Suddenly her blood leaped like fire in her veins. She measured the distance to Sage King. Joel was turning. Then Lucy darted at the King, reached him, and, leaping, was half up on him when he snorted and jumped, not breaking her hold, but keeping her from getting up. Then iron hands clutched her and threw her, like an empty sack, to the grass.

Joel Creech did not say a word. His distorted face had the deriding scorn of a superior being. Lucy lay flat on her back, watching him. Her mind worked swiftly. She would have to fight for her body and her life. Her terror had fled with her horror. She was not now afraid of this demented boy. She meant to fight, calculating like a cunning Indian, wild as a trapped wildcat.

Lucy lay perfectly still, for she knew she had been thrown near the spot where the gun lay. If she got her hands on that gun she would kill Joel. It would be the action of an instant. She watched Joel while he watched her. And she saw that he had his foot on the rope round Sage King's neck. The King never liked a rope. He was nervous. He tossed his head to get rid of it. Creech, watching Lucy all the while, reached for the rope, pulled the King closer and closer, and untied the knot. The King stood then, bridle down and quiet. Instead of a saddle he wore a blanket strapped round him.

It seemed that Lucy located the gun without turning

her eyes away from Joel's. She gathered all her force—
rolled over swiftly—again—got her hands on the gun
just as Creech leaped like a panther upon her. His
weight crushed her flat—his strength made her hand-
hold like that of a child. He threw the gun aside. Lucy
lay face down, unable to move her body while he
stood over her. Then he struck her, not a stunning
blow, but just the hard rap a cruel rider gives to a
horse that wants its own way. Under that blow Lucy's
spirit rose to a height of terrible passion. Still she did
not lose her cunning; the blow increased it. That blow
showed Joel to be crazy. She might outwit a crazy man,
where a man merely wicked might master her.

Creech tried to turn her. Lucy resisted. And she
was strong. Resistance infuriated Creech. He cuffed
her sharply. This action only made him worse. Then
with hands like steel claws he tore away her blouse.

The shock of his hands on her bare flesh momen-
tarily weakened Lucy, and Creech dragged at her until
she lay seemingly helpless before him.

And Lucy saw that at the sight of her like this something had come between Joel Creech's mad motives
and their execution. Once he had loved her—desired
her. He looked vague. He stroked her shoulder. His
strange eyes softened, then blazed with a different light.
Lucy divined that she was lost unless she could recall
his insane fury. She must begin that terrible fight in
which now the best she could hope for was to make
him kill her quickly.

Swift and vicious as a cat she fastened her teeth in
his arm. She bit deep and held on. Creech howled like
a dog. He beat her. He jerked and wrestled. Then he
lifted her, and the swing of her body tore the flesh
loose from his arm and broke her hold. Lucy half
rose, crawled, plunged for the gun. She got it, too,
only to have Creech kick it out of her hand. The pain
of that brutal kick was severe, but when he cut her
across the bare back with the rope she shrieked out.
Supple and quick, she leaped up and ran. In vain!
With a few bounds he had her again, tripped her up.

Lucy fell over the dead body of the father. Yet even that did not shake her desperate nerve. All the ferocity of a desert-bred savage culminated in her, fighting for death.

Creech leaned down, swinging the coiled rope. He meant to do more than lash her with it. Lucy's hands flashed up, closed tight in his long hair. Then with a bellow he jerked up and lifted her sheer off the ground. There was an instant in which Lucy felt herself swung and torn; she saw everything as a whirling blur; she felt an agony in her wrists at which Creech was clawing. When he broke her hold there were handfuls of hair in Lucy's fists.

She fell again and had not the strength to rise. But Creech was raging, and little of his broken speech was intelligible. He knelt with a sharp knee pressing her down. He cut the rope. Nimbly, like a rider in moments of needful swiftness, he noosed one end of the rope round her ankle, then the end of the other piece round her wrist. He might have been tying up an unbroken mustang. Rising, he retained hold on both ropes. He moved back, sliding them through his hands. Then with a quick move he caught up Sage King's bridle.

Creech paused a moment, darkly triumphant. A hideous success showed in his strange eyes. A long-cherished mad vengeance had reached its fruition. Then he led the horse near to Lucy.

Warily he reached down. He did not know Lucy's strength was spent. He feared she might yet escape. With hard, quick grasp he caught her, lifted her, threw her over the King's back. He forced her down.

Lucy's resistance was her only salvation, because it kept him on the track of his old threat. She resisted all she could. He pulled her arms down round the King's neck and tied them close. Then he pulled hard on the rope on her ankle and tied that to her other ankle.

Lucy realized that she was bound fast. Creech had made good most of his threat. And now in her mind the hope of the death she had sought changed to the hope of life that was possible. Whatever power she had ever had over the King was in her voice. If only Creech would slip the bridle or cut the reins—if only Sage King could be free to run!

Lucy could turn her face far enough to see Creech. Like a fiend he was reveling in his work. Suddenly he picked up the gun.

"Look a-hyar!" he called, hoarsely.

With eyes on her, grinning horribly, he walked a few paces to where the long grass had not been trampled or pressed down. The wind, whipping up out of the cañon, was still blowing hard. Creech put the gun down in the grass and fired.

Sage King plunged. But he was not gun-shy. He steadied down with a pounding of heavy hoofs. Then Lucy could see again. A thin streak of yellow smoke rose—a little snaky flame—a slight crackling hiss! Then as the wind caught the blaze there came a rushing, low roar. Fire, like magic, raced and spread before the wind toward the forest.

Lucy had forgotten that Creech had meant to drive her into fire. The sudden horror of it almost caused collapse. Commotion within—cold and quake and nausea and agony—deadened her hearing and darkened her sight. But Creech's hard hands quickened her. She could see him then, though not clearly. His face seemed inhuman, misshapen, gray. His hands pulled at her arms—a last precaution to see that she was tightly bound. Then with the deft fingers of a rider he slipped Sage King's bridle.

Lucy could not trust her sight. What made the King stand so still? His ears went up—stiff—pointed!

Creech stepped back and laid a violent hand on Lucy's garments. She bent—twisted her neck to watch him. But her sight grew no clearer. Still she saw he meant to strip her naked. He braced himself for a strong, ripping pull. His yellow teeth showed deep in his lip. His contrasting eyes were alight with insane joy.

But he never pulled. Something attracted his attention. He looked. He saw something. The beast in him became human—the madness changed to rationality—the devil to a craven! His ashen lips uttered a low, terrible cry.

Lucy felt the King trembling in every muscle. She knew that was fright. She expected his loud snort, and was prepared for it when it rang out. In a second he would bolt. She knew that. She thrilled. She tried to call to him, but her lips were weak. Creech seemed paralyzed. The King shifted his position, and Lucy's last glimpse of Creech was one she would never forget. It was as if Creech faced burning hell!

Then the King whistled and reared. Lucy heard swift, dull, throbbing beats. Beats of a fast horse's hoofs on the run! She felt a surging thrill of joy. She could not think. All of her blood and bone and muscle seemed to throb. Suddenly the air split to a high-pitched, wild, whistling blast. It pierced to Lucy's mind. She knew that whistle.

"Wildfire!" she screamed, with bursting heart.

The King gave a mighty convulsive bound of terror. He, too, knew that whistle. And in that one great bound he launched out into a run. Straight across the line of burning grass! Lucy felt the sting of flame. Smoke blinded and choked her. Then clear, dry, keen wind sung in her ears and whipped her hair. The light about her darkened. The King had headed into the pines. The heavy roar of the gale overhead struck Lucy with new and torturing dread. Sage King once in his life was running away, bridleless, and behind him there was fire on the wings of the wind.

Chapter XVII

FOR the first time in his experience Bostil found that horse-trading palled upon him. This trip to Durango was a failure. Something was wrong. There was a voice constantly calling into his inner ear—a voice to which he refused to listen. And during the five days of the return trip the strange mood grew upon him.

The last day he and his riders covered over fifty miles and reached the Ford late at night. No one expected them, and only the men on duty at the corrals knew of the return. Bostil, much relieved to get home, went to bed and at once fell asleep.

He awakened at a late hour for him. When he dressed and went out to the kitchen he found that his sister had learned of his return and had breakfast waiting.

"Where's the girl?" asked Bostil.

"Not up yet," replied Aunt Jane.

"What!"

"Lucy and I had a tiff last night and she went to her room in a temper."

"Nothin' new about thet."

"Holley and I have had our troubles holding her in. Don't you forget that."

Bostil laughed. "Wal, call her an' tell her I'm home."

Aunt Jane did as she was bidden. Bostil finished his breakfast. But Lucy did not come.

Bostil began to feel something strange, and, going to Lucy's door, he knocked. There was no reply. Bostil pushed open the door. Lucy was not in evidence, and her room was not as tidy as usual. He saw her white dress thrown upon the bed she had not slept in. Bostil gazed around with a queer contraction of the heart. That sense of something amiss grew stronger.

Then he saw a chair before the open window. That window was rather high, and Lucy had placed a chair before it so that she could look out or get out. Bostil stretched his neck, looked out, and in the red earth beneath the window he saw fresh tracks of Lucy's boots. Then he roared for Jane.

She came running, and between Bostil's furious questions and her own excited answers there was nothing arrived at. But presently she spied the white dress, and then she ran to Lucy's closet. From there she turned a white face to Bostil.

"She put on her riding-clothes!" gasped Aunt Jane.

"Supposin' she did! Where is she?" demanded Bostil.

"She's run off with Slone!"

Bostil could not have been shocked or hurt any more acutely by a knife-thrust. He glared at his sister.

"A-huh! So thet's the way you watch her!"

"Watch her? It wasn't possible. She's—well, she's as smart as you are. . . . Oh, I knew she'd do it! She was wild in love with him!"

Bostil strode out of the room and the house. He went through the grove and directly up the path to Slone's cabin. It was empty, just as Bostil expected to find it. The bars of the corral were down. Both Slone's horses were gone. Presently Bostil saw the black horse Nagger down in Brackton's pasture.

There were riders in front of Brackton's. All spoke at once to Bostil, and he only yelled for Brackton. The old man came hurriedly out, alarmed.

"Where's this Slone?" demanded Bostil.

"Slone!" ejaculated Brackton. "I'm blessed if I know. Ain't he home?"

"No. An' he's left his black hoss in your field."

"Wal, by golly, thet's news to me. . . . Bostil, there's been strange doin's lately." Brackton seemed at a loss for words. "Mebbe Slone got out because of somethin' thet come off last night. . . . Now, Joel Creech an'—an'—"

Bostil waited to hear no more. What did he care

about the idiot Creech? He strode down the lane to
the corrals. Farlane, Van, and other riders were there,
leisurely as usual. Then Holley appeared, coming out
of the barn. He, too, was easy, cool, natural, lazy.
None of these riders knew what was amiss. But instantly a change passed over them. It came because
Bostil pulled a gun.

"Holley, I've a mind to bore you!"

The old hawk-eyed rider did not flinch or turn a
shade off color. "What fer?" he queried. But his cus-
tomary drawl was wanting.

"I left you to watch Lucy. . . . An' she's gone!"

Holley showed genuine surprise and distress. The
other riders echoed Bostil's last word. Bostil lowered
the gun.

"I reckon what saves you is you're the only tracker
thet'd have a show to find this cussed Slone."

Holley now showed no sign of surprise, but the other
riders were astounded.

"Lucy's run off with Slone," added Bostil.

"Wal, if she's gone, an' if he's gone, it's a cinch,"
replied Holley, throwing up his hands. "Boss, she
double-crossed me same as you! . . . She promised
faithful to stay in the house."

"Promises nothin'!" roared Bostil. "She's in love
with this wild-hoss wrangler! She met him last night!"

"I couldn't help thet," retorted Holley. "An' I
trusted the girl."

Bostil tossed his hands. He struggled with his rage.
He had no fear that Lucy would not soon be found.
But the opposition to his will made him furious.

Van left the group of riders and came close to
Bostil. "It ain't an hour back thet I seen Slone ride
off alone on his red hoss."

"What of thet?" demanded Bostil. "Sure she was
waitin' somewheres. They'd have too much sense to
go together. . . . Saddle up, you boys, an' we'll—"

"Say, Bostil, I happen to know Slone didn't see Lucy
last night," interrupted Holley.

"A-huh! Wal, you'd better talk out."

"I trusted Lucy," said Holley. "But all the same, knowin' she was in love, I jest wanted to see if any girl in love could keep her word. . . . So about dark I went down the grove an' watched fer Slone. Pretty soon I seen him. He sneaked along the upper end an' I follered. He went to thet bench up by the biggest cottonwood. An' he waited a long time. But Lucy didn't come. He must have waited till midnight. Then he left. I watched him go back—seen him go up to his cabin."

"Wal, if she didn't meet him, where was she? She wasn't in her room."

Bostil gazed at Holley and the other riders, then back to Holley. What was the matter with this old rider? Bostil had never seen Holley seem so strange. The whole affair began to loom strangely, darkly. Some portent quickened Bostil's lumbering pulse. It seemed that Holley's mind must have found an obstacle to thought. Suddenly the old rider's face changed— the bronze was blotted out—a grayness came, and then a dead white.

"Bostil, mebbe you 'ain't been told yet thet—thet Creech rode in yesterday. . . . He lost all his racers! He had to shoot both Peg an' Roan!"

Bostil's thought suffered a sudden, blank halt. Then, with realization, came the shock for which he had long been prepared.

"A-huh! Is thet so? . . . Wal, an' what did he say?"

Holley laughed a grim, significant laugh that curdled Bostil's blood. "Creech said a lot! But let thet go now. . . . Come with me."

Holley started with rapid strides down the lane. Bostil followed. And he heard the riders coming behind. A dark and gloomy thought settled upon Bostil. He could not check that, but he held back impatience and passion.

Holley went straight to Lucy's window. He got down on his knees to scrutinize the tracks.

"Made more'n twelve hours ago," he said, swiftly.

"She had on her boots, but no spurs. . . . Now let's see where she went."

Holley began to trail Lucy's progress through the grove, silently pointing now and then to a track. He went swifter, till Bostil had to hurry. The other men came whispering after them.

Holley was as keen as a hound on scent.

"She stopped there," he said, "mebbe to listen. Looks like she wanted to cross the lane, but she didn't; here she got to goin' faster."

Holley reached an intersecting path and suddenly halted stock-still, pointing at a big track in the dust.

"My God! . . . Bostil, look at thet!"

One riving pang tore through Bostil—and then he was suddenly his old self, facing the truth of danger to one he loved. He saw beside the big track a faint imprint of Lucy's small foot. That was the last sign of her progress and it told a story.

"Bostil, thet ain't Slone's track," said Holley, ringingly.

"Sure it ain't. Thet's the track of a big man," replied Bostil.

The other riders, circling round with bent heads, all said one way or another that Slone could not have made the trail.

"An' whoever he was grabbed Lucy up—made off with her?" asked Bostil.

"Plain as if we seen it done!" exclaimed Holley. There was fire in the clear, hawk eyes.

"Cordts!" cried Bostil, hoarsely.

"Mebbe—mebbe. But thet ain't my idee. . . . Come on."

Holley went so fast he almost ran, and he got ahead of Bostil. Finally several hundred yards out in the sage he halted, and again dropped to his knees. Bostil and the riders hurried on.

"Keep back; don't stamp round so close," ordered Holley. Then like a man searching for lost gold in sand and grass he searched the ground. To Bostil it

seemed a long time before he got through. When he
arose there was a dark and deadly certainty in his
face, by which Bostil knew the worst had befallen
Lucy.

"Four mustangs an' two men last night," said Holley, rapidly. "Here's where Lucy was set down on
her feet. Here's where she mounted. . . . An' here's
the tracks of a third man—tracks made this mornin'."

Bostil straightened up and faced Holley as if ready
to take a death-blow. "I'm reckonin' them last is
Slone's tracks."

"Yes, I know them," replied Holley.

"An'—them—other tracks? Who made them?"

"Creech an' his son!"

Bostil felt swept away by a dark, whirling flame.
And when it passed he lay in his barn, in the shade of
the loft, prostrate on the fragrant hay. His strength
with his passion was spent. A dull ache remained. The
fight was gone from him. His spirit was broken. And
he looked down into that dark abyss which was his
own soul.

By and by the riders came for him, got him up, and
led him out. He shook them off and stood breathing
slowly. The air felt refreshing; it cooled his hot, tired
brain. It did not surprise him to see Joel Creech there,
cringing behind Holley.

Bostil lifted a hand for some one to speak. And
Holley came a step forward. His face was haggard,
but its white tenseness was gone. He seemed as if he
were reluctant to speak, to inflict more pain.

"Bostil," he began, huskily, "you're to send the
King—an' Sarch—an' Ben an' Two Face an' Plume
to ransom Lucy! . . . If you won't—then Creech'll
sell her to Cordts!"

What a strange look came into the faces of the
riders! Did they think he cared more for horseflesh
than for his own flesh and blood?

"Send the King—an' all he wants. . . . An' send

word fer Creech to come back to the Ford. . . . Tell
him I said—my sin found me out!"

Bostil watched Joel Creech ride the King out upon
the slope, driving the others ahead. Sage King wanted
to run. Sarchedon was wild and unruly. They passed
out of sight. Then Bostil turned to his silent riders.

"Boys, seein' the King go thet way wasn't nothin'. . . . But what crucifies me is—*will thet fetch her
back?*"

"God only knows!" replied Holley. "Mebbe not—I
reckon not! . . . But, Bostil, you forget Slone is out
there on Lucy's trail. Out there ahead of Joel! Slone
he's a wild-hoss hunter—the keenest I ever seen. Do
you think Creech can shake him on a trail? He'll kill
Creech, an' he'll lay fer Joel goin' back—an' he'll
kill him. . . . An' I'll bet my all he'll ride in here with
Lucy an' the King!"

"Holley, you ain't figurin' on thet red hoss of
Slone's ridin' down the King?"

Holley laughed as if Bostil's query was the strangest
thing of all that poignant day. "Naw. Slone 'll lay
fer Joel an' rope him like he roped Dick Sears."

"Holley, I reckon you see—clearer 'n me," said
Bostil, plaintively. " 'Pears as if I never had a hard
knock before. Fer my nerve's broke. I can't hope. . . .
Lucy's gone! . . . Ain't there anythin' to do but wait?"

"Thet's all. Jest wait. If we went out on Joel's
trail we'd queer the chance of Creech's bein' honest.
An' we'd queer Slone's game. I'd hate to have him
trailin' me."

Chapter XVIII

ON the day that old Creech repudiated his son, Slone with immeasurable relief left Brackton's without even a word to the rejoicing Holley, and plodded up the path to his cabin.

After the first flush of elation had passed he found a peculiar mood settling down upon him. It was as if all was not so well as he had impulsively conceived. He began to ponder over this strange depression, to think back. What had happened to dash the cup from his lips? Did he regret being freed from guilt in the simple minds of the villagers—regret it because suspicion would fall upon Lucy's father? No; he was sorry for the girl, but not for Bostil. It was not this new aspect of the situation at the Ford that oppressed him.

He trailed his vague feelings back to a subtle shock he had sustained in a last look at Creech's dark, somber face. It had been the face of a Nemesis. All about Creech breathed silent, revengeful force. Slone worked out in his plodding thought why that fact should oppress him; and it was because in striking Bostil old Creech must strike through Bostil's horses and his daughter.

Slone divined it—divined it by the subtle, intuitive power of his love for Lucy. He did not reconsider what had been his supposition before Creech's return —that Creech would kill Bostil. Death would be no revenge. Creech had it in him to steal the King and starve him or to do the same and worse with Lucy. So Slone imagined, remembering Creech's face.

Before twilight set in Slone saw the Creeches riding out of the lane into the sage, evidently leaving the Ford. This occasioned Slone great relief, but only for a moment. What the Creeches appeared to be doing might not be significant. And he knew if they had stayed in the village that he would have watched them as closely as if he thought they were trying to steal Wildfire.

He got his evening meal, cared for his horses, and just as darkness came on he slipped down into the grove for his rendezvous with Lucy. Always this made his heart beat and his nerves thrill, but to-night he was excited. The grove seemed full of moving shadows, all of which he fancied were Lucy. Reaching the big cottonwood, he tried to compose himself on the bench to wait. But composure seemed unattainable. The night was still, only the crickets and the soft rustle of leaves breaking a dead silence. Slone had the ears of a wild horse in that he imagined sounds he did not really hear. Many a lonely night while he lay watching and waiting in the dark, ambushing a water-hole where wild horses drank, he had heard soft treads that were only the substance of dreams. That was why, on this night when he was overstrained, he fancied he saw Lucy coming, a silent, moving shadow, when in reality she did not come. That was why he thought he heard very stealthy steps.

He waited. Lucy did not come. She had never failed before and he knew she would come. Waiting became hard. He wanted to go back toward the house—to intercept her on the way. Still he kept to his post, watchful, listening, his heart full. And he tried to reason away his strange dread, his sense of a need of hurry. For a time he succeeded by dreaming of Lucy's sweetness, of her courage, of what a wonderful girl she was. Hours and hours he had passed in such dreams. One dream in particular always fascinated him, and it was one in which he saw the girl riding Wildfire, winning a great race for her life. Another, just as fascinating, but so haunting that he always dispelled it, was a dream where Lucy, alone and in peril, fought with Cordts or Joel Creech for more than her life. These vague dreams were Slone's acceptance of the blood and spirit in Lucy. She was Bostil's

daughter. She had no sense of fear. She would fight.
And though Slone always thrilled with pride, he also
trembled with dread.

At length even wilder dreams of Lucy's rare moments when she let herself go, like a desert whirlwind,
to envelop him in all her sweetness, could not avail
to keep Slone patient. He began to pace to and fro
under the big tree. He waited and waited. What could
have detained her? Slone inwardly laughed at the idea
that either Holley or Aunt Jane could keep his girl
indoors when she wanted to come out to meet him.
Yet Lucy had always said something might prevent.
He was mistaking his thrills and excitement and love
and disappointment for something in which there was
no reality. Yet he could not help it. The longer he
waited the more shadows glided beneath the cottonwoods, the more faint, nameless sounds he heard.

He waited long after he became convinced she
would not come. Upon his return through the grove
he reached a point where the unreal and imaginative
perceptions were suddenly and stunningly broken. He
did hear a step. He kept on, as before, and in the
deep shadow he turned. He saw a man just faintly
outlined. One of the riders had been watching him—
had followed him! Slone had always expected this.
So had Lucy. And now it had happened. But Lucy
had been too clever. She had not come. She had found
out or suspected the spy and she had outwitted him.
Slone had reason to be prouder of Lucy, and he went
back to his cabin free from further anxiety.

Before he went to sleep, however, he heard the
clatter of a number of horses in the lane. He could tell
they were tired horses. Riders returning, he thought,
and instantly corrected that, for riders seldom came
in at night. And then it occurred to him that it might
be Bostil's return. But then it might be the Creeches.
Slone had an uneasy return of puzzling thoughts.
These, however, did not hinder drowsiness, and, de-
ciding that the first thing in the morning he would

trail the Creeches, just to see where they had gone, he
fell asleep.

In the morning the bright, broad day, with its
dispelling reality, made Slone regard himself differently. Things that oppressed him in the dark of night
vanished in the light of the sun. Still, he was curious
about the Creeches, and after he had done his morning's work he strolled out to take up their trail. It
was not hard to follow in the lane, for no other horses
had gone in that direction since the Creeches had left.

Once up on the wide, windy slope the reach and
color and fragrance seemed to call to Slone irresistibly,
and he fell to trailing these tracks just for the love of
a skill long unused. Half a mile out the road turned
toward Durango. But the Creeches did not continue
on that road. They entered the sage. Instantly Slone
became curious.

He followed the tracks to a pile of rocks where the
Creeches had made a greasewood fire and had cooked
a meal. This was strange—within a mile of the Ford,
where Brackton and others would have housed them.
What was stranger was the fact that the trail started
south from there and swung round toward the village.

Slone's heart began to thump. But he forced himself to think only of these tracks and not any significance they might have. He trailed the men down to a
bench on the slope, a few hundred yards from Bostil's
grove, and here a trampled space marked where a halt
had been made and a wait.

And here Slone could no longer restrain conjecture
and dread. He searched and searched. He got on his
knees. He crawled through the sage all around the
trampled space. Suddenly his heart seemed to receive
a stab. He had found prints of Lucy's boots in the soft
earth! And he leaped up, wild and fierce, needing to
know no more.

He ran back to his cabin. He never thought of
Bostil, of Holley, of anything except the story revealed
in those little boot-tracks. He packed a saddle-bag with
meat and biscuits, filled a canvas water-bottle, and,

taking them and his rifle, he hurried out to the corral. First he took Nagger down to Brackton's pasture and let him in. Then returning, he went at the fiery stallion as he had not gone in many a day, roped him, saddled him, mounted him, and rode off with a hard, grim certainty that in Wildfire was Lucy's salvation.

Four hours later Slone halted on the crest of a ridge, in the cover of sparse cedars, and surveyed a vast, gray, barren basin yawning and reaching out to a rugged, broken plateau.

He expected to find Joel Creech returning on the backtrail, and he had taken the precaution to ride on one side of the tracks he was following. He did not want Joel to cross his trail. Slone had long ago solved the meaning of the Creeches' flight. They would use Lucy to ransom Bostil's horses, and more than likely they would not let her go back. That they had her was enough for Slone. He was grim and implacable.

The eyes of the wild-horse hunter had not searched that basin long before they picked out a dot which was not a rock or a cedar, but a horse. Slone watched it grow, and, hidden himself, he held his post until he knew the rider was Joel Creech. Slone drew his own horse back and tied him to a sage-bush amidst some scant grass. Then he returned to watch. It appeared Creech was climbing the ridge below Slone, and some distance away. It was a desperate chance Joel ran then, for Slone had set out to kill him. It was certain that if Joel had happened to ride near instead of far, Slone could not have helped but kill him. As it was, he desisted because he realized that Joel would acquaint Bostil with the abducting of Lucy, and it might be that this would be well.

Slone was shaking when young Creech passed up and out of sight over the ridge—shaking with the deadly grip of passion such as he had never known. He waited, slowly gaining control, and at length went back for Wildfire.

Then he rode boldly forth on the trail. He calculated that old Creech would take Lucy to some wild retreat in the cañons and there wait for Joel and the horses. Creech had almost certainly gone on and would be unaware of a pursuer so closely on his trail. Slone took the direction of the trail, and he saw a low, dark notch in the rocky wall in the distance. After that he paid no more attention to choosing good ground for Wildfire than he did to the trail. The stallion was more tractable than Slone had ever found him. He loved the open. He smelled the sage and the wild. He settled down into his long, easy, swinging lope which seemed to eat up the miles. Slone was obsessed with thoughts centering round Lucy, and time and distance were scarcely significant.

The sun had dipped full red in a golden west when Slone reached the wall of rocks and the cleft where Creech's tracks and Lucy's, too, marked the camp. Slone did not even dismount. Riding on into the cleft, he wound at length into a cañon and out of that into a larger one, where he found that Lucy had remembered to leave a trail, and down this to a break in a high wall, and through it to another winding cañon. The sun set, but Slone kept on as long as he could see the trail, and after that, until an intersecting cañon made it wise for him to halt.

There were rich grass and sweet water for his horse. He himself was not hungry, but he ate; he was not sleepy, but he slept. And daylight found him urging Wildfire in pursuit. On the rocky places Slone found the cedar berries Lucy had dropped. He welcomed sight of them, but he did not need them. This man Creech could never hide a trail from him, Slone thought grimly, and it suited him to follow that trail at a rapid trot. If he lost the tracks for a distance he went right on, and he knew where to look for them ahead. There was a vast difference between the cunning of Creech and the cunning of a wild horse. And there was an equal difference between the going and staying powers of Creech's mustangs and Wildfire. Yes, Slone divined that Lucy's salvation would be Wildfire, her horse. The trail grew rougher, steeper, harder, but the stal-

lion kept his eagerness and his pace. On many an
open length of cañon or height of wild upland Slone
gazed ahead hoping to see Creech's mustangs. He hoped
for that even when he knew he was still too far behind. And then, suddenly, in the open, sandy flat of
an intersecting cañon he came abruptly on a fresh
trail of three horses, one of them shod.

The surprise stunned him. For a moment he gazed
stupidly at these strange tracks. Who had made them?
Had Creech met allies? Was that likely when the man
had no friends? Pondering the thing, Slone went slowly
on, realizing that a new and disturbing feature confronted him. Then when these new tracks met the trail
that Creech had left Slone found that these strangers
were as interested in Creech's tracks as he was. Slone
found their boot-marks in the sand—the hand-prints
where some one had knelt to scrutinize Creech's trail.

Slone led his horse and walked on, more and more
disturbed in mind. When he came to a larger, bare,
flat cañon bottom, where the rock had been washed
clear of sand, he found no more cedar berries. They
had been picked up. At the other extreme edge of this
stony ground he found crumpled bits of cedar and
cedar berries scattered in one spot, as if thrown there
by some one who read their meaning.

This discovery unnerved Slone. It meant so much.
And if Slone had any hope or reason to doubt that
these strangers had taken up the trail for good, the
next few miles dispelled it. They were trailing Creech.

Suddenly Slone gave a wild start, which made Wildfire plunge.

"Cordts!" whispered Slone and the cold sweat oozed
out of every pore.

These cañons were the hiding-places of the horse-
thief. He and two of his men had chanced upon
Creech's trail; and perhaps their guess at its meaning
was like Slone's. If they had not guessed they would
soon learn. It magnified Slone's task a thousandfold.
He had a moment of bitter, almost hopeless realization
before a more desperate spirit awoke in him. He had

only more men to kill—that was all. These upland riders did not pack rifles, of that Slone was sure. And the sooner he came up with Cordts the better. It was then he let Wildfire choose his gait and the trail. Sunset, twilight, dusk, and darkness came with Slone keeping on and on. As long as there were no intersecting cañons or clefts or slopes by which Creech might have swerved from his course, just so long Slone would travel. And it was late in the night when he had to halt.

Early next day the trail led up out of the red and broken gulches to the cedared uplands. Slone saw a black-rimmed, looming plateau in the distance. All these winding cañons, and the necks of the high ridges between, must run up to that great table-land.

That day he lost two of the horse tracks. He did not mark the change for a long time after there had been a split in the party that had been trailing Creech. Then it was too late for him to go back to investigate, even if that had been wise. He kept on, pondering, trying to decide whether or not he had been discovered and was now in danger of ambush ahead and pursuit from behind. He thought that possibly Cordts had split his party, one to trail along after Creech, the others to work around to head him off. Undoubtedly Cordts knew this broken cañon country and could tell where Creech was going, and knew how to intercept him.

The uncertainty wore heavily upon Slone. He grew desperate. He had no time to steal along cautiously. He must be the first to get to Creech. So he held to the trail and went as rapidly as the nature of the ground would permit, expecting to be shot at from any clump of cedars. The trail led down again into a narrow cañon with low walls. Slone put all his keenness on what lay before him.

Wildfire's sudden break and upflinging of head and his snort preceded the crack of a rifle. Slone knew he had been shot at, although he neither felt nor heard the bullet. He had no chance to see where the shot came from, for Wildfire bolted, and needed as much holding and guiding as Slone could give. He ran a mile. Then Slone was able to look about him. Had he been shot at from above or behind? He could not tell. It did not matter, so long as the danger was not in front. He kept a sharp lookout, and presently along the right cañon rim, five hundred feet above him, he saw a bay horse, and a rider with a rifle. He had been wrong, then, about these riders and their weapons. Slone did not see any wisdom in halting to shoot up at this pursuer, and he spurred Wildfire just as a sharp crack sounded above. The bullet thudded into the earth a few feet behind him. And then over bad ground, with the stallion almost unmanageable, Slone ran a gantlet of shots. Evidently the man on the rim had smooth ground to ride over, for he easily kept abreast of Slone. But he could not get the range. Fortunately for Slone, broken ramparts above checked the tricks of that pursuer, and Slone saw no more of him.

It afforded him great relief to find that Creech's trail turned into a cañon on the left; and here, with the sun already low, Slone began to watch the clumps of cedars and the jumbles of rock. But he was not ambushed. Darkness set in, and, being tired out, he was about to halt for the night when he caught the flicker of a camp-fire. The stallion saw it, too, but did not snort. Slone dismounted and, leading him, went cautiously forward on foot, rifle in hand.

The cañon widened at a point where two breaks occurred, and the less-restricted space was thick with cedar and piñon. Slone could tell by the presence of these trees and also by a keener atmosphere that he was slowly getting to a higher altitude. This camp-fire must belong to Cordts or the one man who had gone on ahead. And Slone advanced boldly. He did not have to make up his mind what to do.

But he was amazed to see several dark forms moving to and fro before the bright camp-fire, and he checked himself abruptly. Considering a moment, Slone thought he had better have a look at these fellows. So

he tied Wildfire and, taking to the darker side of the
cañon, he stole cautiously forward.

The distance was considerable, as he had calculated.
Soon, however, he made out the shadowy outlines of
horses feeding in the open. He hugged the cañon wall
for fear they might see him. As luck would have it the
night breeze was in his favor. Stealthily he stole on,
in the deep shadow of the wall, and under the cedars,
until he came to a point opposite the camp-fire, and
then he turned toward it. He went slowly, carefully,
noiselessly, and at last he crawled through the narrow
aisles between thick sage-brush. Another clump of
cedars loomed up, and he saw the flickering of fire-
light upon the pale-green foliage.

He heard gruff voices before he raised himself to
look, and by this he gauged his distance. He was close
enough—almost too close. But as he crouched in dark
shade and there were no horses near, he did not fear
discovery.

When he peered out from his covert the first thing
to strike and hold his rapid glance was the slight figure
of a girl. Slone stifled a gasp in his throat. He thought
he recognized Lucy. Stunned, he crouched down again
with his hands clenched round his rifle. And there he
remained for a long moment of agony before reason
asserted itself over emotion. Had he really seen Lucy?
He had heard of a girl now and then in the camps of
these men, especially Cordts. Maybe Creech had fallen
in with comrades. No, he could not have had any comrades there but horse-thieves, and Creech was above
that. If Creech was there he had been held up by
Cordts; if Lucy only was with the gang, Creech had
been killed.

Slone had to force himself to look again. The girl
had changed her position. But the light shone upon the
men. Creech was not one of the three, nor Cordts, nor
any man Slone had seen before. They were not honest
men, judging from their hard, evil looks. Slone was
non-plussed and he was losing self-control. Again he
lowered himself and waited. He caught the word

"Durango" and "hosses" and "fer enough in," the meaning of which was vague. Then the girl laughed. And Slone found himself trembling with joy. Beyond any doubt that laugh could not have been Lucy's.

Slone stole back as he had come, reached the shadow of the wall, and drew away until he felt it safe to walk quickly. When he reached the place where he expected to find Wildfire he did not see him. Slone looked and looked. Perhaps he had misjudged distance and place in the gloom. Still, he never made mistakes of that nature. He searched around till he found the cedar stump to which he had tied the lasso. In the gloom he could not see it, and when he reached out he did not feel it. Wildfire was gone! Slone sank down, overcome. He cursed what must have been carelessness, though he knew he never was careless with a horse. What had happened? He did not know. But Wildfire was gone— and that meant Lucy's doom and his! Slone shook with cold.

Then, as he leaned against the stump, wet and shaking, a familiar sound met his ears. It was made by the teeth of a grazing horse—a slight, keen, tearing cut. Wildfire was close at hand! With a sweep Slone circled the stump and he found the knot of the lasso. He had missed it. He began to gather in the long rope, and soon felt the horse. In the black gloom against the wall Slone could not distinguish Wildfire.

"Whew!" he muttered, wiping the sweat off his face. "Good Lord! . . . All for nothin'."

It did not take Slone long to decide to lead the horse and work up the cañon past the campers. He must get ahead of them, and once there he had no fear of them, either by night or day. He really had no hopes of getting by undiscovered, and all he wished for was to get far enough so that he could not be intercepted. The grazing horses would scent Wildfire or he would scent them.

For a wonder Wildfire allowed himself to be led as well as if he had been old, faithful Nagger. Slone could not keep close in to the wall for very long, on account of the cedars, but he managed to stay in the outer edge of shadow cast by the wall. Wildfire winded the horses, halted, threw up his head. But for some reason beyond Slone the horse did not snort or whistle. As he knew Wildfire he could have believed him intelligent enough and hateful enough to betray his master.

It was one of the other horses that whistled an alarm. This came at a point almost even with the camp-fire. Slone, holding Wildfire down, had no time to get into a stirrup, but leaped to the saddle and let the horse go. There were hoarse yells and then streaks of fire and shots. Slone heard the whizz of heavy bullets, and he feared for Wildfire. But the horse drew swiftly away into the darkness. Slone could not see whether the ground was smooth or broken, and he left that to Wildfire. Luck favored them, and presently Slone pulled him in to a safe gait, and regretted only that he had not had a chance to take a shot at that camp.

Slone walked the horse for an hour, and then decided that he could well risk a halt for the night.

Before dawn he was up, warming his chilled body by violent movements, and forcing himself to eat.

The rim of the west wall changed from gray to pink. A mocking-bird burst into song. A coyote sneaked away from the light of day. Out in the open Slone found the trail made by Creech's mustangs and by the horse of Cordts's man. The latter could not be very far ahead. In less than an hour Slone came to a clump of cedars where this man had camped. An hour behind him!

This cañon was open, with a level and narrow floor divided by a deep wash. Slone put Wildfire to a gallop. The narrow wash was no obstacle to Wildfire; he did not have to be urged or checked. It was not long before Slone saw a horseman a quarter of a mile ahead, and he was discovered almost at the same time. This fellow showed both surprise and fear. He ran his horse. But in comparison with Wildfire that horse seemed sluggish. Slone would have caught up with him very soon but for a change in the lay of the land. The cañon split up and all of its gorges and ravines and washes headed upon the pine-fringed plateau, now only a few miles distant. The gait of the horses had to be reduced to a trot, and then a walk. The man Slone was after left Creech's trail and took to a side cleft. Slone, convinced he would soon overhaul him, and then return to take up Creech's trail, kept on in pursuit. Then Slone was compelled to climb, Wildfire was so superior to the other's horse, and Slone was so keen at choosing ground and short cuts, that he would have been right upon him but for a split in the rock which suddenly yawned across his path. It was impassable. After a quick glance Slone abandoned the direct pursuit, and, turning along this gulch, he gained a point where the horse-thief would pass under the base of the rim-wall, and here Slone would have him within easy rifle shot.

And the man, intent on getting out of the cañon, rode into the trap, approaching to within a hundred yards of Slone, who suddenly showed himself on foot, rifle in hand. The deep gulch was a barrier to Slone's further progress, but his rifle dominated the situation.

"Hold on!" he called, warningly.

"Hold on yerself!" yelled the other, aghast, as he halted his horse. He gazed down and evidently was quick to take in the facts.

Slone had meant to kill this man without even a word, yet now when the moment had come a feeling almost of sickness clouded his resolve. But he leveled the rifle.

"I got it on you," he called.

"Reckon you hev. But see hyar——"

"I can hit you anywhere."

"Wal, I'll take yer word fer thet."

"All right. Now talk fast. . . . Are you one of Cordts's gang?"

"Sure."

"Why are you alone?"

"We split down hyar."

"Did you know I was on this trail?"

"Nope. I didn't sure, or you'd never ketched me, red hoss or no."

"Who were you trailin'?"

"Ole Creech an' the girl he kidnapped."

Slone felt the leap of his blood and the jerk it gave the rifle as his tense finger trembled on the trigger.

"Girl. . . . What girl?" he called, hoarsely.

"Bostil's girl."

"Why did Cordts split on the trail?"

"He an' Hutch went round fer some more of the gang, an' to head off Joel Creech when he comes in with Bostil's hosses."

Slone was amazed to find how the horse thieves had calculated; yet, on second thought, the situation, once the Creeches had been recognized, appeared simple enough.

"What was your game?" he demanded.

"I was follerin' Creech jest to find out where he'd hole up with the girl."

"What's Cordts's game—*after* he heads Joel Creech?"

"Then he's goin' fer the girl."

Slone scarcely needed to be told all this, but the deliberate words from the lips of one of Cordts's gang bore a raw, brutal proof of Lucy's peril. And yet Slone could not bring himself to kill this man in cold blood. He tried, but in vain.

"Have you got a gun?" called Slone, hoarsely.

"Sure."

"Ride back the other way! . . . If you don't lose me I'll kill you!"

The man stared. Slone saw the color return to his pale face. Then he turned his horse and rode back out of sight. Slone heard him rolling the stones down the long, rough slope; and when he felt sure the horse-thief had gotten a fair start he went back to mount Wildfire in pursuit.

This trailer of Lucy never got back to Lucy's trail— never got away.

But Slone, when that day's hard, deadly pursuit

ended, found himself lost in the cañons. How bitterly
he cursed both his weakness in not shooting the man
at sight, and his strength in following him with implacable purpose! For to be fair, to give the horse-thief
a chance for his life, Slone had lost Lucy's trail. The
fact nearly distracted him. He spent a sleepless night
of torture.

All next day, like a wild man, he rode and climbed
and descended, spurred by one purpose, pursued by
suspense and dread. That night he tied Wildfire near
water and grass and fell into the sleep of exhaustion.

Morning came. But with it no hope. He had been
desperate. And now he was in a frightful state. It
seemed that days and days had passed, and nights that
were hideous with futile nightmares.

He rode down into a cañon with sloping walls, and
broken, like all of these cañons under the great plateau.
Every cañon resembled another. The upland was one
vast network. The world seemed a labyrinth of cañons
among which he was hopelessly lost. What would—
what had become of Lucy? Every thought in his whirling brain led back to that—and it was terrible.

Then—he was gazing transfixed down upon the
familiar tracks left by Creech's mustangs. Days old,
but still unfollowed!

Chapter XIX

THAT track led up the narrowing cañon to its head at
the base of the plateau.

Slone, mindful of his horse, climbed on foot, halting
at the zigzag turns to rest. A long, gradually ascending
trail mounted the last slope, which when close at hand
was not so precipitous as it appeared from below. Up
there the wind, sucked out of the cañons, swooped and
twisted hard.

At last Slone led Wildfire over the rim and halted for another breathing-spell. Before him was a beautiful, gently sloping stretch of waving grass leading up to the dark pine forest from which came a roar of wind. Beneath Slone the wild and whorled cañon breaks extended, wonderful in thousands of denuded surfaces, gold and red and yellow, with the smoky depths between.

Wildfire sniffed the wind and snorted. Slone turned, instantly alert. The wild horse had given an alarm. Like a flash Slone leaped into the saddle. A faint cry, away from the wind, startled Slone. It was like a cry he had heard in dreams. How overstrained his perceptions! He was not really sure of anything, yet on the instant he was tense.

Straggling cedars on his left almost wholly obstructed Slone's view. Wildfire's ears and nose were pointed that way. Slone trotted him down toward the edge of this cedar clump so that he could see beyond. Before he reached it, however, he saw something blue, moving, waving, lifting.

"Smoke!" muttered Slone. And he thought more of the danger of fire on that windy height than he did of another peril to himself.

Wildfire was hard to hold as he rounded the edge of the cedars.

Slone saw a line of leaping flames, a line of sweeping smoke, the grass on fire . . . horses!—a man!

Wildfire whistled his ringing blast of hate and menace, his desert challenge to another stallion.

The man whirled to look.

Slone saw Joel Creech—and Sage King—and Lucy, half naked, bound on his back!

Joy, agony, terror in lightning-swift turns, paralyzed Slone. But Wildfire lunged out on the run.

Sage King reared in fright, came down to plunge away, and with a magnificent leap cleared the line of fire.

Slone, more from habit than thought, sat close in the saddle. A few of Wildfire's lengthening strides quickened Slone's blood. Then Creech moved, also awaking from a stupefying surprise, and he snatched up a gun and fired. Slone saw the spurts of red, the puffs of white. But he heard nothing. The torrent of his changed blood, burning and terrible, filled his ears with hate and death.

He guided the running stallion. In a few tremendous strides Wildfire struck Creech, and Slone had one glimpse of an awful face. The impact was terrific. Creech went hurtling through the air, limp and broken, to go down upon a rock, his skull cracking like a melon.

The horse leaped over the body and the stone, and beyond he leaped the line of burning grass.

Slone saw the King running into the forest. He saw poor Lucy's white body swinging with the horse's motion. One glance showed the great gray to be running wild. Then the hate and passion cleared away, leaving suspense and terror.

Wildfire reached the pines. There down the open aisles between the black trees ran the fleet gray racer. Wildfire saw him and snorted. The King was a hundred yards to the fore.

"Wildfire—it's come—the race—the race!" called Slone. But he could not hear his own call. There was a roar overhead, heavy, almost deafening. The wind! the wind! Yet that roar did not deaden a strange, shrieking crack somewhere behind. Wildfire leaped in fright. Slone turned. Fire had run up a pine-tree, which exploded as if the trunk were powder!

"My God! A race with fire! . . . Lucy! Lucy!"

In that poignant cry Slone uttered his realization of the strange fate that had waited for the inevitable race between Wildfire and the King; he uttered his despairing love for Lucy, and his acceptance of death for her and himself. No horse could outrun wind-driven fire in a dry pine forest. Slone had no hope of that. How perfectly fate and time and place and horses, himself and his sweetheart, had met! Slone damned Joel Creech's insane soul to everlasting torment. To think

—to think his idiotic and wild threat had come true—
and come true with a gale in the pine-tops! Slone grew
old at the thought, and the fact seemed to be a dream.
But the dry, pine-scented air made breathing hard; the
gray racer, carrying that slender, half-naked form,
white in the forest shade, lengthened into his fleet and
beautiful stride; the motion of Wildfire, so easy, so
smooth, so swift, and the fierce reach of his head shooting forward—all these proved that it was no dream.

Tense questions pierced the dark chaos of Slone's
mind—what could he do? Run the King down! Make
him kill Lucy! Save her from horrible death by fire!

The red horse had not gained a yard on the gray.
Slone, keen to judge distance, saw this, and for the
first time he doubted Wildfire's power to run down the
King. Not with such a lead! It was hopeless—so hopeless.

He turned to look back. He saw no fire, no smoke—
only the dark trunks, and the massed green foliage in
violent agitation against the blue sky. That revived a
faint hope. If he could get a few miles ahead, before
the fire began to leap across the pine-crests, then it
might be possible to run out of the forest if it were
not wide.

Then a stronger hope grew. It seemed that foot by
foot Wildfire was gaining on the King. Slone studied
the level forest floor sliding toward him. He lost his
hope—then regained it again, and then he spurred the
horse. Wildfire hated that as he hated Slone. But apparently he did not quicken his strides. And Slone could
not tell if he lengthened them. He was not running near
his limit but, after the nature of such a horse, left to
choose his gait, running slowly, but rising toward his
swiftest and fiercest.

Slone's rider's blood never thrilled to that race, for
his blood had curdled. The sickness within rose to his
mind. And that flashed up whenever he dared to look
forward at Lucy's white form. Slone could not bear this
sight; it almost made him reel, yet he was driven to
look. He saw that the King carried no saddle, so with

Lucy on him he was light. He ought to run all day with only that weight. Wildfire carried a heavy saddle, a pack, a water-bag, and a rifle. Slone untied the pack and let it drop. He almost threw aside the water-bag, but something withheld his hand, and also he kept his rifle. What were a few more pounds to this desert stallion in his last run? Slone knew it was Wildfire's greatest and last race.

Suddenly Slone's ears rang with a terrible on-coming roar. For an instant the unknown sound stiffened him, robbed him of strength. Only the horn of the saddle, hooking into him, held him on. Then the years of his desert life answered to a call more than human.

He had to race against fire. He must beat the flame to the girl he loved. There were miles of dry forest, like powder. Fire backed by a heavy gale could rage through dry pine faster than any horse could run. He might fail to save Lucy. Fate had given him a bitter ride. But he swore a grim oath that he would beat the flame. The intense and abnormal rider's passion in him, like Bostil's, dammed up, but never fully controlled, burst within him, and suddenly he awoke to a wild and terrible violence of heart and soul. He had accepted death; he had no fear. All that he wanted to do, the last thing he wanted to do, was to ride down the King and kill Lucy mercifully. How he would have gloried to burn there in the forest, and for a million years in the dark beyond, to save the girl!

He goaded the horse. Then he looked back.

Through the aisles of the forest he saw a strange, streaky, murky something moving, alive, shifting up and down, never an instant the same. It must have been the wind—the heat before the fire. He seemed to see through it, but there was nothing beyond, only opaque, dim, mustering clouds. Hot puffs shot forward into his face. His eyes smarted and stung. His ears hurt and were growing deaf. The tumult was the roar of avalanches, of maelstroms, of rushing seas, of the wreck of the uplands and the ruin of the earth. It grew to be so great a roar that he no longer heard. There was only silence.

And he turned to face ahead. The stallion stretched low on a dead run; the tips of the pines were bending before the wind; and Wildfire, the terrible thing for which his horse was named, was leaping through the forest. But there was no sound.

Ahead of Slone, down the aisles, low under the trees spreading over the running King, floated swiftly some medium, like a transparent veil. It was neither smoke nor air. It carried faint pin-points of light, sparks, that resembled atoms of dust floating in sunlight. It was a wave of heat driven before the storm of fire. Slone did not feel pain, but he seemed to be drying up, parching. And Lucy must be suffering now. He goaded the stallion, raking his flanks. Wildfire answered with a scream and a greater speed. All except Lucy and Sage King and Wildfire seemed so strange and unreal—the swift rush between the pines, now growing ghostly in the dimming light, the sense of a pursuing, overpowering force, and yet absolute silence.

Slone fought the desire to look back. But he could not resist it. Some horrible fascination compelled him. All behind had changed. A hot wind, like a blast from a furnace, blew light, stinging particles into his face. The fire was racing in the tree-tops, while below all was yet clear. A lashing, leaping flame engulfed the canopy of pines. It was white, seething, inconceivably swift, with a thousand flashing tongues. It traveled ahead of smoke. It was so thin he could see the branches through it, and the fiery clouds behind. It swept onward, a sublime and an appalling spectacle. Slone could not think of what it looked like. It was fire, liberated, freed from the bowels of the earth, tremendous, devouring. This, then, was the meaning of fire. This, then, was the horrible fate to befall Lucy.

But no! He thought he must be insane not to be overcome in spirit. Yet he was not. He would beat the flame to Lucy. He felt the loss of something, some kind of a sensation which he ought to have had. Still he rode that race to kill his sweetheart better than any race he had ever before ridden. He kept his seat; he dodged the snags; he pulled the maddened horse the shortest way, he kept the King running straight.

No horse had ever run so magnificent a race! Wildfire was outracing wind and fire, and he was overhauling the most noted racer of the uplands against a tremendous handicap. But now he was no longer racing to kill the King; he was running in terror. For miles he held that long, swift, wonderful stride without a break. He was running to his death, whether or not he distanced the fire. Nothing could stop him now but a bursting heart.

Slone untied his lasso and coiled the noose. Almost within reach of the King! One throw—one sudden swerve—and the King would go down. Lucy would know only a stunning shock. Slone's heart broke. Could he kill her—crush that dear golden head? He could not, yet he must! He saw a long, curved, red welt on Lucy's white shoulders. What was that? Had a branch lashed her? Slone could not see her face. She could not have been dead or in a faint, for she was riding the King, bound as she was!

Closer and closer drew Wildfire. He seemed to go faster and faster as that wind of flame gained upon them. The air was too thick to breathe. It had an irresistible weight. It pushed horses and riders onward in their flight—straws on the crest of a cyclone.

Again Slone looked back and again the spectacle was different. There was a white and golden fury of flame above, beautiful and blinding; and below, farther back, an inferno of glowing fire, black-streaked, with trembling, exploding puffs and streams of yellow smoke. The aisles between the burning pines were smoky, murky caverns, moving and weird. Slone saw fire shoot from the treetops down the trunks, and he saw fire shoot up the trunks, like trains of powder. They exploded like huge rockets. And along the forest floor leaped the little flames. His eyes burned and blurred

till all merged into a wide, pursuing storm too awful
for the gaze of man.

Wildfire was running down the King. The great gray
had not lessened his speed, but he was breaking. Slone
felt a ghastly triumph when he began to whirl the noose
of the lasso round his head. Already he was within
range. But he held back his throw which meant the
end of all. And as he hesitated Wildfire suddenly
whistled one shrieking blast.

Slone looked. Ahead there was light through the
forest! Slone saw a white, open space of grass. A park?
No—the end of the forest! Wildfire, like a demon,
hurtled onward, with his smoothness of action gone,
beginning to break, within a length of the King.

A cry escaped Slone—a cry as silent as if there had
been no deafening roar—as wild as the race, and as
terrible as the ruthless fire. It was the cry of life—
instead of death. Both Sage King and Wildfire would
beat the flame.

Then, with the open just ahead, Slone felt a wave of
hot wind rolling over him. He saw the lashing tongues
of flame above him in the pines. The storm had caught
him. It forged ahead. He was riding under a canopy
of fire. Burning pine cones, like torches, dropped all
around him. He had a terrible blank sense of weight,
of suffocation, of the air turning to fire.

Then Wildfire, with his nose at Sage King's flank,
flashed out of the pines into the open. Slone saw a
grassy wide reach inclining gently toward a dark break
in the ground with crags rising sheer above it, and to
the right a great open space.

Slone felt that clear air as the break of deliverance.
His reeling sense righted. There—the King ran, blindly
going to his death. Wildfire was breaking fast. His momentum carried him. He was almost done.

Slone roped the King, and holding hard, waited for
the end. They ran on, breaking, breaking. Slone thought
he would have to throw the King, for they were peri-
lously near the deep cleft in the rim. But Sage King
went to his knees.

Slone leaped off just as Wildfire fell. How the blade flashed that released Lucy! She was wet from the horse's sweat and foam. She slid off into Slone's arms, and he called her name. Could she hear above that roar back there in the forest? The pieces of rope hung to her wrists and Slone saw dark bruises, raw and bloody. She fell against him. Was she dead? His heart contracted. How white the face! No; he saw her breast heave against his! And he cried aloud, incoherently in his joy. She was alive. She was not badly hurt. She stirred. She plucked at him with nerveless hands. She pressed close to him. He heard a smothered voice, yet so full, so wonderful!

"Put—your—coat—on me!" came somehow to his ears.

Slone started violently. Abashed, shamed to realize he had forgotten she was half nude, he blindly tore off his coat, blindly folded it around her.

"Lin! Lin!" she cried.

"Lucy— Oh! are y-you—" he replied, huskily.

"I'm not hurt. I'm all right."

"But that wretch, Joel. He—"

"He'd killed his father—just a—minute—before you came. I fought him! Oh! . . . But I'm all right. . . . Did you—"

"Wildfire ran him down—smashed him. . . . Lucy! this can't be true. . . . Yet I feel you! Thank God!"

With her free hand Lucy returned his clasp. She seemed to be strong. It was a precious moment for Slone, in which he was uplifted beyond all dreams.

"Let me loose—a second," she said. "I want to—get in your coat."

She laughed as he released her. She laughed! And Slone thrilled with unutterable sweetness at that laugh.

As he turned away he felt a swift wind, then a strange impact from an invisible force that staggered him, then the rend of flesh. After that came the heavy report of a gun.

Slone fell. He knew he had been shot. Following the rending of his flesh came a hot agony. It was in his shoulder, high up, and the dark, swift fear for his life was checked.

Lucy stood staring down at him, unable to comprehend, slowly paling. Her hands clasped the coat round her. Slone saw her, saw the edge of streaming clouds of smoke above her, saw on the cliff beyond the gorge two men, one with a smoking gun half leveled.

If Slone had been inattentive to his surroundings before, the sight of Cordts electrified him.

"Lucy! drop down! quick!"

"Oh, what's happened? You—you—"

"I've been shot. Drop down, I tell you. Get behind the horse an' pull my rifle."

"Shot!" exclaimed Lucy, blankly.

"Yes—yes. . . . My God! Lucy, he's goin' to shoot again!"

It was then Lucy Bostil saw Cordts across the gulch. He was not fifty yards distant, plainly recognizable, tall, gaunt, sardonic. He held the half-leveled gun ready as if waiting. He had waited there in ambush. The clouds of smoke rolled up above him, hiding the crags.

"*Cordts!*" Bostil's blood spoke in the girl's thrilling cry.

"Hunch down, Lucy!" cried Slone. "Pull my rifle. . . . I'm only winged—not hurt. Hurry! He's goin'—"

Another heavy report interrupted Slone. The bullet missed, but Slone made a pretense, a convulsive flop, as if struck.

"Get the rifle! Quick!" he called.

But Lucy misunderstood his ruse to deceive Cordts. She thought he had been hit again. She ran to the fallen Wildfire and jerked the rifle from its sheath.

Cordts had begun to climb round a ledge, evidently a short cut to get down and across. Hutchinson saw the rifle and yelled to Cordts. The horse-thief halted, his dark face gleaming toward Lucy.

When Lucy rose the coat fell from her nude shoulders. And Slone, watching, suddenly lost his agony of terror for her and uttered a pealing cry of defiance and of rapture.

She swept up the rifle. It wavered. Hutchinson was above, and Cordts, reaching up, yelled for help. Hutchinson was reluctant. But the stronger force dominated. He leaned down—clasped Cordts's outstretched hands, and pulled. Hutchinson bawled out hoarsely. Cordts turned what seemed a paler face. He had difficulty on the slight footing. He was slow.

Slone tried to call to Lucy to shoot low, but his lips had drawn tight after his one yell. Slone saw her white, rounded shoulders bent, with cold, white face pressed against the rifle, with slim arms quivering and growing tense, with the tangled golden hair blowing out.

Then she shot.

Slone's glance shifted. He did not see the bullet strike up dust. The figures of the men remained the same—Hutchinson straining, Cordts. . . . No, Cordts was not the same! A strange change seemed manifest in his long form. It did not seem instinct with effort. Yet it moved.

Hutchinson also was acting strangely, yelling, heaving, wrestling. But he could not help Cordts. He lifted violently, raised Cordts a little, and then appeared to be in peril of losing his balance.

Cordts leaned against the cliff. Then it dawned upon Slone that Lucy had hit the horse-thief. Hard hit! He would not—he could not let go of Hutchinson. His was a death clutch. The burly Hutchinson slipped from his knee-hold, and as he moved Cordts swayed, his feet left the ledge, he hung, upheld only by the tottering comrade.

What a harsh and terrible cry from Hutchinson! He made one last convulsive effort and it doomed him. Slowly he lost his balance. Cordts's dark, evil, haunting face swung round. Both men became lax and plunged, and separated. The dust rose from the rough steps. Then the dark forms shot down—Cordts falling sheer and straight, Hutchinson headlong, with waving arms—down and down, vanishing in the depths. No sound came up. A little column of yellow dust curled from the fatal ledge and, catching the wind above, streamed away into the drifting clouds of smoke.

Chapter XX

A DARKNESS, like the streaming clouds overhead, seemed to blot out Slone's sight, and then passed away, leaving it clearer.

Lucy was bending over him, binding a scarf round his shoulder and under his arm. "Lin! It's nothing!" she was saying, earnestly, "Never touched a bone!"

Slone sat up. The smoke was clearing away. Little curves of burning grass were working down along the rim. He put out a hand to grasp Lucy, remembering in a flash. He pointed to the ledge across the chasm.

"They're—gone!" cried Lucy, with a strange and deep note in her voice. She shook violently. But she did not look away from Slone.

"Wildfire! The King!" he added, hoarsely.

"Both where they dropped. Oh, I'm afraid to—to look. . . . And, Lin, I saw Sarch, Two Face, and Ben and Plume go down there."

She had her back to the chasm where the trail led down, and she pointed without looking.

Slone got up, a little unsteady on his feet and conscious of a dull pain.

"Sarch will go straight home, and the others will follow him," said Lucy. "They got away here where Joel came up the trail. The fire chased them out of the woods. Sarch will go home. And that'll fetch the riders."

"We won't need them if only Wildfire and the King—" Slone broke off and grimly, with a catch in his breath, turned to the horses.

How strange that Slone should run toward the King while Lucy ran to Wildfire!

Sage King was a beaten, broken horse, but he would live to run another race.

Lucy was kneeling beside Wildfire, sobbing and crying: "Wildfire! Wildfire!"

293

All of Wildfire was white except where he was red, and that red was not now his glossy, flaming skin. A terrible muscular convulsion as of internal collapse grew slower and slower. Yet choked, blinded, dying, killed on his feet, Wildfire heard Lucy's voice.

"Oh, Lin! Oh, Lin!" moaned Lucy.

While they knelt there the violent convulsions changed to slow heaves.

"He run the King down—carryin' weight—with a long lead to overcome!" Slone muttered, and he put a shaking hand on the horse's wet neck.

"Oh, he beat the King!" cried Lucy. "But you mustn't —you *can't* tell Dad!"

"What *can* we tell him?"

"Oh, I know. Old Creech told me what to say!"

A change, both of body and spirit, seemed to pass over the great stallion.

"Wildfire! Wildfire!"

Again the rider called to his horse, with a low and piercing cry. But Wildfire did not hear.

The morning sun glanced brightly over the rippling sage which rolled away from the Ford like a gray sea.

Bostil sat on his porch, a stricken man. He faced the blue haze of the north, where days before all that he had loved had vanished. Every day, from sunrise till sunset, he had been there, waiting and watching. His riders were grouped near him, silent, awed by his agony, awaiting orders that never came.

From behind a ridge puffed up a thin cloud of dust. Bostil saw it and gave a start. Above the sage appeared a bobbing, black object—the head of a horse. Then the big black body followed.

"Sarch!" exclaimed Bostil.

With spurs clinking the riders ran and trooped behind him.

"More hosses back," said Holley, quietly.

"Thar's Plume!" exclaimed Farlane.

"An' Two Face!" added Van.

"Dusty Ben!" said another.

"Riderless!" finished Bostil.

Then all were intensely quiet, watching the racers come trotting in single file down the ridge. Sarchedon's shrill neigh, like a whistle-blast, pealed in from the sage. From fields and corrals clamored the answer attended by the clattering of hundreds of hoofs.

Sarchedon and his followers broke from trot to canter —canter to gallop—and soon were cracking their hard hoofs on the stony court. Like a swarm of bees the riders swooped down upon the racers, caught them, and led them up to Bostil.

On Sarchedon's neck showed a dry, dust-caked stain of reddish tinge. Holley, the old hawk-eyed rider, had precedence in the examination.

"Wal, thet's a bullet-mark, plain as day," said Holley.

"Who shot him?" demanded Bostil.

Holley shook his gray head.

"He smells of smoke," put in Farlane, who had knelt at the black's legs. "He's been runnin' fire. See thet! Fetlocks all singed!"

All the riders looked, and then with grave, questioning eyes at one another.

"Reckon thar's been hell!" muttered Holley, darkly.

Some of the riders led the horses away toward the corrals. Bostil wheeled to face the north again. His brow was lowering; his cheek was pale and sunken; his jaw was set.

The riders came and went, but Bostil kept his vigil. The hours passed. Afternoon came and wore on. The sun lost its brightness and burned red.

Again dust-clouds, now like reddened smoke, puffed over the ridge. A horse carrying a dark, thick figure appeared above the sage.

Bostil leaped up. "Is thet a gray hoss—or am—I blind?" he called, unsteadily.

The riders dared not answer. They must be sure. They gazed through narrow slits of eyelids; and the silence grew intense.

Holley shaded the hawk eyes with his hand. "Gray

he is—Bostil—gray as the sage. . . . *An' so help me God if he ain't the King!"*

"Yes, it's the King!" cried the riders, excitedly. "Sure! I reckon! No mistake about thet! It's the King!"

Bostil shook his huge frame, and he rubbed his eyes as if they had become dim, and he stared again.

"Who's thet up on him?"

"Slone. I never seen his like on a hoss," replied Holley.

"An' what's—he packin'?" queried Bostil, huskily.

Plain to all keen eyes was the glint of Lucy Bostil's golden hair. But only Holley had courage to speak.

"It's Lucy! I seen thet long ago."

A strange, fleeting light of joy died out of Bostil's face. The change once more silenced his riders. They watched the King trotting in from the sage. His head dropped. He seemed grayer than ever and he limped. But he was Sage King, splendid as of old, all the more gladdening to the riders' eyes because he had been lost. He came on, quickening a little to the clamoring welcome from the corrals.

Holley put out a swift hand. "Bostil—the girl's alive—she's smilin'!" he called, and the cool voice was strangely different.

The riders waited for Bostil. Slone rode into the courtyard. He was white and weary, reeling in the saddle. A bloody scarf was bound round his shoulder. He held Lucy in his arms. She had on his coat. A wan smile lighted her haggard face.

Bostil, cursing deep, like muttering thunder, strode out. "Lucy! You ain't bad hurt?" he implored, in a voice no one had ever heard before.

"I'm—all right—Dad," she said, and slipped down into his arms.

He kissed the pale face and held her up like a child, and then, carrying her to the door of the house, he roared for Aunt Jane.

When he reappeared the crowd of riders scattered from around Slone. But it seemed that Bostil saw only the King. The horse was caked with dusty lather, scratched and disheveled, weary and broken, yet he was still beautiful. He raised his drooping head and reached for his master with a look as soft and dark and eloquent as a woman's.

No rider there but felt Bostil's passion of doubt and hope. Had the King been beaten? Bostil's glory and pride were battling with love. Mighty as that was, it did not at once overcome his fear of defeat.

Slowly the gaze of Bostil moved away from Sage King and roved out to the sage and back, as if he expected to see another horse. But no other horse was in sight. At last his hard eyes rested upon the white-faced Slone.

"Been some—hard ridin'?" he queried, haltingly. All there knew that had not been the question upon his lips.

"Pretty hard—yes," replied Slone. He was weary, yet tight-lipped, intense.

"Now—them Creeches?" slowly continued Bostil.

"Dead."

A murmur ran through the listening riders, and they drew closer.

"Both of them?"

"Yes. Joel killed his father, fightin' to get Lucy. . . . An' I ran—Wildfire over Joel—smashed him!"

"Wal, I'm sorry for the old man," replied Bostil, gruffly. "I meant to make up to him. . . . But thet fool boy! . . . An' Slone—you're all bloody."

He stepped forward and pulled the scarf aside. He was curious and kindly, as if it was beyond him to be otherwise. Yet that dark cold something, almost sullen, clung round him.

"Been bored, eh? Wal, it ain't low, an' thet's good. Who shot you?"

"Cordts."

"*Cordts!*" Bostil leaned forward in sudden, fierce eagerness.

"Yes, Cordts. . . . His outfit run across Creech's trail an' we bunched. I can't tell now. . . . But we had—hell! An' Cordts is dead—so's Hutch—an' that other pard of his. . . . Bostil, they'll never haunt your sleep again!"

Slone finished with a strange sternness that seemed almost bitter.

Bostil raised both his huge fists. The blood was bulging his thick neck. It was another kind of passion that obsessed him. Only some violent check to his emotion prevented him from embracing Slone. The huge fists unclenched and the big fingers worked.

"You mean to tell me you did fer Cordts an' Hutch what you did fer Sears?" he boomed out.

"They're dead—gone, Bostil—honest to God!" replied Slone.

Holley thrust a quivering, brown hand into Bostil's face. "What did I tell you?" he shouted. "Didn't I say wait?"

Bostil threw away all that deep fury of passion, and there seemed only a resistless and speechless admiration left. Then ensued a moment of silence. The riders watched Slone's weary face as it drooped, and Bostil, as he loomed over him.

"Where's the red stallion?" queried Bostil. That was the question hard to get out.

Slone raised eyes dark with pain, yet they flashed as he looked straight up into Bostil's face. "Wildfire's dead!"

"*Dead!*" ejaculated Bostil.

Another moment of strained exciting suspense.

"Shot?" he went on.

"No."

"What killed him?"

"The King, sir! . . . Killed him on his feet!"

Bostil's heavy jaw bulged and quivered. His hand shook as he laid it on Sage King's mane—the first touch since the return of his favorite.

"Slone—what—is it?" he said, brokenly, with voice strangely softened. His face became transfigured.

"Sage King killed Wildfire on his feet. . . . A grand race, Bostil! . . . But Wildfire's dead—an' here's the King! Ask me no more. I want to forget."

Bostil put his arm around the young man's shoulder. "Slone, if I don't know what you feel fer the loss of thet grand hoss, no rider on earth knows! . . . Go in the house. Boys, take him in—all of you—an' look after him."

Bostil wanted to be alone, to welcome the King, to lead him back to the home corral, perhaps to hide from all eyes the change and the uplift that would forever keep him from wronging another man.

The late rains came and like magic, in a few days, the sage grew green and lustrous and fresh, the gray turning to purple.

Every morning the sun rose white and hot in a blue and cloudless sky. And then soon the horizon line showed creamy clouds that rose and spread and darkened. Every afternoon storms hung along the ramparts and rainbows curved down beautiful and ethereal. The dim blackness of the storm-clouds was split to the blinding zigzag of lightning, and the thunder rolled and boomed, like the Colorado in flood.

The wind was fragrant, sage-laden, no longer dry and hot, but cool in the shade.

Slone and Lucy never rode down so far as the stately monuments, though these held memories as hauntingly sweet as others were poignantly bitter. Lucy never rode the King again. But Slone rode him, learned to love him. And Lucy did not race any more. When Slone tried to stir in her the old spirit all the response he got was a wistful shake of head or a laugh that hid the truth or an excuse that the strain on her ankles from Joel Creech's lasso had never mended. The girl was unutterably happy, but it was possible that she would never race a horse again.

She rode Sarchedon, and she liked to trot or lope along beside Slone while they linked hands and watched the distance. But her glance shunned the north, that distance which held the wild cañons and the broken battlements and the long, black, pine-fringed plateau.

"Won't you ever ride with me, out to the old camp, where I used to wait for you?" asked Slone.

"Some day," she said, softly.

"When?"

"When—when we come back from Durango," she replied, with averted eyes and scarlet cheek. And Slone was silent, for that planned trip to Durango, with its wonderful gift to be, made his heart swell.

And so on this rainbow day, with storms all around them, and blue sky above, they rode only as far as the valley. But from there, before they turned to go back, the monuments appeared close, and they loomed grandly with the background of purple bank and creamy cloud and shafts of golden lightning. They seemed like sentinels—guardians of a great and beautiful love born under their lofty heights, in the lonely silence of day, in the star-thrown shadow of night. They were like that love. And they held Lucy and Slone, calling every day, giving a nameless and tranquil content, binding them true to love, true to the sage and the open, true to that wild upland home.